AGE OF ATLANTIS
STEPHEN JENSEN

Avalon Books, LLC

AVALON BOOKS, LLC
SALT LAKE CITY

Printed in the United States of America by Avalon Books, LLC

The AVALON CLOCK colophon is a trademark of Avalon Books, LLC. Registration pending

Hardback ISBN 978-1-960860-03-3

Paperback ISBN 978-1-960860-04-0

Ebook ISBN 978-1-960860-05-7

avalonseriesbooks.com

First Edition

Cover Art by Stephen Jensen and Lincoln Writes

Author Photo by Ralph Jensen

Book Design by Stephen Jensen

Maps created by Stephen Jensen

Interior Art by Stephen Jensen

*In Loving Memory
of David*

THE WORLD 1669 PF(2369 BC)

WORLD POPULATION   38 BILLION

ATLANTEAN EMPIRE POP   8.1 BILLION

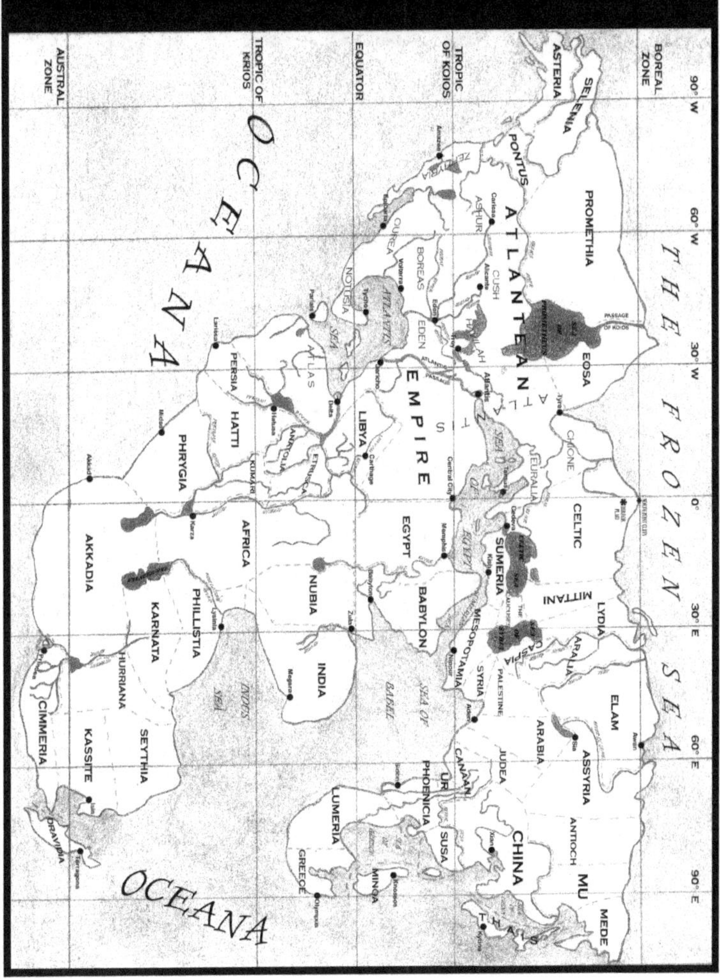

ATLANTIS 1669 PF(2369 BC)
POPULATION 328 MILLION

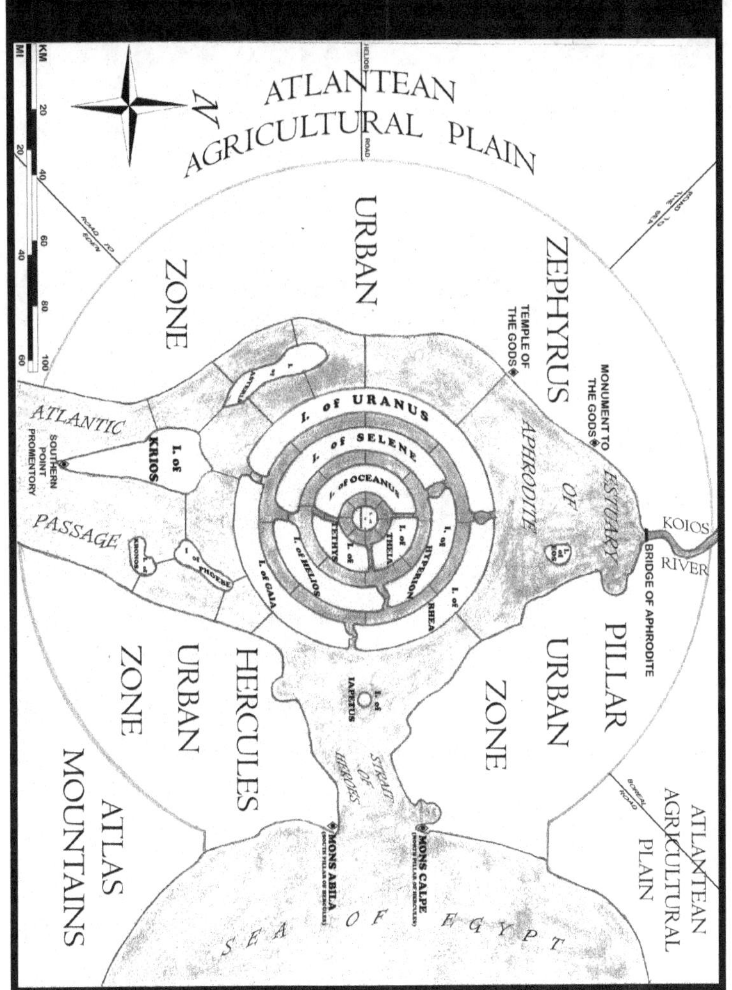

CONTENTS

PRIESTESS OF THE GODS

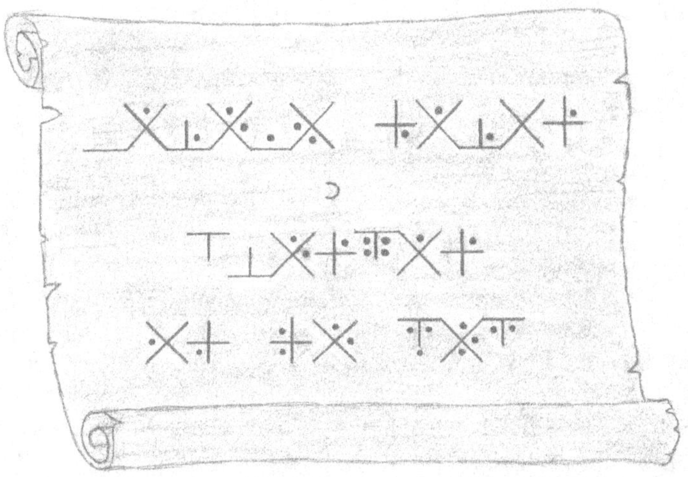

Katherine sat on the bed in a large chamber and tried to make sense of the last few minutes. Lord George Cavendish was just in front of her. There was a green flash and a falling sensation. Then she awoke in this strange place, and no one spoke her language.

"What is your name?" A strangely dressed blonde woman asked.

"Mistress Katherine Snow Talmage."

"So, it is true."

"Of which truth dost thou speak?"

"You speak the words of the gods." Her big green eyes examined Katherine.

"Words of gods?" *Did she mean God?*

"Yes, I have never met another human who could speak it. And I have searched for much of the last 800 years. Where did you learn to speak it? In the heavens? Or did one of the gods teach you?"

"I do beg pardon, what is thy name?"

"Melina Hellas. I am the High Priestess of this temple, The Temple of the Gods."

"Thou dost say my speech is of gods? Which gods?"

"The Gods of Atlantis."

"This place be called Atlantis?" She raised a brow.

"How do you not know this?" Melina's head cocked to the side.

"A mad tale it is..." She paused in consideration. Melina indicated she continued. "I was pulled through a doorway of light, so rapidly did I move, I did lose orientation. There was a bright flash. Then I woke up here."

Melina looked at her in deep consideration. "Perhaps the Gods sent you."

"Nay, it be Lady Avalon. She be responsible for my life in ruins." She clenched her fists. "She is responsible for this." She opened her arms.

"Lady of Avalon? I have never heard of such a person, and I'm 818 years old." Melina shook her head.

"Thou art mad, 800 years lived, thou could not." She laughed.

Melina appeared thoroughly confused. "Of course, I can. Many people have lived for nearly 1000 years. So long as misfortune does not befall them. The youngest priestess currently serving in this temple is 132 years old. How old are you?" Melina raised a brow.

"I am aged 22 years."

"You're just a baby." Melina laughed. "Where is your family? Why can't you speak our words?"

"Only have I learned English. Thou call this place Atlantis, never have I heard. My Ma and Pa and brother passed of the fever. My husband, murdered by Lady Avalon. No children do I have." Tears came to her eyes.

Melina looked at her for a moment. "Follow me."

They walked out onto a balcony, and she could see a massive circular city in the water under a pale green sky. "What year do you believe it is?"

"The year? Well, of course, the year of our Lord, 1697."

"What if I told you the year was 1557 post-fall?"

"Post fall?"

"The purported fall from grace by the elders. Some named them Adam and Eve."

"Adam and Eve? As in the holy Bible?"

"Bible? What is the Bible?"

"The Bible is the holy book of our Lord and Savior Jesus Christ."

"That sounds rather Unitarian." Melina waved her hand. "I know the gods are real. Eight hundred years ago, I was the personal body servant to the Goddess Aphrodite. That is how I speak your words. Aphrodite and the God Koios ruled over the Atlantean Empire for five years. Leading the world into a golden age of great peace and prosperity."

"How could thou be confident they be gods?"

"I was witness to their arrival. They sent rods of flame back to the heavens. They could fly like the birds. They could lift enormously heavy objects with ease. They could shoot lightning out of their hands. And they could speak to all of Atlantis from the sky above." Melina said with excitement as if she were reliving the events.

"To where did these gods go?"

"Too many people stop believing in them. There was much fighting. They returned to the heavens in the Chariot of Kronos. The world became prideful. The prosperous centuries encouraged decadence. People replaced the gods with themselves." Melina's head dropped.

"And thou never lost faith?"

"The world came to a crossroads. The gods returned, it seemed, to restore our greatness. But they refused to rule because humans had left them behind. We are some of the last true believers. If the gods do not return soon, Atlantis is doomed." Melina's gaze returned to the city.

PART I: CLASSICAL ATLANTIS

CHAPTER 1: A WHOLE NEW WORLD

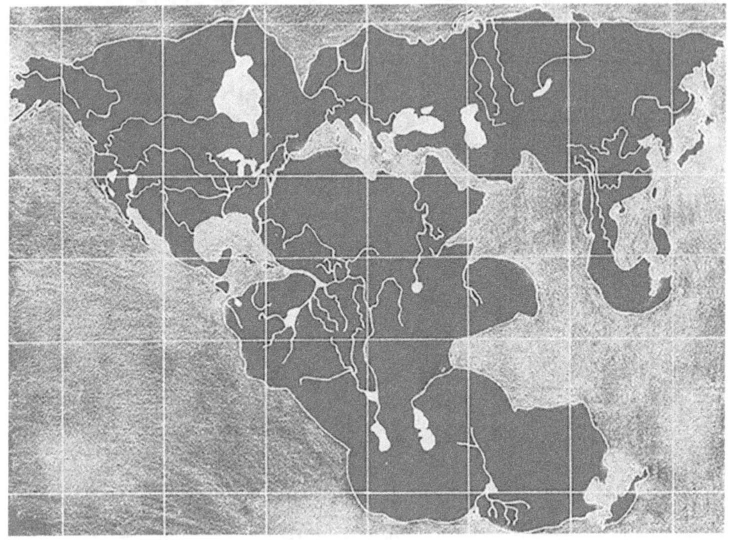

“WHERE ARE WE?” JULIE asked, now that she could finally think again.

“I’m not sure. We were supposed to be somewhere near Halifax, Nova Scotia.” Micheal scanned the area and shrugged.

“Why aren’t you sure?”

“See that, how the coast curves towards the east. It shouldn’t look like that.”

“Maybe it looks wrong because it’s dark. I mean, we only have the light of the moon.”

“And that’s another thing—”

“What is?”

“The sky doesn’t look right either.”

“It’s 5000 years in the past. Perhaps the procession of the equinoxes is different than what they predicted.” She looked at the sky. It did look unusual.

"That's not it. Our position on the surface has to be maybe five or 10 degrees south of where we should be. And see that? It looks like... A glass dome... Or something." He indicated an odd optical element in the sky.

"You think it's a glass dome?" She raised a brow.

He stared at it in consideration. "I doubt it's an actual glass dome, but it certainly appears to be some kind of a shield, maybe it's an energy..." He broke off. "Jules. I don't think we're in Kansas anymore." He indicated the clearing.

She looked to her left, and there was what appeared to be a sloth, but it was the size of a grizzly bear. "Are you sure we only went back 5000 years?"

"Unless the chronometer is malfunctioning. I'm not sure history is quite how historians believed it was."

As they watched the giant sloth, the first rays of dawn broke over the horizon. The sun looked almost silver, and the sky was a greenish hue.

"Why is the sky green?" A feeling of dread was building in her stomach as the overall strangeness of their surroundings was becoming apparent.

"It has to be whatever that force field or bubble or whatever that thing is." He scanned the entire 360-degree horizon. "Where's Cavendish?"

"Cavendish? Why would you ask that?"

"He arrived just as we were about to jump." He continued to scan the horizon.

"You think he came through with us?"

"He was probably near the edge of the fall zone. Let's keep an eye out; anything is possible."

Over the next couple of days, they explored the immediate area.

"I guess there are no villages in the area."

"We've only searched a few miles in each direction. Wait... I think we just found one... Maybe not, it's just a small camp." He crouched to avoid being seen. She could see one young man relatively short of stature with an olive complexion. There were three women, all appeared of similar age with a range from olive to light complexion. There was an adolescent boy, perhaps 12 years old, who had a lighter complexion.

"I can't hear what they're saying." She strained.

"Let's move closer." He ensured they were downwind and then halted their approach around 30 feet from the camp. They observed the camp for several hours. He was clearly logging notes in his head.

"Do you understand anything they're saying?"

"Some of it is becoming understandable, which means my translation of those tablets wasn't far off." There was a hint of pride in his voice.

"How do you know? And you're sure it's the language from the tablets?"

"Because I'm already hearing some of the elements I expected. Okay, hear that? '*Bah-may*', the cuneiform pronunciation in the tablet translation, was 'bow-may'. I had suspected the annunciation of the unknown language had been translated phonetically. 'Bah-may' means fish. They were discussing who had caught the bigger fish." As they listened, he was practicing sounds out loud.

"The wind's shifting. We should go."

———————

The next morning, they returned to the camp and spent more time observing and listening.

"I'm definitely building some associations."

"What do you think the relationship between them is? Are they friends, or siblings, or a combination thereof?"

Micheal shook his head. "It doesn't make any sense."

"What? You can't understand enough to tell?"

"No, I can; it just doesn't make sense..." He paused for a second. "Okay, so the man and the woman with the lightest complexion are a couple. Now, the boy and the woman with the middling complexion keep addressing the couple as mother and father. The couple keeps addressing the woman with the darkest complexion as a mother. The two who address the couple as mother and father address her as grandmother. So, like I said, it doesn't make sense."

"Are you sure you understand those titles correctly?"

"Absolutely. One of the tablets you gave me was a will, which included the titles of nearly every family relationship." He gave a sidelong look.

"Sorry!" She smiled slyly. She always liked to challenge him on his surety. He tended towards arrogance when it came to his statements of fact. "They are breaking camp." She noticed the group preparing to leave. So, they slipped away back to their camp.

"With your template, I could understand maybe a third to a half. How about you?"

"At least three quarters, I need to meditate to see if I can fill in the gaps. Who knew those tablets would be so essential? Then we need to get you up to speed."

"Indeed."

Launch Sequence

MICHEAL made much progress on the unknown language. Julie was far behind but was working hard. But now they had another task to focus on.

"Okay, the inspection looks good. Begin diagnostics, prep the engines to test fire." Micheal instructed Julie.

"Why didn't you go to these extremes before the launch in 1697?" She raised a brow. "It feels like we've unnecessarily wasted the last few days."

"If the launch failed a couple of weeks ago, we would still be able to do our due diligence to try to correct whatever went wrong. With this network and the nanotech involved, that wouldn't be possible. We only get one shot at this."

She picked up one of the micro-sats. "It seems incredible that these tiny things will be able to do everything you say they can," she said, with a look of wonder on her face. "And we were able to engineer these in the 17th century all by ourselves. And they are more advanced than anything in the 21st century."

"That's not actually true. Well, mostly."

"I know I'm not as up on the latest tech as you, but I'm certain I would've heard about something like these."

"I saw some experimental micro-sats of similar size in the late 90s, and I read some articles indicating that they were now being engineered, at least in 2009. It's not about the ability to do this. It's about the most profitable rollout timeline. The only additions I made are the magnetic resonance suspension along with the neural cloud memory storage." He waved it off.

"Oh! Is that all?" She shook her head.

"What's that supposed to mean?"

"It means that even I was having trouble understanding the

exact storage method. It works the same way the brain operates, right?"

"Yes."

"And you think that's a simple process?"

"Well, simple enough."

"I was studying psychology at Columbia when we fell. The complex nature of the brain and the way memories work are still mostly unknown. It's hardly simple."

"Sorry!" He raised a brow. "I think we are ready."

"Then, on top of the sat network, you built these rockets."

"Wow! I built a few rockets." He threw his hands out. "Goddard built the first one in 1926, and Von Brahn more or less perfected them 16 years later. If they could do that 75 to 100 years ago, then it's no big deal."

"Don't you mean 5200 years from now?" she teased.

"Whatever!" He said in frustration.

He looked at her. She was trying not to laugh. He couldn't help but smile.

She came and kissed him on the cheek. "I'm sorry, I couldn't help myself."

"All right. Count it down."

"10, nine... Three, two, one."

"And lift off!"

Micheal was bemused by the fact that it had taken falling back in time to realize his original dream of designing space propulsion systems. And despite his blase attitude, he was proud of this moment.

Even half a mile away, you could feel the force of the launches. "Telemetry looks good. The final launch has reached the thermosphere." Julie said, watching the camera view on her handheld. "The altitude of launch number 20 has passed 60 miles."

"Trailblazer relays are in place. Initiate the dispersion pattern."

"Pattern variation, Mark 0.12."

"Variation in acceptable range."

"Dispersion complete, variation, Mark 0.14."

"Variation still acceptable. Initiating reentry burn."

"Prepping EM constriction."

"Initializing... Now." Micheal entered the sequence.

"Activating primary system... Now." Julie held her breath.

"We are online." Micheal eyed the sky in relief. Then, it was time to test the network. The sky-net was operational. He was mostly confident there would be no terminators this time.

"I'll be back."

"I do hope this helps us get back."

"*Hasta le vista*, baby!" She laughed at the joke.

A New World?

JULIE activated the network interface and couldn't believe what she was seeing.

"This has to be some kind of a mistake."

Micheal returned a look of bewilderment.

"What does this mean? Are we still on earth? Are you sure we didn't travel across the stars and time?" Her stomach was in knots.

"I ran a diagnostics sweep; it indicates all systems are normal. I ran scans of the moon and stars. It is most definitely our moon. And my multiple stellar cartographical scans indicate we are certainly on Earth, and the stellar motion variable is firm that we are in the 33rd century BC." Micheal paused and took a deep breath. "It's not a mistake."

"Then how is there a pangea supercontinent on Earth? Plate tectonics don't move that quickly." She was to convince herself more than anything else.

"Apparently, they can."

"You're just accepting this? I thought you were a scientist."

"I am. You're the one trying to ignore clear evidence. And I thought *you* were a scientist?"

"There has to be some kind of rational explanation." Her mind didn't want to believe the evidence.

"There is! Historians and geologists weren't fully informed about their theories. Everyone was wrong! Obviously, nobody knew this was here. I've studied history my entire life, and the known knowledge about this period is almost zero." He was plainly frustrated. She was a little taken aback by his outburst. He looked at her, then softened. "I'm sorry. I shouldn't have raised my voice." He came over and took her by the hands.

She looked at him. "It's just with everything. The time travel, the Lords of Avalon, and now this? So many things that keep challenging everything I thought I knew." The tears came.

"Come here." He pulled her into him.

"What are we going to do now?" she asked into his shoulder.

"What we always do. Have faith in each other, and everything will be all right." He kissed her. As he pulled back, he said. "We are not alone."

She turned around slowly, and there were a dozen people: seven women and five men who all looked to be in their early 20s.

"Praise to the supreme eminences." She only partially understood the woman at the center. She was obviously the leader; she bowed. The rest followed suit.

"What are they doing?" she whispered to Micheal.

"I think they think we're Gods."

"What are we going to do?"

Micheal stepped forward. "We have been sent to live amongst you." He said in the unknown language. She was only able to make out some of what he said. "What is your name?" He asked the woman.

"My name is Melina." She maintained her bow.

"Rise, you will lead us to your city."

"What are you doing?"

"Going with it." She had to fight to contain her anger. Their 'worshipers' had them wait while a whole bunch more came and packed up all their stuff. Then Melina led the caravan off to the south, down the coast. They were riding in an open carriage. "I'm sorry I couldn't consult with you, but it was necessary to go with it. You've seen Ghostbusters. When someone asks if you're a God, you say yes!" He semi-joked.

"Everything isn't a movie!"

"There is a lot of wisdom in movies. I didn't 'go with it' lightly. I considered all the possibilities. Apparently, they saw the rocket launches and who knows what else. So, they assumed we were gods. They could just as easily believe we are demons or some other mystical evil monster that they might want to kill. I highly doubt they would believe we were just people. Because how did we do those supernatural things?" He tried to justify his decision.

She could see where he was coming from, but she was still upset that he had made such a big decision without consulting her first. "How can we possibly keep up the façade?"

"Before we left Boston, I had been playing around with the KEE extractors. And I was able to make a few... Toys. Here, try these on." He handed her two silver rings.

"What are they?"

"These are lightning gauntlets. Watch this." He tapped a pattern on his silver rings. Suddenly, a spark emerged from his middle finger, connecting to his thumb. He opened his hand quickly, and every finger had a spark that converged over his palm—creating a lightning ball.

"Doesn't that hurt?"

"No, the energy channels on the surface of your skin. Plus, the amperage is fairly low. Try it. Tap shave and a haircut on the crest." The energy sparked in her hand. "Do the other one."

She now had two balls of energy in her hands. She brought them together, and they converged into a large spinning ball of energy floating in front of her. Eventually, she noticed many in the caravan staring frightfully at her. When she closed her hands, the energy dispersed in a flash.

"If they had any doubt, you were a God before, I'm sure they're convinced now."

"Did you make these for this specific purpose?"

"No!" He cocked his head. "I made them to be our stun guns against a major attack."

"So, they can stun people? Can they kill people?" She felt queasy.

"If you amped it up high enough."

She tapped the ring on her right hand. She looked at the ball of lightning in her hand. "So, we are gods then? Like Greek gods?"

"I would presume." He raised a brow.

"What are we the gods of?"

He seemed to understand. "You're clearly the Goddess of Love and Beauty. And I'm the God of Wisdom and Knowledge." He looked up and nodded.

"How come you're not the God of Love?" She gave him a side-long look.

"The God of Love has to be a woman."

"But you're my God of Love." she teased.

"Look at that." He changed gears as they reached the summit of a towering hill.

She looked ahead. There was a massive city. "It looks like..." She began.

"... Atlantis!" He finished for her.

CHAPTER 11: ATLANTIS

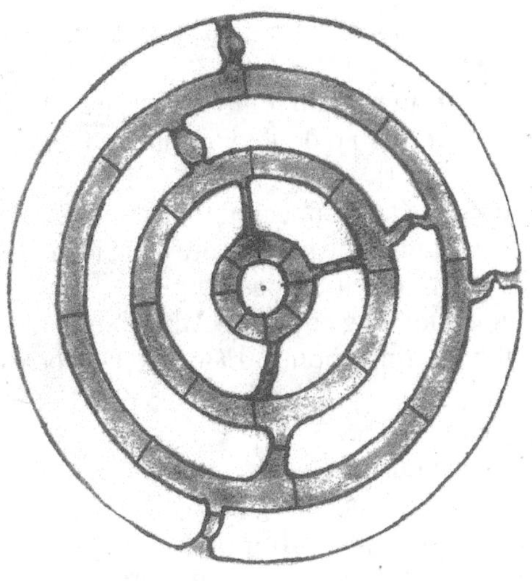

As dawn broke, the caravan began its journey over the extensive bridge leading into the city, its form and structure echoing the ancient words of Plato. MICHEAL observed, however, that the scale of the city stretched beyond the philosopher's depiction, nestled within a channel between two expanses of land. From their vantage point on the rise just before the bridge, Michael had a clear view of the layout – three circular strips of earth embraced a central isle, upon which a solitary mountain stood, unmistakable and majestic.

"This is insane. How long do you think this bridge is?"

"Probably at least 10 miles."

"And it's all made out of stone. Wasn't Atlantis supposed to be like 10,000 years ago?" She furrowed her brow.

"Something like that."

"It makes you question so many things." She stared thoughtfully ahead.

They passed through the first ring of land, it was primarily agricultural, but the road was lined with people either cheering or staring. Word of their coming must've been sent ahead.

"I think I'm having second thoughts again."

"Why?"

"Look at all these people. What if they see through the façade?"

"You are a Lady of Avalon. So that means there's nothing you can't do."

"I'm beginning to doubt I am a Lady of Avalon." She dropped her head.

He pulled her to him. "You're my wife. And that makes you a Lady of Avalon. There is no doubt you can do this." He kissed her cheek.

The second ring of land appeared to have small villages all over it. And the crowds lining the street were even larger. Many people were beginning to bow as they passed.

"Are you understanding any more Atlantean than before?"

"I'm probably getting about 60% of what is being said. How about you?"

"Probably around 90%."

"Atlantean?" She raised a brow.

"Well, now we have something to call it."

"Wow! Look at that," Julie whispered.

There was a massive statue of Uranus, probably about 300 feet tall, guarding the entry to the third ring of land.

"This definitely puts Rome to shame. Those are some massive aqueducts."

"This puts New York to shame."

Buildings completely covered the innermost ring of land. He estimated it to be perhaps ten times larger than Manhattan. As more and more people were bowing, Julie seemed to be trying to give off her best air of godliness.

"So, what exactly are we going to be doing?"

"I don't know. I suppose we will try to do whatever they think Gods would do." He shrugged.

"Yesterday, you said you had a few more kinetic toys."

"Oh yeah, these rings..." He pulled out a pair of black rings. "Can magnetically polarize any magnetic material against the Earth's magnetic field."

"So, it can make them levitate?" She guessed.

"Indeed. And it can generate its own polarized field."

"And what can that do?"

"It could potentially facilitate levitation of... Us." He looked away.

"So now we might be able to fly?" He could feel her eyes on the back of his head.

"It's possible. Now, this last one..." He pulled out a set of copper rings. "Requires remote assist nodes, but it can create a polarized barrier around us. It's basically a rudimentary force field that works against metal or any other magnetized element."

"Are you sure you didn't plan for this possibility?"

"I swear I had no idea."

They were about to pass through the main gate to the central island. Even Micheal was impressed by the massive wall that surrounded the island. It was about 200 feet tall. The gatehouse protruded out about 100 feet into the lagoon. The caravan arrived just as they lowered the massive drawbridge. The gate passage was around 300 feet long. Guards lined the street to the foot of the mountain. Music began to play as they entered the central island. He estimated the island to be similar in size to Manhattan. There was a mountain a few thousand feet tall in the middle with several structures on its plateau; he thought they might be temples. There were skyscrapers, stone skyscrapers, everywhere. Most appeared to be upwards of 500 feet tall.

"It's so weird," Julie said.

"What?"

"I don't think I have seen anyone older than perhaps 30 since we got here."

"I've noticed the same thing."

"How is that possible?"

"I don't know; maybe this culture encourages ritual suicide if you start to get too old. Or maybe they force them into retirement communities. But that's just random speculation."

"Either of those options would be terrible."

"It brings to mind the family dynamic of the people we observed. We are obviously missing something."

Most of the people were bowing as they passed.

"Why couldn't we just be nobody's." Julie's fists clenched.

"Where would be the fun in that?"

"Where do you suppose they are taking us?"

"Probably to the rulers, whoever that is... Take me to your leader." He joked.

"Shut up."

"Sorry." He tried not to laugh.

They came to a stop in front of a large building. On the massive staircase stood a delegation waiting to receive them.

"Here we go." He said as they climbed out of the carriage.

Fallen Gods

As they approached the delegation, everyone went to their knees. Nearly all the crowd followed suit.

"My gods, welcome to Atlantis." The head of the delegation remained bowing. "Your coming has been foretold."

One of the men who remained standing began shouting. "These are not gods, you fools. They're just people. And I'm going to prove it to you."

At that moment, JULIE noticed movement coming from the left. She timed her spin kick perfectly and sent the first attacker flying. She used a flurry of moves from numerous martial arts forms to dispose of about half a dozen more attackers. She activated the black rings and noticed a column had a metal core. As she picked up the column, she could feel the energy flowing. She estimated that the column had to weigh at least three tons. She swung it like a baseball bat, swatting away another dozen attackers. She was trying to be careful not to kill anyone. Suddenly, the number of attackers swelled to more than 100. She looked over, and Micheal was beginning to levitate up about 100 feet in the air. He had lightning sparking in his hands. She activated her lightning and stunned another dozen or so attackers. She looked back at Micheal as he rained lightning down on the attacking mob. They all fell stunned.

The watching crowd was stunned into silence. As Micheal descended, the head guard ordered all the attackers to be arrested. Micheal began walking up the stairs to a central point. She moved to join him. He began to address the crowd in Atlantean. "People of Atlantis, we do not desire to engage in combat against you. Or to sow discord amongst you. We will defend ourselves if attacked. But we do not intend you any harm. We will not hold this assault upon our persons against all of Atlantis. We desire peace." He finished. All present, even those who had at first remained upright, were now united in their bow.

The head of the delegation said. "My holy Gods. Of what do you embody?"

"The Goddess of Love and Beauty." Micheal indicated her. "And I am the God of Wisdom and Knowledge."

The man stepped forward, indicating them. "People of Atlantis, your Gods on Earth, Koios and Aphrodite!"

The people went to their knees again.

Melina escorted them to an extensive suite within the building, where they had been greeted. When they were finally alone. "So, how do you think it's going so far?" Julie gave him a side-eye.

"We managed."

"And what about next time?"

"I don't think anyone will try anything for a while."

"There were about 200 assassins waiting for us."

"They probably gathered every warrior they could find. It obviously wasn't enough. And that show we put on will likely discourage any more attempts for a while, at least. Nice move with the column, by the way."

"I saw the iron core and believed your engineering would work. You could feel the power flowing all around you. And that levitation trick with the lightning would have convinced me you were a God if I didn't know any better." She laughed.

"In a sense, we are like actual gods to these people." He shrugged.

"I don't want this to go to your head. I will concede your worthiness to be a Lord of Avalon. But try to remember you're not really a God." She said, only half joking.

"As you decree, Aphrodite."

She rolled her eyes. "So, they actually address me as Aphrodite." She shook her head.

"You are the Goddess of Love and Beauty."

"I'll make you pay for this."

"Oh?" He raised a brow, then came and pulled her into him. "I don't think you will." He kissed her.

He was right. She would have trouble going without and speaking of which. Before she knew it, their clothes were on the floor. She activated the lightning as they reached a perfect rhythm and were nearing the crescendo. The extra spark of electric energy flowing over their skin sent them over the top. At that moment,

Melina entered their chamber. Melina's eyes widened, and she went to her knees, begging forgiveness.

"You are forgiven; you may depart," Julie instructed. After Melina left, Julie laid her head back, laughing. Micheal joined her, with his head on her chest.

"I suppose word of how Gods have sex is going to get around," Micheal said through the laughter.

He rolled off her, and she rolled over on his chest. "So, I'm Aphrodite. Who are you?"

"Koios, in Greek mythology, was the Titan of Intelligence."

"So, you're a Titan, and I'm a God?"

"Well, depending on which origin you believe, Aphrodite could be both. In the later classical era, she was the daughter of Zeus and Dione. But originally, she's the direct daughter of the primordial Titan father, Uranus. It seems the Atlantean gods might be what would become the Titans of ancient Greece."

"So, what powers does Aphrodite supposedly have?"

"She can make married couples fall back in love, and she has a belt that can make anyone fall in love with the wearer. But I can promise you that however you dress or wear your hair, almost all the women in Atlantis will copy it. You will be considered the ideal." He brushed the hair out of her face.

"Great!" She rolled her eyes.

High Council

The next day, Melina took them to see the high council.

"Your Honorable High Council, may I present their Holy Eminences Koios and Aphrodite," Melina said. The entire council bowed.

After a minute, MICHEAL said, "You may rise." They all stood, then went and took their seats. There were 12 on the Council, seven men and five women. Once again, they all appeared to be under 30 years of age.

One man remained standing. "My Gods, I am Cato. I represent Atlantis proper. I have headed this council since its founding and through centuries of expansion. I will be honored to serve your holy eminences." He bowed.

"Cato, forgive my curiosity. How old are you?" Micheal asked.

"No contrition is necessary, your eminence, I am 612. Will your eminences take your thrones?" He indicated the immaculate thrones on a pedestal.

Solid gold thrones, carved with glyphs and various patterns, stood majestically. Each throne featured a dark purple cushion, seemingly made of soft velvet, for seating.

They took their seats, and then Cato began. "I would first like to apologize on behalf of the Council and Atlantis for the unfortunate attack against your eminences upon your arrival yesterday. I assure you – all will be executed for their evil offense."

Micheal raised his hand. "We thank you for your devotion. However, we will show mercy this one time."

"Your eminences, I'm Helene of Eden. We are pleased about your arrival. Many problems require your attention." She indicated for the woman next to her to speak.

"My gods, I'm Sarai Issedones of Atlas. A terrible plague is gripping the city of Delta, and it is crippling our economy."

Each member of the Council put forward some crisis from their region. It became clear to Micheal, and he believed to Julie that they expected them to rule the Atlantean Empire.

"Leave all your petitions. We will attend them." Micheal said with authority.

As they were nearing the end of the Council meeting, he noticed a young man hiding behind one of the pedestals. At that moment, Cato noticed him also. "Gabriel, get out here!" The young man appeared to be a teen. "My apologies, this is my son, Gabriel... Gabriel, you will show respect for their eminences. And you will apologize for your intrusion."

Gabriel went to one knee. "My apologies, your holy eminences."

"How old are you?"

"18, eminence Koios." He replied, averting his eyes. Then he looked up at Julie, eyes wide. "You're really Aphrodite. Your beauty has enraptured me," he said, unblinking as if hypnotized.

"Gabriel, leave this instant. You make a fool of yourself."

After Gabriel left, Cato once again apologized. And particularly to Julie.

As the Council meeting came to an end, Cato said. "Many thanks, now your eminences. Until your palace is built, we humbly offer the Emperor's Palace." He looked at the ground.

Julie laughed. "This is their humble offering?"

Micheal calculated that the Emperor's Palace was easily 5 to 10 times bigger than Bostonian.

"The Palace of the Gods is going to be about 50 times bigger than Bostonian."

"That's insane! Who could possibly need that much space?" She shook her head.

"I suppose the gods. And we are Gods."

"You're just loving this, aren't you?"

"Maybe a little bit. But it does come with a lot of responsibility." He changed the subject. "I don't know if you understood what I asked Cato. But it might help to explain something, partially at least."

"What?"

"Why there are no old people."

"What did you ask him?" She went and sat on a lounger; he joined her.

"In his introduction, Cato said he led the counsel through centuries of growth. So, I asked how old he was. He said he was 612."

"That's impossible, or maybe you mistranslated it."

"No, I'm absolutely sure."

"You said this might explain no elderly people?"

"What if the Bible is correct, in one aspect at least?"

"The Bible?"

"Genesis says people lived over 900 years. The dates on these petitions say the year is 757 PF. PF, I've come to understand, means post fall."

"Okay?" She shrugged in confusion.

"Post fall? If the fall refers to Adam and Eve, people live upwards of a thousand years. And there's only been 757 years since the fall. There would be no old people."

"Why?" She made a funny face.

"Because, unlike the normal portrayal in movies where anyone over 100 years old is always old and wrinkly, even if they would live for a thousand years. In reality, people would only show signs of aging when nearing death. The process would probably last between 30 and 50 years. So if you lived a thousand years, you would probably be young for 950 of it. And there would be no old people if it had only been 757 years since the fall."

"Wow, I never thought of it like that before."

"Here, study these." He handed her the council's petitions. "We need to get you fully up to speed on Atlantean."

She shook her head. "Oh, all right." She sighed.

Idol Worship

-October 13, 3281 BC

"So apparently I'm Aphrodite, Atlantean Goddess of Love and Beauty. It's so weird to have everyone stare at you with awe. And to know a great deal of them are praying to you. If anyone still doubts our godliness, I haven't seen it. I've become casually fluent in Atlantean. I tried out a new God element that I conceived. We call it the God voice. In secret, we installed resonance posts all over the city. And when you speak with the resonator I engineered, the buildings of the city become like a speaker. When Micheal took a turn, I realized the effect would probably convince anyone it was the voice of a God.

We have adapted the polarization field that usually protects us from metal weapons to buffer the airflow when flying. This has greatly increased the speed of our flight. The suppression allows speeds near the sound barrier. I only use it for long-distance flights. I prefer the wind in my hair.

The Babylonians have been making incursions in the satellite kingdom of Libya on the southeast frontier of the Empire. Next week, we go to put a stop to it. Let's hope the gods show impresses them enough to eliminate the problem.

In the meantime, we need to select the priestesses who will serve us. They've brought them from all over the Empire. I'm not sure what qualifications I'm supposed to look for, but I guess whatever I decide is correct; I am Aphrodite, after all, so how could I be wrong?"

JULIE sat on the throne at the Temple of Aphrodite. The first prospect entered the chamber.

A stunning redhead entered; her sky-green eyes were almost translucent. Her long skirt was split on the side, exposing her leg, and her boosted corset barely contained her chest.

"I, Aquilina, do swear to serve you, Eminence Aphrodite, in the cause of love. I promise to promote the art of seduction and illuminate the joys of bodily pleasure to bind the masculine and feminine in synergistic harmony. I promise to maintain my physical appearance to exemplify the divine beauty of the female form. I offer myself fully to serve your desires or whatever you may require of me."

"What is your age and experience?"

"I am 214 and have practiced with 200 men and 400 women, and I have freelanced 112 women."

As the day wore on, Julie deduced that the minimum age was 14, and each priestess would *practice* with one man and two women per year. And they only ever *freelanced* with women.

The youngest so far was 81, which was more than twice her age. The oldest was 312. It appeared Micheal might be right about the aging element. But the final candidate entered the chamber.

It was Melina Hellas, the head of the discovery party. She'd been the only one to serve them since their discovery. But she'd said nothing about herself.

She was developing a particular fondness for Melina. She was much less intimidated by them than most of the others. She was a petite blond about half a foot shorter than her, with big bright green doe eyes.

She'd definitely dressed to impress. She wore a silky sky-blue corset that emphasized her modest chest. The ankle-length skirt was open in the front, exposing her milky white thighs. A lace choker accented her neck, and her hair was loose curls pulled up in a twist.

Melina gave the same oath as all the rest. Julie was curious about her numbers.

"I'm 19 years old. I've practiced with three men and six women. And I've freelanced with three other women."

"How did you lead our greeting party at such a young age?"

"It was my devotion to the prophecy that led me to you. So, the council appointed me."

"I have determined that you are perfect to serve as my principal priestess. That is all."

Melina suppressed a smile. "I won't fail you, Your Eminence." She bowed, then departed.

A few days later, Julie was beginning to get more comfortable in the role of Aphrodite. She had been practicing the use of the different rings. She had to admit she was most certainly enjoying the flying part. It almost made her truly feel like a Greek Goddess.

She returned from an evening flight, and Melina was sitting in their private chamber.

"My apologies, Your Eminence." She dropped to her knees.

"You may rise." She said in her much-improved Atlantean. "Melina, if you're going to attend me on a regular basis, I would ask you to address me as Aphrodite."

"Yes, Your Em... I mean Aphrodite." Melina stammered.

"Better. Now, you may bring me my dinner."

Melina returned with dinner. "Where is His Eminence?"

"He is tending to the plague in Delta." Melina was about to leave. "Remain... Tell me about you."

"You really want to know?" Melina seemed surprised. Julie nodded. "My parents passed when I was very young. I went to live with my Aunt Dalla. She was devoted to you. I began preparing to be a priestess at your temple in Eden. That's where I'm from. My aunt had a statue of you. It was so beautiful. I mean, you are so beautiful." Melina stammered.

"Thank you."

"After Dalla died, the high priestess sent me away. I moved from place to place until I read the prophecy. I knew the gods would come soon, so I went to Atlantis. That was clearly where you would come from. Then I was on the coast north of the city when I saw Your Eminences arrive out of the heaven's gate. I knew you were the prophecy come true. That's when I knew destiny had called me. The prophecy did not specify which gods it would be. I was overjoyed when I learned it was you, Aphrodite; I am entirely devoted to you."

"Your devotion is appreciated." Julie felt a sense of responsibility on her shoulders to live up to the image of a Greek-like goddess. At least so far, she thought she was pulling it off. She was also curious about the prophecy. "Tell me about the prophecy."

"Twenty years ago, the world was suffering a terrible crisis because of the Great War of Empires, between Atlantis and Babylon. Billions died in the conflict and the plagues that followed. Empress Cyra was executed because of her failure in the war. No one wanted to replace her. People were desperate for hope. That's when Seth, the Great Seer of Eden, made a declaration that when a generation had passed since the Empress lost her crown, the gods would come and usher in a golden age. . . And I'm so blessed to see your arrival. One other omen connects me to the prophecy, but you don't care about that."

"Melina, clearly I see your quality."

"My birth occurred the same day Empress Cyra lost her head. When I read the prophecy, that coincidence made me believe I would discover the gods."

"With expansive lifespans and large families, how is it that you have no family?"

"My family has been devoted to the gods for centuries. That limits how many children we have. All my aunts and uncles had no children. All but my Aunt Dalla perished in the war plagues. My grandparents died long before I was born. My parents never meant to have a child. I was a mistake. So, when my parents died in a flood, I became an inconvenience for Dalla. Then she was murdered." Her eyes were welling, and she was fighting to contain it.

Julie rose and touched her cheek. "Melina, you are not a mistake or an inconvenience."

"Thank you, Aphrodite. May I be excused?"

"Of course."

⁎

The next day, *Aphrodite* paid a visit to her temple. The priestesses were busy practicing their *arts* on each other. They all stopped and prostrated themselves before her. This was her first visit to the temple since she selected her priestesses. It was an odd procession offering their lives to her service. They were all so devout that she didn't want to damage their faith.

"As you were." Julie didn't need any more idol worship. The priestesses reengaged in *practice*.

The temple had three statues of Aphrodite—one for each aspect of love, sex, and beauty running through the center of the main hall. An enclosed sanctuary specifically for her was at the end of the main hall. And flanking the main hall on either side were small chambers, about 5 feet wide, designated by columns. She thought there were 40 or 50 on both sides. So, the main hall was probably 200 feet long by 100 feet wide. And the whole temple was around 250 by 150 feet.

Julie had to maintain her divine aspect in the face of the activities being performed in her name. The side chambers alternated between love, sex, and beauty.

In one chamber, two priestesses were practicing protestations of love. In the next, two more were practicing on each other's pussies. In the next, they were discussing aspects of beauty.

The ladies came and went as she made her way toward the sanctuary. Then, something looked out of place.

It was a man. She moved closer. It was Gabriel Maximus. He appeared quite different than he had in the Council Chamber. He was taller than she originally thought. He was nearly as tall as she was. His long brown hair was held back in a headband. His eyes were sparkling blue. He wore only a loin cloth and a decorative sash that was emblazed with the symbology of Aphrodite.

His body was rather skinny. Obviously, he hadn't filled it out yet. He was only 18.

"Lord Maximus, do explain your presence here."

He dropped to one knee. "Eminence Aphrodite, forgive my intrusion. My father has permitted me an exemption to serve Your Eminence as a priest, should you have me."

Julie didn't know what to do. Clearly, Gabriel had an infatuation with her. And she wasn't sure she wanted to encourage that, but denying him would cause a potential problem with Cato. He was the head of the council so she would deal with him daily. Aside from Melina, she would have more limited interaction with the priestesses. She decided allowing it would be less problematic.

"This is highly unusual, but I'll accept your service if you swear to uphold my tenants. Now follow me."

She led him into the sanctuary, took her throne, and he kneeled before her.

"First, you must swear the oath."

He recounted the same speech all her ladies had before.

"What is your age and experience?"

"I am 18 and have no experience."

"Why do you wish to serve me?"

He looked up at her, then averted his eyes. "I have felt love in my heart since my youth. I studied your divine purpose and knew I was meant for love, not politics. So, when Your Holy Eminence came in the flesh, I knew this was my destiny."

He sounded like Melina.

"Rise. As this is a special circumstance, I have some edicts that will only apply to you. First, you are held to the same love and beauty standards as the priestesses. But pertaining to sex. So long as you are in my service, you are not permitted to freelance. You will practice only with my priestess at the direction of the head priestess. If you violate this edict, the consequences will be harsh. And you will be designated special housing. You will not reside in the main House of Love. See Melina tomorrow for specific instructions. You are dismissed for the day."

"I am eternally grateful. I will endeavor always to honor your divine beauty."

Julie gave him a stern look but said nothing.

"My apologies, Your Eminence." He rose and stared for a long second, then departed.

She sighed and shook her head. How did she become the idol of so much worship? Then she remembered—Micheal's Ghostbusters logic.

An Erudite Priestess

A few days later, Micheal returned from Delta.

"So, how did it go?" He came and joined JULIE in the Roman-style bath.

"My ionization water attractor filtration system works. I had the bores core out a sewer system and clean source water delivery pipes. As soon as the water system was complete, I poured in the penicillin mixture, and within two days, 'the plague' was more or less gone."

"That's great. Guess what I found out?"

"What?"

"Melina saw us come out of the time portal."

"Well, that is something." He put his hand to his chin.

"And there's something else. Cato said Gabriel could serve me as a priest."

"And you agreed?"

She wiped his neck with a sponge. "I didn't want to rock the boat, as it were."

"Oh well, it's just a boyish crush. And you would've still had to deal with it. He's the Prince of Atlantis Proper, the heir to Cato's throne. There was no getting rid of him. Maybe this will allow more control over his energies."

"On a different note, I had wondered about something we discussed a while ago?"

"Okay?"

"Well, first, where did you come up with the concept of the thousand-year lifespan?" She studied him.

"Some documentary I saw on aging." He shrugged.

"I guess you should explain that to me."

"The show talked about a study on rats where they cleansed the free radicals out of one group's bloodstream. The control group lived for about two years. The group with the cleansed blood lived nearly ten times longer, around 20 years. They also demonstrated no signs of aging until shortly before their deaths. So, I speculated that if the effect was the same on humans. The human lifespan being around 100 years times 10 would be 1000 years."

"That's incredible." She wondered at the prospects. "I know about free radicals. But that leads back to my original question. How would it be possible?"

"To that, I've developed a theory. Remember the dome bubble thing in the sky?" He raised a brow.

"Yes."

"I've been analyzing it, and it seems to stop nearly all harmful radiation that generates free radicals. And more than 99% of all free radicals come from the sun. If all of that is being blocked, then I would guess the DNA just runs its normal course. Who knows what that is? But the Bible claims Methuselah lived 969 years. Maybe he really did, or should I say he does. If you believe the Bible timeline, he's alive right now."

That was a lot to consider. Then she remembered another thing.

"I meant to ask about your priestesses. After our selection ceremonies, you left for Delta, and we never discussed it. I was curious why?"

"Because I didn't have time for what would likely be a contentious discussion."

That was concerning. "Why would it be contentious?"

"The erudite philosophy has some interesting quirks-"

"Such as?" She leaned back against the side of the bath.

"They don't believe in clothing. So, the only thing they wear is some kind of undercup support."

"So, they're naked all the time? Why don't they believe in clothing?"

He raised air quotes. "The human body is inherently natural and aesthetically pleasing. Therefore, the only justification for covering it is due to climatic conditions. Otherwise, clothing represents a significant waste of resources and time."

"What did you call it? An undercup?"

"Basically, a bra without cups. Designed to maintain the ascetics of the breast while using the least amount of resources."

He clarified before she ever asked. She decided to move on.

"Any other interesting quirks?"

"They all offered themselves for my use. But thinking about it, that's likely included in all oaths to the gods. Unless you're going to tell me, your priestesses didn't make that offer."

"I think you're right." Julie laughed. "How did we get here? . . . Oh yeah, 'cause one of us watched too many movies."

Micheal rubbed his eyes. "I'm never going to live this down, am I?"

"Not if I can help it." She considered a second. "Fine, now that we are here, I don't think it's our place to mess with the fundamentals of these people's faith. And there is abundant public nudity all over the city anyway. So, when do I meet your head priestess?"

"Her name is Elissa, and now that I'm back, she'll be here tomorrow. But we need to be careful. I chose her because she's clearly an innate genius. And that means she may be intelligent enough to see through our ruse."

"Maybe pick someone else?"

"I can't. While they're all quite smart, she's certainly a step above. If I chose someone else, they would all be confused by the choice and begin questioning my logic. Which could lead them down the very path we want them to avoid."

"Erudites." They shared a laugh.

The next morning, they found Melina laying out their clothing. She was quiet and efficient and then exited the chamber.

When they finished dressing, a stunning woman entered, and she wore no clothes. It must be Elissa. She matched Melina in height. Her chestnut hair was up in a twist. And her hazel eyes were intent on the task of setting up breakfast. Her body was smooth and slim. Her flawless skin was light tan with not an ounce of hair. The undercup didn't appear necessary to support her modest but firm breasts.

Julie told herself there was nothing to worry about because Micheal would never take advantage of the power dynamic with someone who worshipped him. But her beauty was bewitching for such an erudite.

Elissa was all business, and aside from her nod upon entry, she barely acknowledged her.

Once the food was spread, Julie addressed Elissa. "Thank you, Elissa; please remain; I would speak with you." Micheal had gone to his closet to retrieve something.

"Of course, Eminence Aphrodite." She looked at the floor.

"How do you find His Eminence?"

"He is most wise, and his knowledge knows no bounds."

"Is that the only thing you think of him?"

"He exemplifies all I ever imagined he could. I am most honored to serve His Eminence."

"Tell me about yourself."

"I'm from Greece originally. I'm 181 years old, which makes me the youngest in his service. When I was young, my father recognized my superior intelligence and sent me to one of the greatest sages in Celtic. It was halfway across the world, but my father wanted me to utilize my gift. I quickly outmatched him, so I realized there was nothing else he could teach me. I searched for answers to the source of my unique intellect. I was directed to the Temple of Koios in Tyre, on the Frozen Sea. The head priestess explained how the God of Wisdom chose a select few to grant divine intelligence. That was the answer to my quandary. She taught me how to maximize my mental output. Then, after a few years in Tyre, the head priestess in Amazon retired. My mentor nominated me for the position and I served as head priestess there ever since. And, of course, when the call came to serve the god himself, I was a natural choice."

"Quite fascinating. I have a few queries regarding your logic. Is it not a waste of time and energy to maintain your appearance to such a degree?"

"The mind cannot function without the body. It's rational to keep the body in prime shape."

"Removing hair serves no logical purpose. Is that not a complete waste of time?"

"There is a minor benefit in maintaining cleanliness. However, I'll concede to my vanity in this case. I prefer no hair, but regular shaving would be far too wasteful. So, I spent a few weeks developing a cream that removes the hair with a single application. That means on the cycles of the sun, I apply this cream, and I remain silky smooth." She traced the curves of her body.

"Thank you, Elissa."

She bowed, then departed. And Julie thought she would need to borrow this magic cream at some point.

War Games

They flew southeast to Carthage, the capital of Libya, which was technically a satellite territory allied with Atlantis. Babylon had been making incursions, and Libya had appealed to Atlantis for assistance, but the Council was paralyzed on what to do, worried about another war with Babylon.

MICHEAL checked the location of all their magnetized boulders.

"What did the sky-net show pertaining to the siege arrangements?" Julie asked as they hovered a few hundred feet above the ground.

"My analysis indicates around 50,000 in the siege army. And around 5000 Atlantean soldiers and another 10,000 or so soldiers are inside the city." He looked at his handheld. "They've been there for nearly two years. Let's talk to the leaders in the city. Then we will deal with the siege army."

As they flew over the siege zone, Micheal could see that everyone was pretty much mesmerized. They came in to land in the main forum. And everyone went to the ground.

"You may rise," Julie said.

"Your Holy Eminences. You've come to rescue us!" The obvious Lord of the city said with joy.

"People of Carthage, your ordeal will end today," Micheal said pedantically. The entire crowd cheered.

"What will Your Eminences do?" The Lord asked.

"We will instruct them to leave; if they refuse, we will make them wish they had."

They had a similar response on their arrival at the enemy camp.

"You're the gods we have heard about?" The Babylonian general said, unimpressed. "You seem small for Gods. Emperor Samano has priests at his court who can duplicate your levitation stunt. I have seen it. It's a neat trick, to be sure. You are certainly not gods. Kill them."

"You don't want to do that." Micheal threatened, showing no fear.

"If you were Gods, we would never have had this conversation."

"We were just being merciful." Micheal brought lightning to his hand.

The executioners attempted to kill them, but their swords wouldn't penetrate the polarized fields. Julie brought up her lightning and then sent a lightning ball. The energy pulse knocked out the general and his entire council.

They flew out of the general's manor and rose above the siege zone. Micheal could see the walls of Carthage lined with spectators. He flew over to one of their pre-magnetized boulders and picked it up. It likely weighed between 30 and 50 tons. He flew it over and dropped it on a siege tower. Julie began laying waste with her kinetic staff and diamond sword. Then she picked up a boulder and dropped it on another siege tower.

Micheal took a direct hit from a scorpion, but it deflected off. He rose up and used a focused, high-energy lightning pulse to set fire to the rest of the siege equipment. As he approached the retreating siege army, they all froze and began going to their knees, crying for mercy.

Julie landed, carrying the general, then threw him toward the front of the line of bowing soldiers. "You will leave your weapons and return to your lands. If you do not, you will see the end of our mercy."

Micheal gave a long stare to the general. Who appeared genuinely stunned as he looked over the devastation. Then he went to his knees.

As the Babylonians began to depart, Micheal warned. "We will be watching."

"You're letting them go?" The Lord of Carthage asked in confusion.

"They return to Babylon. We desire peace. They will not return. If they deviate in any way on their journey through your lands. We will show no mercy." Julie reproached him sharply.

"My apologies, Your Eminences," he said, bowing. "We give great thanks to Your Eminences for our liberty."

Having broken the siege, they headed to where the Libyan army was sent to meet the invading Babylonians. They arrived on the frontier as the two sides lined up for battle.

"Thank the Gods, Your Eminences, for arriving; we are outmatched. They outnumber us with more than 150,000 to our 50,000," the Libyan general exclaimed with relief.

Following another unproductive parlay, they prepared for battle again. This time, they had no pre-magnetized boulders to throw around, so Micheal knew it was just them and their weapons against 150,000 men.

As they were about to go, the general asked, "What do you want us to do?"

"Watch."

They flew the gap between the armies to meet the Babylonians. He could see that some of them were riding woolly mammoths. Micheal landed right in front of the line, whipping out his kinetic constricting chain mace. He extended it in full 20-foot constriction, swung around, and swept the legs out from under the first three rows in the center.

Julie came down hard in the middle of the rest of the front rows. A flash of lightning generated an electric pulse shockwave that knocked out most of the soldiers in the immediate area. She lit up her diamond sword and charged the nearest line. The light pulse blinded the soldiers, and her sword cut through all their swords and shields like a hot knife through butter.

Micheal flew up and systematically knocked all the riders off their mammoths. He rose over the battlefield with lightning in his hands. Julie came to meet him, and their lightning balls merged. At his signal, they propelled the giant ball of electricity down to the middle of the army now in full retreat. The shockwave was immense, and around half the army dropped stunned.

Micheal had a thought. He flew over the center of the army and activated his voice resonator, hoping the swords would work.

"Halt!" He said in God's voice. *It worked.* Everyone froze in place, then went to their knees.

"In our mercy, we command you. Leave your weapons. Return to your lands. Fail to heed this order, and the limit of our mercy shall be known."

With the war in Libya over, they returned to Atlantis. Micheal had originally been concerned that they'd bitten off more than they could chew. But he found that their superior intellect and advanced knowledge were plenty to deal with whatever Atlantis needed. They could be gods to these people.

CHAPTER III: PLAYING GODS

Global Affairs

DECEMBER 25, 3281 BC

—

"It's our first Christmas in Atlantis. Obviously, no one here celebrates it. But they do have a holiday. The Rebirth Festival is 5 and sometimes 6 days at the end of the year, following the winter solstice.

The Atlanteans had calculated the exact length of the year. They arranged the calendar to have 12 equal months of 30 days, with three 10-day weeks. The festival didn't take place in any month. It was the rebalance of the calendar. Most years, it was 5 days, but every four years it was 6. It was a leap festival, as it were. Nobody works, and it's just a big party until the new year comes. This year is a leap festival, so everyone gets an extra day off.

Being gods gives us the ability to follow our own prerogative. All our servants had the festival off. So, I did the tree. We utilized some of their instrument analogs to play Christmas carols. Micheal recited 'A Christmas Carol' from memory. And, of course, we exchanged gifts.

We emceed the Ceremony of Death, sunset on the solstice. And tomorrow, we will oversee the Ceremony of Life at the dawn of the new year.

The new year will begin the next phase of our rule. We will visit monarchs from across the globe. Micheal will start in Greece, located in future Southeast Asia, on the most distant coast of pangea.

I will tour the most southern stretch of land. The area comprising future South America, Africa, Antarctica, Australia, and the Indian subcontinent, which are all puzzled together in the current configuration. My first stop is in Egypt, which is in the same location it will be whenever the continents shift to their normal locations. Would the ruler match the king's list Micheal laid out?

But this whole pangea situation just gave me a thought. What mechanism could rapidly shift the continents? Whatever is coming will surely end the Empire of Atlantis. Will the 'mythical' city sink into the sea in a day? I pray we don't live to see it, for on that day, we would surely die."

JULIE made the 1300-mile distance in about two hours. She located the royal palace and landed at the entry gate. This was not the Egypt she remembered from her visit in the 21st century. It was still centered on the Nile River, which was actually named the Nile. Many modern rivers and other landmarks already existed but went by different names.

However, the entire region was a lush jungle environment. The palace was located in Memphis. A bit south of the Giza Plateau.

"His Majesty was not expecting your visit. Would you please wait here while I inform the Vizier?" The guard bowed and then departed.

Julie hadn't known what would greet her. None of these visits had been announced. Telephones and the internet didn't exist yet. But they did want to make an impression with the other global powers. They thought that would be the fastest way to guarantee peace.

The guards' reactions clearly showed that the word had spread.

A woman finally approached. She had a dark tan complexion, big brown eyes, and jet-black hair to the shoulder.

"Eminence Aphrodite, I am the Vizier of Egypt. King Khayu welcomes this unexpected visit from the Goddess of Atlantis." She led Julie into the palace.

The court was a murmur of voices that fell silent at their entry.

"Your Majesty, allow me to present Aphrodite, Atlantean Goddess of Love." The Vizier Joined the King and Queen on the dais.

"When I was informed gods had come down to rule The Atlantean Empire, I thought it had to be some fairytale. But then I heard about the war in Libya. Only gods could perform the miracles that were described. So, what can a lowly king do for a goddess?"

"My apologies for not formally proclaiming my visit, but human modes of travel are far too slow, and we desired to personally establish a relationship with the nations of the world to bring harmony to the world."

"There has been some consternation in my court since word of the Babylonian defeat reached us. Some wonder if you plan to conquer the entire world?"

"That was a defensive action. Why would you fear conquest?"

"We have our own gods and our own beliefs. You may very well be a true goddess, but not of Egypt. And many of my advisors saw how easily you could bring us to heel if you so desired. So, their question is, 'Why wouldn't you make the whole world Atlantis?'"

Julie wanted to laugh, but that wouldn't be very godly. The Atlantean Empire, for which they had responsibility, was already a pain in the ass to run. She didn't want to think about dealing with the rest of the world.

It wouldn't just be an administrative nightmare; the disparate religious beliefs would make things even more challenging. Even in Atlantis, where the majority literally worshipped her, there were still sizable minorities of other faiths who wanted her dead. Can you imagine what it would be like to navigate a world filled with such diverse beliefs?

"Our purpose in coming down from the heavens was to help those who believe in us, not force those who lack faith. One of the best ways is to have friendly and peaceful relationships with the rest of the world. If our presence inspires more to believe clearly, we'd welcome this. But force would only lead to conflict, which is deleterious to our cause. We desire peace."

"I understand that even gods require food. My chefs shall prepare a feast in your honor. And until it's ready, we can discuss Egypt's relationship with Atlantis."

Julie wasn't worried anyone would try to poison them on these diplomatic missions. Not only because she doubted they would want to start a war with Atlantis, which would surely come from such an action. But when preparing for their run through the timeline, they weren't sure what they would face. So, she decided to engineer a program in their handhelds that could scan for poisons and toxins. So, she always scanned any food that she was going to eat.

They had primarily expected positive reactions from the various leaders, so they discussed the various nations with the council and prepared proposals for each. This made the discussion go smoothly, and by the time the Vizier notified them about the feast, they had reached an agreement.

The feast ran into the night. She was asked to demonstrate her incredible powers, which almost made her feel like a novelty show. But it definitely served the purpose of legitimizing their identities. And if that could foster peace and friendship, she would play the circus freak.

A Celtic Queen

While Julie was touring the south, MICHEAL was touring the east. He had started in Greece and worked his way back through China, Phoenicia, Assyria, Sumeria, and Mesopotamia, and now he was in Celtic at the capitol of Cedeva, on the Sea of Egypt.

"Queen Kasia is pleased to receive you." He was led into the hall.

Micheal began walking. "Perhaps, Eminence Koios, you would fly?" The Queen requested. She hadn't been the first.

He levitated up to the ceiling and brought lightning to his palms. His audience wore the same gaze of awe of all his past performances.

Micheal couldn't blame them. It's not like they have TV, movies, and other visual means to entertain them. His magic show might be the most excitement any of them ever get.

The Queen rose to meet him as he landed. Her eyes were captivated by the glowing energy in his hands. She reached out.

"Your Majesty doesn't want to do that." Her hand stopped an inch from the light.

"Will it kill me?"

"It's possible. But you would certainly be laid to rest, and I doubt your guards would react well to that situation." He closed his hands, and the electricity dissipated.

"Since word came of the Gods of Atlantis, I have desired to meet you. Celtic has long had a friendship with Atlantis. I had read the prophecy but questioned its validity. You understand how unreliable 'prophets' can be."

"I hope I don't disappoint you."

She looked him up and down. "On the contrary, you're as magnificent as I imagined. And you can count on Celtic as an ally. I look forward to furthering our relationship. No negotiation is necessary. So rather than all the boring politics, join me privately for a more interesting conversation. The feast will be ready by nightfall."

Based on how she was eyeing him, he wondered if she would proposition him. She had no husband and a reputation for a heavy sexual appetite. She actually had her own harem of both men and women.

They retired to her chamber, and she sent all the servants away so it was just the two of them. Then things seemed to be going how he'd suspected they might.

"Allow me to get more comfortable." She began removing all her clothes. Her body was like porcelain, and there was not an ounce of hair. It reminded him of his priestesses. Elissa had engineered a cream they all used to stay 'clean.' Her deep red hair was pulled up in a braided crown, supporting her golden crown. Now completely naked, she then fastened an undercup to support her large breasts. And that emphasized her large, erect pink nipples. She came and presented herself before him. Her stark blue eyes were locked on him.

"I know you won't accept my offering. But just know, I'm always willing." She cupped her breast and pinched her nipple with one hand and rubbed between her legs with the other.

"That's a generous offer, but Aphrodite would disapprove."

"Indeed. I hope you don't think my state of dress was just to please you. The trappings of royalty are so confining and wasteful, don't you think?" She caressed her body.

Queen Kasia reminded him of his priestesses in more ways than silky smooth skin.

"If I hadn't been in line for the throne, I would have pledged my life to you, Koios. While I was only the crown princess, I studied at your temple. That's when I met Elissa. There's no one more worthy to serve you."

And there it was. "She is the ideal servant."

"While I would most like to please you, Eminence Koios, it would be an even greater honor to discuss the nature of life and the world with you."

"Where do you want to start?"

"How do birds fly?" The Queen brought drinks and sat across from him.

The oddity of a stranger casually sitting there completely naked faded away, and the conversation became normal, which made sense. It was the same kind of discussion he would have weekly with Elissa. He would be lying if he said it wasn't a bonus to have a beautiful naked woman on the other side of the conversation. And Kasia proved to match the intellect level of his priestesses.

Following the feast, the Queen requested another private conversation because they'd had to discuss more mundane things in the company of guests.

That conversation ran into dawn. And Queen Kasia finally gave into exhaustion. He signaled her servants.

Three women came to tend the Queen. Two carried her to her bed. "Your Eminence, Her Majesty, prepared this bed for you." The third led him through a curtain to a bed cordoned off from the rest of the Queen's Chamber.

While it was a bit close for comfort, he was too tired to question it.

The next day, Micheal departed late because of the late night. He was concerned that some people might get the wrong idea and that the word could get back to Julie.

A Night Flight

JULIE continued her tour of the South. She had similar receptions at each stop. She visited Nubia, India, Phillistia, Akkadia, Africa, and Persia. The only major nation she skipped was Babylon. She completed the cycle in just 14 days, two faster than anticipated. So, she would have some alone time in Atlantis.

She arrived at the palace. Melina was studying the face of the moon.

"Aphrodite! I did not expect you so soon." She did a quick bow and then was about to go. "I'll prepare dinner for you."

"Don't bother, I already ate."

"Was your mission successful?"

"So much so that I finished early. That's why I returned tonight."

"I can't believe you went all the way to the end of the world. What's it like to soar through the sky?"

"Would you like to experience it yourself?"

"You would fly me?"

Julie stepped to the balcony's edge. Melina hesitated. "Have no fear. It is quite amazing."

She drew Melina in front of her and ran one of her suspension cables below her breasts and the other across her hips. She took her hands and embraced her from behind.

"And here we go."

She slowly rose up over Mount Atlas. She then glided over the skyscrapers of central Atlantis. As they flew, the tension slowly drained from Melina's body.

"Want to go higher?" Julie propelled up to the base of the clouds.

Atlantis became muted rings of light—the glow of the lamplights illuminating the night.

"I never imagined I would experience heaven. But my Goddess of Love has taken me here."

"I haven't taken you there yet. But I can take you close. Get ready; we're about to really move."

She accelerated to full speed, heading toward the western horizon. Then shot up toward space. All the clouds were distant whisps below. The sky had been near the end of twilight when they left, and with their rising the sun came with them.

"How is such possible?"

"Is this more like heaven?"

You could see the glowing curve of the Earth. The silver sun sat on the horizon, beginning to sink again. The clouds helped paint an exquisite pallet.

"Aside from you, my eyes have never seen such beauty." Melina leaned her head back on her shoulder.

They watched their personal sunset, and then it was time to take a twilight dive.

"This is one of my favorite things to do." She deactivated the black rings, and they went into freefall.

Their skydive was over the coast of the Atlantic Passage. She reactivated the rings just before the rushing beach could catch them. She propelled out over the darkening water until a lunar trail stretched toward the eastern shore. She brought them to a pause a thousand feet above the edge of the Atlantean Islands. The Moon was casting shadows in the city.

"This experience has inspired some questions."

"Such as?"

"How high would we need to fly to reach Selene? Is there anything higher? Like the sun?"

"Selene takes care of the night, but she's not the limit. Nor is the sun. For reasons you wouldn't understand, no human could reach Selene. But there are things higher up. You could fly higher and higher forever and never find the end of creation."

They flew a spiral over the city, finishing at the palace.

Julie released her friend.

"I am so honored you would give me this experience. I could feel your power flowing through me. And to go where only the gods can go? I'm unworthy. But I knew I was perfectly safe in your arms." Melina embraced her, and she returned the favor, threading her fingers through her hair.

"Perhaps we can do it again sometime."

"I love you, Aphrodite."

"Thank you, Melina. Now I think it's time for bed."

"Of course." She bowed and departed the chamber.

As she watched her friend leave, Julie wondered how much of the real Julie Melina loved. Or was it just the idealized image she'd created in her head? So, she felt isolated again. She would never be able to be her true self with anyone here. Both the truth and the lie would leave her lonely.

A Babylonian Princess

MICHEAL was flying along the coast of Celtic near the Atlantean border when he saw a fleet of ships that had wrecked upon the rocks. He flew down to investigate and was able to identify the ships as coming from Babylon.

He used the sky-net to do a thermal check for any survivors. He'd already seen some dead bodies in the icy surf. A snowstorm had just left the area, so if anyone had survived, the thermal scan should have no trouble spotting them.

He found only one, and it was a bit small. He wondered if it might be an animal.

Micheal landed at the location and found two frozen men; they were obviously dead. But beneath them was a woman. Only her face was exposed. He checked her, and she had a faint pulse.

As he dragged her from beneath the men who'd sacrificed themselves for her, he wondered if it was for more than simple chivalry. *Who was she?*

At the Atlantean border, another warm spot on the scan was right on the coast. Its size said it was a structure, maybe a light-house.

It was about 20 miles away, but it would only be a few minutes by flight. It was a bit more than two hours to Atlantis, and Julie would be expecting him. But would this woman survive the flight to Atlantis?

He found the lighthouse empty. But a fire was burning in the fireplace. The keeper must have stepped out. It didn't matter. He needed to get her warm as quickly as possible.

He removed her chilly, wet clothing, further establishing her potential importance. The fabric was very high-end, the kind he had only seen on high-level nobility or royalty. She wore a gold necklace that was accented with multiple fine gems. He placed her in a chair beside the fire and searched for clothes or blankets. There were none—only a few dirty rags. There was almost nothing else of use.

He felt her skin, and she was ice cold; he decided he had only one option. He brought her to the floor next to the fireplace and laid her on top of him so she was facing him. He wrapped himself around her to lend as much of his heat as possible. She'd been unconscious the whole time. He might be too late, but he had to try.

After a while, she began to shiver, and her breathing quickened. That was a good sign as her body was coming to life. She began to press into him, looking for warmth.

Slowly, she thawed in his embrace, the shivering subsided, and her breathing became slow and steady. She rose slightly and looked at him. "Thank you. Can we sit?"

"Of course. How do you feel?" Micheal sat up facing the fire, with his legs crossed. She sat in his lap with her legs crossed and pulled his hands down to her breasts.

"I'm so cold." He could feel her icy, hard nipples in his palms. "That's so much better. You have no idea how sore my nipples feel right now."

"At least it sounds like you're going to be okay eventually. But I might want to check your fingers and toes for frostbite." She was moving both extremities, so frostbite was unlikely.

"My fingers and toes are fine. Where's everyone else?"

"It seems you're the only survivor. If I had come by a few minutes later, you wouldn't have."

She dropped her head, and he felt tears on his arms. "Belili only came 'cause I asked her to. She was one of my closest friends."

"I'm sorry." He embraced her a little tighter. She cried for a few minutes.

She finally calmed down. Through the sniffles, she asked. "Where are we anyway? We got totally lost in the storm. We didn't know where we were when we crashed."

"A lighthouse a couple of miles into Atlantis, just past the Celtic border." Her body tensed in his arms, but she said nothing.

"Is there something wrong?"

"I'm in great danger. And I've already failed my father on this mission. I can't afford to be ransomed. You've shown me great generosity so far. Will you help me?"

"Danger? Ransom? Who's your father?"

She turned to look at him. After studying him, she said. "My father is a very rich and powerful man. He will reward you greatly if you help me get back to him."

He took a closer look at her necklace. All the icons of Babylon were present. She quickly grabbed it, protecting it against her chest. He could see the fear in her eyes.

"Is your father Emperor Samano?"

She looked for the exit.

"You wouldn't survive an hour out there."

"Please. A reward is just as good as a ransom."

"Don't be afraid. I promise to return you to your father unharmed and free of charge. Is your name Ishtar? Crown Princess Ishtar Samano?"

She relaxed slightly and started scanning him with her eyes. "Yes. . . Why would you just help me with no catch? Everyone just uses everyone else for their own advantage. You could easily make a fortune off this situation. Or you could try and take something else from me. I'm already halfway there." She ran her hands down her body.

"I would never take advantage of a woman in distress. And I've never cared for money. I would do it because it's the right thing to do. I would do the same for anyone else in this situation. It wouldn't matter if you were a peasant woman or the Princess of Babylon."

"You've never given me your name."

"My name is Koios."

Ishtar's eyes went wide, and she stepped back. "The God of Atlantis?"

"You're lucky it was me. No normal human could've saved you."

"Atlantis is our mortal enemy. You are certainly not taking me home. I'm already a hostage."

Micheal had to laugh.

"You think it's funny to play games with me? The Gods of Babylon never play these kinds of games. They have honor and dignity."

"I play no games. I made you a promise, and I never break my promises."

She was staring at him. "You laid waste to our armies in Libya. No formal peace has been agreed upon. So, I would be a prisoner of war."

He chuckled, shaking his head. "Do you want to be a prisoner? Cause I will take you wherever you like. If you want to be our guest at the palace, I'll take you back to Atlantis with me, and you can stay as long as you like. Although that might make it more difficult for us to make peace with Babylon if we took you hostage. Because that would have to be the story. Or tomorrow, I will take you to Babylon, and whatever mission you failed will pale in comparison to how happy your father will be that you're alive."

"I'm sorry. I was just raised to believe the Gods of Atlantis were evil. But I can see no way you gain from making this offer." She looked contemplatively. "You desire peace with Babylon? Perhaps we can help each other."

"What are you thinking?"

"Your quip about me wanting to be a prisoner. It's not far off. My father controls me like a prisoner. I could really use a break from my responsibilities, and you're wrong about my life, satiating my failure in my father's eyes. But if I were taken hostage, then my failure would become secondary, and my father would be more inclined toward peace with me as a bargaining chip. Negotiations always take a while. So, I get my holiday, and you get peace with my father."

"Are you sure this is what you want?"

"As long as you are as honorable as the Gods of Babylon?"

"I promise."

"I've always wanted to see Atlantis."

"Well then, tomorrow, your clothes should be dry by then. Until such time, as beautiful as you are, we should cover you up."

Micheal removed his tunic and handed it to her. Now, he was wearing only his loin cloth. She was definitely checking him out. "I would try and guilt you into giving me a full look, as you've certainly seen me, but we're friends now so I wouldn't do that."

She sat down and 'accidentally' pulled his cloth loose. He didn't move to cover himself. He'd been briefed on Babylon. They were notoriously conservative—particularly the royal family. Princess Ishtar had been married only once. Her husband died in the plague that followed the Great Atlantis-Babylonian War. The Emperor refused to marry her again. There was a chance he was just the second man ever to see her naked. So, despite the circumstances, he felt turnabout was fair play.

Her face was level with his groin. Her eyes were wide, locked on his dick. After a minute, he slowly spun around for her. Until he was facing her again, she laughed at his performance.

"Did you get the full look?"

Her eyes stayed on his dick. "If it's that big in this chilly room, I can only imagine how Godly it can become."

"I think you've had quite enough." He replaced the loincloth and sat next to her by the fire.

"You're not how I expected a god to be."

"What did you expect?" At this point, he remembered she'd

mentioned the Babylonian Gods.

"The first is the most obvious. You are bigger than most humans, but the gods I've seen are twice your height. But also, you almost seem human by conversation."

"So, the Gods of Babylon. You only saw them?"

"And I wasn't even supposed to do that. I interrupted his sacred meeting, and he nearly beat me to death for it. I wasn't to interact with the Gods until I ever became Empress. And they would come to me. I didn't even know about them for the first 400 years. That's how sacred my father considered them. But he felt I was ready to know when I earned my full awakening. So, for a century, I knew they were real, but I was forbidden from interacting with them."

"But curiosity got the better of you."

"Normally, the visits by the gods only occurred in the Inner Sanctum. But during the war with Atlantis, they made an impromptu visit to my father's chamber, so I took the opportunity to see them for myself. My father considered executing me but settled for the beating."

"Aside from size, what did they look like? Do you know which gods they were?"

"I think it was the King and Queen of the Anunnaki. They both had black hair and light tan skin, and glowing red eyes. And she had what looked like wings on her back."

"So, you don't know how they talk. They might talk just like this."

"I suppose you're right. I hope they're this nice."

Micheal didn't want to push her anymore on these gods. "We should get some sleep."

"I can't sleep in this chilly room."

"I could keep you warm."

"I don't know if I'd be comfortable with that either."

The conservative nature coming out again. "Suit yourself. We'll leave in the morning." He laid down next to the fire.

He began to doze when she tapped his shoulder. "I could really use some rest."

He rolled on his back, and she laid on top of him. He wrapped her in his embrace like spoons. She was tense at first, but then exhaustion won out.

The next day, it was time to show a more divine side of himself.

"So, we're going to fly to Atlantis."

"I heard you could do that. You're going to fly me?"

"We're going to need to get close again."

"I should be used to it by now."

He locked his wrists around her waist. "I'll start slow, then we'll go very fast."

Micheal took her far above the clouds and paused for a moment.

"Is this the god's view?" There was a scattered sea of white, showing intermittent coastline.

"Beautiful, isn't it? Now it's time to go fast."

An hour later, Atlantis stretched below with not a cloud in sight. He paused over Mount Atlas. "You always wanted to see Atlantis? Well, there it is. You never made it here in over 500 years?"

"My father tells me where I can go."

"Just not in this case. I hope you enjoy your vacation. It looks like the welcoming committee is coming to greet us."

Julie flew up to greet them. "You missed our special day."

"I was delayed."

"Who's our guest?"

"Aphrodite, this is Princess Ishtar, Crown Princess of Babylon."

"Highness, welcome to Atlantis. I'm sure there's an interesting story here. Let's have it in the palace." Julie gave him a look.

They descended, and Melina and Elissa met their arrival.

"Well, Your Highness, you're the last person I would've expected." Elissa bowed.

"Elissa, the erudite priestess?"

"You know each other?" Micheal thought, small world.

"Eminence Koios, I briefly visited your temple in Babylon on my way to Amazon. All foreign priestesses must present themselves before the Emperor. Princess Ishtar was there."

"Small world. The Princess will be staying with us for a while. Elissa, will you show her to the guest wing? And select some staff appropriate to her position."

"Yes, Your Eminence." Elissa escorted Ishtar away.

"I'd like that story now."

And now Micheal had more explaining to do.

Divine Rule

JULIE was still trying to decide what she thought about their new guest. But she had other questions on her mind and wondered if they were connected.

"Melina, may we have privacy?"

"Yes, Aphrodite." She departed.

"I was going to ask why you missed such an important anniversary, but first, I want to hear about The Celtic Queen."

Micheal sighed, shaking his head. "I guess word travels fast. Anyway, we have much to discuss."

Julie sat on a couch, leaning forward expectantly. "I'm all ears."

"I'll start with the Celtic Queen. She wanted to be one of my priestesses, but her father wouldn't allow it. She did the training anyway, so she kind of frowns on clothing. When we retired for our private discussions, she removed her clothes. When the agreement was settled, she wanted to have philosophical discussions with the God she most admired, and we talked through the night. The bed she prepared for me was in her chamber, so with all the factors involved, I worried her servants would spread a rumor that we slept together. Obviously, that happened."

Julie had no doubt that he was telling the truth, but she found it funny that he ended up in some of these situations.

"So, how does our Babylonian Princess fit in?"

"I departed Celtic late for reasons just stated, and as I was flying over the coast near the border with Atlantis, I saw a small fleet of half a dozen ships wrecked upon the rocks. When I did a thermal search, there was just one survivor, the Princess. I didn't know that until I'd warmed her up and we could talk."

"How did you warm her up?"

"There was a lighthouse nearby. I brought her there and used the fire."

"I'm pretty sure we're still technically at war with Babylon. Won't this cause some kind of problem?"

"She is technically our prisoner."

"I'm certain we agreed we'd never do that." Julie was frustrated that Micheal constantly made these kinds of decisions.

They had permitted each other to negotiate individually on these diplomatic missions, but she wasn't sure this qualified. And she never thought he would use this kind of tactic.

"She asked me to."

That was a new one. "What?"

"I offered to fly her to Babylon. Because, of course, I would never take advantage of someone in distress. But apparently, when the ships crashed, she failed her mission. She never detailed what it was but said her father would punish her failure. You remember our briefing on Emperor Samanos."

The Emperor sounded like a nightmare.

"So, she said it would be better for both of us if she was our prisoner. During our negotiations with her father, she gets a break from his controlling world. It also lessens the punishment for her failure. And her father would see a gesture of kindness as weakness. He'll be more open to a peace deal if she's a hostage. I'd promised to take her wherever she wanted to go. She asked to come here."

Julie already felt sympathy for Princess Ishtar. She was concerned this was some kind of plot the Princess had cooked up to take advantage of Micheal's kindness, but she could fully believe the stories about her father. Who wouldn't want to escape that environment, even for a little while?

"Any more compromising situations you want to enlighten me on?" He'd said there was much to discuss.

"The most interesting information came out of my discussion with Ishtar. She claims we're not the only gods she's seen. She claims she saw her father talking to the king and queen of the Anunnaki. That they were 12-foot giants with glowing eyes."

"Did she talk to these *gods*?"

"No, and she said her father nearly beat her to death for violating the sanctity of the gods."

"Do you believe she really saw these *gods*?"

"I'm certain she saw something. And she would have no trouble remembering. She's over 500 years old and *earned her awakening,* which means she acquired total recall."

"That's what awakening means?" Julie had heard some of her priestesses speak of their awakenings but wasn't sure what it meant. And a goddess wouldn't have to ask. "Someone explained this awakening to you? And how would it even be possible to acquire total recall?"

"No one explained it, but all my priestesses have total recall, which I found odd. One of the qualifications that all of them mentioned in their pedigrees that made them worthy of my service was when they earned their awakening. Most of them earned it around age 300 years. But the most intelligent like, Elissa, earned hers when she was just 128. How they talk about it to each other indicates a normal person earns theirs closer to 400 years. I determined from these conversations that awakening was total recall."

"Why would that even happen?" She was trying to imagine the mechanism. "Maybe it has to do with the thousand-year lifespan? For the mind to function over such a long period of time. Maybe it needs to awaken the memories when the memory track is too long to remember."

"I think you're partially right. I think it's partially how the brain adapts over time. But I think that adaptation is due to use, not time alone. I think the more someone uses their mind, the more connections are formed. And the capacity for knowledge increases."

"They literally become smarter, and when they reach some kind of critical mass, they earn total recall. Does that mean I'm going to earn total recall?"

Julie wasn't sure she wanted it. She already had an excellent memory. And watching Micheal struggle with the impact of never forgetting made her think the upside wasn't worth the downside.

"If we live long enough, I'm pretty sure you will. And you're at such a high level mentally already that I would think it would happen well before 400 years."

Julie didn't want to think about this anymore, so while she could forget, she changed the subject. "So, what about these gods? What do you think Ishtar actually saw?"

"The world in this time hasn't remotely matched our expectations. So, nearly anything could be possible. The Bible talks about the Nephilim. That's what the wings made me think-"

"Fallen angels?"

"I don't know. Pangea? Atlantis?" He opened his arms. "On the speculative science side, there's aliens. Ancient alien theorists love to talk about the Anunnaki. And back to the Bible, where do the giants come from? Unless you think Goliath's height was misinterpreted, like most historians do. In conclusion, I have no conclusion. It's possible that her mind saw what it wanted to see. I mean, who wouldn't be excited to see their gods?" He indicated their situation.

At the moment, Julie didn't want to explore the rabbit hole of little, or perhaps giant, green men. So, she left it there. Now, they had a guest to entertain.

A few months passed, and Babylon sent their negotiators. Everyone, including the council, believed Ishtar was a prisoner. She was allowed free reign of the city and its surrounding waters. The guarantor of her status was their divine monitoring. She made the most of her vacation, exploring the city, and attending parties and festivals. She was very charming and became immensely popular.

Today was the festival of the sun, and it was JULIE'S turn to address the city. She rose over Atlas just before the first edge of the sun would rise on the summer solstice.

"To the City of Atlantis, I welcome my brother, Helios." Her timing was impeccable. The sun broke the horizon. "He will bless this day with his longest visit of the year. His divine light sanctifies Atlantis." She initiated the mirrors they placed to channel the sun through a series of prisms. The city lit up in a rainbow spectrum of color. "It will be another year of light and prosperity for Atlantis. We bless you all." She severed the light connection, and the effect went dark. But the crowds cheered, and the party was on.

"That was amazing, Eminence Aphrodite. Your dress certainly honors Helios." Ishtar approached in a sunny yellow number. She always dressed appropriately.

"Now you believe in Helios?"

"He illuminates the dark, doesn't he?"

"Most of the Babylonian faith think we are either evil or false."

"I happen to have the best perspective to decide. I absolutely believe in our gods. But after everything I've witnessed since I came to Atlantis, I realized there's no reason any of you gods must be evil. You simply foster different kingdoms, like divine royalty. You play a power game amongst yourselves, but in the end, you're all a part of the same club. Helios and Utu promote the sun. Koios and Nanna encourage knowledge. And you and Inanna promote love."

Julie felt a bit guilty because she was constantly doubting Ishtar's authenticity. But what if her over-the-top enthusiasm came from the responsibility of her status being lifted for the moment? So that even at 528 years old, she was approaching the world like a child.

Ishtar seemed to squint at her dress. "I don't remember your dress being deep purple."

"It changes with the light." Julie stepped into the sunlight, and the EM field flowing through the fabric excited different elements of the light. It seemed to glow in various colors in the light.

"The gods." Ishtar shook her head, smiling. "I'm going to celebrate the sun."

The Princess sauntered off to the Day Gala.

Julie sat and watched the festivities. Gods were above such activities on sacred occasions. So, they were more like glorified emcees.

"Aphrodite, a drink?" Melina handed her a glass.

"Thank you, Melina. Why aren't you at the celebrations?"

"I wanted to celebrate with you. I know you don't rub shoulders with humans, so I came to serve you instead."

"You know we absolved you of your duties on sacred days."

"There's nowhere I'd rather be."

"Do you believe in other gods besides us?"

"I only serve The Gods of Atlantis."

"That wasn't my question."

Melina had been watching the action below but turned at that. "You don't need to worry about Ishtar influencing me or Elissa. Of course, there are other gods. Any honest human would admit that. But Inanna or Hathor don't look after love in Atlantis; you do. And the greatness of Atlantis is because you, The Gods of Atlantis, protect and promote us. I know as long as we honor you, Atlantis will never fall. You would overcome any other gods."

"Aside from serving me, what else interests you?" Julie sat on a bench on the balcony, and Melina joined her.

"I always loved how clothing could compliment beauty. I thought about coming up with my own designs."

"You should do it. Life may be long, but you never know when it might end. So, I will look forward to your fashion line."

"I have actually drawn some things, and I've practiced weaving fabric. I could show you some." The gleam in Melina's eye was what she was looking for.

"I would love to see."

Melina headed off, and Julie was alone with her thoughts again.

How many things about the world did nobody know about? When she woke up at the homestead in 1692, she thought her reality was shaken that day. She'd forced herself to accept that reality. Then in the next five years she'd fought for her life. But also worked her ass off trying to make sure no one could do that to her ever again.

By their departure in 1697, she'd finally accepted the realities of who she'd become—a trained martial artist who would rarely be outmatched. She learned about her inner nobility. And she found a perfect match in love. All these changes were complex but transformed her into a Lady of Avalon.

In tandem with said match, she came to understand time enough to be able to manipulate four dimensions. The centuries in the ether was a devastating discovery. But despite all that, she had found a modicum of peace. Then, this crazy Atlantean world immediately threw everything asunder.

How could such a large piece of history be missing? How could continents be so out of place? How could Ice Age animals be alive? How could lives span centuries? How could this be the same world she'd grown up in? Then, on top of that, she has to play god to this ridiculous world.

Julie felt if she could adapt once again to this situation, perhaps she was a god, but she hadn't discovered it yet. Would that be very much stranger than what this world keeps showing her?

Luckily, Melina returned to save her from her idol reflection.

"These are some of my concepts and some fabrics I've woven. I particularly like this one; it's so soft."

Julie paged through her sketches. "These are all quite impressive. Some are rather unusual. So, you're going to make some samples, aren't you?"

Melina's head dropped. "If you order me to, but the time commitment would detract from my ability to serve you properly."

"Is it the crafting of the fabrics or acquiring the thread?"

"Both."

"Well, I can solve both. If I ensure you have the fabrics, will you make some clothes for me?"

Melina threw her arms around her. "I will effort to honor you." She stepped back. "My apologies."

"Absolutely not. I want you to be happy." Julie pulled her in.

She pulled back. "Now, let's sit and watch the city celebrate. And we can discuss fashion."

They talked and laughed more like friends than a goddess and servant until Micheal closed the official festivities with the setting of the sun. There was a ceremonial release of Chinese lanterns at dusk to give light back to Helios and ensure another year of sunlight.

The next major festival would be a new one to honor their arrival. Julie wondered if the gods would be up to the part. However, it felt like the world was indeed fooled. Maybe playing god isn't so bad.

-September 1, 3280 BC

"We have really taken to our roles as gods, ruling over the Atlantean Empire. Peace has spread worldwide following our demonstration against the Babylonians and our diplomatic tours. Only one agreement remains to be signed. Emperor Samanos, has come from Babylon, to retrieve his daughter personally. The peace treaty will be signed symbolically on The Day of The Gods. So, it looks like today is the last for our guest Princess. She really did grow on me. I will miss having her around—she is the true life of any party. I hope she can retain this zest for life under her father's thumb.

As the Empire goes, we cleaned up the sanitation issues and focused on infrastructure across the Empire. And that, coupled with the peace, has given rise to great prosperity.

Our Palace of the Gods, along with mine and Micheal's temples, were completed in record time with the assistance of maglev technologies. The entire complex was opened officially just before our first anniversary. Married as Lord and Lady. Celebrated as a God and Goddess.

Melina has become a trusted friend, which took much effort due to the intimidation factor. She fashions clothes for both of us and has even updated the look for my priestesses. I do think it's an improvement.

With the minimum effort required to run the Empire, Micheal and I have been able to enjoy each other. I would never have believed you if you had told me this would be the outcome a year ago.

Let's go make a new friend and usher in the golden age we were prophesied to bring."

Peace In Our Time

MICHEAL'S unusual guest was about to return to Neverland, and he was fascinated by how many people in Atlantis were sad to see a Babylonian Princess leave. Apparently, her casual participation in Atlantean society was how 'prisoners' of her standing always operated. In the eight months she'd taken holiday in Atlantis, she had made friends with much of the Atlantean aristocracy and even made a few on the Atlantean Council, including Cato.

He certainly thought that boded well for future relations with Babylon. The Emperor had many physical problems. Echoes of a riding injury he'd suffered. Rumors were going around that he might not live long. In that case, Ishtar would succeed him.

"I do wish the negotiations had taken longer." Ishtar entered his chamber. She was wearing an adapted style of the classic Babylonian Royalty. Clearly, Melina's work.

"Not excited to see dear old dad?"

"He's like a shadow that brings shade to all aspects of court. I don't endorse all the things I've seen in Atlantis, but it's so much more laid back here. You can enjoy yourself without worrying about violating some pointless law that serves no functional purpose."

"Perhaps he'll lighten up without a looming war with Atlantis."

She came over and began fixing his look. "I know it's not the truth, but when I return to the night we first met, I like to tell myself I missed my chance at a divine sexual experience. But the way you pleasure Aphrodite showed me I was never a thought. How could I compare to a Goddess of Love?"

"How many times have you watched us?"

She put her arms around his neck. "As often as I could. At first, I needed to see if the stories were true. But then, beyond the power involved, I saw the truth beneath. In my long life, I've never experienced an ounce of the love and passion you share. I envy Aphrodite that. And if I could never feel what that was like, I wanted to build a file of you to at least feed my fantasies. So, while I know I should apologize for my intrusion, the truth is I'm not sorry." She was staring into his eyes, and he could feel her yearning.

At that moment, he thought about the scene from the Matrix Sequel. And the Merovingian's wife Persephone's plea. It's only a kiss.

"It's true that there was no chance at the lighthouse or any other time. However, I can empathize with your situation and the loneliness you must be experiencing. You've never known true love. While I can't provide that for you, I might be able to offer you a more personal experience related to what you observed."

He didn't know what Julie would think about this. Ishtar was talking like a jaded lover. Perhaps if he satisfied her want, the friendship would be strengthened. He thought Julie would understand his reasoning; after all, it's only a kiss.

Micheal took her face in his hands and pretended she was Julie. He met her lips and after a minute he activated the lightning bringing sparks. After another minute, she broke the kiss, panting. He could tell by the look on her face that he'd given her something even more personal.

Ishtar held on for another minute. Like she worried she'd fall if she let go. "I expected retribution for my trespass. And now you shame my preconceptions again. I felt more passion in that kiss than I've felt from anyone in all my years." Tears streamed.

In her reaction, he wondered if it might have the opposite effect to what he had intended.

"I wish I could do more."

"No. This was perfect. I know you risk Aphrodite's wrath to show me a mercy I don't deserve. I never considered what true divinity looked like. But you've given me a personal taste of what I've witnessed these past eight months. You and Aphrodite utilize your immense power to better the lives of us meager humans. The way you care for all those under your authority is truly divine. When my time comes to rule, I will try to follow your example. And when I meet the Anunnaki, I can only hope they're as worthy of the title *God* as you and Aphrodite."

Ishtar leaned her head on his chest. "Thank you for everything." Her tears wet his shirt.

At that moment, Julie entered the chamber. "I hope I'm not interrupting?"

Ishtar stepped away from him.

"I was just saying a proper farewell to our guest. With a parting gift."

"Must be quite a gift. Can I see?"

"I'll show you later. I think the Emperor is waiting on us."

Julie's eyes shifted between them. "Can't wait to meet your father."

They all headed for the Divine Hall in the center of the new Palace of the Gods. They'd moved into the palace a month earlier, once their private sections were complete. But now the entire palace was finished, and they'd engineered their receiving court to give a divine impression.

When they weren't present, the Divine Hall was designed to look like an all-glass rotunda in the center of the palace. Once seated in their thrones, their rings could work their magic. The thrones could float them anywhere in the chamber they wanted to be. And their electricity would cause the whole chamber to glow, including their thrones.

Their personal access port was at the top of the dome. And they entered, levitating Ishtar between them. On the upper-rimmed balconies sat their priestesses—Julie's on one side, his on the other. Melina and Elissa sat above them on their personal balconies.

On the next rim sat the aristocracy, and the council members sat above them on twelve private balconies. On the ground level was the palace guard lining the chamber. The designers intended the rest of the ground level for visitors.

They descended to their thrones, floating in the center of the chamber. Ishtar landed on a small platform extending from Micheal's throne. As they took their seats, the Hall became a chamber of light. All present went to a knee.

"Rise," Micheal instructed.

They lowered to 10 feet above the ground.

The herald stepped forward. "Your most Holy Eminences, I present His Majesty, Emperor Itu Samanos."

A golden litter was brought in, carrying a man wearing cloth weaved of the same. Micheal felt he was trying to impress them.

His retinue followed him. At the head was a woman who resembled Ishtar. He believed she was the Empress. Next was about a dozen men and women wearing matching attire, likely his council of advisors. The two negotiators were next. Behind them were two familiar faces in the eight men to follow. The two generals they faced in Libya. And finally, the Emperor's compliment of a hundred personal bodyguards.

The Emperor descended his seat with an evident limp and stood before them.

For the first time since they arrived in Atlantis, Micheal felt he could see advanced aging. Itu appeared to be middle-aged, which he found odd. All mentions of the elders highlighted their ability to maintain a youthful appearance despite their status as the oldest individuals on record. According to his information, the elders were at least a century older than he was.

Another oddity of his appearance was that he was rather short and stout. Micheal guessed he was barely more than five feet tall and weighed around 200 pounds. His height was a little below average, and Micheal had only seen a few heavy-set people the whole time they'd been here.

Despite all of that, he definitely had a presence. His head was Bic smooth. He wore a well-groomed, graying beard. And a pair of deep-set eyes narrowed past a large nose with a prominent bridge.

"We bid you welcome." Micheal opened his hands.

"I do wish to commend your show of force in the destruction of my daughter's fleet and her capture. I respect the message you sent."

"We wish no animus in the world. We believe in peace through strength."

"I understand my daughter has conducted herself well, befitting one of her station. I am grateful for her generous treatment. Let us establish this grand peace so she may again enjoy her birthright."

"Princess Ishtar has been a compliment to Babylon and Your Majesty." Julie nodded.

"Bring forward the document."

Cato carried the scroll, followed by the rest of the council. He presented it to the emperor.

Itu dipped the quill and scratched his agreement. The council followed suit. The document was then put before them, and, from a distance, Micheal sparked his electric power; then, just like he practiced, he seared his symbol into the paper. Julie did the same.

"Let there be peace in our time," Julie announced.

"We release her Highness, Princess Ishtar of Babylon. And now that we are friends, let the celebrations begin." They lowered Ishtar to the ground, and she received a simple nod from her father.

As the festivities commenced, a man approached. "This peace is a heresy. I know you won't rule on earth forever, and when I'm emperor, I will see the end to your tyranny."

"That is not how a prince of Babylon conducts themselves." Ishtar scolded the man. "Forgive my son's trespass."

Another woman who was the spitting image of Ishtar stepped forward. "Don't worry about him; he'll never rule Babylon."

"Both of you need to conduct yourselves appropriately."

The daughter headed off. "They're as bad as my father when it comes to the power games."

"At least you're proud of them, right?"

"Gods willing, this peace holds, and no one must face the horrors of the wars I've seen."

"War is part of human nature. Always remember that peace is the divine state. The best you can do is maintain any peace for as long as possible," Julie said.

"You can count on my promotion of these principles so long as I live."

"Hopefully, you can teach them."

"Four hundred years of thought will be hard to change. But at least this treaty is a start. Let's focus on that tonight. And I will worry about my children later."

The festivities ran for a week, and then the Babylonians left to implement the new edict. Micheal hoped they could bring peace to the Atlantean world. If they could do this here, who knows what they might achieve when they get back to the future?

CHAPTER IV: MELINA

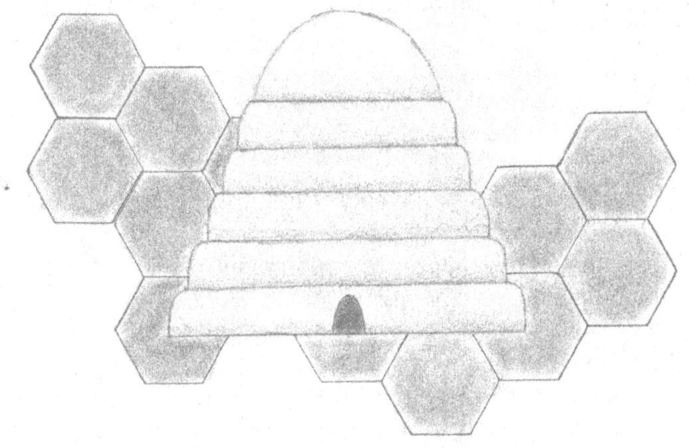

Gabriel

MELINA NOW HAD A new problem to deal with. Aphrodite had permitted Chief Council Cato's son Gabriel to serve her as a priest. It was up to Melina how to implement Aphrodite's decree about his sexual training.

After his initial orientation, she placed him on the rotation, beginning with love, then it was beauty. But the final rotation was now here. He was a virgin, and she didn't want to pass the responsibility of his coming of age on to anyone else. But it was a sensitive subject.

With the celebration of the arrival of the gods about to occupy her time, she felt it was time to address the situation.

Gabriel arrived in her doorway. "You sent for me, Eminence Melina?"

"Gabriel, please sit." He obeyed. "Now, I will get right to the point. It's time for your sex training. And while Aphrodite did give specific edicts pertaining to you. She also gave me some leeway on implementation. I feel it is only right that I will be your instructor for your first sex rotation. However, I realize how special the first time is for every man, and as such, I will relax the edict against freestyling just this once. If there's any pledge that you wish to choose for your first time, I will see it done. But after that, you will be restricted to the priestesses. I will give you a few days to decide."

"I don't have anyone in mind."

"Take a few days to look around."

"I'm not interested in anyone else."

"You're not interested in sex?"

"Oh, I am. But I only have eyes for Aphrodite. She's who I worship."

"Clearly, that's never going to happen. And if you don't choose a partner, it will have to be me."

"That's fine."

"I just thought you might want to choose your first time."

"Who better than the High Priestess of Aphrodite? The one who serves her directly. And who knows, maybe Aphrodite will reward my devotion one day."

Melina sat back, studying him. "Last chance for a different partner."

"Let's just get it over with."

"Meet me here tomorrow at sundown, dismissed."

Melina wasn't sure this infatuation would relent in the future. But the person she thought it would hurt most was Gabriel himself.

The next day, she made sure to dress for the part. She had her hair tied up in a twist and a tight red corset pressing her breasts out in a beautiful display. Her silky stockings ran thigh-high, and she wore tall heels. Her neck was constricted with a tight lace band.

Gabriel entered, and he too, had dressed for the occasion. He wore a white kilt that fell to his knees and a fabric sash draped over one shoulder. The white signifies purity. And the red belt was a sign of surrender. His hair was pulled back in a ponytail.

"Follow me." She led him into her private chambers. "Now, I

will leave the instructions for our sessions, but I will work to make this experience memorable."

"I have been trying to prepare for this."

"Then I hope you're not just trying to get it over with quickly."

"For your sake or mine?"

"You're the one who will remember this forever. It will simply be another time for me. So we'll go as fast or slow as you like."

"Very well, lead the way."

"I see you've been holding to the beauty edicts. You smell wonderful." She nuzzled up to his neck, tracing his arms and shoulder muscles. Then she tasted his lips.

Gabriel's hands found her ass and squeezed. He passionately sucked on her upper lip.

Melina slid his sash off his body and kissed his nipples, then licked down his abs.

"Let's see how excitable you are."

She pushed him back on the bed, then removed his loin cloth. He was already at full attention.

"We're going to need to give you a reset."

She used her mouth to relieve the pressure. Gabriel was sucking air, trying to recover himself. Melina stepped up on the bed and stood over him.

"Now that I've taken some of the wind out of your sails, why don't you see what you can do for me until you've recovered."

He rose to his knees at her chest. His eyes made contact and then focused on her breasts. He untied the laces, releasing her corset. Gripping her tits tightly, he tasted her nipples between his fingers. His mouth remained hungry on her breast, but his hands continued to unwrap her.

The corset fell away, and he discovered a new focus. His fingers found her pussy, and he wanted a taste. He took her legs out from under her, then pulled her to the edge of the bed.

Gabriel kissed her lower lips with passion, sucking her into his mouth, trying to consume her. He was clumsy but earnest. When he stumbled into a pleasure center she responded with body language. He responded to her cues and she found bliss.

Melina caught her breath. "Not bad for a novice."

"I think I've fully recovered." He dropped his kilt to reveal a solid erection.

"Let's hope you last longer than before."

As Gabriel slid in between her legs, preparing for entry, she reflected on the fact that at least he was beautiful to look at. His blue eyes, piercing from beneath a strong brow, and a chiseled jaw trying to grow a beard. His silky black locks were tied back.

She guided his cock inside her and crossed her ankles above his ass. She could better control his wild thrusts.

He started tentatively like he didn't want to break her.

"Harder. I'm not made of glass."

"Like this?" He thrust hard and deep.

"Find a good rhythm, and slowly increase the pace."

Melina matched his rhythm and felt him rubbing against her inner sweet spot. She used this technique to guarantee satisfaction for herself.

"Faster. Faster!"

He complied, and she reached the summit. A moment later, the shudder in Gabriel signaled he'd finished as well, and he collapsed on her chest.

She fingered his hair. After a minute, he pulled himself from her. He was just staring at her.

"Are you regretting the decision not to choose someone else?"

"No. I made the right decision." His eyes traced her body. "I'm regretting that I waited so long." He sat on the bed next to her.

"So you enjoyed yourself?"

His eyes locked on her with hunger.

"Now, don't go falling in love with me. We begin normal sessions tomorrow." She teased him, inserting a few fingers inside and squeezing her tit.

"Are we going to do this again?"

"Not tonight. Tomorrow, I'll begin showing other methods. And positions. Dismissed."

He clearly still wanted more, but that would have to wait.

"Yes, Your Eminence." One final scan of her flesh and he exited the room.

Melina thought she gave him a pretty good first time. She reflected on her own first time.

Five years earlier, she had finally reached the age of maturity, and her aunt allowed her to join the Temple of Aphrodite in Eden. Her aunt handpicked the pledge for her.

She never learned his name, but she would never forget him. He was tall and blond with green eyes. And he was so gentle the first time. His velvet techniques nullified the mild pain of the first penetration.

As a priestess, you weren't to know much about the pledges to limit the urge to attach. She knew firsthand why. She had thought she loved him when the cycle came up. She professed as much. But he had no such feelings for her. It had all been a job for him. This disconnect between their feelings taught her what she didn't understand about love and that recommitted her to her studies.

Now Melina recognized that love was the most rare and valuable of the three virtues. Would she ever experience it firsthand? Was she even capable at this point?

She wasn't sure she trusted herself to connect the virtues. Would she remain loyal to Aphrodite? Or herself?

Fashion

Melina had been able to put her creativity fully to work since Aphrodite had gifted her an endless supply of the most exquisite fabrics. She'd already supplied her priestesses with a wide variety of outfits to promote the principles of love, sex, and beauty.

Aphrodite had requested some looks specifically for her, and Melina had been trying to perfect them, but now time had run out. The Arrival Festival was two days away, and Aphrodite would need to ensure the designs were pleasing.

"I think those are a little big for you." Elissa was always on point.

"They're not for me, they're for Aphrodite."

"And what about these ones? Koios?"

"Aphrodite only asked for herself, but I felt it made sense if they matched."

"These look nice. Are you going to make any for us?" Elissa picked up one of Aphrodite's bras.

"You don't wear clothes, remember?"

"We wear something like this." She held it up.

"It's so small; what difference does it make?"

"You think my tits would be this perky if I didn't wear this?" Elissa gave her firm pair a nice squeeze.

"Remind me why you erudites care what your breasts look like?"

"Clothes, in general, are indeed a waste of time and resources, but there is value in proper presentation. We represent Koios and must present ourselves accordingly. Wearing one of these helps maintain our most overt feminine features. It's a worthy tradeoff for minimal effort. They're still perfect after nearly 200 years, don't you think?"

"They're beautiful."

"Go ahead and give 'em a squeeze; you know you want to."

They were quite enticing. Melina felt the soft firmness and hoped that hers would still be so lovely in a couple hundred years.

"Are we having fun ladies?" Aphrodite interrupted.

"I was proving a point to Melina."

"It appears she's feeling your points."

"Very clever, Eminence Aphrodite. Would you like to feel them?"

Aphrodite took a turn, feeling Elissa's breasts. "So what was the point?"

"Wearing our basic support helps maintain firmness even after centuries. We may even match your divine self." Elissa averted her eyes. "My apologies, Eminence. I meant no trespass."

"None taken. Want to feel?" Aphrodite let her top down.

Elissa looked up. Her eyes narrowed on Aphrodite's perfection.

"They won't bite." Elissa slowly sampled Aphrodite's other-worldly pair that seemed to defy gravity.

"My mistake. That's why you're the goddess. May I take my leave?"

"Of course, Elissa."

"Thank you. Melina, can I expect some then?"

"Sure."

Elissa exited.

"So what are you doing for her?"

"She wants me to make the erudites some support bras."

"Now I understand what I walked in on. She does have an impressive pair, doesn't she?"

"Yes." Melina couldn't stop staring at Aphrodite's perfect, firm breasts.

"You want to feel?"

She took a deep breath and put her hands on the breasts. The skin was flawless and smooth as silk. The shape was unnaturally round and firm. And the nipples were large and solid, piercing into her palms. If the gods crafted the perfection of the female form, this was clearly it. Of course, the Goddess of Beauty.

Melina became enamored, lost in admiration.

"So Melina, what do you have for me?"

"Oh! Sorry." She pulled her hands back. "I thought these colors were most complimentary, and these shapes gave the best emphasis." She led Aphrodite to her samples.

"This one has a beautiful shape and an interesting color dynamic. And this one has a nice color trio. Let's see how they fit."

They spent the next few hours testing all her creations. The goddess was the image of perfection and brought Melina's vision to life.

"A most impressive spread. A few were a bit ambitious, but overall, Melina, great job. And clearly, Koios will have to approve your vision for him. But I feel this one should match the one I'm wearing."

Aphrodite was wearing a purple, pink, and red number with a short front skirt and a long flow in the back. The thin fabric hugged her upper body.

The Koios bodysuit used the same purple, but the knee-length kilt was black and trimmed with silver.

"I will finalize everything with plenty of time before the festivities."

"Are you going to be dressing the erudites as well?"

"If you call that dressing." Melina laughed. "It's just ironic that the geniuses decided clothing was wasteful."

"To be fair, the subject does encapsulate much focus from people in general."

Melina stroked a stretch of fabric. "But it feels so luxurious on your skin. And it can change your mood simply by slipping into different clothes. It's so much more than something to conceal your body."

"If Elissa and her friends want to forgo one of life's greatest luxuries, that's on them. Now I want to see what you've made for yourself and my priestesses."

"While I try on mine, will you showcase the rest of what I've made for you?"

They spent the next couple of hours trying on different outfits. It felt like Aphrodite was simply a friend spending time with her. They would gush over a fabric or discuss the positives or negatives of a specific design. Then Melina lost her proper self.

"I'm still having doubts about Gabriel."

"Is he doing something wrong? Has he violated my edicts?"

"No, he's quite dutiful. It's just, he has a singular focus."

"His infatuation with me? He's young. As he grows under your tutelage, I'm sure he'll move beyond it."

"Perhaps, but he already admits to fantasizing about you during our sessions."

Aphrodite ran her fingers through Melina's hair. "Don't worry, Melina; I'm sure all young men are doing that right now. It's what I would expect with my presence here."

Melina sighed. "I get when they're alone, taking care of themselves. But when I'm actually there with him, he still imagines you. It seems a bit much."

"I'm sorry if you feel slighted, but give it time."

"I guess you're right." Melina set down a pair of shoes.

Aphrodite pulled her chin up. "You're certainly an artist, and I look forward to my wardrobe. Now Koios is probably waiting on me." She flew out the balcony doors.

Melina hoped she was wrong about Gabriel.

The festival arrived and was a veritable fashion show of her style.

Gabriel led her priestesses onto the Plaza of the Gods. The council was overseeing everything from a dais. The Priestesses of Koios entered from the opposite side. The massive crowd went to the ground. She and Elissa met in the middle of the spectacle.

"We bid you all welcome to the celebration of our divine provenance." Elissa began.

"With their blessings, Atlantis' primacy is assured," Melina added. "Your gods of Atlantis. The Goddess of Love, Aphrodite!"

"And The God of Wisdom, Koios!" Elissa reached to the sky.

The gray sky burst to light above the Palace of the Gods. Aphrodite and Koios descended to the plaza holding light in their hands. They pressed them together, and a wave of energy flashed across the plaza.

When Melina's eyes adjusted, the gods were resplendent in the style she'd crafted for them. Complete with the accompaniment of their particular themes.

Koios carried a golden scroll with a feather in one hand and engineering tools in the other. A glowing orb adorned his forehead. Aphrodite wore beautiful white wings and a crown of flowers. A glowing red orb hung between her breasts.

"People of Atlantis, Uranus is well pleased by our progress in the last year. You've done well in devotion to the gods. And for that, we will now bless you with a holy cleansing." Koios turned to Aphrodite, and they pressed energy together until the emanation was blinding.

A wave of light washed over the plaza, and all but the holy priestesses collapsed, including the council. As they found themselves again, they seemed disoriented.

The gods rose above the crowd.

"We will continue our mission for another year. Now, this night is for celebration. Enjoy yourselves." Aphrodite and Koios vanished behind the clouds.

And indeed, the celebration was on. It ran late into the night. Melina's fashion was a significant topic of conversation. She would be busy dressing the nobility going forward.

Elissa

The next day, Melina woke late. It was rare that she took a day off. Aphrodite had granted her the entirety of the festival off, and she had been up managing the party all night.

"Wow! I don't think I've ever seen you sleep in before." Elissa spoiled a perfectly quiet morning.

"We were up all night. Why are you acting like it's a normal day?"

"There's no reason to waste a day because of the previous one."

"It was surprising how much you got into it last night."

"I will have you know I'm quite fun at parties."

Melina laughed. "Yes, all those loud get-togethers at the House of Wisdom. Who doesn't want to spend their leisure time debating the meaning of life."

"We don't debate the meaning of life. In his wisdom, Eminence Koios taught us that it's good to relax the mind from time to time. We play games where you must drink wine if you can't answer the science query fast enough. The more you imbibe, the slower your mind works. The folly of slowed wit is relaxing to the mind."

"Sounds amazing; perhaps you'll invite me next time."

"It's certainly more stimulating than the sex parties at the House of Love. We'll see if you can handle it."

"I'm not sure you understand the meaning of the word stimulating."

"I never use a word out of context. Physical sex is so basic. Come back to me when you've been mind fucked." Elissa raised an eyebrow.

That did sound amazing.

"I look forward to being enlightened." This was a side of Elissa that she'd never seen before. Perhaps there was a fun person hidden behind the wall of stoicism? "And feel free to crash one of our sex parties. We'll see if you really are 'fun'."

"Don't say I didn't warn you."

"Didn't Koios give you the day off?"

"He did, but I still like to be productive."

"Why did you come here?"

"I was going to thank you for the way your clothing accentuated our appearance yesterday. We did truly look divine."

Melina began pulling her clothes on.

"I never understood why you priestesses of love wear clothing."

"Love isn't only about sex. Clothing creates mystery, and that is important for seduction. I don't understand why you erudite don't wear clothing."

"Clothes are a waste of time and resources. The human body is completely natural and aesthetically pleasing. There's no reason to worry about covering it. Perhaps your youth is a factor for you on this subject."

"Why do you think centuries of life will change my thoughts on clothing?"

Elissa slid her hands around Melina from behind. "When you're ten times older, you'll be much more comfortable in your body." Elissa ran her hands up to Melina's breasts. "You'll realize how unnecessarily restricting these are." She untied her corset, and she felt the cool air on her nipples. "Doesn't that feel better?"

Melina turned and pressed her palms down on Elissa's nipples. "Doesn't that feel better?"

"I like how they feel in the cool air. But your hands feel good as well."

"Why don't you try wearing clothes today?"

Elissa released her breast support. "How about this? I will dress like you today if you dress like me."

"So we switch for the day? What do you think the gods will think?"

"I think they will be amused. Now follow me; you'll be easier."

In Elissa's quarters, she removed Melina's clothes.

"We're going to need to take care of this first." Elissa stroked Melina's bush.

"What's wrong with it?"

"You need to be silky smooth, like me." She caressed her skin. "I have a lotion that will do it nice and easy."

Elissa's hands touched every inch of Melina's body for the next few minutes. The only place untouched was the hair on her head. A quick rinse in the baths, and that was the only hair left.

"Wow! I feel exposed." She touched between her legs.

"It's like silk, right? Now, about your hair." A moment later, her hair was pulled up in a twist, matching Elissa's. And the warming day felt comfortable on her bare skin.

"One last thing." Elissa hooked the undercup and adjusted her tits. "You look smarter already."

Melina almost felt fake. The magic cream made her skin look like it was crafted by an artist. No matter what happened after this, she would need to use that going forward.

"So now it's your turn." Melina led the way.

"Let's start with this." She picked a purple satin corset.

As she slid it up Elissa's body, she thought about how this was the most dressed she'd seen her.

"This may feel constricting at first, but you'll get used to it." Melina tightened the garment, and Elissa's breast heaved as she sucked in air.

Melina cinched the garter in place and slid the stockings up to Elissa's thighs.

"What's the point of these? They don't really cover anything."

"They look sexy. That's the point." Melina buttoned a short skirt in place.

"This all seems to be a lot of trouble."

"All of it is designed to accentuate your physical beauty. And play into flirtation." She slid a short shoulder jacket on. "And more to tease him as you remove each piece."

"Some sexy sandals." Melina tied the straps.

"And one final item." She pulled the lace choker pendant tight around her throat.

"Are we finally done?"

"One last thing." Melina let Elissa's hair down, brushed it out, and crowned her with a jeweled chain. Her modest locks flowed behind her ears. But Melina left a couple of tendrils to frame her face.

"You look sexier already."

Elissa seemed captivated by her reflection in the mirror. Melina ran her hands up to Elissa's tits.

"Are we beginning to understand the trouble?"

Elissa stroked her inner thighs. "If anyone is worth the trouble, it's me. But I'm still not sure I'd do it again. But I do look damn sexy. Now, want to take it to their eminences?"

They gathered a lunch meal and went to the chamber of the gods. They were casually talking in their own words. As Elissa approached Aphrodite, Melina went to Koios. His brow went up as he scanned Melina's body.

"I'm pretty sure you're not the Priestess of Koios. Either way, we gave you the day off."

"Elissa and I live to serve you. But today, we wanted to trade places." Melina set the tray down. "Is there any other way I can be of service to you? And I do mean anything." She stroked the sides of her body. She glanced over to see Aphrodite smiling at her.

Koios followed her gaze and laughed with Aphrodite, who signaled them to approach. He took Melina's hand, and they complied.

"Wow, Melina, You must've borrowed some of Elissa's magic cream. Silky smooth."

"Heavenly soft," Elissa said.

"Well, I thought we were on our own for the next few days. But as our most devoted are here so unexpectedly, should we avail them of their most generous offerings?"

"We would be most honored." Elissa sat on Aphrodite's lap.

"Go on, Melina; I am relaxing my prohibition on Koios receiving his full service."

She wasn't sure if this was a test, but all she could do was follow instructions. She climbed on his lap and reached for his dick, but he stopped her.

"Well, now I've seen an interesting side of you, Melina. But the prohibition is also mine." He looked at Aphrodite.

She laughed. "I just thought it would be fun to humor them. And Melina is perfection. Don't you agree? I mean, feel those tits."

Koios's hands warmed her cold nipples.

"Do I properly honor you?" Elissa asked.

"You epitomize love, sex, and beauty. Now, I think the two of you should serve us as you usually do. In the roles you've traded for the rest of the day."

Koios pulled his hands back, and Melina sighed in disappointment as the prospect ended.

The rest of the night was mostly normal, except she served Koios instead of Aphrodite. When she prepared to leave for the last time, Aphrodite called her over.

"This was an interesting experience, Melina."

"I hope we didn't upset you."

"On the contrary, I think it's good to walk in someone else's shoes for a day. It was just unexpected. We had to have a little fun with you."

"Do you want us to come back tomorrow?"

"I want you to spend the rest of your days off however you prefer. You work so hard on my account. I think you and especially Elissa should take a few lazy days where you pamper yourselves. But if you insist on serving us, we won't stop you."

"I will relax for at least half the day, but don't be surprised if I deliver your dinner."

"Good night, Elissa."

"My offer always stands, Aphrodite."

Aphrodite laughed at the statement.

"I think I will take a few days." Melina bowed and left the chamber.

Melina closed her eyes and imagined Koios had followed through. But clearly, Aphrodite knew he would decline. She thought about how her nakedness became normal after only a few hours. She could understand where Elissa was coming from. Maybe there was some wisdom there.

The House of Love

One of the most important days at The House of Love came a few weeks after the festival. Twice a year, the day and the night found equilibrium. These days embody the primary principle of love—balance. Love was meant to balance the hearts of both parties involved. They come together with both hearts, trading equal amounts of give and take.

On these occasions, the Priestesses of Aphrodite revel in the heavenly symmetry and celebrate love. The party was well underway when their expected guests finally arrived.

"Well, Elissa, I was worried you'd changed your mind."

"We also celebrate the balance of night and day. I felt this was the perfect time to see the other side."

"It's a free-for-all, so you can do whatever you want. With one exception, Gabriel is off limits, at Aphrodite's command."

"Hear that, ladies, for tonight, don't think, just act."

The Priestesses of Koios mixed into the party.

"I'm glad you all decided to actually dress for tonight. Clothes are much more fun. The idea is to end the night naked, not begin that way."

"Our trading places was interesting. And we are at the House of Love."

Melina led Elissa into the party.

"This area is the lazy lounge. Usually, people drink and chat here. Over there, it's typically comparing body parts. It's crass, I know, but everyone has a good laugh. The next room is generally random games that are not usually sexual in nature. The room over there is where the ladies compete in the art of striptease. And sex does feature throughout."

"And what's your favorite thing to do?"

"I like to play the game of seduction. I pick someone and attempt to seduce them."

"That's not very challenging. Who wouldn't want to fuck you?"

"Everyone here is completely fuckable. It's a game; you're supposed to play hard to get. And it's more fun when you judge the effort. And when it's us, we refuse sex if we think their effort was weak. As you said before, physical sex is basic, so we make each other earn it."

"Why can't I play with Gabriel?"

"Aphrodite appeased Cato by allowing him to serve her. But she didn't want him to be able to abuse his station, so she limited his options to her other priestesses. So far, I'm the only one he's been with."

"Really? I suppose if it's a God's command. I'm sure that's nice for you."

Melina grabbed a pitcher of wine. "He's my student; that's all there is to it."

"And I'm a damn good one." Gabriel entered the room. "Your Eminence, does Aphrodite's edict extend to Koios' priestesses?"

"No. Just stick to Aphrodite's ladies."

"It's a shame. I would be able to teach you a few things."

"You do always know how to command a room, Elissa."

"So, what are you two up to?" He sat on a lounger in the corner of the room.

"Melina was about to see if she could seduce me. As her student, do you think she has the skill?"

Gabriel sat up with a smile. "I assure you I could tickle your fancy. But as I'm prohibited, I suppose she'll have to do. But trying to impress an erudite is a bit more challenging. Perhaps she's lacking after all."

"Are you up for the challenge? And we'll even have Gabriel as an unbiased judge."

Melina shook her head and sighed. "If you wanted to fuck me so bad, all you had to do was say so."

Elissa sat on the edge of the bed expectantly.

"Sex is a full body experience. It's not only about feeling the wet and warm inside of you. It starts with a simple touch." She began caressing Elissa's wrist with her thumb. "Then you honor the most precious part of her."

Melina kissed Elissa on the temple. "Now, you present a little preview of what you have to offer." She released the bindings on her corset, and her nipples slipped the top.

"Imagine my fingers are magic. Like ten pleasure sticks that are going to rub you the right way." One hand traced Elissa's neck and chest. And the other tickled her inner thighs.

Elissa began breathing deeply.

"They'll feel even better inside you." She whispered in her ear.

"I can follow your erogenous zones all the way to the sweet spot." She kissed the side of Elissa's neck, then smoothly removed Elissa's corset and kissed the small of her back. She bent Elissa over the edge of the bed and slid Elissa's panties to the ground. She kissed the back of her knees, then licked up her thighs up to her sweet spot.

Melina hugged her thighs and made magic with her tongue. Elissa's whole body quivered as she climaxed. Then she caught her breath.

"I thought that was respectable." Gabriel couldn't disguise his approval.

"Very effective. Now, I want to return the favor."

Elissa took her time between Melina's legs with quality results. When sanity returned to her, she almost felt Elissa was trying to one-up her.

They spent some time playing games, enjoying each other.

"I guess we're a lot closer than we used to be." Elissa laughed.

"Was this a basic sex party?"

"The night's still young, but this is a good start. And I look forward to your visit to the House of Knowledge."

"Let's go find some more entertainment." Gabriel held out a hand for both of them. Then, they explored more of what the House of Love had to offer.

The House of Knowledge

The year was coming to an end and Melina was finally going to see how they partied at The House of Knowledge. She arrived, and all of the Priestesses of Koios were on the West Terrace watching the sun.

"Join us for the ceremony." Elissa reached for her hand.

"What's the ceremony?"

"Helios will suffer a little death tonight. And will be born anew tomorrow."

The priestesses were unconventionally wearing a thin shall over their shoulders, except for Elissa.

"Why are they covered?"

"Today, Helios provides his smallest amount of energy. They show a willingness to reduce their need of him."

"But you don't?"

"As the personal attendant of a god, I maintain my personal honors only for him. But as priestesses to the pursuit of knowledge, we celebrate and honor all truths the gods have revealed. So today, we show deference to Helios."

There was a curved post standing on the edge of the plaza. The sun began to dip behind the pinnacle. This was a demonstration that they could predict its descent on this day.

Over the next hour, the sky behind the post changed from green to orange, then red to purple, until night finally overcame day.

"We thank Helios for granting us another year. This night, the world passes as if to death, to be reborn with his blessing of a new day." They all chanted.

The Priestesses of Koios filed inside the House of Knowledge, but Elissa remained.

"So when does the party begin?"

"There's nothing to celebrate yet. We must survive the night and pray Helios grants us another year. If the sun rises tomorrow, we celebrate."

Melina looked at Selene, showing only half her face, and felt comfort that the gods looked after the world.

She thought the party was supposed to be that night, but thankfully, she'd not sent word for the rest of the priestesses to come yet. She spent the night in Elissa's guest chambers. Elissa dressed her in the ceremonial death wear, and she spent much of the longest night sleeping in a ceremonial tomb. It was still dark when Elissa came and retrieved her.

"I sent word for the Priestesses of Love to come any time after dawn. But I want you to complete the Rebirth Ritual."

"What's next?"

Elissa led her by the hand. "We shed our symbols of death." She began undressing Melina. "And at the first sign of the rebirth, we walk the Underworld Pool."

The horizon showed a hint of light. Helios, it would appear, would bless the world for another year. Elissa guided her into the pool. It was quite long and narrow. The water got deeper the further they went.

"Take a deep breath and remain calm."

They descended below the surface until the ground finally began to ascend again. Melina tried to quiet her thoughts as it had been a while since she'd breathed. At last, she could see light at the surface. Her chest was screaming for air, but she focused on the light, the blessing of Helios. Her head broke the surface, and she took the air deep inside of her.

"Very impressive. Most of our priestesses fail our first rebirth." Another Priestess wrapped her in a robe.

The rest of the priestesses completed the ritual and then sat watching the eastern horizon. The sun began to break the edge, and all the ladies rose and threw off their robes.

"Helios grants another year. So now we celebrate." Elissa announced.

Music rose up from the House of Knowledge.

"Who else attends your parties?"

"During year-end festivities, the House of Knowledge is open to all. Many eschew us because they're intimidated by our intelligence. But we get some brave people, mostly men, who want to test themselves with us."

"Are there any restrictions to what's allowed?"

"Only the limits of your imagination. Let's see if you measure up."

Elissa led her in, and the party was picking up. Her priestesses and Gabriel entered with the throng of people, come to let loose. She spent the next few hours drinking and playing brain games. She felt like she acquitted herself quite well.

Melina took a break to get another cup of wine.

"You're not dressed as a Koios devotee." The man was tall with raven hair. His soft blue eyes met hers and he had a pleasant smell of a forest.

"I'm just here for the party."

"I came to see how I measured up to the erudite priestesses. I didn't think I'd meet a true beauty."

"So you're saying beauty conflicts with brains?" She smiled.

He laughed. "I simply meant that you could challenge Aphrodite in divine aspect."

"How dare you insult my patron."

"I was trying to compliment you. I meant no offense."

She laughed. "Aphrodite is quite humble, I assure you."

"You know her personally?" He poured himself a glass.

"Of course, I'm Melina, and I am her personal servant."

"You're the blessed one who found the gods?"

"I suppose I am. And what is your name?"

"I'm Darius. And I practice philosophy at the Academy."

"I see. So, let's go see how you measure up."

***

They spent the next few hours playing brain games. And suffering punishment for their shortcomings. Their final game ended with them going head-to-head. And she lost. As punishment, she had to submit to his every desire. Her hands were bound, and he led her into a private chamber.

"What do you want me to do?"

Darius traced the curve of her chest, then down her arms to her wrists. His eyes studied her body, until he met her eyes, and he began to untie her hands.

"I want you to explain love to me."

"Love comes in many forms. But the underlying principle is selflessness. Giving of yourself with no expectations."

"Is any form superior to the others?"

Melina sat on a lounger. "Superior is not applicable. Love is love, be it familial, platonic, or romantic."

He sat next to her. "It seems that familial is a given. Doesn't that diminish it somehow?"

"Just because you're family, doesn't mean love is a given. But due to the natural connection, it does seem easier. It's a unique kind of bond between mother and child. And that serves a most important function. So I think it loses nothing."

"And what about platonic love?"

"This is probably the most common type. Anyone you choose to be close friends with would fall into platonic love. Most people are closer with their friends than their family."

"And that leaves romantic love." He touched her hand.

"Romantic love is the most rare, but also the most rich. It combines all the tenets of platonic love, with another level of intimacy. It is where two people can become their truest selves. And the synergy allows each party to become more than they could ever be on their own. It is the closest to the divine that we mortals can ever achieve."

Their instant chemistry was now electric. She'd never felt anything like it before.

"Will you show me?"

Melina turned and he met her lips. They went slow and took their time. For the preeminent priestess of love, she felt like she was experiencing a whole new level of love. She wondered if any woman who hadn't personally lived romantic love was qualified to promote it. And now here, in the House of Knowledge, she felt she was receiving her advanced education.

They continued exploring each other and savored every moment. She'd had sex many times, but this felt different. It was a new level of intimacy. The connection was well beyond physical. It was like their souls bonded. When they finished it felt like they'd known each other longer than time.

"I think I finally understand love. And it only took two centuries." Darius ran his fingers through her hair.

"You just needed the right teacher."

He chuckled. "I know it sounds crazy, but I've never felt like this before."

She caressed his arm. "It's not about how much time has passed, it's about the souls involved."

"Well, you have mine." He kissed her temple.

"And you have mine." She kissed his hand.

"Only for tonight." He nuzzled her hair.

"The timing is wrong, but love does find a way."

"Perhaps it will, but let's make the most of this night." And they went for another round.

They spent the rest of the Death Festival making the most of it. As dawn arrived on the new year Melina savored their final moments together.

The concept of love at first sight was always ridiculous to Melina. But now it had happened to her. She almost regretted that she served the gods. Marriage was forbidden for divine servants. Which she found ironic for those in the service of love. It seemed a significant part of the principles of love was missing from their experience. But of course, pure romantic love could divide their loyalties, so she understood the reason.

She hoped Darius would be there waiting for her when she completed her service. But that was centuries away, so the chances were small. She watched him leave with the sun, and she prayed to Aphrodite that they would find each other again.

CHAPTER V: A GOLDEN AGE?

Superiority?

MICHEAL HAD BECOME ACCUSTOMED to his godhood over their more than four-year rule. He had to laugh because he was originally unsure of his nobility. Now, it just felt natural that he should be worshipped. His superior intellect was obvious. And then, through hard work and divine effort, he'd sculpted himself into a physical specimen. If there was anyone worthy of ardor, it was him.

And it's not like he wasn't earning his keep. His clean water systems had probably saved millions. Their combat efforts had secured peace. And the ensuing prosperity had improved millions more lives.

He would attend council meetings, honor his devout priestesses, and routinely inspire the masses. Speaking of which, he'd just finished addressing Atlantis.

Julie flew up to meet him. "That was a rather self-congratulatory speech."

"No more than normal."

"That's my point. I've been meaning to talk to you about this."

"About what?" He squinted.

"I've noticed that over these last four years, you let this Gods thing go to your head. During that first year, when we had so many problems to fix, you remained the humble servant. But once we no longer had to put that much work into earning the praise of our worshipers, you started to demonstrate a superiority complex." She said a bit sharply.

"Complex?" He laughed.

"Yes! You act like you're superior to everyone."

"Well, aren't I? In most ways, at least?" he asked lightheartedly.

"Including me?" She didn't laugh.

"Of course not!"

"You do, don't you?" Her eyes watered.

"That's ridiculous!"

"You hesitated!"

"I did not!"

She flew off with tears in her eyes.

He sighed, then flew back to the palace. She had locked him out of the Chamber of the Gods, their private quarters in the Palace of the Gods.

He went through his memories one by one of his time as Koios to see if she might be right. He didn't feel he had changed much over the past five years. He thought perhaps she must be going through some kind of an episode.

He decided to go for a flight to give her space. As he overlooked the Pillars of Hercules, he once again tried to trace his actions. He still didn't think he had done anything wrong. That evening, he returned to the palace. The chamber was unlocked, and he went inside to discover Julie was gone.

As he sat there with his thoughts, Melina entered the chamber. "My apologies, Eminence Koios." Melina turned to go.

"Melina, stay," he ordered. She stopped. "Come here."

She came over to him. "How may I serve you?" She was shifting.

"While you have served Aphrodite, you have also become familiar with myself, have you not?"

"I have eminence Koios."

"Speak honestly to me. Have I become... More, full of myself over these last years?"

"Well, Your Eminence, no more than any god would."

"I really have." He leaned back, touching his chin.

"You are a God, Eminence Koios." She nodded.

"Thank you, Melina."

"If I may, Your Eminence?"

"Go ahead."

"You are indeed a magnificent god." He noticed her scan him as she made herself more comfortable. "But Aphrodite carries herself more like one of us. Perhaps if you matched her energy, it would appease her."

"She's spoken to you about this?"

Her eyes went wide. "Um, I..."

"No, stay. It's okay."

He studied her. She was quite sophisticated for a 23-year-old. While she always played demure around him, he had always noticed her observational mind working.

"I'm thankful she's had a confidant through our time here. Down here, it can be quite isolating for us. I'm pleased that you are not like everyone else around here."

"You have always been so kind to me since our first meeting. I have always wanted to thank you for gently accepting my failings upon my offering. I really would have been honored to serve you. In whatever way you desired."

His memory flashed to her mousy presentation.

"I appreciate that, and you would have been amazing. Your beautiful mind is quite erudite. But I think you have been perfect for Aphrodite. Thank you for your candor, Melina; good night."

She scanned him again, swallowed, and then took her leave.

He went to try to apologize to Julie, but she was already asleep in the lower chamber. He decided to let her sleep on it. So he went to bed.

***

"Wake up!" Julie yelled, standing over top of him.

As he opened his eyes. "Jules—" He began.

"No! I have a challenge for you." She cut him off. "We spar, no weapons, no technologies. If I win, we return to the heavens. If you win, we stay."

She was in a determined mood. He knew there was no argument. "All right."

"Meet me at Aphrodite's Plaza." She instructed, then departed.

"Begin!" She yelled. They circled for a moment; then she slid in for a sweep. He dodged, then did a rotating counter, taking her down. She was able to pull a dynamic escape. They exchanged multiple attacks, but they were both able to block and counter them. They went back and forth for a while. Then he feigned making a mistake. She fell for it; he was able to get the upper hand and was pressing for a chokeout. Her defenses suddenly failed, and he was sure he'd won. But she suddenly flipped her body out of the lock he had her in. She had reversed him; she brought her elbow down on his head. She stopped as her elbow barely connected. She had played possum, and now he had lost.

"Congratulations, I guess we leave then. You were right. I guess it did go to my head a bit. I'm sorry. It is time to leave."

"It's okay, you're forgiven. It's been one heck of a ride, hasn't it?" She took in their surroundings.

"Indeed, my Aphrodite." He said, taking in her full aspect. "Let's make all the preparations. On a different note, I have something for you."

She took his gift and slowly opened it. "Oh, Micheal." She said with tears coming to her eyes. It was a true-to-life painting of her sister Jessica. He had painstakingly re-created her image from his memory. "Happy anniversary Jules."

After dinner, they began having an extended session of electric sex. "I am going to miss this." He said with a chuckle.

"I would say that perhaps we might still be able to under the right circumstances," she said with a devious grin.

False Gods

-September 1, 3276 BC

"The Gods' reign over Atlantis is nearly at its end. It has been one crazy ride. Our decision to leave appears to be just in time. Some of the opposition voices have been bubbling just beneath the surface and appear to be about to burst. The peace and prosperity

of our reign have allowed them to sit around fat and happy and plot against us. Our tentative departure date is September 8th, the fifth anniversary of our arrival in the city. Final preparations are nearly complete for our dramatic return to the heavens. A swansong worthy of the gods."

A couple of days later, the bubbles began to burst. First, the believers of the Babylonian gods began massive risings all over the city. JULIE wasn't sure what they should do about it.

"We only have five days left, I doubt anything significant will happen before then." Micheal tried to reassure her.

She flew to the administrative palace where one of the major protests was taking place and addressed the crowd. "I have come to listen to your concerns."

"You are false gods. You must die." The leader of the resistance yelled.

"We have made no decree against your faith. We harbor no ill will toward you. We have only sought to improve the lives of everyone."

"Die!" Many in the crowd began yelling, throwing things at her.

As she returned to the palace, Micheal asked. "Let me guess, they were all ears?"

"I don't understand why they hate us so much."

"They believe in the Babylonian gods. We are an affront to that belief system."

"Maybe we should tell them we are leaving. If they knew we were leaving, perhaps they would be satisfied." She suggested.

"I doubt that. They would likely push forward any assassination attempts. Everyone already knows it's possible to kill a God. And this would likely represent their last true chance to kill a rival God."

Two days later, the Unitarians began to rise in protest, declaring that both polytheistic religions were sacrilege.

"What is to be done about these protests?" Cato asked as they held an emergency council meeting. "I know you have always been merciful towards those who have wished ill will upon your eminences. But I strongly believe in making an example."

"Your eminences I beseech thee. Continue in your mercy. We

of the Unitarians have demonstrated nothing but respect for your eminences." Helene of Eden appealed.

Each member of the Council took a turn arguing for their opinion of the matter. When they were done, Julie spoke. "We were unsure of the proper time to reveal our plans to you. And by our decree, this does not leave this chamber. It is not to be that we gods should reign indefinitely over the dominion of men. Three days hence, we shall ascend back to the heavens. Our work here is complete. It has been our honor to serve the people of Atlantis these last five years."

Each member of the Council took a turn paying final tribute.

"How's the mining bore prep going?" Micheal asked her.

"They are well on their way to being established in strategic locations around the world. We should never run out of gold or silver."

"Well, it looks like you finally got your wish-"

"My wish?"

"I don't know how often you wanted to just sail off on the Liberty and leave the world behind."

"It still does have an appeal, doesn't it?" She raised a brow. "I mean, no more lords or gods, just you and me with nothing but leisure time on our hands. I'm sure we could find other ways to fill the time." She pulled him to the bed.

<hr>

The next day, Julie was looking through some of the items they'd accrued over their rule.

"You're really leaving?" She was stunned to hear Melina ask in English.

"You know our words?"

"Aphrodite! Have mercy!" Melina pleaded, falling to her feet.

She reached down and picked Melina up. "Melina, I'm not angry with you."

"You're not?"

Julie shook her head.

"Melina, you are my friend and trusted servant. How long have you known?"

"Only recently in full. Slowly, over time, I would pick up a piece here or there. I just so desired to be like you. I'm sorry." Melina had her head down.

Julie pulled her chin up to look her in the eyes. "My dear friend, it is folly for a mortal to aspire to godliness." Did she ever know that firsthand? "I do admire your desire to aspire to greatness."

"You don't have to go."

She wiped the tears from Melina's eyes. "Sadly, our time here is at an end. I will never forget your friendship. It has been an honor to know you. I want you to promise me you will always strive for that lofty, unreachable greatness."

"I promise."

"I will be looking down on you from the heavens. And perhaps I will come and visit again from time to time; I mean, it does get a little boring in the heavens."

"I will look forward to it." Melina had tears running down her cheeks. And they hugged for a while.

When they first laid out their path home, and she realized they would only be in one place for five to ten years and then move on. She initially decided it would be better not to make friends because goodbyes were difficult. And she knew she was going to face this at every time stop. But it wasn't in her nature. It took every ounce of her to play the God for Melina's sake. Despite the God between them, Melina had become like a sister to her. And her heart was breaking to say goodbye.

My Friend Aphrodite

-Oceansel 13, 762 PF

"I begin this entry with a sense of impending loss. My friend Aphrodite, the Goddess of Love and Beauty, and everything I aspire to, is about to return to the heavens. Of course, this was an inevitable end to such a friendship, but that fact does not diminish the pain. It is unusual to be a full-family orphan at such a young age. No one knows how long people could live, but the elders are over 750. With such a long lifespan, all my known family were gone when I was just 16. Then, my idol came in the flesh and became as a mother to me—a true mother and then friend. I finally found a purpose in my life, in my great and holy honor, to serve Aphrodite. I have studied every aspect and attempted to emulate them. How to comport myself with strength and dignity. How to

treat everyone with gentle kindness. How to show compassion and generosity to the downtrodden. I have faithfully studied Aphrodite and Koios during their warrior sparring and practiced daily to simulate those techniques. So, I might defend myself or those not able to defend themselves. I have also learned to have the grace to show mercy to those who wrong me.

I have learned so much from Aphrodite these past five years. To my utmost honor, I can now speak the words of the gods. I hold that most sacred. I alone can speak. But the most amazing thing Aphrodite taught me is that beneath that perfect goddess ideal is a more down-to-earth, almost human side. The side that became my friend."

MELINA entered the Chamber of the Gods and had to stop and really take it in. She had been here so many times that it had become routine. But now it was ending; she had to consider how amazing the last five years had been. The Chamber of the Gods was a half-dome. It was made of some kind of glass. She had paced out the dimensions of the chamber at 321 paces the long way by 160 paces the short way, which would also be the height. She knew there was nothing like it in the world. It was something only the gods could build.

"Melina?" Koios said as she approached the center of the chamber.

"Eminence Koios, where is Aphrodite?"

"She has gone for a morning flight." He answered, in his own words. She wasn't sure how to respond. "I understand you know our words."

"Um, yes." She shifted back and forth.

"Good, sit with me." She hesitated for a moment, then sat down.

"You are quite resourceful, aren't you?" His beautifully intelligent eyes studied her.

"I am but a meager servant."

"We both know that's not true. You were what? 19 when you came into Aphrodite service? And a full family orphan at that."

"Does Aphrodite speak of me often?" She wondered how he knew so much about her.

"She does, but that's not how I knew such detail. I will let you in on a secret, Melina. I forget nothing. I suppose you don't remember. But five years ago, you told me those details." He said gently.

"My apologies—" She began.

"It's okay, God of knowledge." He tapped the side of his head. "How have you found it? Serving Aphrodite these past years?"

"It has been my singular honor and joy in life!" She sat up straighter.

"I'm glad. As we are leaving, I had intended to thank you for both of us, but for Aphrodite in particular. Being a God amongst men can be lonely. You mean the world to her, and so to me."

"I feel the same, if not more, for her. I might not have a perfect memory, but I remember many of your attempts at humor over the years." She laughed. "Aphrodite always says you're not as funny as you think."

"I know, I'm just too clever for her."

"Yes, I'm sure that's it." She shook her head. "Have you ever felt loneliness?"

"Not since Aphrodite, not here."

"And you have your priestesses to *serve* you? I would *serve* you." Her heart beat faster as she realized her words.

Koios sat back with a smile. "How would you *serve* me?"

Melina didn't know what to do, so she rose and stood before him. She had butterflies. Then she dropped her shoulder straps.

"Stop. What are you doing?"

"I wanted to serve you like your priestesses do."

"They don't serve me like that."

"They don't?" Melina was disappointed.

"I have never been with anyone but Aphrodite."

"I thought it was an erudite duty to give pleasure to you?"

"It is, but I don't have to partake. Don't get me wrong, you are certainly beautiful, as are all my priestesses, and all are willing, but I am committed to Aphrodite."

He rose and came to her. "I told you years ago that your intellect was just as beautiful as your body. And you would have served me well." He drew up her shoulder straps, covering her. "But your heart..." He moved her hand to her chest. "Is why you served Aphrodite so well."

Melina looked up at the god and wished she could have served him in the way she'd always imagined. But discovering he'd never taken advantage lessened her jealousy of Elissa, her counterpart for Koios. She'd always boasted of the god. But somehow, this revelation made Koios even more desirable. His love for Aphrodite remained pure.

She stepped back to break his spell.

"Were you ever lonely before, Aphrodite?"

"Perhaps once or twice in my youth."

"I was loneliness, then Aphrodite came. And now she's leaving. What am I going to do?" She began crying.

He came over and pulled her into him again. "It's okay, everything is going to be okay." It was hard not to feel safe and protected at that moment, he was so big. Then he pulled back. "I know you're going to be all right. You will live a long and meaningful life."

"And you can see the future, can't you?" She looked up.

"I am Koios."

"Will I see Aphrodite again?"

"Indeed, you will." He broke their embrace and indicated Aphrodite, who was standing right there.

"I meant—"

"I know what you meant. And yes, you will. Melina and I were just talking about you."

"Only good things, I hope." Aphrodite raised a brow.

"Are there any other kind? My love." He said elaborately. Aphrodite laughed, shaking her head.

"What else could you say about perfection?"

"You're very sweet, Melina. May I borrow Koios?"

Melina bowed. Then they flew off.

Clash Of Faiths

MELINA began the second to last day as always, preparing everything for Aphrodite. She tried to pretend it was just another day.

"What are you so upset about?" Elissa asked.

"Tomorrow is the last day."

"Yes... They're Gods. Did you think they were going to stay forever?"

"You erudite priestesses have no sentimentality at all, do you?"

"Obviously, not compared to you priestesses of passion. But I will miss his physical perfection."

"You've served eminence Koios for five years, and you feel no affection for him?"

"Of course, I have great adoration and respect for his eminence. His incomparable mind and delicious conversation. And I will have you know I was and still am ready and willing to serve my master in *any* way."

"I have to hear this," Melina said with a grin. She knew what was coming. Elissa was always using innuendo but never explicitly said she'd given him sexual favors. Melina knew better.

"On my very first day, I went to his eminence and offered myself for his full use. He politely declined my offer that day and every other day since. But I maintain my aesthetic aspect for his pleasure." Elissa said, indicating her undercup, supporting her breasts but covering nothing.

"He would never avail himself because of Aphrodite. And he's too romantic for the bare offerings."

"My lack of clothes has nothing to do with it. And it always seems you feel superior about this issue. As I recall, you put yourself up to serve Koios. You would have been naked for that, correct?"

"As the one who discovered them, I felt it was my duty to make the offer. And I would have been happy to serve Koios in *any* way he liked. In his wisdom, he knew I'd better serve Aphrodite."

Elissa smiled. "I'm sure you would, Melina. But he was right about who you should serve. We both know if he's going to use one of our services before tomorrow, it'll be from me." Elissa left for The Chamber of the Gods.

As soon as the gods took their post-breakfast leave, Melina went to Aphrodite's Plaza to practice her warrior skills. While working on her staff strikes, she heard a chaotic murmuring from the city below. She walked to the end of the Plaza and looked down. Fires and smoke were rising from all over the city.

"What's happening?" Elissa asked as she walked to the edge.

"Everyone seems to be fighting."

"What could they possibly be upset about? The gods have brought great peace and prosperity, not just throughout the Empire, but throughout the world." Elissa shrugged.

"There are many people who don't believe in our gods."

"That doesn't make any sense. What they've been doing here has been well-reported all over the world. And everyone in this city has seen what they can do."

"It's religion. Many people here have had well-established beliefs for centuries. They're not going to change their beliefs so easily."

"So, they will deny what their own eyes show them?" Elissa shook her head.

"People will rationalize away nearly anything."

"It just shows you how small-minded normal people are." Elissa walked off with a huff.

At that moment, Aphrodite and Koios appeared and began interceding wherever clashes were going on. The city was quiet by evening, but Melina doubted the battles were over for good.

"Thank you, Melina," Aphrodite said as Melina delivered her dinner for the last time. Melina hesitated for a moment. "Yes, Melina?"

"Do you think the city will return to peace after you leave?"

"Yes, they're fighting over whether we are true gods, or not. Once we are gone, most of the reason for these clashes will be gone." Aphrodite paused. "Melina, what do you plan to do after I'm gone?"

"I will continue to serve you. I will do everything in my power to promote your legacy." She stood up straighter.

"While I greatly appreciate your devotion. You still have a millennium of life ahead of you. Promise me you will take a few of those centuries for yourself. Live a life, have a family."

"I have always wanted a family for obvious reasons, but It also scares me."

"What about that scares you?"

"Is it possible to devote your love to many different things?"

"It's all about balance. You figure out what's really important and be sure to give that the time it requires. Now you can't have too many. But a good few. Live intentionally, and you should be able to spread your love."

"I know how important you are to me. I have spent most of my life studying the edicts of romance and seduction. I bring joy and pleasure to many more people through this work. It will be so difficult to turn to selfishness compared to that."

"What is the first edict of love?"

"First, love yourself."

"I know it seems like selfishness. But the first person you need to show love to is you. When you fully love yourself, your heart can open completely to others. Melina, your heart is bigger than anyone I know. For all that you feed in, you will see a multitude in return to others. So, as your goddess and your friend, I expect you to find love for yourself. We will return at some point. I expect to hear about your great love."

"You will, I promise, Aphrodite."

That evening, all of the servants to the gods were permitted inside The Chamber of the Gods and were given a sendoff feast worthy of the gods. By the deep middle of the night, she and Elissa had finally cleared the chamber.

"Quite the last day, right?" Elissa sighed.

"Yes, it was. I'm sorry Koios never accepted your offering."

"Same for you." They both laughed.

"Five years of miracles and divine leadership is more than enough reward for me. In this position, I have fulfilled my life's purpose."

"So what will you do now?"

"Just because I won't be serving him in person doesn't mean I stop serving him. What about you?"

"I'm being venerated, almost as if I'm divine because I discovered them. I think I need to use that to ensure that the peace they've delivered to the world is perpetuated."

"You know you sound rather erudite."

"Don't start with me, Elissa." They laughed again.

"So, how are you going to perpetuate peace?"

"I think there needs to be a temple built specifically for both of them. Not a Temple of Aphrodite or a Temple of Koios, but a Temple of the Gods. As in both of them. Want to help?"

"We do make a pretty good pair, don't we? And it is another way to serve Koios. Besides, you need my engineering skills. Goodness knows the walls won't stay up if you design the place."

"I don't think we want it to look like a generic box, so we might want to let me handle the overall look."

"I am very artistic."

Melina laughed. "You've said on more than one occasion that simple is elegant. But it's also boring. So I'll handle the artistic side, and you make sure it's well-built. See, we are a good team."

"Well then, we have a new mission. Where are we going to build it?"

"The Overlook of the Gods is perfect."

"See, you do have some intelligent ideas, after all." Elissa headed for the exit. "Are you coming?"

"I will say a bit longer." Melina scanned the chamber.

"More sentimentality. Well, I will leave you to it." Elissa headed off.

A few minutes later, while walking near the center of the chamber, she noticed someone standing near where the gods slept. As she got closer, she recognized him. "Gabriel, what are you doing here?"

"I can't believe Aphrodite is leaving us." Gabriel didn't look at her.

"It is upsetting, but change is inevitable." She touched his shoulder. "You're not supposed to be in here."

"I was worried someone would try to hurt her."

"They're quite capable of defending themselves."

"But what if someone discovered the source of their power?"

"That's not possible. Now, I appreciate your concern, but you really should go."

Gabriel looked at the gods, looked at her, and left the chamber.

Gabriel was the only priest of Aphrodite. Normally, only priestesses were allowed to serve a goddess. But rare exceptions were made if you had the right connections. Gabriel's father, Cato, was the head of the Council, and he wanted to please his son. For the most part, Melina considered Gabriel to be a friend. But his obsession with Aphrodite had always made her feel uneasy.

As she walked the edge of the chamber, it was very dark, except for the great river of stars flowing off towards the dark horizon. Selene, the goddess of the moon, had taken the moon for herself this night. She sat down and stared at the sky, contemplating the enormous grandeur of the gods. And how lucky she had been to get to know them personally. She made her way to the center of the chamber and looked in on the gods. They were already asleep. Aphrodite was sleeping on Koios' chest. She was the ideal image of a goddess. Melina sat in a chair just watching them, but the long day's exhaustion overcame her, and she drifted off to sleep.

The Great Escape

MELINA was fighting scores of assassins in The Chamber of the Gods, fighting to protect Aphrodite. She had just defeated several foes when she felt the blade cut into her throat. She lay gurgling in a puddle of her own blood.

She woke with a start just-in-time. She grabbed the man's arm, preventing him from actually cutting her throat. She did a backflip reversal and jabbed the knife into his chest. She looked over at the gods. A man was standing over them with an obsidian-tipped spear. As he tried to stab Aphrodite in the head, Koios moved her, taking the thrust in the shoulder. Melina ran and kicked the man hard, sending him flying. Aphrodite and Koios rose, and while they had no clothing on, they began laying waste to the oncoming attackers. Melina went to assist them. She picked up two swords and began cutting through waves of attackers. After fighting through hundreds of assassins, the attackers seemed endless.

"Melina!" Aphrodite yelled. Melina ran to her. Aphrodite picked her up, and they flew out the top of the chamber with Koios. They hovered over Mount Atlas, and she could see several thousand assassins. Koios charged a large ball of energy, sent it down on the mass of attackers, and all went down.

"To the overlook," Koios instructed.

As they flew to the overlook, Melina could feel the power running through her. And the city became tiny below her. In the dawn's early light, she could see clashes taking place all over the city, even in the outer rings. She was certainly glad she wasn't down there.

Every time Melina got the chance to see the world from a divine perspective, she always felt insignificant. The city of Atlantis was massive. And the world was even grander still. She thought if only everyone could experience this, the turmoil below would cease.

The trip was short and as they arrived at the overlook Aphrodite went to tend to Koios.

They were both naked. She had, of course, seen them naked many times, but their perfection was always a sight to behold. Once, Aphrodite had mended his shoulder wound. Koios reached toward the ground, and a pod rose out of nothing. It contained a fresh set of clothes for each of them.

After they had dressed, Aphrodite came over to her. "Melina, my dear friend. Our time here is at an end. I noticed that you emulated yet another aspect of me. I have never been so honored. I can't say when, but I will see you again."

"It has been my honor to serve you, Aphrodite. And I will continue to do so after you leave. I will be your legacy."

"I have some gifts for you," Aphrodite said. She reached toward the ground, and a pod rose. Inside was a veritable mountain of gold. In the next was a statue of Aphrodite. "Something to remember me by," Aphrodite added with a smile. For possibly the first time she could remember, she saw tears running down Aphrodite's cheeks. "I will miss you." Aphrodite pulled her in.

They embraced as the tears continued to flow down Melina's face. "Farewell, Aphrodite."

"Farewell, Melina." Aphrodite released her and began drifting toward the sky. A moment later, she turned, and she and Koios flew away towards the city. Melina watched longingly until they were out of sight.

A little while later, she saw lightning balls flying out from the center of the city to nearly every part of it. Finally, she saw a massive ball of light spinning over the city. It descended rapidly to Mount Atlas. A wave of light spread all across Atlantis. Everything became calm as if the city took a deep breath. Finally, she heard Koios's voice. "People of Atlantis, our time here has ended. You must end your enmity towards each other." Aphrodite picked up the message. "I admonish you, love your neighbor as yourself. Living in harmony will allow for continued prosperity. A better life for everyone." Then Koios continued. "It was our honor to serve you these past five years." Then Aphrodite finished their message. "We return to the heavens; your fate is in your hands. Goodbye and farewell." Then, the voices fell silent.

A short time later, Melina saw brilliant light ascending from Mount Atlas. It climbed rapidly through the clouds and disappeared. She couldn't keep the tears back and wondered when she would see Aphrodite again, but she felt lucky to have witnessed the rule of the gods.

CHAPTER VI: VOYAGES

Return to the Heavens

"ALTITUDE IS 50 MILES, velocity has reached 17,000 mph. We are approaching orbital velocity. 1000 miles down range. About to break the threshold... Velocity has increased to 18,000 mph, altitude 60 miles, 1300 miles down range."

MICHEAL was pulled from his astronaut mentality by the reality of his location. He gazed out at the curve of the Earth's surface. There was a translucent purple bubble surrounding the green multi-shade surface below. It wasn't the blue orb he was used to from his childhood.

Ten years earlier, he'd thought his dream of going to space had passed him by. The realization that it only took him five years to develop the technology in the wilds of the seventeenth century made him want to kick himself for his depressive idiocy.

But 2010 was a different world, and a different life. If he'd stayed and it was now 2020, He'd likely be that same depressed loser. Not achieving a lifetime goal.

Micheal initiated the sequence, and the world fell silent for a moment. "Afterburners off. Altitude 250 miles, 3000 miles down range, velocity is 17,500 mph. We've reached a stable orbit. How are you holding up?" He sighed to steady his stomach.

Julie closed her eyes and sucked in deeply. "A little woozy and nauseous, but at least I haven't thrown up yet."

"I've wanted to do this my whole life." He released the buckle and floated into the center of the pod. It was different than the M-pulse flight. It was a true suspension of gravity. "I'm glad we built it as big as we did."

The spaceship was an orb approximately 20 feet across. Most of the systems were built into the walls. There were also several large windows.

Julie floated past with her hands behind her head. "I think I've finally found equilibrium."

"So this won't be the vomit comet after all?"

"Thank goodness! Now, let's have some fun."

They played around in zero-G for a while.

"Catch this." He sent some chocolate drops toward her.

She caught them in her mouth. "I'm already a pro. And would you look at that?" She floated to the window; he came to join her. "I still can't get over the fact that this is earth." She shook her head. You could clearly see the Atlantic passage below them.

"It certainly is beautiful." He remarked as they were about to cross the terminator to the nightside.

"Ready to join the 250-mile club?" She gave a sly smile as she began removing her jumpsuit. He did the same and floated over to her.

Suspended in the center of the ship, he began kissing her, then moved on to her neck as he removed her sports bra. Her breasts floated, two perfect mounds in the zero-G. He traced their shape with his fingers. He pressed them together, then proceeded to take her irresistible nipples into his mouth. He worked his way down, pulling her legs over his shoulders. He buried his face in her pussy, tasting her sweet lips.

Micheal took his time bringing her to multiple levels of heaven. His hands wandered across her silken skin. When he brought her up and down and pushed her to the max, her thighs were quivering, and she was out of breath.

The feast between her legs had him at full attention. Apparently, she noticed. "You took me to heaven. Now, it's your turn."

Her mouth consumed his dick. He leaned back with his hands behind his head. She worked her magic mouth while she took a firm grip around the base of his cock. She teased him up and down. Then she latched on and sucked him like a straw until he popped. His next stop was cloud nine, though he didn't remember the details. When he got his wits back, she swallowed, sucking until he was dry.

She finally released him. "We wouldn't want to make a mess now, would we?"

Julie climbed him up to eye level. "We really did return to heaven, didn't we?"

"When did we ever leave?" Micheal slowed it down by accepting a mission to rediscover all the beautiful contours of her.

After reloading, it was time to explore inside. He entered her as she wrapped her legs around him. They were able to sync up in a perfect rhythm. He generated more force, and they began slowly rotating in the air. He brought her to the brink and then tried to pull her back, but she lost control. Her pussy spasmed, pulling him to nirvana with her.

"You don't know how amazing that was." He sighed.

"I think I have an idea." She caressed his face.

"I'm pretty certain we're the first." He released her hair from its binding, and it moved like smoke in the air. She was like a dream.

"What are you thinking?"

"I never thought I would find heaven. And I certainly never thought an angel would let me inside."

"You are definitely still inside." Her pussy contracted around his dick. They were still connected, body and soul. "Feels like you want to go deeper." She smiled.

"Will you take me there?"

And they tested the depths of heaven the rest of the night.

Micheal woke in near-complete darkness. Julie was still asleep. He released his footholds and drifted over to the window. He cracked the shade and saw the night side sparkling with lightning flashes. He chuckled at the fact that his mission to space took place 5000 years in the past.

He caught a glimpse of Julie's reflection in the window—the angel of his life.

"I never thought I'd be here."

"Neither did I." He could see her reflection looking at him.

"There should be wrinkles and gray hairs. Signs of the passage of time." She ran her fingers through his hair.

"You don't want to be eternally youthful?"

"Won't you get bored of my changeless appearance?"

"Your timeless beauty isn't just about your flawless complexion. I can see your heart through your eyes, and that aspect of your beauty is dynamic."

"We have so long to go. What is even the point of returning to the 21st with how much we'll change."

"One thing that will never change is you are Julie Buckingham, and I'm Micheal Hall. One year or a thousand, our core selves will never change. My memory gives me a different perspective. Whenever we happen to return, it won't seem so long. And those we're missing will be waiting to absorb us back in as if we never left."

Micheal drew her into his embrace as the sun began to rise over the curved glow. She leaned her head back, and he kissed her ear.

Their space vacation continued, and the time was incalculable.

"Those two weeks really flew by, didn't they?" Julie was distracted by the window.

"You want to stay longer?"

"It does have its appeal."

"One way in particular." He winked.

"Are you thinking what I'm thinking?" She bounced her brows.

"One more for the road?" He floated over to her.

The one more, lasted a few orbits around the world.

"Definitely isn't a normal life up here," Micheal said.

"It is certainly a unique experience."

"Ready for reentry?" He raised a brow.

"Not the kind you're thinking. Now, let's return to solid ground."

Micheal laughed, then said. "Vector bearing 0.8."

"Preparing for descent burn. In 10 seconds."

"Mark."

Julie hit the switch, and the ship began a gradual descent.

"Atmospheric burn in five seconds."

"Angular bearing is good. Variance is 0.02°."

"Adjusting." He looked out the window, and it was a wall of flame. A few minutes passed. "We are about to go subsonic."

"Preparing to activate the M-pulse system," she said.

The M-pulse system channeled kinetic energy to generate a magnetic repulse polarized field inverse to the Earth's magnetic field. It was designed to slow the ship to a soft touchdown. It was the same technology that was in their black rings. The one that allowed them to fly. She activated the system.

"Targeting system... On." He said as they began vertical descent.

"Altitude 1000 feet. Rate of descent 10 ft./s. 100 feet, 10 seconds to soft touch."

"We have a soft touch within 10 feet of the bull's-eye."

They felt a bit heavy for a few days, but they were still able to bury the spaceship. And prepare their Atlantean yacht for the voyage ahead. It was 120 feet long. Constructed in the Atlantean style, it was reminiscent of a Viking longship. But it had all the same technologies as the Liberty. They boarded and headed for open water.

"I'm sailing away!" Julie sang. All he could do was laugh.

Vagabonds

-November 12, 3276 BC

"We sailed from our desolate cove on the coast of the Frozen Sea in the wildlands on the north end of the pangea. We skirted the coast for weeks before heading south around China to the north coast of Greece, which, in the insane arrangement of our current time, is where Indonesia and the Philippines will be in the future.

This crazy life of mine continues, and I try to keep a true sense of who I really am. The longer we are out here. The more things I experience, the more likely it becomes that I might begin to lose myself in whoever I'm pretending to be. At what point does acting end and life begin?"

PS: Happy 41st!

"This is only our second run of the Atlantic Passage," JULIE said as they passed between the Pillars of Hercules.

"We were lucky last time; no one tried anything. But it's been years since the gods ran the pirates out of the passage."

The next morning, they awoke to a small pirate fleet stocking them. Three in front, three behind. They were closing in on all sides.

"Cut to starboard!" Micheal yelled.

She turned the wheel hard to the left. The Avalon beelined straight toward one of the ships. It tried to turn, but there wasn't enough time.

"Brace for impact!" Julie yelled.

The impact sent the ship, which was only about half the length of the Avalon, into a careening spin, which caused it to roll. The impact also caused the Avalon to lose momentum. Just as they began accelerating, they were hit from behind. The two ships in front of them tried to cut off their escape path. She swung hard to port and rammed the side of one of the ships. It ruptured a gaping hole in the side and began to sink. One of the trailing ships moved to lend aid. Another trailing ship rammed the Avalon in the side. But instead of damaging the Avalon, the front of the ship cracked. She accelerated again. The last ship in front threw a hook line that caught onto the back of their ship.

The ship began to be dragged by the Avalon, slowing them down significantly. Micheal ran to the back to attempt to free them. Suddenly a seventh ship approached. It was nearly as large as the Avalon. It had to be the flagship. It began to pull up to the side of them. She could see that many men were preparing to board. At that moment the anchored ship was released, and the Avalon began accelerating. The flagship tried to keep pace. The Pirates tossed over anchor lines, and several began to board. But Micheal kicked them back one by one. As the Avalon started pulling away, Micheal systematically severed all the anchor lines.

Now at a safe distance, Julie looked back at the mess of ships left in their wake.

"That was a close one," Micheal said as he joined her on the bridge.

"The closest in the three years we've been at sea." She sighed.

"It has been a good three years, but I think we are at the end of our vagabond ways."

"We still have time."

"You did want to check out Eden, right?" He raised a brow.

"Oh yeah... Do you really think it's the Eden from the Bible?"

"Nothing would surprise me at this point."

"The location is wrong, isn't it?" Eden was not in the Middle East.

"I don't think so. The Mississippi in this time is called Pishon in Atlantean. And, of course, no one knew there was a pangea supercontinent either."

"I suppose we'll find out."

-January 12, 3272 BC

"So, we go to Eden. Is it the fabled Garden of Eden? Will we find Adam and Eve there? And what if we do? What does that indicate about all the religions that we know about? So many questions.

It has been a crazy eight years so far here in Atlantis. As we begin to prepare to leave this time period, how much crazier could it get?

Today marks the 14th anniversary since we fell through time. It also happens to be my beloved husband Micheal's 41st birthday. How the time flies."

Quest to Eden

A week later, they sailed up the Pishon River en route to Eden. MICHEAL had never had any kind of faith. He wondered if whatever they found in Eden could change that. It's not like the bible was very specific about much of the Genesis Era. If there really were a couple of 765-year-old *elders*, would that convince him?

"Isn't this the Mississippi River?" Julie asked.

"Sort of, the course is actually different than it will be in our time. The Pishon runs up the lower Mississippi area, then transitions to the course that will become the Ohio. The Pishon is also the main river mentioned in Genesis. The three primary tributaries, the Gihon, the Chidekel, and the Phirat, are also mentioned in the Bible. In our time, the Gihon is the upper Mississippi; the Chidekel is the Missouri, and the Phirat is the Arkansas."

"So, you really believe this is the Eden from the Bible?"

He shrugged. "It does seem quite the coincidence if it's not."

"If you really thought that, why didn't you visit Eden when we ruled over Atlantis?"

"Honestly... That's part of the reason I didn't. If it is the true Eden and the famed Elders are actually Adam and Eve. I felt it would be sort of sacrilegious to visit when I was pretending to be a God."

"I didn't think you cared that much about religion. You never showed much interest. Isn't that why we've never discussed it before?" She raised a brow.

"Part of the reason I never brought it up was because of Jessica. You told me how that affected your faith in the catholic church, and I wasn't sure I wanted to open the religious can of worms. I found it a little odd you never broached the subject when we were going to get married, for real I mean. But when you never asked about my religion, I thought it must be a sore spot, so I thought it best not to bring it up unless you did."

Julie laughed. "I had the same thought about waiting for you to bring it up. Honestly, I did imagine you might be a Mormon because you were from Salt Lake City. I don't know much about that faith, but I thought they were pretty devout. And when you never brought it up, I thought, maybe you had a good reason. So why bring a potential controversy into our marriage?"

"I was raised in the LDS Church, but I have been inactive since I was 12. I have never had anything that would be called faith. Now, in the LDS Church, you are supposed to get baptized when you turn eight. And one thing about that is that you're only supposed to do it if you truly believe the church is true. So, when I was seven, I researched every major religion, from other Christian faiths to Buddhism and other religions such as Judaism and Islam. I even researched Native American religions as well as Hinduism. In the end, my analytical mind decided that they pretty much all had too many flaws to be true. But if there was a correct one, the LDS Church made the most sense from an analytical standpoint. I can explain my reasoning for that later. But with that, I went through with the baptism, hoping I would gain a testimony at some point. When it never came in concert with my severe depression, I stopped going."

"Do you believe in a God?"

"According to the known laws of physics, the Big Bang would require a God power to ignite. So that tells me there has to be some form of a God. Only the nature of God would be the true question." He shrugged.

"In the heresy trial, you made some pretty compelling arguments that would seem to indicate a belief in the Christian God. Was that all for show?"

"No. The only faith of any kind I actually have is in provable science. There has to be some kind of a God. And my arguments were true to the concept that God would be a perfect scientist. If someone understood every aspect of how the universe works, including the missing piece of the unified field theory, you would likely be what most people conceive God to be. That is the conception of God that makes the most sense to me. Do you believe in the Catholic God?"

Micheal had been curious about her thoughts on religion for some time but didn't want to risk messing up the best thing that had ever happened to him.

"When I was young, I had a strong faith in the church. But after what happened to Jessica, I did struggle to believe that God wouldn't answer my prayers that day. It made me question everything I thought I knew." She clenched her fists. "I wasn't sure I could believe in a God like that. And even if I allowed myself to entertain the idea..." She trailed off, tears coming to her eyes. "I was too angry at God to attend mass or go to confession... After my time with Jessica on the other side, I felt a sense of closure. But I'm still ambivalent about the church, and about God."

While in Boston, they had just kept up appearances by regularly attending an Anglican church in Charlestown. But aside from that, they had not been overly religious. This discussion seemed to emphasize why.

They came around the bend in the river, and a wall stretched as far as the eye could see. As they neared, they could see the massive river gates. The wall over the river was perhaps 200 feet high. In contrast, most of the wall was closer to 100 feet tall. There were three statues above the gates. A man and a woman walking with what Micheal believed was supposed to be God. The statues were perhaps a few hundred feet tall themselves.

"They don't do anything small in Atlantis, do they?" Julie chuckled.

"I'm guessing Adam and Eve walking with God." She matched his conclusion.

"I think you're right. This is certainly a Unitarian stronghold."

They passed through two sets of gates per wall, both the outer and the inner walls. Their satellite images of Eden indicated the outer wall was a rectangle that ran 30 miles north to south and 40 miles east to west. The inner wall was 13 miles north to south and 20 miles east to west. The Pishon branched into three Rivers inside the inner walls. The Pishon went east into the region of Havilah. The Gihon went north into the region of Cush. And the Chidekel went to the region of Ashur. There were many islands. Within the inner wall, it was reminiscent of central Atlantis. Stone skyscrapers were reaching upward of 500 feet high. They had done a census while they ruled the Empire; the city of Atlantis had approximately 40 million people. And the city of Eden had nearly 35 million people. The Empire, on the whole, which spanned about 5000 miles in each direction, had approximately 2.5 billion people. A satellite data analysis produced a global population estimate of roughly 10 billion. All with Romanesque-level technology. By comparison, Rome's estimated population at its peak in the ancient world was around 1 million. The Roman Empire reached its peak with a population of approximately 60 million. It was almost hard to fathom how so many people could live in one place with Romanesque technology.

As they disembarked in central Eden, the streets were wall-to-wall people. "This reminds me of New York," Julie said of the chaos swarming around them. "At least no one thinks we are Gods yet."

"I'm sure we will be crowned king and queen soon enough." Micheal laughed.

"How will we ever find the elders in this mess?"

"I suppose we'll just ask around. I'm sure someone knows where they are. However, there's a good chance we won't be allowed to meet them."

"Let's go in here." She said, indicating a large marketplace. They walked around perusing the various shops. As they moved through the market, Micheal realized they were being followed. They turned into a shop, and Micheal waited momentarily in the doorway. As the woman passed, he grabbed her and pulled her into the door.

"Please don't!" The woman yelled.

"I wasn't going to hurt you!... Why are you following us?" he asked sharply.

"I was sent for you."

CHAPTER VII: ADAM & EVE

Expected Arrival

JULIE GRITTED HER TEETH at the woman's statement. All this chosen one bullshit was growing a bit thin. First lords, then gods, now whatever this was.

"You were sent for us? How would you even know we were coming here?" Julie asked.

"Who sent you?" Micheal asked.

"My name is Evelyn. My parents, the Elders, sent me to invite you for a visit... Now, I don't know all the details, but my father asked me to come to the market today. He said, just after midday, to look to the southwest entrance of the market. For two people of your description. I followed you to try to confirm in my own mind that you were who I was sent for." Evelyn shifted her eyes.

Julie assessed Evelyn. She was about five-foot-nine, of slender build. And, of course, she looked to be in her early 20s. She had strawberry-blonde hair and blue eyes with a slightly tan complexion.

Micheal seemed to be studying her also. Then he looked at Julie. "So, what do you think?"

She looked at Evelyn again, then said, "I believe her."

Micheal turned back to Evelyn. "One question. Do you know our names?" He raised a brow.

"Oh yeah, Micheal and Julie."

"Nice to meet you, Evelyn. Our apologies. Now lead the way." Micheal gestured.

"It will be easier to get there on your ship."

Julie shook her head.

"Very well," Micheal said, and they headed for the docks.

They headed up the Gihon River, following Evelyn's directions.

"So, your parents are the elders. Why are they called the Elders?" Julie asked.

"While many people no longer believe it. They are the first man and woman." Evelyn looked away, shaking her head.

"They are Adam and Eve?" A nervous knot formed in her stomach.

"Some used to call them that, but that's not their real name. Those are just titles."

"Titles?" Micheal glanced from the wheel.

"Adam means first man; Eve means first woman. They said they're titles like king or emperor."

"You say you're their daughter. How old are you?" Julie asked.

"I'm 758," Evelyn replied casually. "I am one of the oldest people in the world. Very few people have crossed the seven-century mark."

"What's it like to live that long? I mean, what do you do for seven centuries?" Julie asked.

"My childhood was quite simple. We lived in a small settlement. And there were only about a dozen of us. Can you imagine being one of only 12 people in the world?" The look on her face reminded her of how Micheal looks when he's living in a memory.

"Sounds lonely."

"When it's all you know. You don't really think about it that way. It's crazy to think that there are billions of people in the world today."

"Did you ever get married? Have children?"

"Of course," Evelyn said, with a look that indicated it should have been obvious. "I was with my first husband Jacob for almost 400 years. We had 23 children over about 300 years. Jacob was murdered about 250 years ago. Most of my children from him are still alive. Then, I was married to Ezra for a little over a century. We had four children. They're all still alive. Ezra died in an accident about 100 years ago. After that, I decided to come help my parents out."

"That's quite a life."

"How about you? How old are you?"

"He's 41, and I'm 44, and I don't have any children."

"Not to worry, you're just a baby. You have a long way to go."

"Don't I know it?"

They docked at an island in the middle of the Gihon River. It was fairly sizable. Maybe a couple of miles in length.

"Is this where you grew up?" Julie asked as they walked onto the docks.

"No, I grew up around where that market was. My parents moved here when the city began to grow too large."

"How far is the garden?" Julie inquired nervously.

"The garden? Oh, no one believes that anymore." Evelyn waved it off.

"Do you believe that story?" Julie raised a brow.

"I generally don't give my opinion about some of this stuff. The only thing I sometimes say, only half seriously, is. I wouldn't be here if it weren't true." Evelyn gave a snide laugh. "This way." She led them down the right fork of the path.

"You've been rather quiet," Julie said to Micheal. "Nervous?"

"Maybe a little. But you seemed to be having a nice conversation with Evelyn, so I decided not to interject."

The pathway opened to a clearing. There was a large mansion, almost a palace. It was probably one-third to one-half the size of Bostonian. They were led into a lounge of some sort.

"They will be in shortly." Evelyn departed.

Julie found her nerves were also tense. What would they be like?

Adam and Eve

MICHEAL was truly nervous. If he became convinced this was the real Adam and Eve, what would that do to his 'beliefs'? His train of thought was interrupted by the doors opening. He and Julie stood to greet them. 'Eve' entered first. She was about five-foot-ten, with a fair complexion, blonde hair, and hazel eyes. And she did look to be in her early 20s, 'Adam' followed. He was nearly as tall as Micheal, probably six-foot-three, and he had a brown complexion, similar perhaps to someone from South Asia. He had black hair and hazel eyes. And, of course, he appeared to be in his early 20s.

"Welcome to our home." Eve gave a smile.

"Yes, welcome. My name is Michael, and this is my wife, Julie," Adam (Michael) said.

Julie laughed. Micheal had to try not to join her. "Thank you, and while I'm sure you already know, I'm Micheal. This is my wife, Julie. It might be easier if we called you... Adam and Eve?"

"So, you are believers, after all? Because that wasn't clear to us."

"I suppose as belief goes." Micheal shrugged.

"We all struggle with our faith from time to time." Eve smiled.

"How much do you know about us? And how did you know about us to begin with?" Julie was examining them.

"About a week ago, I had a dream." Adam began. "I saw you, just as clearly as I see you now, arriving in the market. When I awoke, I knew it was a vision. A voice inside me indicated the time and said I was to send for you."

"How did you know our names?"

"Each night of that week, I had another dream, which told us more about you. We know you're from another time, from the future, correct?" Adam's eyes shifted.

"We are from approximately 5300 years in the future," Micheal confirmed.

"I was not sure of the years, but I was shown you are traveling through time. And to many places."

"Does this mean we were chosen for this somehow? Like destiny?" Julie pressed her eyes closed.

"No. The series of events that have put you on this path were completely by chance. But the Lord does try to utilize unusual opportunities to serve unique purposes." Eve explained.

"So does this mean we will definitely get home?" Micheal asked.

"There is no guarantee. As far as I was shown, the purpose of this request is to serve in a unique role for as long as you are able." Adam shook his head.

"So, this isn't like a calling?" Micheal asked.

"No, this is a request, and it will require a certain amount of faith. You are not obligated to do this. The choice is entirely up to you." Eve said.

Micheal sat there, considering everything. Then Julie said. "Did you see anything else about us?"

"You have been in our time for eight years. And you have had quite the impact, we would say." Eve gave a sly smile. "Your reign over Atlantis greatly improved life for billions of people around the world."

Julie stuttered, then said, "It's not like we intended to... How did you know?"

"Aphrodite, relax. We didn't learn this directly from the visions. Years back, when word of the gods' rule over the Empire spread to Eden, we were naturally just as curious as anyone would be. It wasn't long before temples honoring Koios and Aphrodite sprung up here in Eden. We visited some, and I will say the likenesses of your statues are pretty striking. So, when... 'Adam' Had his dreams, he said in jest that the gods were who we were meant to meet. How did you become the Gods of Atlantis?" Eve smiled with a raised brow.

"Micheal?" Julie glared at him.

"Well..." Micheal began while averting his eyes. "Apparently, there was some kind of prophecy. That said, the gods would come and rule over Atlantis. The day we fell through the temporal portal. Someone happened to see it. They went to Atlantis and notified everyone that the gods had come. We didn't know anyone had seen us when we launched our satellite network."

Adam and Eve passed a look, then looked at him.

"It's not important." He waved it off.

"When we launched the network, the entire city saw it happen. A delegation of people came and said we were gods..." He paused. Julie was looking at him with a smirk.

"I thought it might be too dangerous to deny it. I had no idea they wanted us to rule. But we just went with it." He shrugged.

"Like you always do." She laughed. That made everyone laugh, including him.

"We heard all kinds of stories of the great feats of the gods... First, are any of them true? And if so, how were you able to do it?" They had an expectant audience.

Micheal took a deep breath. "I wouldn't know what stories you've heard, but whatever you heard was likely true." He brought lightning to his hand. They looked stunned.

"How?" Eve asked, mesmerized.

He shut it off. "These rings are actually very advanced machines. You might be familiar with how a waterwheel moves the gears of a mill—to grind the flour. These are of a similar concept, just vastly more advanced."

Julie took over. "Each ring pulls energy out of the air in the same way a cloud generates lightning. This silver ring does that exact thing." She brought up a ball of electricity.

"And how does a cloud generate lightning?" Eve opened her arms.

"The air is filled with almost infinite tiny objects called molecules. When they rub against each other like this." Julie was explaining, rubbing her hands together.

"You try it." She indicated for them to mimic her. "Feel that heat? That is friction energy. It builds up in the clouds until the air can no longer hold it. And then it is released as lightning. All of these rings channel that energy. The silver ring generates lightning. The black ring generates a polarized magnetic field; it would be too complicated to explain."

"But it allows us to do this." Micheal took over the explanation and began to levitate.

Then Julie walked over to a decorative column like the one from their first day in Atlantis. "And this." Julie picked up the column that probably weighed two to three tons.

"I can see why they believed you were gods." Eve shook her head.

"What does the copper ring do?"

"It creates a polarized magnetic field around us." Julie picked up a knife. "Watch this." She attempted to stab Micheal. The knife deflected off the energy field.

"Three years ago, when the gods, you, left Atlantis. There were rumors that someone had stabbed a God and drew blood." Eve said. Micheal pulled his shirt down from his left shoulder, revealing the scar. "How?"

"They used an obsidian-tipped spear. The energy field only protects us from metal weapons." Micheal explained.

"I see... And what about the fourth ring?" Eve asked.

"That is our wedding rings; they are carved diamonds." Julie held out her wedding band for Eve.

"There's some kind of inscription glowing."

"It says 'Micheal and Julie forever in love' in our original language 'English'." Julie explained.

"You don't normally speak like this?" Adam was confused.

"In 1100 years, there will be a time when most people are wicked. They will try to build a tower to heaven. God will punish them by confusing their speech. So, no one except the righteous will be able to communicate with each other. After that, it will take another 3500 years for our natural language to emerge from one of those confused tongues," Micheal said.

"That is so fascinating. I was curious about how you were able to make rings out of diamond?" Eve asked.

"We developed a material out of the mixture of multiple other materials that complement each other very well to create a new material capable of carving diamond," Micheal explained.

"Your intelligence is quite apparent. We will discuss further what is being asked of you in the days ahead. For now, Evelyn will show you to your accommodation. It was a pleasure to meet you." Adam and Eve rose from their seats.

"The pleasure was ours," Micheal said as they were escorted out.

Chosen Ones

Their private accommodation was a guesthouse perhaps 100 yards from the main house. It was a large mansion in its own right. It was square in shape. JULIE thought it was probably 100 feet in each direction. It was two floors high with a courtyard, perhaps 30 feet across, in the middle. It was quite ornate. And they had their own private staff.

Once inside, Julie asked. "So what do you think?"

"They seem very nice."

"I don't mean that. I meant doing this quest or whatever it is."

"I don't know; I guess I need more details about it." He shrugged.

"Why doesn't it ever bother you that all this crazy crap keeps coming our way?" She huffed.

"I suppose because I spent the first 27 years of my life doing absolutely nothing of note. So, a little craziness has mostly been a good thing."

"Well, I can say definitively that for the first 30 years of my life, never once did anyone try to kill me. In the past 14 years, it's happened so many times that I've lost count! And one time, they even succeeded!"

Micheal averted his eyes. "There have certainly been too many negative events to be sure. But they are outweighed by the positive."

"How?!"

"I met and fell in love with you. I wouldn't trade that for anything." He came over and put his arms around her waist. "We don't have to do this if you don't want to. You don't need to feel like you owe anyone anything. Whether they are Adam and Eve or not, we don't owe them anything."

"While I've always been different for obvious reasons, I was still more or less normal. But the series of roles I've had to play since we fell has made me feel like I'm losing myself. The real me I was before all of this."

He traced her face. "No one ever completely remains the same. I fell in love with all the amazing aspects that make you, you. The rest is just fluff whether you're Lady Avalon, Aphrodite, or the chosen one. You always remain Julie Buckingham. And that's the most important thing you need to remember." He kissed her temple.

<hr>

The next day they were invited to the garden veranda overlooking the river, and then Adam spoke. "I would like to better explain what you are asked to do. There are particular artifacts that contain a special holy energy. They can influence certain important events relating to the gospel. We do not know which artifacts they are or which events they can affect."

"Then how would we know what to search for? Or which events to intervene in?" Julie cut in.

"The best I can do is tell you to reference the Bible. That's one of your scriptures, correct?"

"Yes, that's how we knew about you."

"How much do you know about us?" Eve asked.

"Not a lot. The Book of Genesis in the Bible states that you lived in the Garden of Eden. The Lord gave you two commandments. The first commandment was to be fruitful, and multiply, and replenish the earth. And the second, do not eat from the Tree of Knowledge. For on that day, you would surely die. Then it said a serpent convinced you..." He indicated Eve. "To eat of it. As a result, you were to be expelled from the garden. So, Adam also ate of the fruit so that you would remain together. That's pretty much it. Then it moves on to your children."

"First of all, that's not exactly how it happened." Eve began defensively. "We had actually discussed both of our commandments. And we realized that they conflicted. So, after a while, I became convinced that the first commandment outweighed the second. I tried to convince him to do it, but he declined, so I did it to force his decision." Eve gave Adam a sidelong look.

"I totally understand."

"What's that supposed to mean?" Micheal asked.

"You know!" Julie stared him down.

"We women have to direct our men to do what's necessary," Eve agreed.

Adam apparently, decided to right the ship, as it were. "So anyway, that's more or less it. It's actually fairly simple; there's just no one else who can do it."

"That's not true. We already know we aren't the only ones who have fallen through time." Julie protested.

"The falling through time aspect is really the least important reason for this request." Eve countered.

"How?"

"You are right; people apparently fall all the time. But not the two of you." Eve paused for a second. "We are smart enough to recognize genius. Both of you are likely in the top 10 of the most intelligent people of all time. What are the odds of the two of you falling together? I can't say how, but we were shown that it has not or will ever happen again. You are the only ones. If you decide not to do this. There will not be anyone else capable of doing this. But the decision is entirely up to you. We do hope you will not take too long to decide."

***

"How can we possibly say no now?" Julie asked as they entered their private chambers.

"Because it is our choice. Don't feel obligated to do anything you don't want to do." Micheal pulled her into him.

"What do you think?"

"I was already planning to collect artifacts from throughout the timeline. So that aspect was more or less already there." He shrugged. "So, what do you want to do? That is the only thing that matters."

The next day, they had made their decision.

"We will do it. So, what do we have to do?" She asked.

Patriarch

Following their decision, Julie split off with Eve, and MICHEAL went with Adam. He supposed, to be prepped for their mission. But what was there to prepare for?

"Do you feel like you're superior to other people?" Adam asked as they sailed down the river in Adam and Eve's boat.

"Not particularly, well... Maybe in a few ways..." Micheal shrugged.

"You think you're smarter than everyone else."

"I just consider that to be a fact."

"And how have you come to that conclusion?"

"I have all the hallmarks of genius. My inability to forget anything, including the day I was born. I can understand how things work nearly effortlessly. Solving problems is like breathing... but that doesn't mean I'm better than anyone else."

"So, you're intelligent. In what other ways do you feel superior to other people?"

"I'm a better combat fighter than just about anyone. But that has taken a lot of work over the last 14 years."

"Anything else?"

"Not really."

"Do you feel you have any weaknesses?" Adam raised a brow.

"A whole lot... I used to think everything about me was bad except my intelligence. Now I see myself more clearly, but I still recognize my many shortcomings."

"As in?"

"Before we fell through time, I didn't like myself at all for about 20 years out of those first 27-"

"Why wouldn't you like yourself?"

"It started because I was a chubby kid. Everyone made fun of me for being fat. And fat was ugly, so I was fat and ugly. Everyone told me I was a loser and worthless. Eventually, I started telling myself the same things. I shut down emotionally. I decided emotions were bad. It stunted my emotional development. So that's one weakness. I don't relate normally to people. Around the time this all began, I realized God wouldn't care about the worst person in the world, so any faith I could muster evaporated away. And I stopped caring about religion. So, there is another weakness."

"You cared enough to read this Bible of yours."

"I was raised in the Church of Jesus Christ of Latter-Day Saints. And you are expected to study the scriptures. So, I had to read parts of them. When I was seven, I realized I never had the kind of faith most people do. The laws of thermodynamics say there had to be a God of some kind. So, I decided to research every major religion in the world to see if any of them were believable. I spent most of that year going to the library and reading everything I could find about different faiths, and in the end, they all seemed too flawed to be correct. That year was the only time I read the scriptures all the way through."

"You say Eve and I are from these Scriptures. If you believe that, how does that affect your faith?"

"Many of my experiences since falling through time have challenged things I had always believed. But the one thing for sure that I do have faith in is my own five senses. Coupled with my mind's ability to interpret what I sense. So, if the evidence supports one possibility more than the other. Well..."

"I have a better question. You say you have faith in the evidence. What evidence led you to conclude that we are 'Adam and Eve'?"

"There were several things that led to that conclusion. The first thing was that the year on the calendar was around 760, which, when run back, closely matches the biblical timeline. And when we heard that the Elders were around that same age, the full speculation began. Particularly because you were in Eden. The river names and the surrounding lands all fit the description in Genesis. Then there's the fact that you knew we were coming. And you knew who we were, as well as some other details you would probably only know if it was shown to you. Those are far too many coincidences to ignore. So..." Micheal opened his arms.

"I can say definitively that we are the Adam and Eve from your Bible's Eden. Your genius causes you to move towards pride very easily. That arrogance is the primary thing that hinders your faith. You need to fight that tendency. Much of your road ahead is going to require more humility."

As the days turned to months, Adam seemed to peel away his layers of emotional baggage. He had routinely mocked the concept of therapy for most of his life. But now, he had a slightly different perspective on the subject. Adam truly defined the word patriarch. Nearly a thousand years of experience coupled with great intelligence gave him a seemingly superhuman insight into almost every aspect of life. During nearly six months of, for lack of a better word, therapy, it had felt like Adam always knew just what to say to inspire new ways of thinking about things. He had a great sense of humor, that he would interject at just the right moments to diffuse a potentially negative line of thought.

"So, I realize we are almost out of time. How do you feel about faith now?"

"I don't have anything like a burning of the bosom. But I do feel I have something that could be called faith."

"I'm not completely sure you're ready, but you are almost out of time. So, I will put my faith in you that you are ready."

"Ready for what?"

"We need to go to the Garden."

"The Garden of Eden?" Micheal raised a brow.

"That's what these past six months have been about. I hope you're ready." Adam stared at him.

"So do I."

Matriarch

-January 21, 3272 BC

"So now I become the latest version of myself. The ordinary girl from Virginia became the genius of Harvard, then the world. She then grew into the business mogul as a woman. She was married to a great guy with many future plans. Her life was just as it should be. But then, life almost never goes how you think it should. One fateful day in January of 2010 would change everything, forever.

That ordinary woman from New York would become an executed witch. Who returned from the dead to meet a new man who would turn her into a noble Lady of Avalon.

In the years since she entered the Age of Atlantis, she became the goddess Aphrodite, who ruled the Empire from on high. And now, the apparent first woman, Eve, is about to attempt to turn her into the chosen one. I have been forced to accept that I am no longer the girl from Richmond. I have succeeded so far through all the challenges and versions of myself. I have always succeeded in convincing everyone around me that I'm something I'm not. On some occasions, I have nearly convinced myself. Now, I must do it all over again. But faith is what I lost all those years ago at the lake. Can I find it again? Or do I just have to play the part in an attempt to fool myself once again?"

"What are we even doing here?" JULIE asked Eve as they sat in a cove in the gardens on the north end of the island.

"Just relax, calm your mind."

They had been 'calming their minds' for at least an hour.

"I don't understand—"

"So impatient! The purpose is that you have lost faith. It's one of your challenges. Your analytical mind desires proof."

"That's only part of the reason."

Eve looked at her. "You lost someone." Julie looked away. "You blame yourself... And God."

Everything, the whole situation at the lake, came flashing back. Julie closed her eyes. Eve remained silent.

"Jessica said I needed to forgive myself for what happened to her. I have tried, but it was my idea to go to the lake..." Julie paused. "How come God didn't answer my prayers that day?... When I died, I didn't see God; I saw Jessica." Some long-buried anger came to the surface.

"And it was Jessica who helped me find Micheal when he almost drowned in the hurricane, not God." She covered her face as the tears began to flow. "I think I'm done for the day." She left quickly.

As the days turned to months, it felt like she was in therapy. Eve slowly drew out every major issue that was haunting her. The more she got to know Eve, the more her ancient wisdom began to show through. Behind the youthful façade, the experience of nearly eight centuries of life slowly became obvious. It was a strange combination. Sometimes, Eve could've come off as a stodgy old coot. Then, in others, she would act more like a college coed. Julie felt that if she was the Eve from the Bible, she was perfect for the role. She was amazingly beautiful, intellectually on par with Julie, had a clever sense of humor, and genuinely cared for everyone around her. All of that certainly made her worthy of being the mother of all humanity. Some had termed her the matriarch. The title fit like a glove. They say the eyes are the windows to the soul. As she looked into Eve's, she could see the soul of the perfect mother.

"How do you feel?" Eve broke her meditation.

"I feel like me again, like Julie Buckingham Hall. I can't thank you enough for what you've done for me these past six months. I honestly thought I would never feel like myself again."

"That's good, it means you're ready."

"Ready for what?"

-May 24, 3272 BC

"After spending six months with the biblical Eve, it's like I have a second mother. She has taught me so many things about life and myself. With all the crazy things that have happened to me over the past 14 years, I never thought I would be able to find the real me again. I thought she was gone forever. But Eve showed me she was still there, deep inside me. Piece by piece, she stripped away the 'fluff' Micheal had talked about. And now I truly feel like myself again. Just Julie Buckingham Hall, a regular girl from Richmond, Virginia."

CHAPTER VIII: THE GARDEN

T HEY GAVE AN EXTRA set of black rings to Adam and Eve. With a quick tutorial, they were all able to fly. The next day, they left before sunup to conceal their movement. The journey would've taken six hours on the Avalon. It took about an hour by air.

"Wow! This flying thing is quite exhilarating!" Eve said as they began to descend.

"Isn't it amazing, the power flowing through you?" JULIE asked.

"I can see how someone might let this power go to their head," Eve said, referencing something Julie had told Eve about Micheal. All Julie could do was laugh.

"This is the place," Adam said as they landed.

"I hope you're ready. This will be our first visit in nearly 800 years." Eve took a deep breath.

"Let's go," Adam said.

The Garden of Eden

They followed a path through the woods. As they rounded a bend in the path, two personages were floating above the ground. They looked like teenage girls, perhaps 16 years old. They were glowing. And as Julie got closer, she could see they had ethereal wings. The one to the right of the path flew toward her. She stopped in her tracks. She thought these must be the cherubim mentioned in Genesis.

"Your faith is weak, but it is growing." The cherub said telepathically. "Your husband lacks faith, but he is pure of heart." The cherub continued without speaking.

The one communicating with her had golden hair, copper-colored skin, and golden eyes. "You are deemed worthy to enter," The cherub finally said.

With that, a gateway appeared as if from nothing. It looked like an arbor tunnel. The most beautiful flowers and vines covered the tunnel arch. They sauntered through as they crossed the threshold at the end of the tunnel. The color of the sky changed from the current normal green to a shade of lavender. The sun looked silvery purple, much the color of lightning. The flowers ranged from pastel to neon. There were bushes with all different sorts of flowers on them. She saw trees with a rainbow of different colored leaves. Other trees had numerous different kinds of fruit on them.

"Are we able to eat any of this?" Julie asked Eve, referencing the fruit.

"Of course, that is what we will eat while we are here." Eve picked one of the fruits and handed it to her.

"This was one of my favorites," Eve informed her. "Anything you can remove without harm to the plant is okay to eat. So, fruit, berries, nuts, flowers, and leaves are okay. There is no poison in the garden."

The fruit tasted like watermelon lemonade. But it looked like a blue grapefruit. "Micheal, you have to try this." Julie handed him one.

"That's amazing," Micheal said. "What is that?" He pointed to the sky.

Julie looked up, and there was what appeared to be a pegasus flying above them. "Eve, want to get a new perspective of the garden?" Julie indicated the sky.

"I would love to."

All four of them lifted off towards the pegasus. As they got closer, the immense size of the animal became obvious. The body portion was about the size of a thoroughbred horse. But the wings were huge, at least 20 feet long each. Julie estimated the full wingspan at about 50 feet. It was white in color. When they caught up to it, it was gliding. The feathers were the largest she had ever seen. Perhaps up to 10 feet in length.

She matched its movements, and then the pegasus spoke, "You can fly?"

Julie was momentarily at a loss for words, then she said, "You can talk?"

"You are welcome here," the pegasus told her. "Dominus, Domina," The pegasus said to Adam and Eve, then descended toward the ground.

"The garden is definitely different from up here," Eve said.

They were hovering some 1000 feet above the ground. "The animals can talk?"

"Yes. Now, you can't have a complex conversation with them. It's like talking to a two-year-old... Oh, and some plants can talk," Adam explained.

"Really?" Micheal asked.

"They have to have a way to generate sound. And they are of varying levels of intelligence," Adam said.

"Why did the pegasus call you Dominus and Domina?" Julie asked.

"They know us as the Garden Masters," Eve said.

They spent the rest of the day and the next two days exploring the garden. There was a fantastic panacea of plants. There were also several animals considered fantasy, like dragons and unicorns. But the pegasai were still Julie's favorite. There was no fear in the garden; they could walk right up to any animal, and the animal would never run. On top of exchanging pleasantries with many animals, she talked to a couple of flowers and one tree, which was a unique experience. They slept on the ground on top of various lush grasses. It was very comfortable. The air temperature was always perfect, and with no danger, she could understand why it was described as paradise. She felt beyond honored to be allowed to visit.

Adam and Eve decided to go on their own. On day four, there was a planned meeting location for that evening. Now she and Micheal were alone. Julie sat there gently stroking a baby pegasus in her arms. It was black, and it was tiny – about the size of a small dog, like maybe a Jack Russell terrier. It was extremely lightweight, perhaps five pounds. It was probably the most adorable thing she'd ever seen. If the weight of an adult were comparable, then an adult pegasus the size of a thoroughbred would probably weigh between 200 and 300 pounds.

The garden was so serene and peaceful that she almost didn't want to break the pleasant silence. But she wanted to discuss everything with Micheal. "Can you believe this place is possible?"

"Obviously, you know the way my mind works. I've been observing everything and trying to determine how it all works." Micheal paused.

"And?"

"This has to be another dimension. And, of course, I already believed the Bible would have to have some basis in history. And while so many crazy things have been proven to be real. I have yet to witness anything that would violate even the laws of physics as we know them."

"What about me going to the other side? Or when you saw Jessica under the water?"

"There are possible explanations for both of those."

"Like what?"

"I believe that the place you met Jessica was another dimension. The dimension that, in the past, I have called the Soul Dimension. The dimension where your soul technically lives."

"You're saying you think we are multidimensional beings?"

"Well, there is some kind of soul."

"I thought you were basing your conclusions on science?"

"I am, haven't you ever heard of 21 grams?"

"I thought I heard that that study was flawed?"

"From all my research on it. The only true criticism was that it was unethical. So, for that reason, many people were trying to cast aspersions about the results. Some were threatened by the potential positive results from the study, those who had an anti-religious motive. It didn't seem like he just randomly pulled 21 grams out of thin air." Micheal paused. "So yeah, I think there is a good chance we are multidimensional beings."

"What about when you saw Jessica?"

"Remember the radio station analogy? I think it's like that. I probably wasn't all dead; I was mostly dead." He laughed.

"The Princess Bride?" She smiled and shook her head.

"Anyway, Jessica had come to your call, and I was between life and death. It's sort of a transition zone between dimensions. The portion of that zone closer to our dimension is likely where ghosts live." He said matter-of-factly.

"So now you believe in ghosts?"

"Just like with alien UFOs or Bigfoot, there are far too many sightings and pictures for it all to be BS."

"I suppose that is at least logical."

At that moment, a large black pegasus landed in front of them. Then it said. "It's dinner time." Julie set the baby pegasus down. Micheal stroked it a few times. Then it went to its mother.

"I think it's time for us to go meet up with Adam and Eve."

They flew to the meeting place.

"Just-in-time. Micheal, do you have the Ring of Destiny?" Adam asked.

"Yes, how did you know? But of course, you know."

"You're going to need it tomorrow. It's the only way to access the Fountain." Eve said.

"I wasn't even sure if it was real; I thought that story might have been made up."

"It's real. We will go to the Fountain tomorrow," Adam said.

The Fountain

MICHEAL and Julie woke up earlier than Adam and Eve.

"What do you think the ring has to do with pulling out the flaming sword? Do you think it's like your great-grandfather Arthur and the sword and the stone?" She raised a brow.

"I don't know. You think there was a sword in the stone?"

"Do you doubt it after this..." Julie indicated where they were. "It's quite the coincidence. This ring and the flaming sword sound a lot like the sword in the stone... And then there's Atlantis. You didn't know you were the heir to Camelot. Do you think there's some connection between the garden, Adam and Eve? And Camelot and Avalon?"

Micheal had just been thinking while she was speculating. "The whole ring situation is an intriguing piece of evidence. I suppose we will have to see what exactly it does."

They flew for about an hour, and then Micheal saw it. There was what looked like a dome made of liquid fire, around a quarter of a mile wide and 700 or 800 feet tall. Adam directed them where to land.

"This is the place," Adam said as they landed.

"Hey, dragon," Micheal said as he walked up to a dragon on the ground right next to the dome.

He patted it on the side of the face. It felt like petting an alligator, only far bigger. Its head was about five feet long and three feet across. It had horns on top of its head and smaller spikes coming off its chin. Its neck was around five to ten feet long. The body was also about ten feet long but slender. The tail was similar in length to the body. It moved in a fashion that led Micheal to believe it was about to leave.

Micheal stepped back, and the dragon said, "Master!" with an apparent bow.

Its mouth opened and closed. When it did, one of its teeth broke off. It rose to its full height and spread its wings. It was about 20 feet tall, and its wingspan was about 80 feet across. With a few bats of its wings, it took flight, generating massive wind gusts in the process. As he went to pick up the tooth, he noticed a claw stuck in the ground and pulled it out. It was around eight inches long and six inches wide at the base. It was red with black trim, and it curved to a point. Julie picked up the tooth. It was pitch black in color, around six inches long, with a slight curve. They placed the dragon elements in their bags. Then Micheal turned to the task at hand.

The Flaming Sword had been hidden behind the dragon. It stood to hilt up. It was about five feet tall. The liquid flame seemed to emanate from the blade. Micheal began to approach. The temperature started to increase rapidly at a distance of about 20 feet. It felt like being next to an open oven.

"How am I supposed to reach the sword?" Micheal asked Adam.

"The ring will protect you. It should begin to suppress the heat as you approach."

Micheal looked at Julie. "Good luck... Chosen one." She smiled.

He kissed her. "For luck." Then returned the smile.

He began moving toward the sword. The closer he got, the less heat he could feel. The purple stone on the ring began to glow. And then the sword was right in front of him. The blade looked as if it was made of liquid metal, like the T-1000 from Terminator 2. It was pulsing. As he reached out his hand, a hole began to open in the wall of flame. He reached inside and grabbed the handle. As he pulled the sword out of the slot in the stone in which it was standing. The entire dome rapidly dissipated.

The Fountain came into focus in front of them. There was a plateau, perhaps a thousand feet wide. It was around 100 feet tall, and water cascaded down the slopes. There was one tree on either end.

"The tree to the north is The Tree of Life. The tree to the south is The Tree of Knowledge." Adam explained.

They made their way up a path through the cascades. As they reached the top, Micheal could see that the plateau was completely flat. It looked like a shimmering mirror. There was what appeared to be a literal fountain springing up from the center of the plateau.

"This is incredible!" Julie said.

"Isn't it?" Eve agreed. "That is The Fountain of Eternal Youth."

They made their way over to the fountain and took turns taking a drink. "It's sweet," Micheal said, taking another handful.

"It's bitterly cold."

"This is how water should taste."

They filled their bottles from the Fountain.

"So, which tree should we go to first?" Micheal asked.

Both trees looked nearly identical. Except, the bark on The Tree of Life was white, and it was black on The Tree of Knowledge. The leaves on The Tree of Life were lavender; the leaves on The Tree of Knowledge were red. They both had vines draping down from them, which made them resemble a weeping willow.

"The Tree of Life." Adam indicated.

As they drew near to The Tree of Life, Micheal estimated it was perhaps 100 feet tall, and the branches were around 100 feet wide. The fruit was nearly perfectly round, about the size of a baseball. And it was turquoise in color.

"It's so soft," Julie said, holding one of the fruits in her hand.

"One thing to note before you taste it," Eve interjected. "Eating from The Tree of Life will return all physical aspects of you to youthful perfection. In approximately two to three days, the body will eliminate any physical maladies or scars. You did indicate that you were past your physical prime, and I'm sure you have many scars. Now, you certainly appear to be physically similar to everyone else, so you likely won't look too different, but you may feel quite different."

"Are you ready?" Julie asked Micheal.

"Indeed." He bit into The Fruit of Life; it was so juicy and sweet. It tasted like kiwi guava with some kind of berry. It was probably the best fruit he had ever tasted.

"Oh, my goodness, this is heaven and my mouth." Julie closed her eyes.

"Have you ever tasted anything better?"

"I can't think of anything at the moment."

"From my memory, I can only think of one," Eve stated.

"The forbidden fruit... From The Tree of Knowledge." Julie said.

"Indeed."

Knowledge

They spent about an hour eating The Fruit of Life. Then, they traveled across The Fountain to The Tree of Knowledge. The Fruit of Knowledge was a yellow-orange color. And nearly identical in every other way to The Fruit of Life. JULIE thought it tasted like a peach mango with some kind of citrus flavor.

"Now I see why it's the forbidden fruit." Julie quipped as she took a bite. Within moments, she had a splitting headache. She closed her eyes to fight it. When she did, a sudden flash of memories overwhelmed her. She fell to her knees, covering her face.

"Julie!" She heard Micheal yell through the chaos in her mind. He caught her as she was falling to the ground. "What's happening to her?" Micheal asked. He sounded far away.

The flood of images and sounds felt like a tsunami battering her head. It felt like the whole world was pressing down on her. Then everything went dark.

"She'll be all right. I assure you." Eve sounded muffled. "The same thing happened to us."

"What exactly is happening?"

"Total recall, we should've warned you," Adam said.

"So, it didn't affect me because I already have it? Is it permanent?"

"No, it will last for a while, then it will fade, and finally, it dissipates completely. Unless you continue to eat from the tree." Eve explained.

All the voices sounded distant. Then she passed out again.

"Where am I?" Julie asked as she opened her eyes.

"We are under The Tree of Life. How do you feel?"

"How do you live like this?" All the worst memories she had blessedly forgotten were now foremost on her mind.

"I don't know, I've never not had it... I guess the first thing to do is to decide how important that memory is to you."

"And how do you do that?"

"You decide that regardless of what happened, it's not a big deal."

"Oh, is that all? Now I understand why you were depressed. I can't believe you're not depressed now!" The tears came. So many horrible memories. So much negativity. She was now honestly surprised he had been able to pull out of his depression.

"Come here." He pulled her to him, wrapping her in his warm embrace. He began gently stroking the side of her neck. His tender, loving touch brought the most tender moments between them to the forefront. "How do you feel now?"

The tears came on again as the force of his love for her became apparent. "How can you love me this much?" Julie shook her head. All the little moments that meant so much, that created the synergy of love, were laid out literally before her. When contrasted with all the bad thoughts and memories. She felt unworthy of such complete, honest love. Micheal came around to face her. He took her by the hands. As she stared into his eyes she felt that, for the first time, she was seeing him the way he saw her. "I'm not good enough for you." She dropped her head.

He cupped her face with his hands, turning her up to look at him. "No one is perfect in this life, but you have given me the honor to get to know the most amazing, genuine, good person this world has. Everyone has negatives. But you have far more positives."

"If that's true, then why don't I feel worthy?"

"That's the nature of a perfect memory."

This made her realize something. "You still don't feel worthy of me? Do you?"

"Any day now, I try to tell myself. I continuously effort to improve myself so that perhaps one day I will be."

For the first time since they met, she felt she had some true understanding of the way he thinks.

"Okay, Jules…" He said as he sat down behind her. "The key to managing this is compartmentalization. Learn to focus on the good. Move the good files to the top." He took her hands from behind. "Close your eyes, find your center, just breathe slowly. Focus on the good."

As they meditated, she began to gain better control over her memories. She decided she would be the master, not the subject.

Reflections

The next day, Julie was in a much better state as MICHEAL had helped her weather the storm of memories. At least her emotions were not so erratic now as they once were.

"You do look younger, not by a lot, but younger," Micheal said as they sat under The Tree of Knowledge at the edge of the fountain.

"You prefer that?" Julie raised a brow.

"I prefer you… In whatever package that comes in."

"Good answer." She kissed him. "I am going to miss the scar."

She ran her finger from the corner of his eye. The scar from when she shot him was gone, but the hair had yet to grow back.

"And just when I thought you couldn't get any more flawless. You go and put perfection to shame." He outlined her face.

"It's crazy to think we've changed so much in the last four days. It's even crazier to imagine what I would've looked like if none of this had ever happened. I'm 44 and look like I just got out of high school." She shook her head, then paused for a second. "Yup, I just confirmed it. This memory thing is really handy for some things. I just went back to the day I received my PhDs at Harvard. I saw myself in the mirror when I was 17 and I looked almost exactly like I do now." Julie looked at her reflection in the fountain.

Julie suddenly broke down in tears. He pulled her into him. "And then there's the downside." He realized an unpleasant memory must have surfaced.

"Well, this certainly has been an interesting stopover in the timeline. Nothing we would've expected."

"You mean like sabretooth tigers and mastodons. Or dragons and pegasi? Oh, and don't forget unicorns." Julie laughed.

"All. And how about the reign of the gods? Aphrodite?"

"What about the green sky? Or the pangea supercontinent?"

"It certainly has been an amazing nine years."

"Only 140 more to go." Julie quipped. "On a different note, I can't believe they're letting us take all this stuff out of the Garden."

Micheal shrugged. "I'm sure there's a reason. I doubt they're just souvenirs. What is that?"

Julie pulled the object out of the fountain. It was a unicorn horn. Now unlike in the movies, real unicorns are massive animals. When measured in horse parlance, every unicorn they had encountered would measure between 25 and 30 hands and likely weigh between one and two tons. An adult horn would be three to five feet in length. The horn Julie had pulled out of the fountain was obviously malted. It was around four feet in length.

"That's a beautiful unicorn horn," Eve said as they returned from The Tree of Life.

"Can we keep it?" Julie asked.

"Of course, but just like everything else, they are for you and you alone. The responsibility is yours."

The horn was around four inches in diameter at the base. It was a twisting spindle spiraling up to an extremely sharp point. It was translucent like a crystal. In the shimmering light of the Fountain, it sparkled prismatically.

"Tomorrow, we leave The Garden," Adam said.

"It has been a most singular experience." Micheal reflected.

The next morning, they ate a breakfast of life and knowledge. As Micheal drank one last gulp from the fountain, he noticed his reflection in the water. Any indication of age was entirely gone. The Fountain of Youth, indeed.

He had never been as concerned about his apparent age as Julie, but his youthful reflection in the fountain did seem strange. Normally, a man of more than 40 might be graying and have deep wrinkles from father time. Now, he looked younger than he had in nearly 30 years. And the road to 2015 still had 135 years to go—the oddities of time.

Micheal grabbed the sword, and his ring began to glow again. "Stand back." He warned. As the sword slid into the slot, the shield of flame blossomed out of it. He almost felt like he was in the scene at the end of the movie 'Sunshine' where the nuclear bomb the size of Manhattan explodes to restart the sun. Kappa is standing there as the flames envelop him. It's like time stands still.

They flew most of the day and reached the tunnel arch by sunset. There was a large black pegasus next to the entry. As it took flight, one of its feathers was shed. Micheal picked it up. It was the largest feather he had ever seen in his life. It was eight feet long, around one and a half feet wide, and the shaft was about two inches thick at the base. And the whole thing weighed about a pound. Giving new meaning to the saying, light as a feather.

"Hey Jules, you should write with this," Micheal suggested.

They took a moment to savor one last look at paradise. Then, they exited through the tunnel.

Parting Gifts

They returned to the island in the city of Eden. JULIE felt she didn't want to leave, but time was calling.

"It has been our great honor to get to know you," Julie said as they prepared to leave Eden.

"Did we live up to your expectations?" Eve asked.

"I truly don't know what I expected. But I would say you surpassed any possible expectation I could've had."

"I hope you think of us as friends," Eve said.

"We most certainly do." Julie smiled. "Which makes this that much harder." Julie always hated goodbyes. Eve, in particular, was like a sister to her. Eve had helped her with so many things over the last six months.

"We have some gifts for you to help with the road ahead. These are from The Tree of Knowledge. If there's ever a time when you need a memory boost to help enlighten your mind for the task at hand, these will provide it." Adam presented a small black case with six small bottles containing The Nectar of Knowledge.

"These are from The Tree of Life. They can restore you to health from any injury or return you to a state of youth." Eve presented a small white case with six small bottles containing The Nectar of Life.

They placed the black and white cases in a larger case that was made from both the Tree of Life and the Tree of Knowledge.

Adam and Eve walked over to Julie and Micheal, respectively. "We present these amulets..." Adam said as he put the amulet around her neck.

"They represent the dichotomy between life and knowledge. Forged from the flesh of the same." Eve finished. "These we also bestow unto you..." Eve said as they presented two more cases. The first case had two more amulets. The second contained three.

"These are for others of worth; you will know who to gift them to." Adam finished. "And finally, we present to you, the original *Book of Eden*. Written in our own hand..." Adam began. The book was leather bound, parchment paper. About six by four inches and two inches thick.

"Our most prized possession. Our holy scriptures, written at the direction of God himself. We are so grateful for the opportunity to get to know you. It has been our most interesting times in centuries." Eve said with a smile as tears ran down her cheeks.

"And many thanks to you for the wonderful opportunity to visit The Garden again," Adam added.

"We will miss you." Julie hugged Evelyn. "You've become as family."

"Farewell and good luck on your long journey ahead." Adam bowed.

"Always remember, you are what you do, all of it. That's what makes you, you. Never think you're not worthy." Eve said as they shared a farewell hug.

-June 12, 3272 BC

"Today, we leave the 33rd century BC. Despite ruling over Atlantis for five years, our return to the city nearly four years later was uneventful. No one recognized us, thank goodness. We hid the Avalon, along with most of the rest of our stuff, in a secret vault. Our total acquisitions are voluminous.

We did make a one-day visit to Melina, a trusted friend. And Elissa, as well. They were living together at a palatial villa in central Atlantis. And they accompanied us to the area where we arrived to see us off. I promised to visit again. I feel particularly bad for Melina because it will be over 400 years for her. While for me, it will be nearly instantaneous. I will be interested to see how she changes in that amount of time."

So, this is farewell to the 33rd century BC. I'm Julie Hall|Aphrodite|Lady of Avalon. This is The Book of Avalon: Volume 2 ...

CHAPTER IX: A QUIET STOP

Temple of the gods

T HEIR SECOND TIME JUMP went smoothly and after a couple of weeks to establish a baseline in the 29th century, it was time to reunite with Melina. They wanted to maintain a lower profile so they would need to avoid the city of Atlantis. With potential thousand-year lifespans, many people in the empire might recognize them. But one place that wouldn't matter was the temple on the hill where they first saw the famous mythological city.

Melina had put their gift to good use. They flew up above the palatial compound. Some priestesses were matriculating the grounds. One of them, JULIE recognized.

"Aphrodite!" She dropped to her knees. The rest of the priestesses followed suit.

"Ashera, you may rise."

Micheal landed at this moment.

"Koios!" And the whole yard of ladies repeated the exercise.

"As you were!" Micheal commanded.

All the women rose but stayed put, averting their eyes.

"Ashera, is Melina here?"

"Right this way." She led them inside a massive cylindrical tower. All of the priestesses walking around the temple were dressed for different gods of Atlantis.

"She's on the top level." Ashera indicated the top of the atrium over the rotunda.

"Thank you, Ashera."

Julie flew up to the top; Micheal remained on ground level. Melina was consulting a scroll. "I like what you've done with the place."

She looked up. "Aphrodite!" She rushed over and Julie caught her embrace.

"I was worried you'd never return."

"I promised we would."

Melina looked around. "Where's Koios? I received his gift nearly 200 years ago. So now I remember all our time together like it was yesterday."

"He's exploring the grounds. He wanted us to have some time together. I hope you took my advice."

Ashera delivered refreshments.

"I remain your most devoted servant. And that meant I needed to find my own love and legacy. It took 200 years to plan and build this temple. But we couldn't start right away. Elissa and I were removed from our positions as heads of your temples so we could advise Emperor Kalin. For 100 years we served him. So, my own life kept being put off. But 200 years ago, a chance reunion changed everything."

"Reunion?" Julie snacked on some fruit.

"His name is Darius. And we first met at one of Elissa's parties over 450 years ago. But obviously, I was unavailable. Then we both served the emperor for 80 years. And we got to know each other quite well. We fell in love. But the fates had different plans for us." Melina's eyes welled up, and she had the same expression Micheal gets when he returns to a memory.

"I thought he was your husband?"

"As imperial advisors, we were forbidden from marriage. So we were in all but name. Then the emperor sent him as an ambassador to Greece. On the other side of the world. Eventually, I received word that he had wed another. A Princess of Greece who fancied him. I was devastated. Shortly after that, I convinced Kalin to let me go. And I devoted myself, once again, to your purpose. For 200 years, Elissa and I perfected this monument to your honor."

"It's very impressive. And I appreciate the effort. But you did get a family for yourself, right?" Julie studied her friend.

Melina was now 487 years old. She still looked the same physically. Except for her eyes. The platitude that they're the windows to the soul was clearly true. She could see the centuries of life and experience. She wondered if it would be more difficult to pretend to be an immortal goddess.

"A few years after the temple was finished, I was visiting the Emperor's Palace. I learned that Darius's wife had passed and his children were all over a century old. He had recently moved to Eden for a fresh start. So, I went to Eden to see him. And it was just like old times. And finally, there were no impediments. So, we wed, then moved to the temple. And that was over 150 years ago. We have five children."

"I'm happy for you. I think you understand love better now. Wouldn't you agree?"

Melina took a sip. "It's the most amazing feeling to hold your child in your arms. If only I could experience that again. But alas, my time has passed."

Julie felt a pang of regret. She wanted a child. But she would have to wait another 150 years. It had been nearly 15 since she and Aiden had been planning on one. And now the chance may have passed her by. Time was dangerous and making it through the gauntlet was uncertain.

The next thing Julie knew she was flying Melina above the ringed city. They paused above Mount Atlas. Atlantis had completely filled out. The rural outer rings we're now completely cosmopolitan. Julie used the sky-net to run a scan and it said there were over 100 million people in the capital city. Three times more than the last time they were here. And it was bigger than any modern city by at least three times. That made her wonder about the global population. The next scan said the current global tally was just above 30 billion. Nearly four times the population in 2010. And the technology at the temple indicated it was early industrial, similar to the late 18th century.

"Okay, Melina we are going to go much higher."

She made sure the EM field generator was at max, and she jetted them through the spotty clouds and into the stratosphere. Julie turned them to the sun, hanging low over the horizon.

"I completely forgot. Today is the balance of night and day. I'm supposed to conduct a ceremony at sunset."

"Well then, we don't want to keep them waiting. It's time to dive." Julia allowed them to go into freefall. Melina tensed in her arms she activated the rings as the surface of the Atlantic Passage came up fast and they jetted across the surface buzzing past some ships, before climbing up to the Temple of the Gods. The priestesses were all gathered in the courtyard. Micheal was in a conversation with Elissa. Julie landed them right in front of Micheal.

"Wow, do I get to go for a flight?" Elissa asked.

"I think that can be arranged," Micheal said.

"I love the views, and Aphrodite gives a hell of a ride."

"I saw that. It looks thrilling. I can't wait. But it looks like Helios is about to go to the underworld."

Elissa took Melina's hand and led her to an altar. The priestesses of Helios circled the altar. They were surrounded by the devotees of the other gods. There was a crystal ball on a staff that Elissa planted in a stand behind the altar. Melina placed scrolls in a teepee formation on the altar. The priestesses of Helios were all holding large crystals in their hands. Then Melina spoke.

"Today we honor the sacrifice of the night for the day. On the day of the sun. Helios and Nyx will trade their balance and be at peace once more. On this day we are honored by their kin, Aphrodite and Koios. They have returned from the heavens to pass judgment on the decadence that our world has fallen into. If people do not change, there will be dark times ahead. We offer these prayers to the God of the life-bringing sun."

A beam of light pierced the clouds on the horizon. It entered the crystal ball and divided the light between the gems the priestesses were holding. And that light redirected to the scrolls on the altar, as pinpoints of light. In mere seconds the scrolls went up in flames.

Julie was amazed that the priestesses were able to orchestrate such a display.

The light faded with the Sun's dip below the horizon. The priestesses of Helios parted, and the priestesses of Nyx closed around the altar. They dropped a white ball into a goblet and a fog began to roil over the top. They blew the vapors over the altar and the burning embers were snuffed out.

"Now comes the darkness of equilibrium. When Helios returns, the day we'll begin to cede some light to the blessed night. For this is the beginning of Nyx's increasing dominion." Elissa closed the ceremony.

They took up residence at the Temple of the Gods and for the next four years lived a mostly quiet life. They got to learn about Melina's family. They visited old friends from the past. Like the Queen of Celtic. And Empress Ishtar of Babylon.

After a year or so away, word came from Babylon that Ishtar wanted to see them.

Empress of Babylon

It had been four years since their return and MICHEAL had continued his friendship with Ishtar. She had now been Empress of Babylon for 468 years. And now she was the oldest person known to history. She was 999 years old. He wondered if this was about the momentous occasion of being the first person to reach four digits of life. They flew to Babylon to see her. They landed on her private balcony overlooking the mega city.

Babylon was the second largest city in the world after Atlantis, with a population just north of 100 million. It was 20 million short of the crown, but it was quite impressive, Stretching some 100 miles across. It was located in what would be modern-day Djibouti.

The Babylonian Empire covered most of what in modern times would be northeast Africa, stretching from Niger to Somalia and up to the modern-day Mediterranean Sea. But also included the Arabian Peninsula, which on the Atlantean pangea map, was attached to the southern continent. Which was an amalgamation of Africa, South America, Antarctica, Australia, as well as the Indian subcontinent.

The only area in that great expanse that wasn't part of the Babylonian Empire was Egypt. Out of all the modern civilizations, Egypt was the only one that was in its precise, modern-day location. Sumeria was also in its modern-day location, but it covered a much larger area.

"Koios, Aphrodite, thank you for coming." Crown Princess Kissare bowed. She led them into the empress's chamber.

"Thank you, Kissare." The Princess left. "My apologies, I can't get up."

"So, this isn't about the big milestone?"

Ishtar sighed. "No Koios, I'm afraid I won't quite make it."

"Do you want us to try and help you?" Julie asked.

"I think a millennium of life is plenty."

Micheal sat next to the bed and took Ishtar's hand. "You want to say goodbye."

"That was my primary purpose. But I wanted to tell you how grateful I am for the person I became. And it was because of you. You saved my life that day. Then you saved my soul with your generosity. That year in Atlantis taught me about life, the gods, and how to lead an empire. And that led to 450 years of peace between Babylon and Atlantis. It has been such a joy for me in your return."

Micheal touched her shoulder. "You are the exact type of leader the gods hope for. And Kissare shares your quality. Your legacy is secure."

"Speaking of the gods, I finally let her meet the Anunnaki. The king and queen, at least. And I want to say that Queen Inanna shares your quality. I have met all 12 of the Council of the Gods. And while they maintain their mystery, Inanna clearly cares deeply for the people."

"How often do you speak with the gods?"

"Marduk and Inanna come twice a year. Then they and the others come occasionally unannounced. The frequency has been around once every other month. I'm surprised that after all this time you still haven't come across each other." Ishtar began coughing.

" Obviously, we keep to ourselves... Would you like some water?" Julie grabbed the goblet.

Ishtar cleared her throat. "No. Bring my daughter in."

Micheal found Kissare on the balcony. "It's time, Your Highness."

The Princess joined them. "Kissare, I am so proud of the woman you've become. There's no one better to succeed me. The eternal dynasty of our family lives on in you. I only have one piece of advice. Love the people, as I have loved you."

Ishtar breathed deeply, then went still, eyes open.

"Utu welcomes you."

"She's going to live amongst the gods?"

"Her peaceful reign brought a golden age to Babylon, earning her place. Take heed of her example and you may as well, Your

Majesty. Now we take our leave. Your gods will come shortly."

Micheal led Julie out of the chamber, his vision blurred. He felt a particular connection to Ishtar since he saved her life in Celtic. He was happy that this unusual meeting had brought out the best in her. And that led to centuries of peace. He was pleased that Kissare took after her mother. He had come to know her well after Ishtar introduced her to them. So, Babylon and Atlantis would continue in peaceful coexistence. They paused on the balcony. Micheal turned back for a moment. A bright light burst around the edges of the closed door. It was intense for a few seconds, then slowly dimmed to nothing. Perhaps the Babylonian Gods, the Anunnaki, had indeed come.

He felt, that as a God of Atlantis, he should respect the Babylonian faith. Despite his curiosity about these gods. "Let's go."

He flew up to the lower cloud deck; Julie paused with him. "What just happened?"

"The Anunnaki came to usher in the new empress."

Julie laughed. "You know we're not gods, right?"

"That doesn't mean the gods aren't real."

Julie laughed again, shaking her head. "So, you actually believe that mythological gods exist?"

"Let's just say that the history and the world we thought we knew are different. If there can be a pangea supercontinent in 3000 BC, then I think powerful beings being worshipped as gods is perfectly possible. It doesn't mean they're the ones who created the universe, or that someone named Apollo rides a chariot with the sun across the sky every day. We're pretending to be gods with advanced technology. Why couldn't someone else do the same?"

"But Ishtar said they're giants. That they have wings."

Micheal shrugged. "I don't know what to make of that. I mean, time travel, aliens, angels and demons, or mythological gods? Who knows? Whatever they are, they haven't bothered us yet. They are unknown to history, except perhaps as the gods of the various pantheons of mythology. So, I don't think it's anything we should worry about. If we learn more in the future, that might assuage my curiosity. But until then, we just do our best to deal with our own situation. Now let's go back to Atlantis."

The entire way back, Micheal considered the possibilities. He came to no conclusions, for now.

Family

MELINA mourned the passing of Empress Ishtar. They had become friends during Ishtar's visit to Atlantis centuries earlier. Back when lifespan was unknown. And people thought eternity might be possible. Then in PF 912, during a visit to Eden, Melina met the elders.

The patriarch, Adam; and the matriarch, Eve, were both odd in appearance. They claimed 912 years of life and they both had wrinkled skin. Their hair was gray in color, and the patriarch was missing the hair on top of his head. Melina had asked if they were sick and they said they were simply old, that their lives would end soon.

That made Melina consider natural mortality. They both died 18 years later. They were the Unitarian prophets. But they were generous with her despite her religious differences. They said she was doing God's work. But of course, there was more than one God.

The elders were thought to be the first people, as they were the oldest. And some senior priestesses at the temple of Aphrodite in Eden even claimed they were the elder's daughters. At that time, when Melina was just 16, they were almost 400. So, this Adam and Eve were likely the first man and woman, created by the gods. And now with Ishtar's passing, the God's limit of life seemed to be 1000 years. Ishtar was 999, only a month short of 1000. Melina realized that she had lived nearly 500 years, her life was half over. And she wanted to maintain her family's bond.

Today was Founding Day. And not just any Founding Day, it was the millennial celebration of the founding of Atlantis. That event brought civilization to the world. Her children would be visiting for the occasion.

"Everyone should be here soon. They were clearly held up by the throngs of people coming for the festivities." Darius entered the chamber. She gave him a kiss.

"They were supposed to be here yesterday. I hope it is just a delay."

"Of course it is. Don't worry. Are the gods going to attend the festivities?"

"In a limited fashion. They want to maintain a low profile, but this is a momentous occasion."

At that moment they flew onto the balcony. She and Darius bowed.

"So, we finally get to meet the family?" Aphrodite said.

"They wrote to say how excited they are. It's a long road from Amazon, Tycho, and Eden."

"I can't wait to meet them."

A large caravan was visible, approaching the gate. An hour later everyone was settled in. Now they were all gathered in the main hall. Melina was now the matriarch of this rabble. They numbered more than 300, composed of six generations. Melina and Darius entered the hall, and all of her family went to their knees. Due to the circumstances of her marriage, they were more than 300 years older than their children. And in such a family gathering they were regarded as almost divine beings. She imagined this must be how Aphrodite and Koios feel all the time.

"We bid you welcome to the temple of the gods. It is a joy to have our entire family together once more. And for such a momentous occasion. Today we celebrate one thousand years of Atlantis." Darius raised a glass; a cheer was their response.

Melina rose next. "This is indeed a special time, and we are honored by the presence of my divine friends. Aphrodite and Koios are here to bless Atlantis. To another thousand years." Melina raised a glass, as Aphrodite and Koios floated into the chamber.

Some of her kids were skeptical of her association with the gods. She was happy they could finally see them for themselves.

Koios spun up a ball of light. "We are pleased that the peace we forged some four centuries ago, has held out. Part of the credit for this state of affairs belongs to Melina and Darius. Who both helped maintain the relationship with Empress Ishtar, who earned her exaltation. And with such a fine legacy of theirs before us, it is hopeful that the challenges ahead may be weathered. And Atlantis will remain strong."

Aphrodite picked it up. "While it is said that our return is to pass judgment on the rising decadence that is permeating the world. We also desired to reconnect with the humans who served us so vociferously. To my friend and loyal representative, Melina, it's a pleasure to meet your greatest accomplishment. Five generations of family. And family is what provides the greatest purpose to life; love and legacy. So now, let's celebrate that special bond."

The priestesses of the gods began playing music and serving platters of food. And the party was on.

Aphrodite and Koios made the rounds they took time to talk with many of her kin. They gave some divine performances. Then they finally worked their way back to Melina and Darius.

"You have so much to be proud of." Aphrodite sat next to her.

"I am so very lucky. And I try to enjoy these rare times of reunion. But I fear that it won't last."

"Why would you say that?"

"Centuries are too long. And people grow past their forebearers. It's only a matter of time before my children become their own elders. The time when they earn their awakening is usually when it happens. It was such a major transition in life. As a woman, your fertility dries up. And then your memories awaken to the forefront of your mind. And the things that are important to you, change."

"You're worried you'll lose them?"

Melina sipped her wine. "It's a certainty. The last time I visited Ishtar, a few years ago, she talked to me about legacy. She knew the end was near and so that was weighing on her. She said that life is too long to maintain relationships with your children. They, of course, will always have some connection with you. But when they have centuries under their belt, and generations expanding geometrically, you grow too insular. She said that even with the dynastic anchor holding her generations together, she barely knew her children anymore. She had become isolated and lonely in her later years. Kissare was the only one she felt she could talk to. I love my children so much. And to think that they will become strangers. And I will die alone, terrifies me."

Aphrodite touched her shoulder. "I don't know what the future holds but I promise you, when your time comes the people you cared about the most, who transitioned to the afterlife before you, will welcome you to the other side with open arms. Love crosses time and outlasts this life. It is the most powerful force in the universe."

Melina leaned her head on Aphrodite's shoulder. "I love you, Aphrodite. I know that our connection will transcend life and death. We will be friends forever."

Melina wondered if life was different in Elysium. Did everyone live happily with their family forever, like Aphrodite seemed to indicate? She looked back into her memories.

Her parents died when she was very young, so she only had a few fond memories of them. And now, after five centuries of life, she wondered; if they had lived, would she have drifted away from them? If that was the normal fate of longevity, was it better in a way that they had died? Because all her memories of them were evergreen. The brief time together was so precious. Melina pulled herself from the past and enjoyed her family in the present. While it lasted.

Dynasty

-December 20, 2806 BC

"Our time is short, here in the 29th century BC. We leave in four months. The Babylonian Empress Kissare wanted us to visit one final time before we leave. We are coming for the Death Festival. The Empress is her mother's daughter, so the golden age of peace and prosperity is likely to continue going forward. On our last visit, we met Kissare's daughter, Crown Princess Zelia. She also supports the friendship with Atlantis.

It's amazing that one ill-fated encounter with Ishtar some 500 years ago, forged a stable peace that could last a millennium. With such long lifespans, peace in the world could be determined by a single person in charge of one of the major countries of the world. I'm proud of the legacy we established during our rule. May it continue in perpetuity."

The next day they arrived in Babylon. They spent the next five days visiting with Empress Kissare and Princess Zeila. Now on the final night of the Death Festival, they were eating a farewell dinner.

"I first want to say it's been a pleasure to host you for the festival. I know the community of gods maintain their mystique. But I'm certain that Negral welcomes your blessing of another year of peace between Babylon and Atlantis."

Kissare raised the glass and everyone toasted. It was an intimate dinner, just the four of them. While in Babylon, Kissare, like Ishtar before her, maintained a sacred element with them. As if they were practically the Anunnaki. So only immediate family, and her personal attendant, were allowed to be in their presence.

"We care deeply for the Babylonian people. And so, the mutually beneficial relationship will continue from our side." JULIE said.

"And I am very excited to see Atlantis for myself." Zelia smiled.

"When are you going to Atlantis?" Micheal asked.

"Empress Regina has invited me to a summit in Atlantis on the anniversary of the signing of the Perpetual Peace Agreement. The one you signed with my grandfather all those centuries ago."

Julie was served another glass of wine by Kissare's attendant. "How well do you know Regina?"

"We've met twice before. 70 years ago, when she first came to the throne, my mother invited her to Babylon. At that time, we met her and some of her children. And then 26 years ago, there was a global summit in Central City, to mark 1200 years since The Fall. So, I met many world leaders there. She was one of them. She's quite close in age to Zelia and Melina Hellas. So, they all got on quite well. I consider Regina a friend."

Kissare's attendant cleared the table. Julie and Micheal rose to leave.

"Well, Kissare, Zelia, we've enjoyed our visit this past week, but we must return to Atlantis. Melina is expecting us tomorrow."

"Yes! Return to Atlantis." Prince Daon entered the chamber with an entourage of a dozen guards. "Your presence here is sacrilege."

"You're out of line," Kissare warned.

"No dear sister, you are. I've had to suffer this persistent insult for all of Mother's reign. This ends now."

Prince Daon stepped up and slashed Zelia's throat. Kissare Moved to aid her and the guards seized her. Before Julie or Micheal could react, he cut Kissare's throat.

Julie fired up her electricity and began to move in an effort to aid the women. Suddenly, she was pierced in the shoulder with an arrow. She pulled it out and blood was dripping from a glassy black tip. Micheal had an arrow in his forearm. She looked back and saw six of the guards with arrows drawn. Prince Daon had his fist up, holding their fire.

Julie looked at Kissare and Zelia. Zelia was already dead. And Kissare was gurgling blood. A crimson puddle was expanding around them. She noticed a similar bloody mess through the open door, featuring Kissare's attendant. It appeared Prince Daon wanted to talk.

He looked at his sister for a minute then looked at Julie. "I've finally cut the heretics out of this dynasty."

"No, you've destroyed your dynasty."

"You're going to threaten me? Clearly, I know your weakness. You only live because I allow it. If only our assassins had been successful 470 years ago. The sacred glass could have cut the heretical gods from this world."

Micheal extracted the arrow. "It wasn't a threat; it was a statement of fact."

"I must hear this explanation." He seemed amused.

Julie took the mantle. "In the nearly 1200 years of your dynasty, there's only been 3 emperors. And every transition has been peaceful. Your actions here will set a new standard. Your rule will be short-lived. Someone will follow your example and remove you."

"No, they'll thank me—"

Micheal cut him off. "For what? Destroying the centuries of peace and prosperity. For bringing death and destruction in a war with Atlantis? Yes, I know your mind. This coming war will consume you along with your ambitions."

Prince Daon's eyes narrowed. "No. They'll thank me for killing the heathen gods who murdered the Empress and her daughter."

Julie thought this was where he would give the signal. She flew quickly, low to the ground, and the arrows buzzed above her. She released a blast of lightning shocking the guards. She saw that Micheal had evaded the attack to the opposite side.

Prince Daon was huddling on the ground. Julie and Micheal landed in front of him.

"Rise, Your Majesty," Micheal commanded.

He was gritting his teeth as he came to his feet.

"We are leaving now, but before we do, I want you to remember this day." She indicated Kissare and Zelia, who's dead eyes were staring blankly, framed in blood. "Today began the countdown to the end of your family, and this dynasty. Because when your rival takes you down, they will slaughter your entire family. They'll be viewed as a threat. Just remember, you did this."

They levitated up, preparing to leave.

"This is your fault! You held my mother for ransom! You forced my grandfather to kiss your feet!" Prince Daon clenched his fists.

"If that makes you feel better. You dug your own grave. Maybe your gods will have words to comfort you." Micheal said, and then they flew out to the safety of the skies.

"How's the arm?" Julie felt the shock and adrenaline were wearing off, and the pain in her shoulder was beginning to throb.

"It hurts like hell. We need to get back to Atlantis to treat these wounds properly."

"But first, do you really believe a war is coming?"

"We weren't just saying those things for his benefit. He will blame us for killing Kissare and Zelia. And use that as an excuse to start a war."

Julie felt partially responsible.

"If we hadn't come here. If we weren't pretending to be gods. He wouldn't have murdered them. And now there's going to be a war... Because of us." The tears came.

"No, Julie, you can't blame yourself."

"But this wouldn't have happened if we were never here."

"Our rule brought peace to the world. We saved the world from war and pestilence. Billions of people are alive today because of us. Everyone alive today is better off because of us. And while we pretend to be gods, we aren't all-powerful. People are responsible for their own decisions. People choose to murder, hate, steal, and wage war. It's human nature. All we can do is try to influence people; mitigate the damage. And we have been a force for good. We're not perfect, we're only human."

Julie wiped her eyes. "Well, we better get back to Atlantis."

She winced from the pain as they accelerated to the north. They arrived at the Temple of the Gods a little before midnight.

***

Micheal went to work on her shoulder wound. Julie grit her teeth to bear the pain of the cleaning of the wound. As he was injecting the penicillin, Melina entered the chamber.

"What happened?!" She said in English.

"Prince Daon attacked us," Julie answered, in kind.

"How could he know how to hurt you?"

"He was behind the attack on us just before we left last time. And it was simply a coincidence that the assassins were using sacred glass for their weapons. So, he learned we could be hurt by them."

Melina scowled. "I'm sure Empress Kissare punished him."

"Melina, Kissare is dead. So is Zelia. Daon cut their throats."

A tear came to Melina's eye. "How could he murder his own family?"

"He felt their association with us was sacrilegious. Including his mother. He's always hated Atlantis. And now that he's emperor, war is coming."

Micheal finished wrapping her shoulder and she began on his arm.

Melina sat down and the tears were streaming. "Kissare and Zelia were friends. And I represent the Gods of Atlantis. Am I partially responsible for what happened?"

"You don't control the evil in another person's soul."

"Why do people wage war? Is it because of religion?" Melina looked despondent.

"People wage war for power. They use many excuses, but it's always about power. When one ruler wants what another one has, they go to war. But wars are fought by common people. And common people don't care about how much stuff one ruler has compared to another. So why would they fight and die for their war? Religion, greed, national pride. They must motivate the warriors with something bigger than a power game. Religion is just the easiest way to motivate them."

"I wish people would just love each other."

"If only I had that power in this world. But love does win, in the end." Julie certainly hoped so.

CHAPTER X: THE ORACLE

Heaven's gate

FOUR MONTHS PASSED AND their physical wounds healed but MICHEAL could tell that Julie still felt guilty for the war. Since the spring equinox, seemingly endless columns of soldiers had been marching south from Atlantis.

The time had come for them to leave the 29th century. Everything had already been set up for the transition. And now it was a three-hour flight to the island that would be modern-day Key West. It was the location of their jump. But they weren't going alone.

After having more casual interactions with Melina and Elissa over the past seven years, they decided to let them come and see them off.

Julie was at a girl's luncheon with her priestess friends. So, Micheal was enjoying some quiet meditation on his own. He thought about Daon killing Kissare and couldn't understand how someone could kill their own sister. Family was such an integral part of his life. He would do anything for his family.

———————

That brought his sister to mind, and he went back to 1999.

"I don't wanna go back to the hospital!" Amanda complained as Micheal was driving to the park.

"It's only going to be for a little while then you'll be good as new. And I promise by then, I'll find a permanent cure."

"What's taking so long?! The treatments are going to make my hair fall out. I'm going to look like a freak!" Amanda started crying.

"I'm sorry. There are just many complications in making the body recognize that the cells are a threat. It will take a little bit longer." They pulled into the parking lot and he found a stall to park in. "I won't let that happen."

"I'm not stupid you know. If all those doctors can't save me, how can you?"

Micheal draped himself over Amanda. "I don't know if I can solve cancer. But I promise I will never stop trying to help you."

They held each other for a while, then he finally pulled back.

"Well Mandy, it's your last day before all the doctors, and Mother Nature played an April fool's joke on us with half a foot of snow. Let's go see how many times we can ride the big hill."

"Okay. I love you, Micheal."

"I love you... Now let's go have some fun."

———————

Micheal came out of his memory at the sound of footsteps approaching.

"My apologies, your eminence."

"No, it's okay Elissa, come sit with me."

She sat across from him. "So, today's the day."

"Indeed, it is."

"Then we won't see each other again. Before I die, at least."

"You're right. And I would like to express my gratitude for your superior embodiment of wisdom."

"I've gained so much understanding from our vigorous discourses. Would you humor me one final time?"

"What would you like to discuss?"

Elissa pursed her lips. "Is it possible to find true happiness?"

"If you imply some form of permanent happiness, the answer is no. But it is possible to find contentment within yourself."

"Why isn't happiness achievable?"

"Do you have any regrets in your life?"

"Of course, doesn't everyone?"

"What's your biggest regret?"

Elissa looked away for a moment, then she returned to eye contact. "Not having a family of my own."

"That's just one example of why happiness is never a perpetual state. We may accept the consequences of our decisions, but they persist. And happiness would require a life fulfilled, lacking any detrimental consequences."

"But flawed decisions aren't the only impediment to joy. There's also jealousy."

"Indeed, comparison is the death of happiness. No matter how good you have it, there's almost always someone who has it better."

"I'm fortunate that I haven't had to worry about how much I have in relation to other people. As your representative, I prosper off your gift of knowledge. People from all walks of life sponsor us to imagine beneficial technology. To solve difficult problems. And that has been so fulfilling." Elissa's eyes dropped in introspection.

"But you sacrificed one major aspect of life in that pursuit."

"It was all-consuming. As time moved forward, all I ever thought was, there's not enough of it. There was always another challenge on the horizon. A new idea for some machine that could make life easier for everyone. And then one day I realized that in 657 years of life, I have no one who was born to love me. I have a tremendous legacy of accomplishments. But did I sacrifice my humanity in the process? My chance at happiness?"

"With such a long memory happiness can seem elusive. But in the end, happiness is a choice. Happiness is an inward journey. By deciding to focus on the good over the bad. It is certainly not easy, but it's worth the effort."

Elissa stared in silence for a moment. "I'm supposed to be so wise, and yet I allowed myself to lose track of time. In seven centuries, I should have found some time for family."

"Having people who share familial bonds is something special, but family doesn't need to only include those birthed from the same parents. One great source of happiness is interpersonal relationships. And that includes friends. I'm sure you have many people who can trust you wholeheartedly. That's what family is."

"Many of the priestesses at the temple I've known for centuries. And perhaps, half a dozen of them I trust implicitly."

"They are your family, and you need to work to maintain those relationships. Accept that some things are past your control, and you may find contentment in yourself. Don't compare yourself to others. And accept that you made the best decisions in your life, in each of those moments, and live with no regrets. Do these things and you may approach happiness."

"Do you live with no regrets?"

"As you know, while the gods possess superior power, we also possess the same range of emotions you do. So, in that way we are vulnerable to regret. But I only have one."

"What does a God regret?"

Micheal closed his eyes and the previous memories flashed.

"I failed to save my sister. I'm knowledge personified but I still came up short."

"I know Gods can die but who killed her?"

"Mother Nature."

"Why would Gaia do that?"

"I don't know. Perhaps to see what would happen. She cursed her with a unique pestilence."

"I didn't think gods could get sick."

"If you turn the body against itself, it's much harder to recognize there's a problem."

The cryptic way he was discussing Amanda's death reminded him he still hadn't told Julie about Amanda. How could he bring it up now? After 15 years of marriage? He understood that the longer he waited, the worse it might be. But everything was so perfect right now. How could he take that risk?

Their session was interrupted by Julie and Melina.

"It's time."

"You've so rarely taken me for a flight. And never long distance."

"I'm sorry Elissa. Hopefully you'll enjoy this one."

Micheal stepped behind Elissa and put his arms around her waist.

"This won't be a leisure flight. We will push the maximum safe velocity."

"I didn't know you had a limit."

"I meant for you."

"Of course."

Julie flew Melina out of the oculus in the central tower of the temple. Micheal followed. He accelerated rapidly until he felt the pressure waves of the sound barrier. Flying at around 10,000 feet meant they were going about 730 miles an hour. It would take two and a half hours to reach modern-day Key West. The departure point from this time.

Micheal thought about what his rings made possible. If they ever made it home, how different might life become? Obviously, they wouldn't just immediately mass-produce this technology and sell it to the world. They would need to be more judicious. But even only 20 years into their adventure in time, they'd already produced game-changing technology. What would they invent in the next century?

The hours flew by and the south tip of Florida came into view. A few minutes later, Micheal pulled up over the string of islands running into the gulf.

"It's hard to fathom that we've traversed much of the empire so quickly. It would take over a week by boat. So divine."

"I should have given you more divine experiences. You've been such a loyal friend."

"It's been divine enough to know you. Although, speaking of regrets, I do regret that you never took my offer to serve you properly. But I do hope that you appreciated the care I took to keep myself aesthetically pleasing."

"Indeed, I did. And under different circumstances, I would have allowed you to honor me properly."

"I received special training from Melina, so you know I have the skills."

Micheal laughed. When he thought about his younger self, such an offer from the likes of Elissa, Melina, or any of the hundreds of his priestesses, would have been impossible to deny. But he had, somehow, married the most beautiful woman he'd ever seen. And on top of that, she was his equal in all the most important aspects. He could honestly say there was no temptation.

He landed them at the departure point. It was the most southern point on the island. Their ship was docked about 100 yards down the shore. It was there so Elissa and Melina could return to Atlantis. And now it was time to say farewell.

Julie was saying goodbye to Melina, and he was saying farewell to Elissa.

"I know you're not big on sentimentality. So, I'll just say this. You have utilized your mental gifts very proficiently. You will leave a lasting legacy in knowledge and wisdom. As well as the good you have done to practically help the world through technological application. You honor me beyond all others. So farewell and continue to pursue contentment." He nodded to her.

"It has been a most particular honor to know you and to serve you. And I will continue that effort till the end of my days." She bowed. "Now I do tend to eschew sentimentality, but if it's amenable to you, might I have a hug?"

"Of course, you may, Elissa."

This was the first time she'd ever hugged him in an emotional fashion. He'd always suspected there was a softer core to his loyal stoic servant and friend. After a long embrace, she pulled back. She had tears in her eyes. "Now I fear Melina has rubbed off on me." She laughed.

"I will miss you as well. And I shall never forget you. It's not a bad thing to experience your emotions."

Micheal and Julie said farewell to each other's principles.

"It is time. Stay beyond the barrier. Our portals pose a danger to humans."

Micheal found his position. Julie stood about five feet away. They turned and faced their friends. A moment later, Elissa and Melina were illuminated by a bright green light. This was the first time he wasn't facing the vortex for a jump.

A brilliant flash pulsed across the landscape and Micheal felt the pull of time behind him. Just before the tunnel took him, he saw a surge pulse out and hit Melina. Then the rush of the tunnel blew past him. The final flash washed his vision out, and everything went black.

Visions

MELINA said her goodbyes and Aphrodite and Koios turned one

final time. Against the twilight backdrop, a green light seemed to pierce a hole in the orange-purple mural. It expanded into a spinning gate, like the one she witnessed when the gods first arrived. It began to engulf the gods. She was in complete awe and felt privileged to experience another divine event. There was a green flash, and everything went dark.

"Melina!" She woke to Elissa shouting.

"What happened?"

"The gods struck you with divine energy."

"My head hurts."

"Let's get you to the ship."

Elissa assisted her to the Ship of the Gods. She laid down on a bed. When she woke, she clearly remembered the most terrible dream. It was of a coup in Babylon. The entire royal family was slaughtered. On each of the next four nights of their voyage back to Atlantis, she experienced another strange dream. A vivid dream.

They reached the Temple of the Gods and retired to Melina's private chambers.

"Do you think the gods can bestow power on humans?"

"Of course they can, why?" Elissa cocked her head to the side.

"I think they gave me a special power."

"You think the divine energy that struck you at the heaven's gate was them imbuing you with power?"

"That's the only thing that makes sense."

Elissa shook her head. "This is about your dreams?"

"I don't think they're dreams. I think perhaps they're visions."

Elissa laughed. "What possible reason would lead you to that conclusion? Didn't you say the Samano dynasty was wiped out in one of these dreams? They've dominated Babylon since the beginning. I don't see that one coming to pass. And the rest are just random. Besides, if Koios was going to give the gift of sight to one of us, it would have been me."

"It all just feels so real. Like I'm actually there."

"Obviously the divine energy has damaged your mind. They're just dreams. So, stop worrying about it."

"I guess you're right."

"Of course, I am. Now I need a hot bath." Elissa exited the room.

Melina wasn't so sure Elissa was right. Unless she could confirm that one of her dreams was actually a future event.

The years passed and none of the events could be confirmed. She became more and more convinced they had to be prophetic because several of them repeated. Usually with more details. And now the dream about the coup in Babylon had come for a fourth time.

The war had been raging for four years and billions had died. Atlantis was now pushing toward the Babylonian capital of Babylon. Atlantis had lost around a billion people, but Babylon had lost perhaps 3 billion. Melina hoped the slaughter and destruction would soon end.

Melina joined Elissa for the celebration of the coming of the gods. It was 480 years since the prophecy had proven true. After a day of ceremony, they retired to Elissa's chambers.

"This day reminds me that it is possible to see the future."

"Melina, don't you think if you really could see the future, we would have confirmed one of these visions by now?"

Melina rubbed her eyes. "I saw the royal family of Babylon get slaughtered again last night. It felt so real. This was the fifth time."

"I'm sorry about your dreams. But you need to let this go."

"Melina, Elissa, Empress Regina Seneca is here to see you."

"Your eminence." They bowed.

"As you were. I have a favor to ask of you. This war is at a critical moment. And I can use your help to boost morale in the people who believe in the old gods."

Regina was the 4th emperor to lead the empire and the second since the rule of the gods. Melina knew her well. They were just 30 years apart. Regina was from the powerful Seneca clan. So, after Melina's ascension into the upper class, they attended many of the same events.

They'd met for the first time at the 25-year celebration of the coming of the gods. Regina was only 13, and it was her first formal function, but that hadn't stopped her from voicing her skepticism of the reality of the gods. That opinion hadn't changed in the 455 years since. Despite that, they'd become good friends over the years. But there had been a chill in the friendship after Regina took the throne 75 years ago.

"We're happy to help," Elissa said.

"What's going on? Are we losing the war?"

"No, but with a billion dead, and the years piling up, much of the populace is turning on our campaign. But a major event just went down in Babylon. If we push our advantage, this war may end before the year is out."

"What happened in Babylon?" Elissa asked.

"Emperor Samano is dead. His entire family was slaughtered in a coup. That makes me a bit sad. I liked Ishtar and Kissare, and now their legacy is over. But the new emperor in Babylon may be more tenable to peace than Emperor Daon ever was."

Melina looked at Elissa. "Okay Regina, what do you want us to do?"

Regina laid out her plan. Then returned to the city.

Melina was joined by Elissa in her chambers. Elissa was studying her.

"Are you going to say anything?"

"I suppose I'm just jealous. This gift clearly comes from Koios. So, I wonder why he chose you and not me?"

"I don't know, but it's a curse, not a gift."

Elissa came and embraced her from behind. "I can understand your trepidation. But you were given a gift of divine power. I will help you deal with this."

Melina touched Elissa's hand. "What can we do?"

"Maybe I can figure out a way to channel this power, to better control it. In the meantime, I will help you determine the when and where of these future events, so we can change them."

"Thank you, Elissa." Melina sighed, hoping for some relief.

The weeks passed and it became clear there was no easy solution. She continued to have the dreams.

Melina had to lean on Darius to try and deal with her visions. Elissa did help interpret the dreams and prevent future tragedies.

She went to sleep and found herself in Regina's chambers at the Emperor's Palace. Regina was consulting some scrolls by candlelight. Melina looked out past the balcony and saw the half-moon hanging just above the horizon.

A man dressed in black climbed over the rail of the balcony. He crept up behind the Empress and drew a rope out of his pocket. He looped the rope over Regina's head and quickly lifted her out of her chair by her neck. She kicked the table, but the sound was muted.

She couldn't scream due to the strangulation. The man took her to the ground then rolled over on top of the Empress. He straddled her back and pulled her chest off the ground with the ligature. Regina was helpless against him. A few minutes later she went limp. The assassin tied the rope as tight as he could, then he slipped off the balcony and into the night.

Melina woke with a start.

"Is everything okay?" Darius mumbled.

"I need to talk to Elissa." She made her way to Elissa's chambers. She stirred on Melina's entry.

"I need your help."

"Can it wait till morning?"

"I don't know."

Elissa rubbed her face and led Melina out onto the balcony. "So, what happens this time?"

"Regina will be assassinated."

"Tell me everything you saw."

When Melina finished, Elissa turned and studied the moon. "Was the half-moon the top or the bottom?"

"The bottom."

"You have eight days. Go warn Regina tomorrow. Goodnight Melina."

Elissa returned to her bed. Melina looked at the full moon and thought she should have realized that.

———————

Melina was finally given an audience with Regina.

"Welcome Melina, before you say anything, I want to thank you and Elissa. Those who worship the old gods are rising for the cause. Now tell me why this meeting is so urgent?"

"You're going to be assassinated."

Regina leaned back. "Why do you think that? I am quite well protected."

"This may be hard to believe, but I can see the future."

"Like the God, Koios?"

"He gave it to me."

"I know you claimed to have directly served the gods, but I've never seen any evidence. Their supposed reign was decades before I was born. And if you've had this gift since then, why is this the first time you've told me about it?"

Melina wasn't sure she should say this but. "The gods returned 10 years ago. Koios gave me the gift before he left. That was four years ago."

"The gods returned, and you didn't introduce me?"

"They didn't want everyone to know. But we need to prevent this attack. Seven days from today is when it's going to happen."

"It's okay Melina, you have nothing to worry about. My security will protect me." Regina rose to leave.

"You don't believe me, do you?"

Regina sighed. "The gods were a propaganda fabrication. No one can see the future. It was good to see you again." Regina exited the chamber.

Melina tried to follow, but the guards stopped her.

⸺⸺⸺

Over the next week, Regina rebuffed all her attempts to see her.

"It's going to happen tonight. Regina refuses to see me."

Elissa shrugged. "She doesn't believe in the gods. I guess she'll find out the hard way."

"She'll be dead."

"You tried your best. What else can you do?"

Melina looked at the half-moon, high above the oculus. It was beginning to shine in the last light of twilight. "I'll stop him."

"How?"

"Let me worry about that."

Melina dressed in a black body suit. During the three-hour ride on horseback, the moon began to drift closer to the horizon. She needed to hurry. She used her knowledge of the Palace of the Gods to slip past the guards and enter the long empty monument. She crossed the top of Mount Atlas until she was above the Emperor's Palace on the other side.

She repelled down, until she was on the west side, above the empress's chambers. She slipped between the guard patrols, and she was in the gardens below the balcony. A rope was already hanging down from the rail. She looked at the moon. She might be too late.

She scurried up the rope and saw a dark figure throttling Regina in the candlelight. Melina rushed and struck the assassin with a baton. He dodged the next strike and drew a dagger from his belt. She slid under his thrust and jabbed him in the groin with the baton. He dropped the dagger, and she went into a handstand wrapping her legs around his neck. She dropped him to the ground.

Regina coughed and sat up. Melina kicked the man in the face. She retrieved the rope and bound him. Regina grabbed her neck.

"I should have listened. Thank you, Melina. Now you must leave the way you came. Your presence here will be difficult to explain. I will come by the temple to discuss your gift from the gods."

Melina whacked the assassin on the back of his head with her baton as she headed to the balcony. She slipped past the guards and scaled the mountain to the Gods Plaza, on Mount Atlas. She looked back at the palace. And Regina was watching from the balcony. She vanished inside and the alarm was raised.

Melina went back to the temple and crashed. The sun was already rising.

The next day Regina came to talk. She was wearing a scarf to hide the bruise on her neck.

"Thank you for protecting me. One of the guards was a deep plant by Babylon. He was put there centuries ago by Emperor Daon. With him dead and Babylon losing the war, he decided to murder me, hoping to affect the outcome of the war."

"I'm glad you're okay."

"Where did you learn to fight like that?"

Melina stepped over to her display of weapons and traced the blade of a sword. "When Aphrodite and Koios ruled, before you were born, they trained in martial skills on a regular basis. I wanted to emulate Aphrodite. So, I studied her movements and practiced in my spare time. And now I've practiced regularly for centuries. I know I can handle myself in any situation."

"You were amazing." Regina studied her for a moment. "Had you introduced me to the gods, I might believe. But it's hard for me to take anything on faith. No matter where your visions come from, I'm grateful for it. Do you have other visions?"

"Nearly every day. The first one that proved they were visions was actually confirmed by you."

"By me?" Regina sat in a chair.

"I saw the coup in Babylon well before it happened."

Regina rose and touched her shoulder. "Be careful Melina, if word gets out, they'll be calling you the Oracle. Perhaps I'll consult you from time to time... Thanks again." Regina left the chamber.

Melina hoped she wasn't prophetic.

The Oracle

As the months turned into years, and then decades, MELINA wondered if she and Elissa could ever reign in her visions. Perhaps the power of the gods was beyond mere humans. No matter how intelligent they were. But Melina made the best of it and tried to use her visions to help the world.

Over time the word did get out. Her newest moniker was the Oracle of Atlantis. Many world leaders wanted her to peer into their futures, but she had found limited success trying to control the power. Faith in the gods had waned significantly in the 130 years since she'd been given the sight. But she was being venerated as a divine figure and carried a global reputation.

She started taking years-long sabbaticals to escape all the noise. But the 600-year celebration of the departure of the gods was approaching, so she returned to the Temple of the Gods.

Melina settled in then went to see Elissa.

"Welcome back sis." Gabriel came and gave her a hug.

"What are you guys working on?"

"We're trying to prevent the dead from wasting away," Elissa said.

"I think we are quite close," Gabriel said.

"How fascinating."

"Well, I must go. There's a council meeting in a few hours. And, of course, I'm head of the council."

Gabriel always complained about the promise his father Cato had guilted him into. He had agreed to serve on the council for a century. And he was 36 years into his sentence. Gabriel left the chamber.

"Well Melina, I solved your predicament. While you were gone, I was able to find a way to channel temporal energy. You can see the future, so I did a deep dive into how time works and discovered its source. After playing around with many materials, I found one that acts as a conduit for temporal energy. The chamber was completed about a week ago. Want to see?"

Melina followed Elissa into a new building that was attached to the main temple. The room was circular and curved on all sides.

It was like the inside of an orb. The walls were dark gray and had a metallic shine to them. There was a round stool in the center, elevated above the entrance by five concentric stairs. The walls had ornate patterns engraved throughout.

"Try it out. See if you can view something on purpose."

Melina sat on the stool and concentrated on the festivities that were two days away. She felt a surge of energy, and a green glow, reminiscent of a God's portal, swirled around her and she elevated up to the center of the chamber. She locked eyes with Elissa and the images began to flow. She closed her eyes and saw the ceremony underway. It was at the steps of the Council Dome. The place where Melina first presented the gods to the people. Regina gave a speech, then announced Melina, and as she stood in acknowledgment, the modest crowd of the faithful bowed down to her. As the Oracle, she was worshipped as divine in her own right. She pulled out of the vision.

"You did it, Elissa. I can focus on a time and place, or event, and I can see it."

Melina drifted back down to the stool while the green mist evaporated.

"And now you truly are the Oracle of Atlantis."

The celebration came and went, and Melina returned to the temple. But Elissa didn't come with her. She said she was going to her research institute on the south side of Atlantis. A few days later Melina had a terrible dream.

She saw Elissa in a large chamber. She was with a man, but he was a shadow.

"Well, well, well, the supreme erudite, Elissa figured it out." His voice was muffled.

"My gift was given to me to advance the world. How can you use knowledge for evil?"

"There is no good or evil. There's only power. The gods don't care about people. They care about power. You've been corrupted by Unitarian thought. With your genius, you could have been a goddess. I will be a God, but you will only be an impediment to that. So, you must die."

Elissa tried to run but the man was too fast. He tackled her to the ground and pinned her down. He wrapped a wire around her throat and then sexually assaulted her as he strangled her to death.

Nothing about the chamber or the shadowy figure gave her any clue as to when or where this terrible event would take place.

Melina woke and went to the Oracle Chamber. She focused on Elissa, and she was back in that chamber. She watched Elissa die again and tried to find anything useful. Nothing about the killer was meaningful, he was a muffled shadow. The chamber reminded her of one of Elissa's research chambers. The ambient glow in the room must be coming from one of the energies that Elissa had discovered. The illumination was divine in nature. It wasn't coming from a flame. Other than that, the chamber was a nondescript room. The location was a dead end.

She went back to the event and tried to feel the relative temporal force. The best she could figure was the event would happen sometime in the next week. How could she locate Elissa?

Melina visited Regina and received imperial assistance to try and locate Elissa. Melina visited all of Elissa's known properties. But time pressed forward mercilessly. The weeks passed and Elissa was a ghost. Melina returned to the temple in defeat.

In the chamber, she tortured herself one final time and she knew her best friend was gone. She was overcome. The person she had known longer than anyone else, over 600 years, was gone.

Life became a haze. It was like a part of her was gone. Elissa was honored by both the temple and Atlantis itself. A statue of her was placed in front of the Palace of the Gods.

Melina tried to find normality in the arms of Darius. And then, on Death Day, she woke from one nightmare to another. Darius was dead. While he was older than her, he had yet to reach 900. So, his sudden death was a shock.

Melina fell into a washout of melancholy. She lost all reckoning of time. In three months, she'd lost both of her rocks. The two people she relied on most. And the visions were relentless. Her mind became a mess of confusion. The perpetual sadness eased, and she tried to rein in her splintered memories.

Ashera brought some food. "You look much improved, Your Eminence."

"Ashera, what day is it?"

"Today is the Day of Helios."

"Has it been so long?"

"It's okay, Your Eminence, I have ensured that all the honors for the days of the gods have been observed."

"Thank you, Ashera."

Melina went to her study and found a quill. She drew a scroll and began writing.

-Theasel, 30, 1357 PF

"As the fog in my head has finally lifted, I've turned to this long-forgotten journal in an effort to organize my memories. I abjectly failed as an Oracle. My "gift" was unable to find Elissa in time. She's technically missing but I saw how she died. She solved my quandary, but I couldn't solve hers. And then after three centuries of marriage, I lost Darius so abruptly, I don't think I was able to register that in my head. It still seems like someone else's dream.

Unfortunately, it appears Empress Ishtar was prophetic. It feels like I've become the old woman, and I'm only 624. I may have centuries still to go, but Darius and Elissa are gone.

The wars, the pandemics, and general turmoil that's gripped the world have caused my children to drift away. I only see two of them regularly anymore. And I rarely see any grandchildren.

Gabriel is the only person I feel I have a strong connection to, that remains. I feel isolated. I would hope for the gods to return but Koios's blessing has caused such strife in my head that I fear I may become resentful of my association with them. But when I stop to think of my good fortune in life, I realize I owe much of that to the gods. So, I can't complain too much.

And now that my direction in life seems so uncertain I think I should embrace my role as Oracle. I wouldn't want to insult Elissa's memory by not utilizing the last gift she ever gave me. I will try to embrace the power the gods have given me. And see if I can help make the world a better place. Or at least improve individual people's lives. So now it's time to become, the Oracle of Atlantis."

Melina dusted the scroll and set it aside, then headed off to the chamber to peer into the future once more.

PART II: ADVANCED ATLANTIS

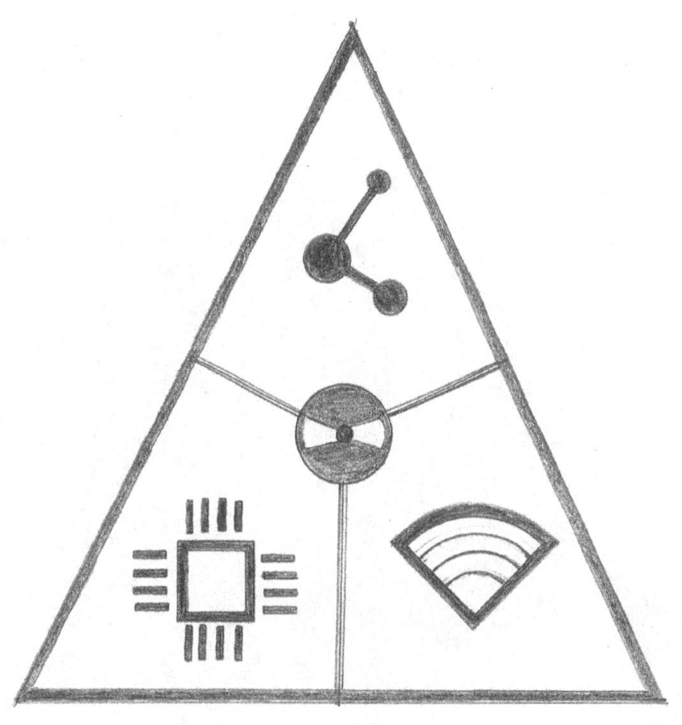

CHAPTER XI: A STAR IS BORN

Alias

APRIL 8, 2378 BC

"Seven years of mostly peace and quiet. Our time in the 29th century BC was relatively uneventful. Particularly following the craziness of the 33rd century BC stop. The belief in the Gods of Atlantis had begun to wane. So, almost no one recognized us as Aphrodite and Koios.

I was happily able to reconnect with Melina. I had considered telling her the truth, but she has spent nearly 500 years believing in us. I felt that shattering that belief was more harmful than continuing the ruse. It was nice to have a familiar friend. While the centuries definitely changed her, at her core she was the same devoted friend.

Micheal and I passed several major milestones. We celebrated our 10th and 15th anniversaries. And I celebrated my 50th birthday. Still blessedly living in perpetual youth.

We arrived in the 24th century BC. And to our amazement, but not to our surprise. The world has greatly advanced. There are flying cars, regular space travel, and the whole society is powered by a much more rudimentary version of kinetic energy. They use pyramids to channel kinetic energy out of the air.

Upon our arrival here, I discovered, to my disappointment that Melina was gone on a multi-year sabbatical. I do hope to reconnect at some point."

"So do you think this will work to get our identities into the government databases?" Micheal asked JULIE.

"I don't know. Do you think they detected our sat network yet?"

"I don't think so. I ran a full diagnostic sweep after we woke up. And aside from its passive monitoring of the heavens and the earth, there is no indication that it has been accessed at all for the last 427 years."

"I will attempt to use a carrier bypass wave to circumvent the Atlantean government mainframe firewall." Her fingers moved like lightning. "I'm sending a counteragent virus to divert attention from my Trojan horse." She was attempting to hack into the main data storage network controlled by the central government. "I've been detected!" She focused intently, as she went to battle against a government hacker. She wasn't an expert hacker by any means, but she had parlayed her software coding classes into a passable capability. And with the help of their sky-net... Not the one from Terminator... She was at least able to compete. The opponent was crazy good, nearly severing the uplink on several occasions. "We've been located!" Her heart began to race.

"How much longer?"

"30 seconds!" She defended the uplink with everything she had. "The files are planted... The fox is in the henhouse. Activating the stunner!" She said sending a final virus to short-circuit the government mainframe and confuse the storage memory.

"Did it work?"

"I need more time to confirm. . . What's that?" She could hear the noise getting closer.

"Run!" Micheal yelled. "It's the feds!"

He ran for the door. She was right behind him. They ran straight into, two agents. They quickly disabled them and ran full speed up the stairs. She could feel the other agents breathing down their necks. They burst through the door and onto the roof. The chase was on. In this section of the city, the buildings were very tightly packed. While it wasn't easy, they began building hopping. Jumping from one roof to another. Their speed and parkour skills began to leave most of the agents in the dust. But the two remaining on the chase were relentless.

"Micheal! There's a problem!" Julie yelled breathlessly.

"Think The Matrix!" He yelled back. The gap was enormous, about 80 feet. "Aim for the center window!"

He accelerated ahead of her. Put his hands over his head like a diver and jumped. She was two steps behind. She flew like a dart. Micheal broke the window in front of her. Even using a break fall she landed hard rolling down the hallway.

"Oh! Ow!"

"Okay, we have to move." Micheal pulled her to her feet.

"We should lose our catsuits."

"Good idea."

They slipped into a side alley and threw their catsuits into a homeless person's fire. Then casually strolled into the busy street and walked naturally. Several agents ran right past them. A flying unit arrived, and many agents swarmed the building. But they slipped away undetected.

"The sky-net still hasn't been detected. And all the test uses of our planted identities have not raised any red flags with the central government. I think we're home free." Micheal was studying his phone.

"So, you're saying we can just be ourselves."

"Yes. Just two insignificant people among the 330 million people in this city."

His statement brought a smile to her face.

The Piano Bar

With their identities secured, they were able to casually blend into the modern Atlantean society. They spent the next year continuing to lay down the foundation of their history.

The advanced version of Atlantis was amazing. MICHEAL'S knowledge of energy made him wonder why the 19th-century industrial revolution didn't follow the more logical steps that Atlantis did. While the government heavily controlled the flow of kinetic energy it was still far superior to the wired power grid of their time. And it fed an invention tree that had magnetic levitation, a version of force fields, and opened up the realm of space so that there were already lunar stations and asteroid mining. There was even space tourism, but it was heavily regulated and anyone who went received much publicity. So far Julie had wanted to wait until they could do it privately. So, he would need to be a bit more patient.

They founded a finance firm called The Investment Hall and gradually transformed their mining assets into company equities. Julie was a wizard. Her market instincts were uncanny. Whenever they went head-to-head on investing, she always at least doubled his efforts.

Julie was busy analyzing company reports. And her latest successes.

"Jules, I think it's time to take a break."

"I'm on a roll."

"You've been on a role for quite some time." Micheal had felt she was a little too focused on it.

She looked up at his tone. "I'm sorry, Micheal. It's just that 20 years was a long time, and it was so good to be back in the game. You have no idea how much I had missed this."

"While I think you spend a bit too much time on the investments, your market genius means we don't have to worry about our mining operations anymore. But that's not why I said that."

"Okay?"

He smiled. "Happy anniversary, Jules."

"It's not our anniversary."

"What were we just discussing?"

Her eyes shifted. "Has it been a year?"

Micheal laid the annual report down. "And I doubt you'll weep when you read this."

Julie laughed. "Let's celebrate!"

They went to a Broadway-style matinee show. And then went to dinner at a fine dining establishment. Following dinner, they took a walk. "This looks perfect," Julie said, pulling him into The Piano Bar. It advertised live music. They ordered some drinks from the bar. Micheal looked around. No one was playing music on the stage. And it seemed no one had for a while. There were perhaps only 20 people in the bar.

"Sparse crowd," Micheal said.

"It looks like no one's used those for a while," Julie said, referring to the instruments on the small stage.

"If you're looking for music, the stage will be quiet tonight, sorry." The bartender said sadly, then she went to tend to another customer.

Julie looked at Micheal; she took his hand. "Come on." She pulled him onto the stage.

As they began to tune the piano and the guitar, the bartender seemed like she was going to stop them, and then she indicated they could proceed. Julie started to play the piano; she began the melody to *I'm Your Angel* by Celine Dion and R Kelly. Micheal immediately recognized it and picked it up with the guitar in complement. They sang in perfect harmony to the delight of the two dozen people in the bar. Julie seemed to be enjoying herself. So, she moved on to *From This Moment On* by Shania Twain. They continued to sing. Sometimes Julie would sing alone, or Micheal would. Then, they would intersperse duets occasionally. As the night went on, the bar began filling up with more people. By closing time, the place was packed. It truly felt like a real concert. Everyone was so into it. Julie appeared to be fully engaged with the crowd of about 500. And it was a unique experience. They hadn't performed since Europe in 1696. And never an impromptu concert. It was highly enjoyable.

"Apparently, it's closing time," Julie announced to the disappointment of the crowd. "So, we will close with a song called *Everything I Do*." They did a duet version of the Bryan Adams song.

"That was quite the performance. Are you professionals?" the bartender asked.

"No, we just love music."

"I used to be famous 50 years ago. Zara Zepata? No? Oh well, and this bar used to be popular 20 years ago. But time and memory move on. Thank you for giving me a taste of the past." She gave a smile.

"She certainly was. Bellatrix Bonaventure, most people call me Belle or BB. And you are?" another woman at the bar said.

"Micheal Hall and my wife, Julie."

"It's a pleasure to meet you both. I represent Sky Records. My job is discovering new talent, and you have everything I'm looking for."

Micheal looked at Julie. He could tell she didn't want to go down this road. "I'm sorry, Belle, we will have to regretfully decline. Thank you for the offer."

"You have the "it" factor. With my help, you would be the most famous people in the world. I promise."

"Thank you again, but we must still decline." Micheal began leading Julie through the crowd, most of whom remained.

Belle chased them down through the crowd. "If you change your mind." She handed Julie her card.

They returned to their penthouse in central Atlantis.

"That was so much fun. I have always enjoyed playing to the crowd."

"Do you wish we hadn't said no to Belle?"

"No, it was the right decision. I don't need, popstar, added to the list of things I pretend I am that I'm not." She laughed.

"Okay then. This has been a great celebration, but no celebration is complete without dessert. And I am definitely ready for mine." He pressed Julie down on the bed.

A Star Is Born

Three days after The Piano Bar, JULIE had a special gift for Micheal.

"Wake up! We are going to be late."

"Late? Late for what?" He was still half asleep.

"For our recording session at Sky Records." She'd decided to turn the tables on him. So, he'd know how she felt the numerous times he'd made decisions for both of them.

"A recording session?"

"I told Belle we could begin recording today."

"You decided to do it after all? And you didn't even consult with me about it?"

"I just went with it." She shrugged.

"So, this is payback?"

"Of course not. How could you possibly think that?"

"It's not too late to cancel, is it?"

"It is absolutely too late; we are doing this." She stared him down.

They recorded all day. Finishing their entire first album in one recording session. It included 12 songs by artists from their time and eight original songs written by them.

"Wow, I don't think we have ever had anyone record an entire album in one day. And it was all so amazing. This means I can move forward with so many things." Belle was furiously entering all kinds of information into her touchscreen tablet computer.

"Move what forward?" Julie sighed her turbulent stomach.

"Well, when you came in today, my original plan was to go through a few months in the studio. Then, it would be a couple of months to tune the work for release. Then, we would lay the promotional framework down. But the perfection of your session today opens up the door to laying that down immediately. So, I'm moving the release of the first single, *Need You Now*, to the beginning of next week and initiating a marketing push to accompany it. You will need to do a video shoot in the next couple of days so the video release can coincide. Then, at the beginning of next month, the album will hit the shelves. I've arranged for you to debut on *After Hours with Zoe Cirillo* to complement that. Why? Is there a problem with moving this fast? Cause we have an opportunity to move your entire rollout up at least half a year, and it will give you the most prime release schedule. If you really want to be the world's biggest stars, now's the time." Belle looked between them, then gave a long pause.

"Okay, let's do this."

After the long recording day, Micheal and Julie returned to the penthouse. "Well, this is all moving at lightning speed. Aside from punishing me, why did you change your mind?"

"Well, it occurred to me we wouldn't likely have this opportunity again for centuries... It is also true I was enjoying turning the tables on you." She laughed. "But more seriously. I had really enjoyed myself the other night and thought it wouldn't be such a bad way to spend the next few years."

"What's it like to be a celebrity?"

"You know just as well as I do."

"I was never Julie Buckingham of *Bull Markets*."

She huffed. "We were bigger celebrities in Boston than I ever was. And we were literally worshiped in the 33rd Century."

Micheal laughed. "So, Belle's going to make us Elvis or the Beatles? And there are nearly 50 billion people on Earth. Are you ready for that level of fame?"

"That level is extremely rare. So, Belle's intentions aside, I'm okay with whatever level. It'll be fun to play popstar for a few years."

"Did you consider that we will need to disappear in a few years?"

"Celebrities have vanished before; what's one more? We'll be Atlantis' Elvis."

"You mean people will swear they see us around long after we're gone?"

"Indeed."

A few weeks later, *Need You Now*, was number 1, on all charts. They had arrived in Delta for *After Hours with Zoe Cirillo*. Delta was the Atlantean version of Hollywood. The shoot was set for the next day. Micheal had gone to The Pinnacle. It was one of the favorite places he'd discovered during their previous stops. Julie didn't feel like going, so she stayed behind. It was late, and the hotel had a rooftop pool, so she decided to go for a swim.

The pool was empty, and it went to the very edge of the building. There were incredible views of all the bright lights of stardom. She swam a few casual laps, then relaxed back and could also see the stars above. As she was pondering her new reality, he spoke.

"Am I interrupting?"

She righted herself and leaned on the glass edge. "No, there's plenty of room."

The man stared at her for a second. "You're Julie Hall, right? *Need You Now* is a great song. And by the way, I was at The Piano Bar the night you broke out."

"I'm glad you liked it. What's your name?"

"Thomas Fields. You know, I dabble in guitar myself. Maybe I could sit in with Avalon sometime?" He entered the water and moved to the edge.

"That might be fun." Julie wasn't sure what she should do. She wanted to return to her room but didn't want to seem rude.

"You're going to be on Zoe's show tomorrow, right? That's why I'm in Delta. I'm going to the show. I have front-row seats."

The back of her neck tickled, and she looked closer at Thomas.

He raised his brows and opened his arms. "I don't want you to think I'm stalking you now. We had these plans weeks ago. You were only announced a couple of days ago. It was a happy surprise. Your show at The Piano Bar was amazing."

Julie sighed. "Who's we?"

"My daughter. She's a huge fan, also. I totally understand your defensiveness. There's a lot of psychos out there."

"How old is she?"

"14, and her name is Penelope."

"Well, I hope we don't disappoint her. I'm turning into a prune. I wouldn't want to risk tomorrow?" Julie climbed out.

"That would be impossible." He up-downed her.

She wasn't sure what was causing the goosebumps. She wrapped her towel and headed for the exit.

Paparazzi greeted their arrival at the show. Julie was a little nervous about the front row now, but was a bit excited as well. She knew that Kelsie Ambrose and Emeric Salvator were going to be the other guests. Kelsie was the most famous actress in the world, and Emeric was the leading man. They were the King and Queen of Delta. As they entered the green room, Emeric was nowhere to be seen, but Kelsie was just as stunning as advertised, five-foot-eight with dirty blonde hair, sky-blue eyes, and a perfect figure. And every other aspect of her was picture-perfect. In the year and a half they'd been in the 24th century, she'd seen at least ten of Kelsie's movies. She was disappointed Emeric was absent.

"Kelsie Ambrose." She gave her hand to Micheal; he kissed it.

"A pleasure, Micheal Hall, and this is my wife, Julie."

"The pleasure is all mine." Kelsie demurred, and then she took Julie by the shoulders. "Wow, how do you look so perfect? You're even more stunning than your music video. And those videos of your performance at The Piano Bar; amazing. I can't wait for the album. You don't happen to have an advanced copy?"

"Absolutely. And we loved you in *Eclipse the Darkness*." Julie went to retrieve one.

"Knock-knock." Zoe Cirillo entered the room. "Micheal and Julie Hall, welcome to *After Hours* I can't wait to hear you play. Now, about that. Emeric canceled a few minutes ago. If it's okay with you, we will have you perform two extra songs in an early segment. Then I will interview you on a middle segment."

"Julie?"

"We would love to."

"Emeric canceled? What about the skit?" Kelsie asked.

"I guess we will just have to call it off."

"Wait, maybe Micheal can fill the role." Kelsie smiled at him. "What do you say?"

Micheal looked at her. "Go win that Atlas."

"I hope you can pick up the lines quickly."

"That won't be a problem."

After Zoe's monologue, the first segment was the skit.

Julie was surprised at how good of an actor Micheal was. Then, she thought he should be. They had both been acting to one degree or another since they fell. The skit was quite funny. Both Kelsie and Zoe were pretending to fight over Micheal. Near the end of the skit, Kelsie kissed Micheal on the mouth. A moment later, Zoe kissed him as well. And finally, at the end of the skit, Kelsie tackled Micheal to the couch, kissing him again. Even in the circumstances of the skit, pangs of jealousy ran over Julie. Until this moment, only she had ever kissed Micheal on the lips.

For the two additional songs, they each did a solo vocal.

Thomas was indeed on the front row with a beautiful young woman. During her opening solo, she made a point of singling out Penelope. The girl was properly thrilled.

The late night plus the excitement of their first show caused Micheal to sleep the whole flight home. Now, they arrived at the penthouse.

"Well, that was interesting. And who was that girl you focused on?"

"Her name's Penelope and I met her father at the rooftop pool while you were at The Pinnacle."

"A coincidence that he just happened to be in the front row?"

"Yes, he's just a random fan."

"Okay, so how do you think we did?" Micheal was casually undressing.

"So that's how you want to play it?"

He stopped. "What am I playing?"

"Did you enjoy yourself?" Julie gave a side-eye.

"The skit?"

"That was our special thing."

"I'm sorry, I had no idea they were going to do that."

"Oh, but I'm sure it was so terrible to kiss Kelsie Ambrose and Zoe Cirillo?"

"Those kisses meant nothing. I'm sorry I'm not your virgin lips anymore, but you have nothing to be jealous about." He brushed the hair out of her face. "And you're a thousand times more beautiful than Zoe Cerillo and Kelsie Ambrose combined. Come here, my Aphrodite." He showed her with more than words.

The Storm

Two months later, they were the biggest-selling artists in the world. They graced numerous magazine covers, appeared on a parade of talk shows, and were now being chased everywhere by paparazzi. MICHEAL had no conception of how famous they might become. It felt surreal.

"How long before you will be here?" Micheal asked through the phone.

"I'm stuck here until tomorrow at the earliest."

"Okay, I will see you then. Love you, Jules."

"Love you, Micheal."

Micheal went to the overlook to take in the Mirror Plain. It was to be the setting of their latest music video. Julie and Belle unexpectedly experienced a delay, leaving him stuck with the band and crew and Kelsie Ambrose, who had requested to be in one of their videos.

The Mirror Plain was amazing. It was a thin piece of crust over the internal aquifer. This moderated the ground temperature so that snow would constantly melt and refreeze. The effect was that during winter, it became a massive mirror. It was located in what he thought would become northern Europe or Russia, up by the Frozen Sea.

"So, how much longer will Julie be?" Kelsie asked.

"Tomorrow at the earliest."

"I know how we can kill the time. We could go to North Point."

"What's North Point?"

"You've never been to North Point Cliffs? Now, we absolutely must go."

"I don't know."

"We'll be back before nightfall, I promise. And it's the most incredible views from the top of the world."

"Okay."

They boarded an automated hover limo. Kelsie laid in a course, and they flew into the sky.

Micheal awoke in a field of snow. Giving him a striking feeling of *déjà vu*. It reminded him of that day nearly 23 years ago. Then his mind came back into focus, and he remembered the crash. The air temperature was around -20 (-5°F). The Atlanteans had basically developed the Centigrade Temperature System, where 0 was freezing, and 100 was boiling for water.

He felt his arm. It was becoming cold. Then he suddenly re-membered Kelsie. As he sat up, most of his body was sore. He forced himself to his feet. He peered through the falling snow and saw Kelsie partially covered in snow.

"Kelsie! Kelsie!" he said as he knelt next to her. He checked her pulse. It was elevated.

"Kelsie, wake up!" He gently shook her. He physically inspected her; she didn't appear to have any serious injuries.

He needed to find some shelter; he scanned the area around them. Then, he noticed what appeared to be a small cave. He carried Kelsie inside, out of the snow and wind. She felt ice cold. He knew he needed to warm her up.

"Kelsie, wake up!" He shook her again, and she finally roused.

He sat down and set Kelsie in his lap. He wrapped his body

around her to lend her some of his body heat.

"Kelsie, stay awake, don't fall asleep." She kept wanting to fall asleep, but he knew if she did, she may never wake up.

"Kelsie?"

"Yes, Micheal?" She was shivering.

"How do you feel?"

"Still a bit cold, but much warmer, thank you."

"I need to make a fire before nightfall." He rose to his feet. "Just stay here. I will be back soon."

He fought through the blowing snow. The storm was getting worse by the minute. He dug through what he thought was a pile of wood. Buried in the middle, he found some that were mostly dry. He didn't know how long they might have to stay there, so he brought back as much wood as he could get. During his second run, he stumbled on something in the snow. Upon closer inspection, it proved to be the courtesy snack box from the autonomous limousine.

"I found some food."

Once he had a fire going, he retrieved several large logs to close off the opening to the cave and shield them from the storm. Then he went and sat next to the fire.

"I'm still cold."

"Come here."

Kelsie came and sat in his lap. "It's a good thing you were with me; otherwise, I would be dead." She leaned into him.

"Dinner?" He handed her a few snacks. "We need to ration the food. We don't know how long it will take for them to find us."

"It's a good thing I don't usually eat much." Kelsie opened some chips. "So, how long have you and Julie been married?"

"17 years."

"And you are 50?"

"I will be in a couple of months. And you are 332?"

"Indeed, and it only took 120 years to become a star." She had a smile in her voice.

"Well, I'm sure it's late. We should get some sleep." Micheal laid down, spooning Kelsie. He wrapped himself around her. It would certainly be warmer, sharing body heat.

Micheal spent much of the next day trying to dig them out. The storm had snowed them in. Luckily for them, the rising heat from the fire had melted a chimney of sorts through the top of the opening to the cave. So, at least, they wouldn't suffocate. But his attempts to dig them out were all in vain. They might just need to be found.

"Are you all right?"

Kelsie had gone to the back corner of the cave to clean herself with some water he had warmed on the fire. She had been back there for a while.

"I'm all clean now." She emerged completely naked.

"I think you forgot your clothes." He averted his eyes.

"They're still all wet. I'm cold; will you warm me up?" She demurred.

Micheal sat down. "Come here."

She walked over and stood in front of him. Her pussy was at eye level. He was having trouble not looking. He grabbed her hips, and she sat on his lap, facing him. As she did, her breasts brushed his face. Her rock-hard nipples pierced softly into his lips. She stared longingly into his eyes. He would've been lying if he said he wasn't getting turned on.

"Let's get you warmed up." He said, pulling her into him so they were body on body. Her nipples poked through his shirt.

She pulled back a little. "Doesn't it work better without this shirt?" She removed his shirt. As she pressed against him, her silky soft yet firm breasts pressed pleasantly into his chest. She kissed him on the mouth as she reached up the leg of his shorts and began stroking him down there.

Micheal grabbed her wrist as he broke the kiss. "Kelsie, I can't do this."

She pulled her hand back and then stood up. Her pussy was once again at eye level. It was close enough to kiss. "I think I'm all warm now. I will go check on my clothes." She stepped forward, and her pussy pressed into his lips. "We can continue this anytime you want." She stepped away to retrieve her clothes.

Micheal wasn't sure how to proceed. He knew they would have to spend at least one more night together, sharing body heat to stay warm.

"I'm sorry, Kelsie, we're out of food."

"I know something that would take our minds off of that." Kelsie opened her top.

A noise from outside came to his rescue.

Rescue

The delay in Delta was frustrating. Julie took a walk down the waterfront. The Pinnacle was silhouetted against the setting sun. The green sky was shifting toward orange. All she wanted to do was go for an evening flight like she'd done as Aphrodite, but the risks were much too significant.

Maybe The Pinnacle would have to do. She started walking toward the outcropping when a man stepped into her path.

"You're Julie Hall of Avalon, right?"

"Hi, do you want an autograph? Or maybe a photo?"

"I heard you were shooting the final video for your latest album sometime this week, and I was wondering if you would be willing to feature my wife in the video?"

"I'm sorry, that role has already been given to Kelsie Ambrose. But if you submit her portfolio to Bellatrix Bonaventure at Sky Records, perhaps she could be featured in one of the videos for our next album."

"We've already done that for two years. That's why I came to you."

"Did you know I was going to be here?" She clenched her fists, ready for potential defense.

"I didn't know what else to do. You always seemed so nice. I thought if I talked to you, she would actually get a chance; no one ever gives us a break. Please?"

She felt sympathy. "What's her name?"

"Ruth Woods and I'm Daniel. Can you make a secondary role in this next video? She could compliment Kelsie Ambrose, not replace her."

"It's too late to change the concept for this one, but I promise she'll be in the next one, okay?"

He flexed his fists. "You're lying. This is just a ploy to shove us aside to wait for a call that will never come. You're just like the rest of the phonies in this joke of a City of Dreams. Just a self-centered whore!"

She tried to contain herself. "I can see why you've had no

success in this town. If this is how you treat someone who was going to give you a break, how do you treat people who slam the door in your face? I was going to keep my word and feature Ruth in the first video of the next album but now I can promise you, she won't be right for any of our videos." She began to walk away.

"Please. I'm sorry for my outburst. It's just been so hard these last three centuries. If she doesn't get in soon, she'll never get the chance. Please?" He went to his knees.

She did feel bad but didn't think she could work with him based on her reading of him.

"You stalked me to have this conversation. And then you exploded when I didn't give you exactly what you wanted. I can't deal with someone like that. You did cost her a real opportunity. But if she's failed to break through during the entire history of Delta, it wasn't meant to be."

"You're going to regret this!" He rose up.

"What are you going to do? Kill me?" She held her hands out, staring him down.

He dropped his shoulders and averted his gaze. So, she walked off toward The Pinnacle in case he tried to follow her, though he might know her hotel.

Julie was shaken by the encounter. She was distracted as she prepared for bed, and then the voice on the TV gave her a sinking feeling. The TV said. "The craft went down in a storm..."

"Turn that up." She instructed Belle.

"The craft was carrying Kelsie Ambrose and Micheal Hall of Avalon. Rescue crews are still searching..."

"We have to go immediately."

They boarded a hover limo and flew all night, arriving at the search headquarters in Celtic.

"Have you found them yet?" she asked as she entered.

"Mrs. Hall, I assure you; we are doing everything in our power to find them." The Foreign Minister promised.

"What exactly happened?"

"Director Keilis said they were making their way from the Mirror Plain to North Point Cliffs. But they never checked in."

"Why were they going to the Cliffs?"

"You were delayed, so Kelsie offered Micheal a tour of the Cliffs." Xenia Keilis entered the room.

"So why have they not been found yet?"

"There is a terrible storm passing through the area. We have to wait until it breaks." The Minister said.

The storm had passed, leaving a blanket of around 6 feet of snow covering the whole area. And there were drifts dozens of feet high. They searched all day to no avail. As evening began to set in, Julie was beyond frustrated. "Has anyone found anything yet?!"

"We have thoroughly searched the primary search zone; But with 6 feet of new snow, anything out here would be buried," the Minister said.

"So, you think they're dead?"

"The wind chill factor dropped to -60°. Anyone exposed to that would likely not survive. But we are not giving up, I assure you, Mrs. Hall." The Minister explained.

As day three of the search wore on, they were getting nowhere. Then, a thought occurred to Julie. Perhaps the sky-net could help. She chastised herself for not thinking of it sooner. She knew Micheal was the ultimate Boy Scout. If anyone could survive this, he could. But he would still need to find shelter.

She used the sky-net to scan the area using thermal contrast imaging. She detected several dozen anomalies. They must be caves, she thought. She closely inspected each potential candidate and narrowed it down to two.

"We need to check over here!" She instructed the pilot. To her utter disappointment, they dug out a cave; it was empty.

"Head five miles to the northwest." Time was getting short; it was maybe two hours to nightfall.

Half an hour later, the opening was clear. One of the first people through was Julie. "Thank goodness!" She threw her arms around him. "Looks like you're no worse for wear." She looked him up and down.

"It was touch and go there a couple of times."

"Thank you again, Micheal, you saved my life." Kelsie was escorted past them. She winked at him.

"Let's go." He suggested.

They were flying back to The Mirror Plain.

"So, you saved her life?" Julie winked at Micheal.

"She wouldn't have survived without me."

"And the..." She winked again.

"She was quite thankful."

"So, she tried to *reward* you?"

"She was in an odd state. I calmed her down and shut her down."

Micheal put his arm around her. "You understand what it's like to think you're going to die. And how you feel when you're protected. She wasn't thinking straight."

"It's obvious she wants to fuck you."

"The whole world seems to want to fuck both of us. We can't allow that to cause jealousy between us. There will be forces trying to come between us because we're in the spotlight. We need to keep faith with each other. Who cares what anyone else tries or says about us."

Julie hadn't really thought about it that way. She considered the fact that she had been propositioned by multiple leading men in Delta herself, including Emeric Salvator, the male equivalent of Kelsie. It occurred to her that her jealousy of Kelsie was clouding her judgment.

They reached the medical center. Micheal and Kelsie were in such good condition it was decided to go ahead with the shoot. The Mirror Plain was spectacular. And the video for *Reflections* was terrific. It was the theme song for Kelsie's latest Film, *Through the Mirror*.

The Consequence of Fame

When they returned to Atlantis, they visited the Sky Records Studios. After they entered, Bellatrix's personal assistant, Collette, told JULIE, "Mrs. Hall, someone who claims to be a friend, is waiting for you in the office."

As she walked into Belle's waiting room, "Gabriel!"

"Aphrodite! It's an incomparable honor to be in your presence again. I apologize for my unannounced intrusion. I saw your Eminence as a music star and had to say hello." Gabriel Maximus admitted. "I would've thought you would have gone to the temple."

"We did stop by, but Melina was gone on a sabbatical. So, we decided to pursue other experiences.”

"Of course, Eminence Aphrodite. It is a goddess's prerogative."

"It was good to see you again, Gabriel. Koios is waiting on me." She left the office.

"That was creepy," Julie said as she entered the studio.

"What?" Micheal asked.

"Remember Gabriel Maximus?"

"The priest of Aphrodite?" Micheal chuckled.

"Yes, Cato's son. He was waiting for me when we got back."

"What did he want?"

"To say hi. He's been obsessed with Aphrodite, me, for centuries." She shook herself.

"I'm sure he's harmless." Micheal tried to reassure her. "We've known him on and off for 900 years. He hasn't tried anything before, has he?"

"No." She shrugged.

"Okay then, don't worry about it."

They were interrupted by Belle. "You leave on your world tour starting at the end of the week. We are pairing you with the Aquarius twins, Aeliana and Ameliana." She introduced the twins.

"A pleasure." Micheal kissed their hands.

"We are honored to be paired with Avalon," Aeliana said excitedly.

"We love everything you've done so far," Ameliana added.

The Aquarius twins were among the other top new artists.

"*Two Hearts* is a great song," Julie said.

"Perhaps we'll have greater success now that we're paired with you. It's amazing how fast your star has risen." Aeliana said.

"And now we get to play the Megadome. Can you imagine a million people cheering for you?" Ameliana was positively giddy.

Julie on the other hand was a bit intimidated. She and Micheal had attended about a dozen events at the Megadome, but it was always as a spectator. And always from a luxury box. So, the true grandeur of the million-seat stadium had barely been experienced. And now in a week, she would be the focal point of that mass of humanity.

When Julie "went with it", and decided to go the pop star

route, she never conceived that they might headline million-seat stadiums. And that they would be swamped by people in paparazzi everywhere they go. And the fact that this meteoric rise happened in just a few months.

At least when they were the gods, there was always a natural separation. The gods were sacred. Any interaction was always at their discretion. As a normal person celebrity, people feel entitled to your time.

Eight days later they had a meet and greet outside the Megadome. It was all good for the most part. But there was one man who had come through for a photo op, who hung around just watching them. He seemed quite nice, but now she felt the creeps. She maintained her composure, then he disappeared shortly before the event wrapped up.

Micheal left to deal with an emergency business situation, and she remained to inspect the security plan for the concert. Now she was being driven back to the penthouse.

The privacy barrier of the limo lowered, and she discovered that the driver was the man who had been staring at her.

"I must say it was a pleasure to meet you Miss Hall. I can't wait for the concert tomorrow."

She maintained her composure. While she felt it was inappropriate for a driver to engage their guests, she decided to let it go. Perhaps he had simply been waiting for them to finish in order to take them home.

"Thank you, Kingu, I hope we don't disappoint you."

"You remembered my name... Oh, there is no way you could disappoint."

"Thank you. I don't mean to be rude, but it's been a long day, if you don't mind?"

"Oh, my apologies." He went quiet but kept the barrier down. He was watching her the rest of the way home.

She tried to ignore it because she was worried about looking rude. She thought asking him to raise the barrier might cause a reaction. It would only be a few more minutes to the penthouse.

After their arrival, the driver opened the door.

"Well, here we are. Miss Hall, might I make one small request?"

"A request?"

"Could you sing *Secret Love* tomorrow? It's my favorite song."

"I suppose you'll need to wait until tomorrow. Thank you, Kingu." Julie went inside.

In the end, she felt bad that she'd judged him harshly. One of the consequences of fame was fans. Some who may not realize where a line of comfort might be. She knew how people saw her. She had received extra attention since she attended graduate school at Harvard. And while she was an emancipated minor, she still needed to learn to accept that reality. So now she was used to it. And fame had its perks as well. Not all the consequences were bad.

CHAPTER XII: THE TOUR

The Megadome

M ICHEAL LOOKED DOWN FROM a sky box in the roof of the Megadome. The stage on the floor, nearly 1500 feet below, looked like it was only a few dozen feet away. It was thanks to a new technology that made the Megadome possible.

The Megadome was the new premier venue in Atlantis. It had opened ten years earlier and could entertain more than one million spectators. The dimensions were nothing short of incredible. It covered a circular area totaling over 120 acres. The Dome spanned about half a mile across, and a quarter of a mile tall. It was nearly as tall as the Empire State Building.

There was a 1000-foot oculus in the center of the Dome that could open to the sky. The dome soared 1800 feet above the field level. Which was five hundred feet below ground level. The structure dug another twenty stories below the field. That was where the performers would dress and relax before and after the show.

Megadome was the largest building in the Atlantean world by volume. It was over 7 billion cubic feet. Put another way, it could fit 15 Boeing factories inside it. The Boeing factory in Everett WA was the modern equivalent, and it was only 472 million cubic feet.

He rode the magnetic inclinator down to field level, to double-check all of the instruments.

"Can you believe this place?" Julie asked as he joined her on stage.

"It is amazing. And you've seen the view from on high?"

"I have indeed. It makes you a little more self-conscious of anything you're doing because a million people are going to have a prime view."

"Well, there is no bad view of you." He kissed her.

"Thanks. But I certainly took that into account in my wardrobe selection."

"All five look stunning."

"I can't believe we sold out this place with nearly 1.1 million tickets."

"You're not intimidated, are you?" Micheal tested a guitar.

She sighed. "It will certainly bring our newfound stardom into focus."

"Everything looks good, now let's go relax until showtime."

They went to their dressing room. They chatted casually with their band. And the stadium feed showed the arena fill up in less than an hour. Then they enjoyed the set played by the Aquarius twins.

Their band members went to take up their positions. Then it was showtime. The lights went out and as the core of the stage brought them up from below, the Dome was gently illuminated by the glow of people's cell phones.

Micheal struck the first chord on his guitar and the lights slowly came up with the music. A roar from the crowd greeted the song. And the stage shook from the artificial earthquake. They fed off the electric atmosphere and sent the crowd on a roller coaster of emotions with a dynamic first set.

The lights dimmed and the band played an extended intro to the next set while Micheal and Julie did a wardrobe change, designed to fit the next theme.

Four more sets and three more hours later, they reached the final two songs. Their current number-one hit, *Need You Now*, was followed by an electric, up-tempo song called, "To the Heavens".

As they left the stage the energy inside the Megadome was palpable. Now the concept of the encore was not a modern convention. The crowd began stamping their feet until they found a harmonious rhythm. The quaking of the Dome had a music of its own.

They let the apprehension rise for a couple of minutes, then a fog rose upon the stage and a flash of green light revealed their return and the crowd roared.

Micheal and Julie alternated on vocals before bringing the house down with an epic duet. They soaked in several minutes of thunderous adoration then descended with the stage one final time.

"That was amazing!" Ameliana gushed.

"Why haven't you shared all those incredible songs with the world before now?" Aeliana asked.

"Our music was always simply a fun hobby. If it wasn't for Belle's intercession, we would still be making music, except it would only be for us." Julie said.

"Well, I'm thankful for Belle then," Ameliana said.

"There's plenty more in our catalog. And we will be quick-releasing albums over the next few years to bring it all to the people. Until then, that will be a perk of attending our shows. You'll get to be the first to hear some of our songs." Micheal smiled.

"And we get to be there for all of it," Aeliana said, then the twins headed off.

Micheal and Julie retired to their dressing room.

"That was amazing. I'm so glad we did this."

"So you liked the Megadome?" Micheal unbuttoned his shirt.

"Not just the Megadome. The pop star idea. My original purpose was to get back at you, but I also love to perform. That's why the Megadome was so amazing tonight. I've never felt energy like that before."

Micheal did enjoy the experience. It fueled him to play it up that much more. "So you enjoy the adoration?"

Julie sighed. "It's not only the fame. I have been some form of famous for 40 years. It's the magnitude. A million people cheering you all at once, it's a whole 'nother level."

Micheal hadn't been famous much before. The Lords of Avalon was his first taste. But the nobility in the 17th century kept most people at bay. Playing gods in Classical Atlantis was certainly a step up. But divinity kept people at bay. In this time, they were just normal people. And he was getting a true taste of fame. The Megadome was a magnifier, elucidating the concept.

"The Megadome showed an adoration for our talent. Not some aloof status as a God or a Lord."

Julie smiled. "A good consequence of fame."

"I think we're going to enjoy this tour."

Foreign Lands

-September 1, 2376 BC

"Eight months of our tour has taken us all around the empire and now we venture to the foreign lands. We begin on the far side of the world. We are in Olympus, the capital of Greece. Greece covers modern-day Southeast Asia. While it's the opposite side of the pangea supercontinent, they ascribe to the Atlantean gods. Today brings the 905th festival of the gods. Ironically celebrating our arrival in Atlantis. And nine centuries later we're headlining the musical aspect.

We're going to be given a special tour of the Temple of the Gods. It features larger-than-life statues of us. I wonder if anyone will suspect us? With our star burning so bright, and lives spanning the better part of a millennia, there's a real risk of us being recognized. Let's find out."

The head priestess of Aphrodite, and the head priestess of Koios, were giving them a private tour of the Temple of the Gods.

"Today's festivities celebrate the coming of the gods. The divine couple of Aphrodite and Koios came to Gaia, to bring peace and prosperity to the entire world. Not just for those who believe."

Aphrodite's representative passed it off to Koios's representative.

"Koios himself signed the perpetual peace agreement right here on this location. That's why this temple was built here."

"These statues are copies of the ones at their temples in Atlantis."

Aphrodite's representative looked at the statue and then looked at JULIE. And her words faltered. She looked back and forth, then said. "You look just like her."

"That's very kind, but how can I compare to beauty herself?"

After a couple more glances, she said. "My apologies, Miss Hall." She went speechless again, so Koios's representative took over.

"None other than Elissa, personal servant of Koios. And Melina, personal servant of Aphrodite, oversaw the plans for the construction of this shrine."

Koios's representative squinted at Micheal. Then looked back and forth at the statues. "Your holy eminences!" She went to Micheal's feet. Then Aphrodite's representative went to her feet.

"Rise," Micheal commanded. They complied and stepped back. "What makes you believe we are the gods?"

"You both are a striking image of your statues. And the odds that two random people would do that defeats logic."

Micheal looked at Julie and then back again. "Your logic is sound. We visit periodically, in disguise, to get a more personal experience of humanity. But this knowledge does not leave this chamber."

"Of course, your eminence." They said in concert.

"Eminence Koios, might I make a request?" He nodded. "Elissa spoke of her regular discourses with you. Might I have the pleasure?"

He looked at Julie and then back. "What would you like to discuss?"

"Ways to travel faster than the light constant."

They headed off for a more comfortable forum. Julie remained with her representative.

"I failed you, your eminence."

"How so?"

"I've loved Avalon since your debut, but I never put it together."

"We are in disguise. You're not meant to recognize us. Is there anything you would ask of me?"

Her acolyte looked at her, then turned away shyly.

"You've been a devout servant for centuries. What is your wish?"

"Melina spoke of the times she flew with you. I have greatly desired that experience."

Julie saw a courtyard, beyond the statue hall. "Give me your hand."

Julie pulled her into position, then flew them up and out through the courtyard. She shot them quickly up through the clouds, above the flying traffic lanes, to avoid being vulnerable to spectators. They flew high above the city of Olympus. And the noise of 150 million people went silent. They paused when the curve of the earth became apparent. All the clouds were far below them. Julie estimated they were perhaps 30 miles up. The sun was brilliant with no occlusions. And Oceana was greenish-blue, speckled with white, stretching to the eastern horizon.

The high-altitude Superman view was always inspiring. But the force field would only hold out the harsh environment for so long, so it was time to dive.

"Now for the fun part," Julie said as they went into freefall. A few minutes later the Olympus beachfront what's coming up fast. Julie jetted them out over the ocean. She climbed back up to the cloud deck and paused on the edge of a billowing cloud.

"Watch this."

She generated an electric current, then sent it through the conductive water vapor. A rumble of Thunder rolled across the sky. Then Julie took a leisurely flight back to the temple.

"Thank you for the tour." She said as they landed.

Micheal emerged with Koios's representative. "We must go now."

Their priestesses bowed and then escorted them out.

***

The concert was a smash for over half a million people at the festival. Over the next seven months, they visited every country on the eastern continent. Now they crossed the Sea of Egypt to the southern continent.

It was their first visit to Egypt. As the limo flew into Memphis it was worlds removed from Julie's visit, a few years before The Fall. The pyramids of Giza were far different than in modern times. They were white with what appeared to be glass at their pinnacles. And a purple glow ran up the edges, coalescing into beams that pierced the heavens. And while the plateau was cleared out around them, beyond it was a thick jungle. It wasn't the arid desert of modern times.

Memphis was a mega city of 200 million people. They landed at the entrance to the royal palace. The purple carpet path they walked to reach the central building was lined with alternating sphinxes and obelisks. They were greeted by a well-dressed man.

"I am, Ihy, vizier of Egypt. Welcome to Memphis. His Majesty is very excited to meet you."

The vizier led them through numerous halls until the guards opened two enormous doors. The pharaoh was seated on a throne, wearing a pschent.

"His Majesty, Unas, King of Egypt, welcomes Micheal and Julie Hall." The herald announced.

The grand hall was lined with many attendants. They walked up together and bowed before the pharaoh.

"As you were."

They stood up.

"I am honored by your visit. Your music is most divine. And I can't wait for tonight's show. Originally, I had considered requesting a private performance, but then I decided to experience your show in all its glory at the Eye of Ra. I've been wanting to see a performance there since it opened during the Death Festival. And I thought this was the perfect opportunity."

"We are most honored, Your Majesty," Julie said.

"So, as that creates a few hours of time, I would like to personally give you a tour of the pyramid complex."

"That sounds amazing," Micheal said.

"Right this way."

The Pharaoh rose and shed his ceremonial garments. They boarded the Pharaoh's private transport, and a few minutes later they were next to the Great Pyramid.

"This is where modernity began. King Khufu's vizier, Prince Hemiunu, had a brilliant idea. He believed that energy could be harnessed from the air itself. The king had begun to age and so he wanted a grand burial site. Hemiunu saw that the stone pyramid might be perfect to channel the power of the gods. Khufu agreed to allow the prince to make the attempt. Over a few decades, we worked to implement his vision."

"You were there?" Julie asked.

"Yes, Hemiunu was my cousin. He was a genius. That's why he

was in charge of all royal projects. I was always fascinated by the mysteries of the world. But I didn't have the mental wherewithal to envision such greatness. Still, Hemiunu encouraged my efforts. And after so many years of work, it was magical when the divine light emanated."

"How long ago was this?"

The pharaoh gave an amused look at Micheal.

"I understand you're young. This was 176 years ago. It took some time to catch on, across the world, but I felt fortunate to witness Hemiunu's legacy become realized. I grew up in a world without electricity. Without telecommunication. Or M-Pulse transportation. And especially space travel. Despite the protestations of my Advisory Council, I recently visited the moon. What a time to be alive."

Unas was clearly reliving memories. "Come, I want to show you how it works."

Pharaoh Unas proceeded to go over everything about the pyramids and how they sparked the industrial revolution. It was clear he was more proud of these accomplishments than being pharaoh. They were given the royal treatment before and after the concert.

According to Micheal, King Unas was the last pharaoh of the 5th dynasty. They, of course, knew that this version of Atlantis would end. Likely in the Flood of Noah. What seemed most intriguing was how the history of Egypt would transfer to the Post-Atlantean Age. Because modern history believed there was an unbroken line of kings going back to the late 4th Millennium BC. But the king lists were an artifact of the New Kingdom. Over 1000 years after their present day. So clearly much of the knowledge makes it through the Atlantean apocalypse.

But it seems the creators of the lists constructed much, based on their own life experience. Lifespans in the New Kingdom are much better documented. People only live an average of 30 to 40 years. Not the nearly 400 years that King Unas had lived.

Perhaps the 5th Dynasty ends because of the apocalypse. And just like Atlantis, the real history is lost to time.

A few weeks later they had finally returned to Babylon. The last time they were here, Empress Kissare had been assassinated and her brother had tried to kill them. But now they weren't enemy gods. Babylon was one of the few megacities in the top 10 that wasn't in the Atlantean Empire. Its population was well over 250 million. And now they were flying over some of the tallest buildings they'd seen since leaving Atlantis.

The towers flanking the central harbor were upward of a mile and a half tall. Then Julie saw their destination. The Orb. The Orb was the second-largest venue in the world. It could seat over 800,000 people. The Orb was, in fact, an orb, 2000 feet in diameter. It was glowing purple as twilight was falling over the city. Their hovercraft docked at the base. And they were escorted to their dressing room.

"Finally." Emperor Egino Rainard greeted them.

"Your eminence." They both said.

"I realize that tensions are high right now. And Atlantis and Babylon aren't as friendly as we once were. But that's the precise reason I invited you for this festival. The Equilibrium Rising Festival. This is one of the only two days a year when the day and the night find equilibrium. That harmony reminds us that the world is bigger than our differences."

"Well said, your eminence. We hope to inspire the same." Julie nodded.

"Well, if anyone can unite the world it's the golden couple of Delta. I look forward to your performance." The emperor left the room.

Julie and Micheal dressed then it was showtime. The stage elevated out of the floor just like in the Megadome. But this one could also levitate anywhere inside the Orb. Seats were covering most of the inner globe.

Julie started on the piano. And the roar of the crowd fueled her performance. The Orb was perfectly oriented to conduct electricity. She activated her rings and shocks of lightning radiated out from every keystroke.

Micheal picked up on her action and his guitar riffs electrified the crowd, literally. They were using harmless voltage, but the effects were impressive.

The Orb looked like they were inside a massive Tesla plasma orb. They utilized the levitating stage to full effect working the crowd in every part of the Orb.

The Emperor invited them to an afterparty that ran late. Julie couldn't help but imagine this visit if Zelia was Empress. If Daon hadn't murdered her and her mother, Zelia would be Empress right now. But after Daon's betrayal, and the Samano family's annihilation, there had been more than 50 emperors and empresses of Babylon.

The party was winding down when Julie noticed a woman. She'd seen her earlier. The woman was still seated in the same place she had been earlier. She was just staring at Julie. A closer look gave her an odd thought. The woman resembled Empress Ishtar.

Julie approached and the woman began to scramble to her feet. "Wait!"

The woman froze, then slowly turned, but didn't look at her.

"Did you enjoy the party?"

"It was nice. Your show was amazing."

"Thank you. I must say, you remind me of someone I once knew."

The woman looked up at that.

"What's your name?"

"Mylitta Samano." She locked eyes.

Julie was certain Mylitta must be from the founding family.

"Who was your mother?"

"Princess Zelia."

"You know who we are?"

Mylitta averted her eyes. "I snuck in and spied when you visited my mother and grandmother. I saw when my uncle murdered them."

"How did you survive the purge?"

"I wasn't here when that happened. I was only 14 when my uncle took over. I stowed away on a ship and ended up in Celtic. Why didn't you protect my mother?" She began to cry.

"Your uncle knew one of our weaknesses. And we didn't think Daon was a threat when he entered the chamber. There was nothing we could do."

"You're the gods of Atlantis. I know you could have saved them."

"When we are living amongst you, our powers are limited. I'm sorry."

"Why didn't the Anunnaki protect them?"

"We don't know them. But the gods rarely intercede directly in human affairs."

"Of course." She shook her head. "I've had to live a lie for the last 400 years. If anyone learned my true identity, I'd be dead."

"A name doesn't define you. Who you are in here…" Julie touched her chest. "Is what matters."

"The gods should intercede more often. Your last true intercession brought peace to the world. Maybe you should do it again." Mylitta walked out of the room.

Julie felt guilty all over again about Kissare and Zeila. She wished she truly was Aphrodite. But she was just a normal person. Micheal always says that with great power comes great responsibility. But how much power did Julie really have? She had spent decades training in martial arts, and they possessed special technological rings that allowed them to pretend to be gods. But beneath all of that, she was just as much flesh and blood as any normal person. What could she actually do? But more importantly, why was it her responsibility?

The fact that they were portraying themselves as gods, made Julie feel that perhaps she did have some responsibility. But at this point, all she wanted to do was go out and perform and entertain people.

They spent the next eight months touring the southern continent, then it was time to return to Atlantis.

Empress Regina

-February 14, 2374 BC

"For the past two years, we've barely seen Atlantis. We've literally toured the entire world. At least that allowed us to see what the Atlantean world is really like. There have been many ups and downs. But now the tour comes to an end today.

We officially returned to Atlantis last night. And today we perform for the Empress. It's her 895th birthday. Our world tour was nothing short of crazy. We are mobbed everywhere we go. We are now said to be at the top of the Delta A-list, the Atlantis version of Hollywood. I have done numerous magazine spreads declaring me the sexiest woman alive. You would think Aphrodite would have been the pinnacle of adoration. But this current spotlight is so much brighter. And I am somewhat ashamed to admit I am enjoying it quite a lot.

Micheal, of course, has been declared the sexiest man alive. I very much wish that hadn't happened because it's hard to keep my jealousy in check. And I have to try to ignore every tabloid article proclaiming he has been having affairs with half the actresses and singers on the A-list, which I am confident, are all bullshit.

On the other hand, all the women are so gorgeous. And Micheal has been married to me for nearly 20 years. And I am the only woman he has ever been with. Is there a chance he might be curious about what it would be like with another woman? And with so much temptation around all the time, can he really resist it all?"

PS: Happy Valentine's Day, Micheal.

MICHEAL and Julie were escorted to a fancy door in the Emperor's Palace. They'd lived here when they first came to Atlantis. But this section of the palace had been fully renovated. The doors opened and the Empress was standing in front of a large desk. All of the seats lining the edge of the office were occupied.

Micheal thought Regina greatly resembled Julie. She was around five and a half feet tall with fair skin and raven hair. Her deep blue eyes were the only part of her that reflected her nine centuries of life.

"Please, come in."

As they reached the desk she said. "Welcome Micheal and Julie Hall, I'm Regina Seneca."

"Your eminence." They both briefly bowed.

"We have a gift for you." Julie withdrew a scroll.

"What is it?"

"See for yourself," Micheal said.

"This looks like an original of the Perpetual Peace Treaty with Babylon."

"Indeed, it is." He confirmed.

"Where did you get this? Those who ascribe to the old gods, deem this too sacred to share."

"We happen to know someone who owned this copy. And we know how much you love history."

Regina fingered the signatures of the gods. "You know Melina

Hellas? She wouldn't even let me see it."

"We do know Melina. But she's not the one who gave it to us. And we are not at liberty to reveal the source." Julie said.

"I'm afraid I can't accept this. Melina would never speak to me again. While I don't believe in the gods of old, I do fear to upset their devotees."

Micheal touched Regina's hand. "We do believe in the gods. And I promise, that if Melina knows this was a gift from us, she will not have a problem with it."

"If you consider this a sacred document, why would you give it to me?"

"As the ruler of the greatest empire on the planet, you deserve solemn veneration. In your role as Empress, you do serve the gods. And we are aware of your love for history. And your desire for artifacts from the time of the rule of the gods. But due to the sacred nature of that time period, all documents are kept safe even beyond your reach." Julie nodded.

Regina reexamined the document. "This is the greatest gift I've ever received. I hope this isn't some ploy to convert me?"

Micheal shook his head. "We'd never dream of such machinations. As a person of such esteem and long life, it is very likely that you have nearly everything you desire. So, we thought to present you with something you weren't likely to be able to acquire on your own."

Regina smiled. "If you're close with Melina, I know we'll be great friends." She examined the scroll one final time, then rolled it up. "I shall cherish this forever. Now about my concert, I desire a small intimate affair. I know your band arrived earlier. I spoke with them and thanked them for their offering, but I sent them away. I hope this is not an issue."

"Of course not." Julie smiled.

"I didn't need another big concert. I attended your inaugural performance at the Megadome, amazing. I had planned this introduction at that time, but I was pulled away on important state business. Your music is so fresh and dynamic. Such diversification of sound. I have practiced many of your songs on my guitar and piano. Would you indulge me?"

Multiple instruments were brought in. Regina sat on a bench and began strumming a guitar, then transitioned into the beginning riff from the song *From Time to Time*.

Julie found harmony with a violin. Micheal added in the piano attribution. Then he began to sing.

The Empress was quite talented. This was no surprise to Micheal, as it was her 895th birthday. He would hope anyone that old would have used some of that time productively. They should have a diverse array of talents.

Regina alternated between the piano and the guitar, for three more songs. Then sat back and enjoyed their improvised concert. She would make requests or ask for new unreleased music. There was much banter and laughter. It was surreal that this vibrant "young" woman was turning 895.

While Melina was older, they had yet to see her in this time period. They knew Ishtar when she was nearing 1000, she definitely showed her age.

After several hours of music, it was time to present Regina's lifeline. This was an Atlantean tradition where the person to be honored, was gifted a fancy ribbon marking the person's length of years.

Following this presentation, there was a short ceremony. Afterward, Micheal and Julie did a meet and greet for all the other guests, most of whom were family members of Regina.

With the party over, the rest of the guests left. Now it was just them and Regina.

Regina went back to a previous topic. "I was curious how you know Melina?"

"We worked together a while back. She's a good friend." Julie said.

"With how quickly you've risen to prominence, I was surprised you had a connection to her. I've known her since my coming of age. And she pretty much only serves the old gods anymore." Regina paused. "I do have to admit she's become a bit more distant over the past few centuries. I wonder if it has to do with her Oracle powers?"

Micheal's stomach dropped. He realized that if Melina had developed some kind of foresight power, it must have something to do with them. "How long ago did she seem to change in your mind?"

"I understand you're both young, only in your 50s. She's probably always seemed the same to you. But she was a kind, happy person for the first five centuries I knew her. Then came her visions, around 400 years ago. That was the first time she became more distant, closed off. She seemed like she finally adjusted to her role as Oracle. But then, a century ago something changed. I've never pressed the issue, but clearly something's wrong."

"You believe she sees the future? Isn't that crazy?" Julie poured a drink.

"You don't? I thought you were friends with her?"

Micheal set his drink down. "Oh, we believe she does. It's just that we thought you didn't believe in the mythology."

Regina rubbed her eyes. "I've lived a very long life. But I've never witnessed anything that affirms the old ways. Melina's visions are the closest thing I've ever seen. We simply disagree about where they come from."

"Where do you think they come from?" Julie asked.

"I grew up Unitarian. So clearly it must be God who gave them to her. But she claims it was the gods. Have you never discussed this with her?"

"It was never brought up. We didn't feel it was our place to investigate a gift from the gods. But it does seem like there's another reason you believe she has divine sight."

Regina sighed and grabbed her neck. "I'm only alive today because she sees the future. A little over 400 years ago, when Atlantis was about to defeat Babylon in the Great Atlantis-Babylonian War, Babylon tried to assassinate me. Melina tried to warn me, telling me about her vision. But I thought she was crazy. I refused to take it seriously. Then, on the precise night she said it would happen, I was viciously attacked. The man nearly strangled me to death. But Melina decided that she would protect me anyway. She infiltrated the palace defenses and subdued my attacker. It was hard to have doubts after that. But she said Koios, God of Wisdom and Knowledge, had given her the ability. She said that 430 years ago, Aphrodite and Koios had returned to Gaia. They came to more closely assess the decadence that humanity had fallen into. But how could I believe they returned when they never came to the palace to see me. I was already Empress at that time. And with the sacred shield over the time of their so-called reign? I was never able to see any documentation. Or any other evidence. I need actual proof. That's the reason the gift you gave me is so amazing. For the first time, I can touch with my own hands something that the gods actually signed." She unrolled the scroll and studied it closely.

Micheal thought about Melina and wondered if she was correct. Were they the cause of the visions? Melina had been at three of their temporal jumps. And the timing of her visions matched their last departure. Could temporal energy cause Melina to see the future? If so, why didn't they have temporal powers? They'd been exposed to more temporal energy than anyone they knew.

Micheal felt bad if their actions had brought a burden to Melina. But at least it seemed that she tried to use it for something good. But what about this change a century ago? It sounded bad. He hoped Melina would return soon, so he might learn more.

This whole situation challenged how much they thought they knew about temporal mechanics. They would need to study this further.

They spent the night at the palace, then it was a true return to their penthouse. Home sweet home.

The Fan

-February 28, 2374 BC

"The last two weeks we took a break, to decompress, after years on the road. But we didn't take it alone. Our new friend Regina spent much of her concurrent vacation visiting the penthouse. She always came alone. No security, no advisors. I think our friendship with Melina engendered trust. Regina wanted to jam together and have deep conversations.

She told me she has no friends, other than Melina. That her long reign has caused her children and generations to all drift away. The only ones who regularly interact with her are the ones who desire power and influence. They've become strangers. She said she felt like she could be herself around us. That she believes we can be true friends.

I can say, that the way she talks to me, feels like she's been holding everything in. She's dumped a lot on me in her comfortable state. It could be because, I in fact, do you understand her feelings of isolation. When living as a goddess, Micheal was the only one I could be completely me with. So going forward, I will try to be a friend to her.

The lazy days, away from the bright lights of stardom, have also been cathartic. I do feel refreshed. Ready to face the spotlight again. We are approaching the midpoint of this stop. Our time as true celebrities will end with this stop. So, I do want to revel in it while I still can."

JULIE and Micheal were dressing for a movie premiere. It was called *The Reign of the Gods* starring Kelsie Ambrose. It was a period piece about her and Micheal's reign as Aphrodite and Koios. It was ironic that Kelsie had played her. Julie was curious how accurate the portrayal would be. Avalon had written three original songs for the picture. So, of course, they were invited to the premiere.

As she slid her shoulder straps up, she heard the TV say. "... Kiri Ashur was found strangled in her home in Delta. She is the 12th actress from the Delta A-list who has been murdered in the past few months, and in that same time, eight of the top female music artists have also been murdered. It is believed to be the work of the same person. This celebrity serial killer is being dubbed the Phantom..."

Julie muted the TV. "Micheal!"

"What's wrong?" Micheal asked with worry.

"Look at this." She un-muted the TV.

The TV continued. "... The killer has not left a single piece of evidence. Despite clear evidence that he raped Kiri, the samples were completely useless. There have been no hair samples, no skin samples, and no fingerprints. And stranger still, no video. The killer is truly a phantom..."

Micheal muted the TV. "Kiri was murdered?"

They had become friends with most of the people in the Delta community. They knew Kiri well.

"He's lucky he hasn't crossed you yet," Micheal said sadly.

"Do you think he will try?" A bit of fear filled her stomach.

"If he's not stopped. And at this rate, the Bureau seems help-less." Micheal said seriously. "We will need to be extra vigilant."

Micheal zipped her up and they flew to the Poseidon Theater. They were walking the carpet, posing for the cameras, when Julie noticed a man mirroring their movement down the carpet. Before entering the theater, she realized it was Kingu, the limo driver who drove her home the night before the inaugural Megadome concert. She shook off the goosebumps. Perhaps this celebrity serial killer had her on edge. But his actions were still creepy.

They found their table and following a short introduction it was showtime. The movie was very well researched. It included their arrival, complete with a green vortex. Their procession into Atlantis. The battle and siege breaking against Babylon. Their diplomatic travels. And the coming of Princess Ishtar. It all culminated with the Perpetual Peace Treaty with Babylon.

Delilah Sabel was spot on as Melina. Julie's friend Adelaide Scharless had fun playing Elissa. Emeric Salvator played a decent Koios. Although he could never fully measure up. And then there was Kelsie. Julie appreciated the effort but felt she played it too stoically. She supposed that was how people envisioned a goddess to act.

The biggest criticism Julie had was in the portrayal of Koios's sexual exploits. They had him avail himself of his priestesses' sexual offerings. There was a sex scene with "Elissa". And even more ridiculous was Koios's dalliance with Princess Ishtar. It implied that her friendly reign as Empress of Babylon may have been due to such a relationship. And of course, they had to include an electric sex scene between Aphrodite and Koios.

Despite such problems, the film was well-made and quite entertaining. It was surreal seeing a quasi-biopic of her own life. Afterward, she approached Kelsie. "Wow, that was a divine performance."

Kelsie laughed. "I mean, how do you live up to the Goddess of Love and Beauty?"

"How do you research a role like this?"

"I talked to the priestesses at the temple of the gods. And Gallia Karallis, a member of the 900 Club who was alive at the time. There are only six people in the world who lived at that time."

"Well, you were quite convincing."

"Hopefully Aphrodite won't come and strike me down. I tried to be as respectful as possible."

Julie laughed. "I think you'll be okay. Do you believe in the gods?"

"I was never that religious, but after my research for this role, I think they could be real."

Julie touched her shoulder. "I think the gods appreciate your respectful efforts." Julie headed off to congratulate Adelaide.

———————————

After the party, she and Micheal were in the limo, heading home.

"Koios was the real ladies' man." Micheal shook his head.

"It's ridiculous. But with the oath, I can see why they would think that. And to be fair, they did have Aphrodite do the same thing with her priestesses. Did that actually happen with Melina?"

Julie laughed. "Obviously not. But it's not like I wasn't tempted."

"Really?! You've never indicated such interest before."

"I didn't want to put that thought in your head. And she's my best friend. The goddess/priestess thing makes it complicated enough already. But seriously, she's stunning. And her body is perfection."

Micheal was giving her a side-eye.

"Don't look at me like that. I'm sure you have imagined that three-way." She shook her head laughing.

He laughed as well. "You're right. But that fantasy doesn't compare to the real Goddess of Love and Beauty." He kissed her.

As she sat back, she tried to pretend the sex scene between Aphrodite and Melina hadn't happened.

When the limo door opened, once again, it was Kingu. "Miss Hall."

"Kingu, nice to see you again."

Micheal stepped out. "Thank you." He took Julie's hand and led her inside.

The man was watching the entire time. Kingu's return was creepy.

———————————

A few weeks later, Micheal went to Amazon to deal with one of their business interests. Julie went to dinner with her friends at a new fancy restaurant that was opening on the outer ring.

"We are celebrating Adelaide, and her amazing performance in the biggest film in the world right now." Julie raised a glass.

Adelaide laughed. "I got so used to walking around naked, I almost forgot to wear clothes tonight."

Everyone laughed.

"I don't know how you did that?" Rosalyn said.

"I was trying to accurately portray a true erudite."

"Don't let her fool you, she would do that regularly if it was socially acceptable." Corra laughed.

"To be fair, I think if you've lived for seven centuries, you should be comfortable in your skin." Belle took a sip.

They enjoyed an amazing dinner to the setting of the sun. The Atlantic Passage became a canvas of light.

Julie used the bathroom, then stopped at the rail, overlooking the Passage.

"Beautiful, isn't it?" Julie turned to the man's voice.

"What are you doing here?" It was Kingu, the limo driver.

"Is that any way to greet a friend?"

"Friend? We're not friends."

He tried to touch her hand and she stepped back.

"We've known each other for years. You've always been kind to me. And I know why."

"You need to leave me alone."

"I just wanna keep you safe. With the Phantom out there, you need someone to protect you."

She studied Kingu. Could he be the Phantom?

"I can take care of myself." She hurried to the table. "I'm sorry, I have to go. You should all come with me."

She looked over and Kingu was watching them. Her friends looked at him.

"Who Kingu? He's harmless." Belle argued.

"I've had multiple creepy encounters with him. I think he's stalking me."

"He can be creepy sometimes," Rosalyn said.

"We've all had awkward interactions with him, but I don't think he's dangerous," Corra said.

"So, he's had multiple interactions with all of us? He could be the Phantom. We need to go."

"That's ridiculous. He's not the Phantom." Adelaide shook her head.

"Fine, I'm leaving."

Kingu was still staring. Julie looked at her friends once more, then headed home.

As she got home, she thought that perhaps she had overreacted. Maybe Kingu was simply concerned for the celebrities. But whoever this Phantom was, she needed to find out.

Julie plotted the last few murder locations on the map. Then she connected to the sky-net and ran an analysis. She saw the victims come, then eventually the investigators. But just like all previous scans of the murder sites, there was no sign of the killer coming or going.

She ran diagnostic scans of the sky-net's systems. Then she ran control scans of non-investigatory sites and there was no indication of any malfunctions. The killer truly was a Phantom.

Micheal's efforts in Amazon ran into complications and he was delayed. By the time he had finished, he needed to go straight to Tycho for his photo shoot. It was located on the modern-day Yucatan Peninsula, near where the Mexican city of Merida would eventually be founded.

So now Julie would be missing him for nearly two weeks. Julie had her own photo shoot. She traveled past the Pillars of Hercules, which was located at the Gibraltar Strait. It was the farthest East extension of the Atlantis mega city.

She dressed in a bikini and walked across the powdery sand until the waves from the Sea of Egypt teased her feet.

"Wade into the water." The photographer directed. The waves topped her knees. "Okay, look back over your shoulder... Turn to me... With your hands, flick the water at me... Now, slowly walk out... Sit down... Lean back... Arch your back... That was great."

It was time for a wardrobe change. Julie went through multiple changes and hundreds of photos, until the sun hung low over the Bay of Hercules. As the shoot was coming to an end, Julie noticed a man taking pictures from a yacht nearby. He was a silhouette. She couldn't make him out.

The yacht came in, to dock, as she walked to her personal transport. The man intercepted her.

"Miss Hall, let me help you get safely home."

She stepped back, fists at the ready. "Kingu, this must stop!"

"I just want to keep you safe."

"You're stalking me. You may very well be the Phantom." She was formulating a plan of attack.

"Stalking? I would never. I love you."

"You can't love someone you don't know."

"But I do know you. And when Micheal leaves you, you can

count on me. I'll protect you from any harm."

He stepped toward her, and she lightly punched his nose. "Don't come near me again."

Security finally arrived.

"Call the police. He might be the Phantom."

"Julie, I would never hurt you."

The police arrived and took Kingu into custody. After she gave her statement, she flew home.

The latest encounter with Kingu had shaken her. She tried calling Micheal, but he didn't answer. She didn't like sitting there doing nothing. She used the sky-net to review all her encounters with Kingu.

She was able to see him at the Megadome before the first incident, but after that there was nothing. It didn't see him at the premiere. Or the restaurant. Or the photo shoot. All that evidence convinced her that he had to be the Phantom.

She did deep-dive research on Kingu. He was over 600 years old. He had been married several times. He had dozens of children from all of his marriages. But on his 600th birthday, his entire family had gathered for the momentous occasion. A transport vessel crashed into the party killing everyone except him. This was about five years ago. The trauma from this tragedy must have caused him to snap.

Julie felt bad. To lose everyone who mattered to you, all at once. That was so terrible. She could understand how his mind could be twisted by trauma.

She breathed a sigh of relief that the Phantom had been stopped.

Micheal should have been back by now. She texted a few more times with no response. She reached out to the magazine that had sponsored the photo shoot. They said that Micheal and Kelsie had missed a press event that had been scheduled for earlier that day.

Julie was tired from the long day and the encounter. She tried to sleep but it was restless. Because she couldn't sleep, and she wanted a distraction. She turned on the TV.

The TV said. "... So once again, Adelaide Scharless is the latest victim of the Phantom..."

Julie couldn't believe Adelaide was dead. Kingu was stopped too late. Her body went numb. Adelaide wasn't a close friend, but she was still a friend. And if only her friends had taken her warning more seriously, Adelaide might not be dead. The static noise of her shock was broken when she saw a picture of Micheal kissing Kelsie.

The TV was saying. "...On a different note, we have exclusive pictures of a potentially scandalous weekend Kelsie Ambrose spent with Micheal Hall..."

Julie was outraged. Ever since they were stranded together in Celtic, in the cave, there had been various rumors of them having an affair. Kelsie had been around periodically over the years. Julie had even come to consider her a friend. But Julie could no longer ignore the likelihood they might be having an affair. She stewed all night, waiting for Micheal to come home.

Julie became momentarily distracted by a news report saying Kingu was released for lack of evidence. Just another thing to worry about. Micheal finally returned.

The Pinnacle

"How could you?!" Julie yelled as MICHEAL walked in the door.

"What did I do?" He was confused.

"You're having an affair with Kelsie!"

"I am not!"

"And now you're lying about it!"

"I am—"

"Admit it, I've seen the pictures, so don't try to deny it." She charged him.

"Nothing has happened—" He retreated.

"No more lies! I will give you one more chance to tell me the truth!"

"I am—"

"Get out!"

"Jules—" He pleaded.

"Get out!" She yelled at the top of her lungs.

So, Micheal did. He walked out, boarded his hover car, and flew off into the night. A few hours later, he was in Delta. When the numerous calls and texts he sent to Julie went unanswered, he went to The Pinnacle by the sea for some solitude.

"Want some company?" Kelsie asked as she walked up.

"What are you doing here?" he asked a little sharply. It seemed rather suspicious that she would show up at this moment.

"I was just coming for some solitude; I thought you were in Atlantis. And after the report, I'm sure I'm the last person you want to see." Kelsie stated sadly. "I've wanted you for years; I've never tried to hide that from you. I guess I'll go."

"No... Stay." Micheal grabbed her hand. "Your place?"

Micheal sat on the couch in Kelsie's loft a few minutes later. She unzipped her dress, and it fell to the floor. She pressed her breasts together as she walked over to him. He examined her soft, firm breasts both with his eyes and his hands. After a moment, he slid his hands down and slowly removed her panties. She gently rubbed herself. She then climbed onto his lap, facing him. He kissed her nipples while Kelsie pulled his shirt off.

He closed his eyes, and Julie came to mind. Memories of her passed quickly through his mind. As Kelsie began kissing him.

"I'm sorry, Kelsie, I can't do this." He stopped her.

"Julie thinks we are having an affair, and I assume she kicked you out," Kelsie asked in exasperation. She pulled his face into her breasts. "Why do you remain faithful to her? It makes me want you that much more, but I realize now I will never compete."

As he stood to go, she wrapped her arms around his neck. "Just one more for the memory?" Kelsie pleaded. He considered for a second, and then he kissed her deeply. Then, without one more word, he left her naked and alone.

CHAPTER XIII: AN APOCALYPSE?

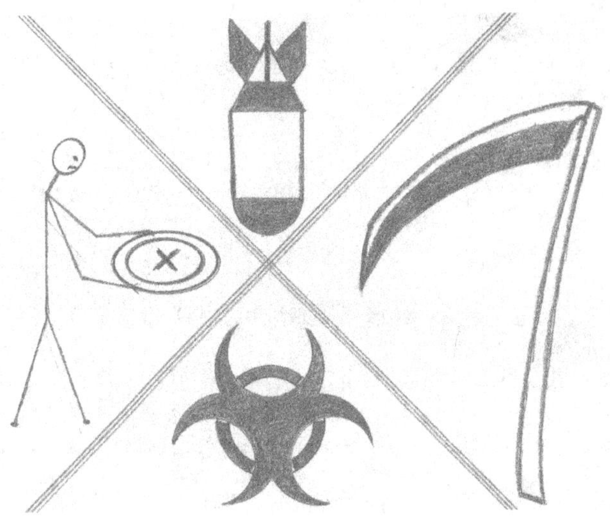

Time Cops

"**S**O AGENT GILLAM, YOU lost them?" KATHERINE said.

"Agent Cavendish, they were on a whole 'nother level. Without hesitation, they jumped from that roof to that window." Gillam said, indicating the buildings on opposite sides of the street. "They had to be Babylonian spies."

"How long after this amazing feat did the containment units move in?" George inquired.

"Maybe two minutes, Agent Cavendish."

"And still, you lost them." Katherine accused.

"You would've lost them too." Gillam flared.

"Why don't you step aside, Agent Gillam? The professionals will handle this from here." Katherine pushed past him.

She had been an agent for the Time Enforcement Agency of Atlantis, or TEA, for over 50 years since its founding. And she had more than a century of martial arts training taught by Melina, the famous priestess of the gods. Everyone knew she was the best agent in all of Atlantis. After she fell through time, Melina took her under her wing. Helped give her life meaning.

"Do you think this is time-related?" Lord George Cavendish asked.

"It's hard to say, but the extraordinary circumstances are enough for me to take jurisdiction."

"Do you think it's possible this is Avalon?"

"George, you need to drop this Avalon thing. I spent a century looking for that bitch, training, preparing. I became obsessed. It nearly consumed me. Don't let that happen to you. If they show up at some point, we will definitely kill them. But until then, drop it."

"Did forensics turn up anything?" Katherine asked the scene commander.

"There's nothing that would relate to our suspects."

Katherine scoped out the scene and determined where they would go. She followed the stairs to an exit door into an alley.

"Which way do you think they went?" George asked.

She saw some vagrants talking around a fire.

"Hello, did any of you see two people come through here in the last hour?"

"We didn't really get a good look at them," one man said.

"All we can say is it was a man and a woman," another man added.

"Did they happen to dispose of anything in your fire?" Katherine inspected the ash at the bottom of the fire.

"They threw some clothes into the fire." The first man admitted. She looked toward both ends of the alley. The streets were packed with people. She looked back at the fire.

"Want us to take them in for questioning?"

"Yes, and confiscate the contents of this fire."

"What did you find out?" Secretary of Defense Amelia Marino asked as Katherine entered The Central Defense Administration building. "Did you apprehend our assailants?"

"They eluded the hapless Central Intelligence agents, leaving behind no trace of evidence—no footprints, fingerprints, or forensic clues. The only available leads are surveillance videos capturing their distant leap across the street and accounts from a few vagrants who witnessed their departure from the building. However, none of these witnesses managed to get a clear view," Katherine said.

"Sounds like the super top-secret agents of Babylon. Do we know what information was stolen?"

"None. From what we could find, nothing was taken or left."

"Nothing?" Secretary Marino squinted at her.

"We had tech do a full sweep scan of every file in the main frame, which matched the previous audit. We must have found them before they could take anything."

"Do we know how they beat the firewalls?"

"It was sourced out of a Babylonian tech firm."

"So, do you think it was Babylonian spies?"

"Maybe, or maybe that's what someone wants us to think."

"All right, keep me apprised of your investigation."

"Will do." Katherine stepped out into the hallway.

"I swear, it's amateur hour in our intelligence agencies. Why do I always have to do everyone else's job for them?" Katherine was frustrated.

"Katherine, you know the answer to that question. You're obviously the most talented agent in the world," George was trying to cheer her up.

"Thanks, love. Now I think we deserve a break." She led him into her office.

He picked her up and cleared her desk with one swipe. He laid her on the desk and then ripped her blouse open. She wrapped her legs around his waist. They proceeded to make use of her entire office. He grabbed her breasts from behind and pushed her to the couch. He bent her over the arm and took her from behind. He was rough with her, and that was how she liked it.

As they lay exhausted on the couch. George asked. "Ever think of going back? To our time period, I mean."

"At first, I did, but the longer I was here, the more I realized there was nothing to go back to. Then you came, and it didn't matter after that. And there is also the fact that here in Atlantis, women are accepted doing nearly anything," she replied in consideration. "That still doesn't mean I hate that bitch any less," she added, with a hint of fire in her voice. "After I fell to this time and place. The transition wasn't easy. Lady Avalon still ruined my life; she took everything from me." Katherine was becoming angry. "I digress... I've lived here for over a century. There's nothing to go back to." There was fire in her voice.

"Right you are. We shall devote our efforts to the forthcoming Apocalypse."

"Agreed. Stop this doomsday we must," Katherine looked out of the window.

An Apocalypse?

"This council is convened to determine the veracity of the Time Enforcement Agency." The council chairwoman, Parisa Maximus, said in opening. "Lady Cavendish, I have long doubted the validity of the evidence of temporal marauders."

"Madam Chairman, I myself am a temporal marauder," Katherine said in annoyance.

"That has long been your claim. Is it possible you fabricated the story?"

"Absolutely not! I didn't realize, Madam Chairman, that you had decided to become a science denier. We already possess a foolproof method for detecting interlopers."

"I've reviewed all of the scientific data. And it's all conjecture," Councilwoman Kiya Rashida challenged.

"Kiya, we've known each other for nearly a century. After all these years are you now going to call me a liar?"

"And what about me?" Lord George interjected. "I know some of you have tried to say that because Katherine has been here since before solid record-keeping and the creation of the agency. That there is room for doubt. But I am certain that you have all seen my file. I did not exist in this time and place before three years ago."

"That's quite enough, my Lord," Parisa said loudly. "You were not addressed. Glitches in the data files could explain the absence of your documentation. The central government can no longer waste resources on unnecessary agencies like yours, Lady

Cavendish."

"So you're not concerned about temporal interlopers?"

"Even if they are coming here, we fail to see a significant threat." Councilwoman Sinaya Ozeri said directly.

"What about the forthcoming Apocalypse?" Lord George cut in.

"The Council need not concern themselves with crazy theories." Katherine gave him a sharp look. "It is important to understand who these people are. And what kind of threat they might pose."

"Wait, what Apocalypse?" Parisa asked.

"It's nothing but wild speculation. Nothing to concern the Council."

"My Lord George, you will explain yourself," Kiya ordered.

"Kiya—"

"Katherine... I was addressing your husband."

Lord George looked nervously at Katherine, then said. "There's a prophecy, around a century old. That says, Atlantis is doomed."

"A prophecy?" Councilwoman Gloria Speier interjected.

"It's not just a prophecy. Time travelers like myself have no knowledge that any of this society was ever here. And I'm from the future. So obviously, all of this gets destroyed, somehow," George concluded.

"Aside from my skepticism of your claim to being from the future, who is the purveyor of this prophecy? Some charlatan?" Councilman Raiden Hirano challenged.

George looked at Katherine. She considered for a moment, then said, "Melina Hellas."

The members of the Council were suddenly much more interested.

"Melina is the prophet? I expected you to say it was this Noah or some other doomsday zealot." Councilwoman Speier raised a brow.

"If Melina is the prophet, then we must take it seriously," Councilwoman Ozeri stated with certainty.

"We must question Melina directly regarding this matter," Chairwoman Maximus agreed.

"Madam Chairwoman, Melina is currently incommunicado," Katherine informed them.

"Do you know her whereabouts?"

"She is on a multi-year sabbatical. She did not inform me of her intended destination."

"I will instruct Central Intelligence to locate Melina Hellas."

"In the meantime, Katherine, we will hear your version of this prophecy," Councilwoman Rashida instructed.

"All of you know of Melina's reputation as the Oracle. She has a nearly perfect record of foresight. The very first time I met her. She told me that Atlantis might be doomed. Over the last century, she began giving me more detailed predictions. I will summarize what she has told me over the years. The last time I talked to her, she told me it would be sometime in the next ten years. The cause was unclear to her, but she was certain that it would cause absolute and total destruction of the entire world. She said there would be survivors, but they would number less than 100." Katherine paused to determine if the Council believed her. "This is one of the primary missions of the Time Enforcement Agency."

"If that's true, how come this is the first time we're hearing about this?" Parisa asked skeptically.

"With the likes of this Noah running around spreading dooms-day propaganda, I was worried this wouldn't be taken seriously."

"May I speak?" Lord George asked.

"My Lord." Kiya Rashida indicated for him to proceed.

"Whatever this apocalypse is, it dramatically changes the face of the earth. In our time, in place of the Atlantic passage, there is an ocean. And the color of the sky is blue, not green. The only reference to Atlantis is from a Greek philosopher, some 2000 years before our time." He indicated himself and Katherine. "Most people think Atlantis is a myth."

The Council whispered amongst themselves. "My Lord and Lady Cavendish, this Council orders you to redouble your efforts in this matter." Councilwoman Speier instructed.

"We must locate Melina Hellas." Councilman Hirano stated definitively.

"While I remain rather skeptical of all of this, we will err on the side of caution. You will have all the resources you need... At least until we question Melina. This Council is adjourned." Chairwoman Maximus stated affirmatively.

Prophecies

"Why did you do that?" Katherine asked GEORGE, a little sharply for his taste.

"Do what?" He replied in turn.

"You risked making us look the fool to the Council."

"I did what was necessary, and you only look the fool if you are wrong. And I am never wrong."

"Lord Avalon made you look the fool."

"He was an arrogant liar. Those fools on the jury believed the lie."

"If that makes you feel better." She just had to have the last word.

"Whatever, where are we going?"

"Eden, we need to talk to this Noah."

A few hours later, they arrived in Eden. "El Bio Laboratories? This is where we are going to find our prophet?" Lord George was confused.

"This is where they said he was. Mr. Noah El?" Katherine inquired at front receiving.

"Do you have an appointment?"

"We are with the Central Bureau. Agents Cavendish."

"Ariella El, at your service." A woman emerged from an office. "Right this way." Ariella led them to an elevator.

"Do you own this place?" George asked.

"My father does. What do you want to talk to my father about?"

"His prophecies," George replied simply. He didn't appreciate the amused look on her face.

"My father gave that up years ago."

At that moment, a man met them, coming in the other direction. "Mr. El? A few moments of your time?" Katherine said.

"Thank you, Ariella." Mr. El dismissed Ariella. "What's this about?"

"We are from the Central Bureau... You spent the better part of the century proclaiming the world would end if people didn't repent their wicked ways." Katherine began.

"And now the government has decided to take it seriously?" Mr.

El laughed.

"Why did you stop evangelizing? What, did the world finally correct their evil ways?" George asked snidely.

"No, not that it matters."

"You honestly believe it? Don't you, Mr. El?" Katherine charged.

"You don't have to believe me. I gave up the campaign five years ago. The world's fate is already set. Nothing can prevent what's coming."

"And what is coming?" George asked nervously.

"A reckoning for the wicked. And Lord and Lady Cavendish. Those badges won't protect you from God's wrath."

"And when should we expect God's wrath?" Katherine asked.

"I cannot say, but in less than a decade, of that, I am certain. Now, if you will excuse me, I have much work to do." Mr. El walked into the labs.

"So what now?" Lord George asked.

"Onto the next. He's not the only doomsayer."

They spent the next couple of years tracking down every soothsayer and charlatan on the planet.

They arrived at a notorious prophet's compound in China. "Hold your fire!" Katherine yelled. "We just want to talk!"

"Sure you do!" A man said behind them. George heard the click of the gun.

"Lower your gun, and we will leave," George said calmly.

"You're not going anywhere."

"You will release us, or something bad will happen," Katherine warned.

The man ignored the warning. He pushed them with his gun from behind, through the gate and into the compound.

As the gates closed, Katherine suddenly confronted the man. She swiftly slid down in front of him, turned his gun upward, and shot him in the head. They drew their guns and methodically swept the compound, eliminating the enemy. George sometimes questioned Katherine's excessive response. But Katherine never took kindly to being fired upon. This wasn't the first time she had gone total war on an enemy.

As they were leaving the compound, George turned to Katherine. "Was it necessary to kill everyone?"

"If you leave one alive, they might come seeking vengeance in the future. I have no interest in constantly looking over my shoulder," Katherine replied sharply. "If they hadn't shot at us, we wouldn't have killed them."

George did love Katherine, but it was only after they were married that her bloodthirsty side had come out. And she was by far the most lethal killer he had ever seen. He certainly never wanted to be on the wrong side of her.

As they were returning to Atlantis, Katherine informed him, "We are making a stop at The Temple of the Gods."

Upon entering the temple, Katherine asked. "Is Melina back from her sabbatical yet?"

"Yes, she returned last night; she's in the inner sanctum." The receiving priestess, Reilia, directed them.

"Katherine, am I to believe you've been waiting for me?" Melina asked in English as they entered the sanctum.

"Melina, long have we awaited thy return."

"You are concerned about the prophecy? The God's failure to return has doomed Atlantis. The impending apocalypse is now inevitable."

"There is not that can be done?" George asked with alarm.

"That is why I took an extended sabbatical. I return now to make final preparations." Melina had an air of resigned finality.

"Something can be done! Surely." Katherine argued.

"It is now our fate. I am occupied." Melina indicated for them to leave.

They nearly ran into a man as they walked out of the chamber. "Gabriel?" Katherine said in surprise.

"Lady Cavendish, as fiercely beautiful as ever."

"How dare you address my wife in such a fashion!"

"Oh, I apologize, my Lord, Gabriel Maximus, at your service. Lady Katherine and I go way back." Gabriel gave a devious smile, and then he winked.

Lord George was incensed. He tried to hit Gabriel. Gabriel caught his fist and easily overpowered him. Gabriel had him around the neck. It felt like he might break it.

"Gabriel, stop!" Katherine grabbed Gabriel's arm.

"Katherine, when you're finished with your toy, you'll be back." Gabriel laughed, then threw George to the ground. George saw him give Katherine a wink, and then Gabriel left.

"You were with that psycho?"

"That was a long time ago. But you should be careful. Gabriel is a cold-blooded killer. He won't hesitate for a second to kill you." Katherine had a slight quiver in her voice. In the entire time he was with Katherine, George had never seen her afraid of anyone before.

"We need to warn the Council of Melina's warning," Katherine stated as they left The Temple of the Gods.

CHAPTER XIV: RECONCILIATION

The Cult of Tartarus(Mars)

MELINA returned to The Temple of the Gods after explaining her visions of the impending doom before the Council of Atlantis.

"Melina, there are some people here who wish to consult with you," Reilia informed her.

"Send them in."

Melina sometimes grew tired of the nearly constant requests for her advice. Over the past few centuries, she earned the moniker "The Oracle" as her prophetic dreams consistently became known to come true. Coupled with her association with the gods and her status as the world's oldest woman, people from all walks of life desire to consult with her about their endeavors.

"Mrs. Camilla Salenius, it is the height of honor to come before the Oracle." Mrs. Salenius said, bowing before her. There were a dozen or so followers behind her, mimicking her. "We have come seeking the priestess to the gods' wisdom. We prepare to embark on a perilous voyage to the solar system's fourth planet, Tartarus, which we believe is the literal abode of the God Iapetus. Do you have any visions to share concerning our pilgrimage?"

Melina went into her special meditation chamber. She sat cross-legged and closed her eyes. She felt herself float up; she opened her eyes. The green vortex of the gods swirled around her. In the vortex, she saw a large face buried beneath the sand. It must be the face of Iapetus, she thought. She saw an advanced space station on the adjacent plateau; it was circular and had a large glass dome. And there was a city of pyramids next to it on the plateau.

"You will be successful on your pilgrimage. The face of Iapetus shall you see. Great honor will you bring him." Melina prophesied from her Oracle circle.

Melina came back down. "Camilla Salenius, go and bring honor to the gods."

"Praise be to the Oracle," Mrs. Salenius said, bowing. Then, the group left.

As the long day of foresight ended, Melina just wanted to relax, as she walked into the rotunda.

"Melina Hellas, it's been too long." She heard Gabriel say.

"Gabriel, I wish I could say the same."

"You're not still upset about the last time, are you? That was five years ago."

"You nearly killed me. And I haven't lived nine centuries to have you kill me with your overzealousness. Or maybe it was more sinister than that."

"You think I was trying to kill you?"

"For a minute there, I wasn't sure." Melina rubbed her neck.

"We've known each other for 900 years. We are like family."

"Sometimes I wonder if you actually see it that way. Sometimes, you scare me."

Gabriel squeezed her shoulder. "I apologize if I've ever made you feel that way. On a different note, I bring great news. Our Goddess of Love and Beauty has graced us again with her presence."

"Aphrodite has returned?"

"For almost four years now."

"Four years? Have you seen them?"

"I had no interest in Koios. But I have visited Aphrodite. She is now, of course, the most famous singer in the world."

"Where are they?"

"They live in The Penthouse of the Gods. At Gods Plaza in central Atlantis."

"I have to go!"

Melina landed on one of the landing pads at The Penthouse of the Gods. As she stepped out, a servant came to greet her.

"Melina Hellas!" The servant reacted in surprise. Then she led Melina inside. "Right this way... Mrs. Hall, Melina Hellas is here."

"Melina?!... Thank you, Bernice." Aphrodite said, dismissing her. "So you have returned from your sabbatical?"

"My apologies, Aphrodite, I needed to get away. I'm under a lot of pressure." Melina closed her eyes.

"What's burdening you?"

"Ever since we last parted ways almost 450 years ago, I have had visions. They call me the Oracle. I can literally see future events. There is a looming apocalypse. And now you've returned, but it's too late. There's no stopping it. And the burden is mine to bear. Where's Koios? He will know what's coming. The force of the future overwhelms me."

"Koios is... Pursuing other interests."

"When will he be back?"

"I don't know, he's been gone for a couple of weeks now. How did you know where I was?"

"Gabriel, he gave me a visit. He said he had visited you. Aphrodite, he's dangerous. And he's obsessed with you. Belief in you has become so small. You may be vulnerable in your weakened state." Melina warned. She could tell something had happened between Aphrodite and Koios. "I will let you get back to whatever I interrupted... I'll see you soon?"

"Of course, it was good to see you again Melina," Aphrodite said obviously distracted.

Melina wondered what could have come between Aphrodite and Koios. They had been together for thousands of years. She would never presume to intrude into the business of the gods. But she did need to find Koios as soon as possible. Only he would know the truth of the coming apocalypse.

Separation

JULIE woke up to an empty bed again. She realized she knew Micheal well enough to know he may be gone for good. She wasn't sure how to feel about such a possibility. If it remained a permanent arrangement, was she now stuck in the 24th century BC? But she also knew she would have trouble forgiving him for his likely betrayal.

Further study of the evidence wasn't as convincing as she had originally thought. But she still leaned toward the idea he had cheated. She hadn't heard from Micheal in over a month and, despite everything, she missed him. So she had taken to watching the Delta tabloid shows, hoping for news of him.

She turned on the TV.

The TV said. "... Obviously, the daily headline... Which Delta star was murdered by the Phantom today? ...Gisilia Marshall has been one of the top-selling vocalists for decades. And it still appears that the authorities are helpless to stop the slaughter... The only person of interest, Kingu Valor, is still avoiding the media since his release. And so is his accuser... And that brings us to the ongoing saga of Delta's golden couple, Avalon. All appearances are canceled until further notice. Julie Hall has locked herself away in her ivory tower in Atlantis. And sightings of Micheal Hall have been exceedingly rare. But we did track down the other woman, Kelsie Ambrose, for comment. "I had thought of Julie as a friend, but I have been enraptured with Micheal since our first meeting." "Is there any truth to the rumored affair?" "All I will say is I did pursue it..."

Julie shut off the TV in frustration.

Several more weeks passed with desperately little new information. Julie was barely sleeping as the nightmares of old came back to haunt her. The longer this situation went on, the more she missed him and the less she cared about his violation of trust. She just wanted him to come back to her.

Julie had been cooped up in the penthouse for weeks, so she wanted to do something else to take her mind off the situation.

She had spent a few hours visiting Melina and other priestesses at The Temple of the Gods. She used her special access to visit Empress Regina.

She went back to the penthouse. After another sleepless night she decided to try something different. She went to the Southern Point Promontory, on the Isle of Krios. It was the southern tip of the southernmost island in the Atlantean Megacity. It was similar to The Pinnacle in Delta, and it was reserved exclusively for the upper class. So, she might find some solitude.

Julie stepped out of her hover car and the wind gusted to meet her. Musty humidity tickled her tongue as she breathed deeply. To the west, she saw an anvil climbing into the sky. A shelf cloud rapidly slid in, overhead. And the misty darkness foretold rain. She figured, just as well. The sky reflected the way she felt.

What was her life going to be now? She was trying to contemplate an answer when the first drops disguised her tears. She closed her eyes and let the rain and wind clean her mind of her thoughts.

Julie's storm therapy was interrupted. "The whore of Delta reaping a taste of her comeuppance."

She opened her eyes and found Daniel Woods looming nearby. He was the man who exploded on her a few years earlier when she didn't immediately accommodate his request to give his wife a break into Delta.

"You have no right to be here." She took a defensive stance.

"The bitch still thinks she's superior. Thanks to you, I had plenty of time to work my way into the inner circle of the Imperial Council. And you don't need to worry about me harming you, yet. I'm content to allow you to suffer your bastard husband's infidelity. Love the constant speculation about your shattered life."

Julie realized he was still threatening her. But he was also accusing her of something.

"Wow, a pathetic loser who can't accept reality, and blames everyone else for his problems. And threatening celebrities when the Phantom is on the loose. People might come to some dangerous conclusions."

"Your rejection caused Ruth to kill herself! Justice won't be served until the photos of your corpse are splashed across the tabloids. The Phantom is vengeance sent by the gods. I have celebrated the death of every one of those whores. But make no mistake, it will be me who stands over you, gazing into your lifeless eyes."

She felt sick for a moment. She had no reason to doubt his claim about his wife.

"I'm going to notify the authorities about your threats."

"By all means, see what happens. I'll see you soon."

Daniel winked, then walked off, washing out into the rain.

Julie took a deep breath, then quickly found her transport.

On her way back to the penthouse, she researched Daniel and confirmed Ruth's suicide. She also learned that he was in a relationship with Parisa Maximus. She was Gabriel's daughter and head of the Atlantean Council. No wonder he felt immune. She would need concrete proof. Was he the Phantom? Or could it be Kingu? Or perhaps someone else?

She felt more alone than ever. Where was Micheal?

MICHEAL spent nearly two months avoiding the paparazzi by living in his stretched limo. With the autopilot, he was able to avoid people nearly completely. When the bullshit story first broke, he was completely innocent. And he had intended to go away for a few days to let her cool down. But then his solitude had been interrupted by Kelsie, and in a moment of weakness, he had nearly slept with her.

Even though he stopped, it was too late. The more he thought about it, the more he realized he had violated his vows to Julie. If he had had doubts before about his worthiness of her. They were gone. He knew now he wasn't worthy. He knew he couldn't face her. But the fact that they were inextricably tied at the hip by temporal mechanics would have to be dealt with. But at least he had about five years to do so.

He decided he would sneak into the penthouse when she wasn't there. Gather a few of his things. And leave a note explaining their new arrangement. He circled over Atlantis a few times until he saw Julie's car leave the penthouse.

He went and landed; then he quickly went through his stuff. He loaded up all his most prized possessions in the limo. Then, he made one final trip to place the letter on her bed. He grabbed the last couple of things and headed for the landing pad.

Reconciliation

JULIE returned to the depressing penthouse as she exited the glass-floor courtyard. She thought she might have heard something. She followed the noise to the Lord's suite. As she exited the staircase, he was there.

"Micheal?" Julie said to stop him in his tracks.

He didn't look at her. "Just pretend you didn't see me..." He replied sadly. "Please?"

She ignored it. "How are you?"

He was quiet for a minute. "You don't want to talk to me." He said with certainty. "Everything is explained in the letter on your bed," he said dismissively, as he began to head to the stairs.

"Micheal, stop! Will you talk to me? Please?"

"What's there to talk about?" he asked, finally turning to look at her.

"We've been married for 20 years. It should be discussed before one of us just decides to end it."

"I am not worthy of you; that's clear now. The last 20 years were all a sham. So what else is there to talk about?" Micheal averted his eyes.

"I decide who is worthy of me... What happened in Tycho with Kelsie? And I want the truth."

He seemed to consider whether to 'discuss this'. "We did the photo shoot. And she, as usual, was trying to seduce me. I, as usual, denied her. Then she kissed me in front of the cameras, likely on purpose. Then I left... Are you happy?"

She wholeheartedly felt he was telling the truth, but she was confused by his protestation of unworthiness. "I want you to tell me every lurid detail of the interactions between you and Kelsie over the years."

"Not that it matters. But since you asked."

She closed her eyes, preparing for the onslaught.

"Kelsie said our kiss in the skit, swept her off her feet. So when we were trapped in the cave in Celtic, she removed her clothes in an effort to seduce me—" He was saying.

"That bitch!" Julie interrupted. "Sorry."

"So I, of course, rejected her out of hand. Then, she made another attempt every time we were alone together, and every time I rejected her. Then the picture circulated and you assumed the worst. Then you don't let me explain myself."

"Why were you delayed in Tycho? Both of you missed a press event."

"Kelsie earned her awakening, the night after the shoot. I helped her transition."

"After my experiences with that, I can understand her heightened desire for you. If you always rejected her, then how are you not worthy of me? And also, if you're so innocent, why didn't you inform me of her relentless pursuit of you?"

"In hindsight, maybe I should have. But there was never a chance I would give in, so I considered it mostly harmless. Hence meaningless. So, I wasn't forthcoming with you, contributing to my lack of worthiness. But the primary reason is that after you kicked me out, I flew to Delta, not necessarily intentionally. I just flew at random and happened to end up in Delta..." As he was explaining, her stomach began to sink. Because the photos, apparently innocent photos, were not the end of the story. "When I realized I was in Delta, I went to The Pinnacle for solitude, to think. Maybe half an hour later, Kelsie showed up—"

"That bitch is relentless."

"Not this time. She honestly was surprised to find me there. She apologized for her actions and was about to leave. In my despair and anger towards you, I decided that if you were going to believe that about me. And not let me explain that I might as well get the experience of which I was convicted."

She had to fight to control the thoughts and feelings welling up inside her.

"I told Kelsie to take me back to her place. We kissed; she took her clothes off. She climbed on my lap, facing me as I sat on the bed... I had my hands all over. We kissed again, Then I realized I couldn't go through with it. I apologized to her and left..." He paused, shaking his head. "As I flew around in the limo that night, I realized that even though I had stopped, it was too late. I have violated your trust. So, any doubts I still had about my unworthiness of you were gone. And I had to accept that the illusion I have lived in for the past 20 years had crumbled to the ground."

Her fury had risen as he had been detailing his interactions with Kelsie. She was about to explode when he described his withdrawal. And now she truly feared he was saying goodbye.

"We both know the times and locations. There is no obligation for us to be together all the time." He was saying goodbye.

"The hell there isn't!" She cut in sharply, surprising him. "You swore an oath, till death do we part. You promised to love me now, and till the end of time. Are you going to go back on your word?"

"I already did. That's why I'm not worthy. You have to release me of my vows."

"I refuse! I declare your protestations of unworthiness to be a lie. You swore to me, and I still hold you to your vows. Are you a man of your word or not?" She challenged. He hung his head, not looking at her. "Micheal, answer me," she demanded. "Swear to me again,"

He closed his eyes, took a deep breath, and then looked at her. He seemed to be studying her face, deciding on how to respond. Then he said. "Julie Alexandra Buckingham Hall, I love thee now and till the end of time." The tears on his cheeks were contagious.

Her tears flowed as her façade of strength came crashing down. "Micheal William Hall, I love thee now and till the end of time." She promised in return.

He dropped what he was holding and met her in the middle with his lips. She jumped up, wrapping her legs around his waist. He carried her into the Lord's suite. They were passionately kissing the entire way. He set her down, and she began ripping his clothes off while he was ripping hers off.

Months of pent-up passion erupted to the surface like molten lava as they couldn't keep their hands off each other. He delved into her mind, body, and soul without exchanging a word. He turned her around and took her from behind, handling her roughly by grabbing her breasts and pulling her close, their bodies pressed tightly together, showing his impressive stamina even after another release. Then, it was her turn. She pushed him flat on the bed, mounted him, and went full cowgirl.

He was like the Energizer Bunny as they tried to fit the last two months' drought into one night. After utilizing nearly every position in *Kamasutra*, they were thoroughly spent. Exhausted by a cathartic release, they collapsed together.

Julie woke to Micheal looking at her. "How can you forgive me?" He looked away.

"Am I happy you did what you did? No. But I know you wouldn't have done that if I had put more trust in you." She shook her head. "I suppose my jealousy of Kelsie clouded my judgment. I should have let you explain."

He brushed the hair out of her face. "You have nothing to be jealous of. You're a thousand times more beautiful than she is. I was never once tempted."

"Until that night."

"That wasn't a temptation. I wanted to punish you for your lack of faith in me. But then I couldn't go through with it."

"She is a beautiful woman and in your state of mind and her naked at your disposal, most men couldn't have stopped. It reminds me of that one night between us, maybe 25 years ago. I still can't believe you were able to stop." She shook her head, smiling. "I realize you have likely punished yourself more than I ever would have. And I understand your desire to punish me. And I am even more grateful that you stopped yourself." Julie sighed deeply.

"So am I."

"But one last thing. Don't you ever leave me like that again. I might say things when I'm emotional that I don't entirely mean. But when we've settled down. You come back, and we talk about whatever our problems are."

"I'm still not sure—"

"And don't you dare say such a thing to me again!" She interjected sharply. "It's you and me, forever."

"I love you, Jules, more than words can say." He said, seemingly relieved. He began running his fingers through her hair.

"I will never stop loving you," she said softly. After a moment of quiet consolation. "There's still something I need to know?" She looked up at him.

"Okay?"

"Where have you been living these past two months?"

He considered for a moment. "The limo." He shrugged.

"Micheal!" She shook her head. "Silly man." She laughed.

The Cavendishes

"What is Babylon planning?" KATHERINE demanded.

"I will never tell you anything." Babylonian agent Kishara Iltani stonewalled. "You know I can't."

"Kishara, the world is at stake. Tell me what I need to know, or I will have to eliminate you." She had Kishara bound to a chair.

"Katherine, we've known each other for decades. I've helped you time and again. You know I can't tell you that kind of information."

"Our friendship doesn't change what I will have to do. Kishara, last chance."

"I can't, Katherine."

"This saddens me, Kishara, but I have to."

"Katherine, please—" Kishara began to plead.

Katherine wrapped a thin wire around Kishara's neck a few times and began to strangle her to death. A few minutes later, Kishara stopped kicking. She held it another minute to be sure. Katherine confirmed Kishara was dead, then left her body so the Babylonians would find it.

"Darling wife, what joy thy return brings. Didst thee kill anyone this day?" George asked in English as she entered their home. They always spoke English at home.

"I did kill Kishara Iltani."

"Sadness does that bring. I did like Kishara." George said sadly. "Supper have I made thee."

"My Lord does spoil me." Katherine smiled.

"My Lady Cavendish, thee is above all else."

"Obvious, that is."

"As a princess, thee should be treated."

"My dear, no progress hast thou made in discovery of our impending doom?" They cut into their stakes.

"Darling, might I have salt? And nay... Madmen have been spent. Other paths do I tread. Theory, have I developed. Of men do I see this apocalypse spring forth."

"Deep cover spies thou pursue in effort of information."

"Many friends might I needs kill in pursuit of knowledge," Katherine said with a sense of sadness. Many of her associates she had known for decades. Her superior nature precluded friend-ships with nearly all government agents of Atlantis. They were far too beneath her to be worthy of her attention. Does a person have care of a fly? Her top-level counterparts in foreign governments were the only ones worthy of her friendship. She had enjoyed their company regularly over the years. So she was slightly trepidatious at the likelihood she would have to kill most of them.

"My dear, more wine?"

"Darling, I thank thee." She accepted gladly. "Does thee know if Melina has gone to council?"

"Indeed, My Lady, council redoubled our efforts as response. Await here, my Princess, a delight of sweet have I made." He exited to the kitchen.

The dessert was heaven. "'Tis sinfully sweet." She took the last bite.

"Thy lips be sweeter still." George kissed her deeply. "My dessert requires dessert." He said, going to his knees and helping himself to the sweet spot between her legs. Right there at the table.

They proceeded to work off their indulgence for much of the rest of the night.

"How didst thou sleep, my darling," George asked as Katherine came to the breakfast table.

"My Lord of love, 'twas I utterly spent of the night. A sweet slumber did I take." She smiled slightly.

"Thy breakfast, my dear." He sat her down at the table.

As she was finishing her breakfast, George changed the subject. "Hast thou heard of this killer of celebrities? The Phantom, do they call him."

"I care not for celebrities. Nor for he who would kill them." She waved it off.

"Impressed thee will be of this Phantom. In the last year, he has done away with nearly 200 Delta actresses and singers." He tried to convince her.

"Impressive, that is my love, show me."

He turned on the TV. "... Now, for an update on the Phantom. He officially claimed his 200th victim. Dalilah Sabel was found brutally raped and strangled in the Phantom's signature style. Investigators have found no DNA evidence, no forensic evidence, and no fingerprints. The only evidence is the semen samples, but there is not an ounce of usable DNA. Investigators continue to be baffled. The killer truly is like a ghost. So is fittingly dubbed the Phantom..." The TV was saying.

"Were not I so occupied, might I take the challenge of worthy foe," Katherine interjected.

Then she heard the TV say. "...And in happier news, Delta's golden couple of Avalon have survived a rough patch and are about to launch to the moon..."

Katherine couldn't believe it. That bitch Lady of Avalon was here, in the 24th century BC. She turned up the TV. "George! Come see!" She yelled.

The TV said. "...Here are the Halls themselves... We are beyond honored that the Jericho Corporation asked us to be the first to experience the luxury of their new lunar station, the Selene. Lord Avalon said. To experience the amazing array of expeditionary options, we can't wait. The bitch added... They will launch from the God's Portal launch site north of Atlantis in about an hour. now for other news..." She muted the TV.

"How, do I ask, didst we fail to encounter them in plain sight?"

"My dear, care not for celebrity; thou does." George pointed out.

"Kill them, we will. Due diligence must we take."

"Avalon, have I seen in combat, formidable they were. Many years past that was, many more years have they trained."

"Then careful our plans must be. Research Avalon online, we will." She stated definitively. After a century of waiting, the thought of snuffing out that bitch once and for all, sent a thrill through her.

"Three years past, Avalon came, as if from nowhere. Have now moved to the top of the Delta A-list. Presenting themselves as Micheal and Julie Hall. Founders of finance firm 'The Investment Hall' four years past."

"My Lord, apologies do I give to thee. Believe do I that our mystery assailants of building jump some four years past, very likely were Lord and Lady Avalon."

"Should teach thee, my dear, to question my intuition." Lord George stated proudly.

"'Tis why, perfection we make as one."

George came over and wrapped his arms around her from behind. "Pleasure does this opportunity give unto me. Primarily for my Katherine to thy justice. After such delay of patience." He said lovingly. "Of which plan do we employ? Phantom killer shall have them on high alert." She was considering for a moment. "Might I propose the Atlas Awards? Event on Day of Death, security shall have their guard at ease. In for several awards, they are."

"Such a public event?" She questioned with consideration. "I do propose. We commandeer oversight of security. Utilizing element of surprise, do we ambush them. Just enough time shall we have to extinguish them and escape authorities. Deserved public execution, shall they have." She detailed her plan with glee. "Vengeance shall be ours."

"Justice?" George raised a brow.

"No luv, sweet vengeance." They shared a sweet laugh.

To The Moon and Back

-November 12, 2374 BC

" 'Fly me to the Moon'. Never could I have conceived that I would be going to the Moon for my birthday, my 56th birthday. And I have to stop and appreciate the life I have lived. Despite all the horrible things I have gone through over the past 26 years, I have also been able to experience some of the most amazing things that anyone could possibly experience. From meeting my childhood idol Issac Newton. To flying as the goddess Aphrodite. To playing with pegasi in the Garden of Eden with Adam and Eve. Now, I get to take 'one small step' on the moon. What a life I have lived.

Micheal and I went through a rough patch recently. I hope that after 20 years of marriage, we don't begin to tire of each other. We still have more than a century before we get home. I still need to work on my forgiveness for his mild dalliances with Kelsie. I've had my own share of propositions over the last three years. But never let it go that far. I just need to remember to breathe and calm myself.

I look out the window and see how tiny and fragile the Earth looks. I can almost hold it in my hand—a tiny blue ball floating in the vast emptiness of space. I think about how small and insignificant I am; we all are. But I also feel that makes all of us that much more special. And how much I appreciate my life."

MICHEAL looked over, and Julie looked longingly out the window as if something was on her mind. Even though they had made up, he was still unsure how to talk to her. His feelings about the betrayal of her trust had persisted. He closed his eyes and thought of her. How could she still love him? His many horrible shortcomings and weaknesses. He knew still, more than ever, that he wasn't worthy.

"We are on final approach," the Captain announced, breaking his train of thought.

As they touched down, Micheal couldn't help but say. "And the Eagle has landed." He gave a mild laugh.

"Can you help me with my suit?" Julie asked.

"Of course." He lent a hand. "It's time to put on our Avalon faces."

He took his first steps on the Moon. He stared across the crater floor toward the horizon, and the first thought that came to mind was 'magnificent desolation'. A slight thrill ran down his spine. When he was young, he had dreamed of going to space. When he dropped out of high school then never went to college, he saw that dream disappear. Then, 15 years ago, he was finally able to get there. But even then, he never thought he would be here.

They did some publicity for a few hours before finally entering the space station.

"Meet in the observatory in one hour," the PR rep for Jericho Corporation instructed.

"Pretty nice for a space station," Micheal commented in English. Their suite had four rooms. The entry lounge was 10 by 20 feet, and at one end was a kitchen. Behind the kitchen was the bathroom, which was about 10 by 10 feet and included a jacuzzi. Behind the bathroom was the bedroom, which was also perhaps 10 by 20 feet. Across the hall from the bathroom was an airlock, about 10 by 7 feet, providing private access to the outside. The entire suite was approximately 20 by 30 feet or about 600 feet squared.

"Micheal, we can't continue like this."

"Like what?" He feigned ignorance.

"Don't play stupid with me. You forget, I know how you think. The one who needs to forgive you is you."

"I know that's not completely true. You still haven't fully forgiven me, and I completely understand."

"You're right. In spite of everything, you still hurt me more than

I could have imagined." tears came to her eyes. "But I truly and completely forgive you. And the only thing I want for my birthday is my Micheal back. And he will always be distant until you forgive him."

"How can I forgive him?" He dropped his head.

She came over and took his face in her hands, bringing him up to look at her.

"Because, Micheal William Hall, I know what is in your heart. I know how much you love me. You're a good man. And I do forgive you. And I love you with all my heart. And that is the only thing that you have to think about. My forgiveness reaches into your flawless memory and washes the slate clean. So, in my eyes, you never broke trust. We both made mistakes, but after it all, what remains is 20 years of the most tender love any two people could ever share. I love you, and you love me, and that's all that matters." She kissed him. "Come back to me, please."

He couldn't stop the tears from flowing. The power of her forgiveness overwhelmed him. How could he deny her plea? He would fight his inner demons for her.

"I will try with everything I am to be worthy of such love, of such forgiveness. I love you, Jules. And tonight, we will celebrate the most special day in the history of the world."

They just held each other for a while. Finally, she said, "I think it's time to go."

"Greetings from Selene; here on the Moon, we are in the observatory and have the most amazing view of a crescent Earth," Julie said with a smile.

"And here in the observatory, we can take full advantage of the low gravity field. Now, on Earth, I can jump around four to five feet. The top of the observatory dome is about 35 feet high. And on the moon, I can jump six times higher. Can I touch that ceiling?"

Micheal jumped, floated up to the top of the dome, and easily touched the glass.

Upon landing. "That was about 10 seconds of air time," he said with a smile.

They proceeded to take the viewers back on Earth on a tour of the space station, The Selene. When they were finished, they returned to their suite.

"Do you wanna take a walk?" Micheal asked Julie.

They suited up and exited through the airlock.

"This is so amazing," Julie said as they walked along the crater floor.

"It feels like we're the only people in the universe right now."

"If we were, I would still be the happiest woman. My Micheal has come back to me."

She had felt that he was mostly back to his old self again.

"I do always try to give my love what she wants on her special day," he replied tenderly. "Wanna test the jet pack?"

They flew up for a few minutes before landing on the crater's rim. They sat on the rim, looking across the crater. The Selene was glowing in the lunar night. Then, in an instant, the sun rose on the black horizon. A shiver passed through her as she considered all the incredible things she had experienced. Then, as if reading her mind, Micheal said. "Hell of a life"

"Hell of a life."

Upon their return to Earth, they spent a week in adjustment to the heavier gravity field. Then, it was on to the press circuit.

"Welcome back to Atlantis Today, joining us now, just returned from the Moon, it's Delta's golden couple, Avalon. Julie, Micheal, thank you for being here."

"Thank you for having us again, Ellencia," Julie replied.

"So what was the moon like?"

"It was like a world of extreme juxtaposition. During the day. The two-week day. The sky is always black except for the sun. And the surface is always bright," Micheal commented.

"Now, on the first day, you claimed you could jump five feet on Earth. Now you've been on this show a few times, and somehow this never came up?"

"Well..." Micheal demurred.

"So I'm about five and a half feet, care to demonstrate?" Ellencia challenged. The crowd cheered.

"Ok, just stand perfectly still," Micheal instructed. He took three big steps and jumped. Bending his knees, he cleared her head by a few inches. To the delight of the crowd.

"That is incredible!"

"Stay there," Micheal instructed. "Wanna see something even more impressive? Julie?" He focused it on her.

She shook her head as she assumed the three quick steps and bound up and over like Micheal.

"As if our favorite couple couldn't be more amazing. Now Avalon is up for three Atlas awards. Do you think you've got it in the bag?"

"We are more than honored to be nominated. All the other nominees are amazing. to be considered in the same company." Julie demurred.

"Now Avalon just passed a milestone. All sales of your first three albums have now surpassed a billion. Only three other albums in history have surpassed a billion in sales. To what do you attribute your incredible success?"

"We have been blessed to have a very close personal connection to our fans." The crowd cheered. "We feel they're like family to us." Julie said to the delight of everyone.

"We wish you the best of luck on death day. And I look forward to seeing your fashion looks. Always a great interview. And when we come back, Avalon will take over the plaza with one of their newest songs." The audience roared, then it cut to a break.

CHAPTER XV: AVALON VS CAVENDISH

ROUND 1

AVALON

VS

CAVENDISH

The Atlas Awards

"**L**ADY AVALON... I CANNOT bide that whore!" KATHERINE seethed in English as she turned off the TV. The whore preening on Atlantis Today, after returning from the Moon.

"Three days longer, my luv."

"Such a fraudulent up-jump." Katherine's hate stewed.

"Plan fully prepared, has it been."

"Three days more and vengeance, shall I have." Katherine's heart raced faster at the thought of throttling Lady Avalon to death.

"You look nervous," MICHEAL pointed out as the limo approached the Pinnacle Theater.

"You know I'm always nervous for a purple carpet walk," Julie explained.

"You know you're a fashion icon."

"That's exactly my problem, knowing everyone is scrutinizing every aspect of me."

"Well, my Aphrodite, the fawning masses await." The door opened.

Three days later, LORD GEORGE did a thorough security walk-through of the Pinnacle Theater. He used it to set the trap for Lord and Lady Avalon. Making sure the back-channel escape was cut off. He locked all the exit doors to the back of the theater.

"So we're going to get that bastard tonight, aren't we?" he asked rhetorically to one of the security lieutenants.

The ruse they were using to get the security team to abandon their positions was that they were laying a trap for the Phantom.

"Julie! MICHEAL! Over here!" The paparazzi screamed as they struck their poses along the purple carpet.

"Avalon!" Ellencia of Atlantis Today summoned them for an interview.

"Wow! Julie, you look amazing! Who are you wearing?"

"Ellencia, it's good to see you again. Avita Leventis is so inspired. I had to have her artistic eye for this most special night." Julie smiled to disguise her aversion to the spotlight.

"I love the lavender, off-the-shoulder look. You are always the epitome of fashion. That clutch is so elegant. Are those diamonds? Such a compliment to the look."

"Accessories make the outfit shine." Julie held out her handbag.

"Julie, how can you stay upright with such a stone on your necklace?"

"Well, I was going to wear my larger version, but there's only so much weight a girl can carry."

"And you're not going to try and jump over me again, are you?" Ellencia pretended to duck.

"Not in this dress."

Ellencia laughed. "Julie, you are the Queen of Delta! The icon of our time!"

"You are too kind, thank you Ellencia."

"And the Prince of Delta, dashing as ever." Ellencia admired Micheal.

"This old thing?" Micheal balked. Everyone laughed.

"I'm not the only fashion maven here." Julie indicated Micheal.

"Good luck tonight... The golden couple of Delta," Ellencia said as they moved on down the carpet.

Julie was basking in the flashes of the paparazzi's cameras. Micheal saw her smile fade and followed her eye. He noticed Kingu in the back of the pack of photographers. He was annoyed that they would let a Phantom suspect be anywhere near such an event.

KATHERINE went over the plan one more time. "So, when they announce the winner of Entertainer of the Year—"

"Which they will certainly win."

"Yes. In the middle of their acceptance speech, I will swing down from the rafters. And using the Babylonian shock technique, I will stun Lady Avalon's legs. When Lord Avalon attempts to intercede, you ambush him. You can at least, with the element of surprise, subdue Lord Avalon, correct?" Katherine pinched her brow.

"Yes." He tried to convince them both.

"I will be sure to knock him off balance for you. Then perhaps with both advantages, you can win."

"You never believe in me."

No, I'm realistic about your capabilities."

"You—"

"Don't you even say it. You know what will happen."

Anytime George wanted to get back at her, he would remind her of how she was from the lower class of society. And the few times he had said it, she retaliated by withholding sex. She deserved to be addressed by Lady. She Knew she had earned it.

Micheal and JULIE sat in the front row. They had already won 'Song of the Year' and 'Music Artist of the Year'. Now they had performed *Faithfully* as one of the finalists for 'Entertainer of the Year'. It was the pinnacle of The Atlas Awards. The winner of Music Artist of the Year, which was them, were up against Screen Artist of the Year, Stage Artist of the Year, Published Artist of the Year, and Tech Artist of the Year.

The host, Apollonia Mencius, one of the top comedians, was in the middle of announcing the finalists. "Screen Artist of the Year, Kelsie Ambrose. And Music Artist of the Year, Avalon." She paused, then announced. "And the winner is... Avalon."

They rose to the celebratory hugs of those in their row. As they made their way to the stage, the side announcer said. "This is Avalon's third win of the night."

As they turned to the crowd, she noticed Daniel Woods sitting with Parisa Maximus in the Imperial Box. He waved at her with a half-smile. She took a deep breath and clenched her fists to maintain her composure.

"Wow! This is such an amazing honor." Micheal began.

"We are blown away by this recognition." Julie took over. "We would like to thank—"

A sudden blur came from her left, interrupting their speech. Julie tried to turn to see what was happening when her legs failed her, and she fell to the stage. She looked over to her left, and Micheal was struggling on the ground with a figure in a full-body catsuit. She looked to the other side, and another figure pulled out a gun and fired it into the air. The theater turned to a panic. Her legs felt numb; she fought desperately to get to her feet. The figure threw the gun away and pounced on her.

KATHERINE was a little surprised by Lady Avalon's skill. Despite her legs hardly working because of the Babylonian shocks Katherine had applied. And despite being dressed in an evening gown. Lady Avalon was still a formidable opponent.

Katherine had to block a torrent of blows. Several even connected. A blow to her face dazed her little. She would need to exploit her minor advantage before it was gone. Luckily, Lady Avalon's slow-reacting legs caused just enough imbalance to allow Katherine to shock her left arm. And yet she still put up an amazing fight. Katherine felt honest respect for such skill. But she still hated the bitch.

Katherine was able to shock her right arm. This increased the advantage, and she was able to sequentially shock the rest of the pressure points on her body. Katherine removed her mask and looked Lady Avalon in the face. "Remember me? I used to be Katherine Talmage. In 1692, you killed my husband. You ruined my life. And now I'm going to take yours in return."

JULIE was confused for a second, then she remembered. It was the wife of Mr. Talmage. He was one of the men she had killed defending herself in the woods outside Boston. Before she could contemplate anything else, Mrs. Talmage pulled out what appeared to be a thin wire and attacked her with it.

Whatever Mrs. Talmage had done to her made her whole body unable to move. Mrs. Talmage sat on her stomach, straddling her, then wrapped the wire around her neck three or four times. As a thin wire bit sharply into her neck, the pain was blinding. When her vision finally cleared, they were face-to-face. There was a look of satisfied glee on Katherine's face.

Julie tried to activate her rings, but they didn't work. She didn't understand. She tried again to no avail. They had always worked before, so it was confusing. Of all the times for the gods' rings not to work, it couldn't be worse.

As the strangulation dragged on, Julie tried to fight through the searing pain. Her legs finally responded, and she temporarily threw Katherine off her. Katherine's attempt to hold on ripped the top of Julie's dress down.

The bitch kicked her off. "No, you don't; this is your public execution." KATHERINE gleefully told the bitch as she reestablished control. She wrapped the wire around her neck a couple more times. Then, straddling her from behind, shoving her knee into Lady Avalon's back, she pulled as hard as she could on the garrote handles.

She saw a beautiful image on the display screen of the camera. A face full of terror and desperation. And the wire was cutting beautifully into the bitch's tender neck. Every time the bitch clawed at her neck, Katherine would shake her to cause her arms to fall to the floor again.

After a few times of this, Katherine pulled the bitch up so her hands couldn't touch the stage. The bitch had given up the struggle. There was one last action to finish the bitch off. She yanked the bitch up hard until her back was pressed against Katherine's stomach. Then she got a good grip on the handles of the garrote and lifted the bitch off the ground, suspending her in the air.

With her last breaths of life draining away, the bitch had one last desperate surge and began kicking desperately for the ground. Feeling the life draining out of Lady Avalon brought a rush of excitement through Katherine.

JULIE clawed desperately at her throat, but Katherine kept jolting her to make her arms fall to the ground again. It had been so long since she had been able to breathe that she found no more fight left in her. She made no further attempt to fight. Katherine throttled her so hard that Julie thought wire would slice right through her throat. But instead, the pressure only increased. She couldn't believe that was possible.

The pain was so terrible that she just wanted to die. Then, it only got worse as she was lifted completely off the ground. She kicked frantically in response. But there was no relief to be found. After what seemed to be another agonizing eternity, the world closed in around her, and everything faded to black.

Lady Avalon's body went limp in her arms. KATHERINE felt total satisfaction as she felt the last breath of life leave the bitch. She decided to hold the bitch high for at least one more minute to be sure she was dead.

There was a sudden movement from Katherine's right. Before she could react, a figure in black plowed into her from the side. She was momentarily stunned. Before she knew what had happened, the figure was on top of her. He neutralized any ability for her to fight back. In a distorted voice, he said. "That is my victim. Only I have the right to kill her." He slipped behind her, putting her in a death grip. He had his arm wrapped around her throat and pushed her head forward with his other arm. After a few moments, she felt her brain shutting down and everything went dark.

Assassins

The TV says: "...Our top story. The Phantom attacked The Atlas Awards last night. The one confirmed victim, Ellencia Beila, long-time host of Atlantis Today, was found in a back room brutally raped and strangled. And there was also a very public attack on Avalon. In front of billions of viewers on live TV, Julie Hall was savagely attacked. An unidentified woman attempted to throttle her with some wire garrote. An unknown individual interceded, but Julie Hall is in critical condition at Delta Central Hospital..."

"The bitch survived!" KATHERINE screamed in frustration.

"Of what dost thou mean?"

"Lady Avalon lives still! And I needn't remind thee of Lord Avalon's survival." She glared.

"At the moment in which I was about to finish him, thee were attacked. To thy aid, did I come. To where dost thou go?" He followed her to the car.

"To Delta Central Hospital, we shall go; we shall finish that which we started last night. Short of all else, Lady Avalon dies!"

MICHEAL woke with a pounding headache. His memory began to return. They were attacked at the awards show. He quickly scanned the room; he didn't see Julie anywhere. He pulled the IV out of his hand and sat up. He took a deep breath and squeezed his eyes tightly to help quell his raging mind.

After a few minutes, he rose to his feet. His head was beginning to clear. Upon returning to the fight in his head, he was certain that the man who attacked him was Lord George Cavendish from the year 1777. He was never able to get a good look at the woman who was attacking Julie. All he needed right now was to find Julie, to make sure she was all right.

KATHERINE and George systematically searched the executive wing of Delta Central Hospital. They eliminated all the security. Then Katherine used her special access clearance to lock down the wing.

She found Lady Avalon, or Julie Hall. Or whoever she claimed to be, it was irrelevant. She looked over the charts and was still confused as to how Lady Avalon was still alive. Not only that, but she was breathing on her own.

Lady Avalon must truly be a witch. But she knew witches could be killed. She turned off all the emergency alert alarms. Then, she removed the tubes and monitoring attachments. Even in a medicated state of rest, Katherine wanted to look at Julie's face as she snuffed the life out of her.

She pulled a clear plastic bag out of her purse and slipped it over Julie's head. Then she made a slipknot out of a power cord and tightened it around Julie's neck. Constricting the bottom of the bag around her throat in the process. Now, she could just sit and enjoy the show as she finally extinguished the witch for good.

A few minutes later, the bitch began to squirm as the plastic became stuck to her mouth and nose. The suffocating whore kicked desperately. Katherine laughed in delight. Then, the door began to open.

MICHEAL carefully opened the door. As he peeked into the hall-way, he was alarmed when he saw Lord George a few doors down the hall. Was that Julie's room? He thought. He stealthily made his way down the hall. He snuck up behind George, and in one quick, silent movement, he got his arm around George's neck and choked him out. He knew George might wake up in a minute or so. He decided he needed more time, so he kicked George in the side of the head. He knew it could kill him, but he wasn't overly concerned. George had tried to kill him at the awards show.

Micheal made his way back to the room George seemed to be guarding. He slowly opened the door, not sure what he would find. As the room came into full view, he saw a woman on the bed. He realized it was Julie. A plastic bag was over her head and a slipknot was around her neck. A woman was pulling on the ligature. Then he realized it was Mistress Katherine Talmage from the heresy trial.

"George, come for the party?..." Katherine turned and looked at him.

His rage overtook him, and before she could react, he pounced on her.

⸻ ◆ ⸻

KATHERINE was stunned by a powerful hit to her face. For a moment, she didn't know what hit her. The next thing she knew, she realized it was Lord Avalon, and he wrapped an IV tube around her neck several times.

She flexed her neck against the ligature as she had trained. The key was not to panic. But she had to act fast. She pulled a reversal escape. She saw him move towards the bed, so she tripped him. He turned back on her. Before she could untangle the IV tube, he was back on top of her.

She felt the tube bite hard into her neck. He brought an elbow down hard on the back of her arm, stunning it into a useless state. He kneeled hard on her other arm. As she attempted an escape, she felt her arm break.

Her attempt to squirm out of his death grip only succeeded in her ending up on her back. She saw the same rage she felt inside her, staring down at her through the fire in his eyes. The situation was becoming desperate. She hadn't been able to breathe in at least a few minutes. Where the hell was George?

Lord Avalon tried reaching Lady Avalon on the bed with one hand. She tried to use the opportunity to escape, but his reaction hyperextended her knee. Now, she was helpless. His strength was imposing.

With one hand, he dragged her by her neck to the bedside. With the other, he pulled the bag off Lady Avalon's head. He then picked Katherine up by her neck. With her one good leg, she tried to kick him. He punched her inner thigh, and her leg went numb. Then he carried her by the neck to a hook on the wall and hanged her from it.

None of her limbs could save her now from almost certain death. As the tube cut like a knife into her neck, the pressure inside her chest increased dramatically. With her last clear thought, she only hoped she had done enough to kill Julie. But now, more than five minutes without air put her strangulation training to shame.

The unbelievable pain, searing through every cell of her body, overcame her bravado. She was overwhelmed by terror and desperation. She was sure her head would be severed from her body. The agonizing pain seemed to last for an eternity. Then everything faded to black.

Avalon vs. Cavendish Rd. 2

-May 1, 2373 BC

"It's been a long, hard road to recovery. While I have been given a clean bill of health, I'm not who I was on Death Day. That feeling of hopelessness I felt all those years ago in Salem has returned to haunt my dreams. The psychological scars feel too deep to ever heal.

I am taking the first step today. I am going to visit Katherine Talmage Cavendish. Who sits in prison for her multiple attempts on my life. Micheal very nearly killed Katherine and Lord George Cavendish in defense of my life. I don't think I can forgive Katherine even though that is part of the idea of going and seeing her."

"Are you ready?" Micheal asked JULIE.

She closed her eyes, and the wire bit into her neck again. She breathed deeply in and out a few times to calm her pounding heart.

"I'm ready," she said doubtfully. Micheal pulled her into him more tightly to comfort her.

The fire and rage built inside her as they walked through the door.

"Good morrow, Lady Avalon," Katherine said in English.

"Lady Cavendish, is it?" Micheal asked in kind.

"It is." Lord George answered for her.

"My Lady Cavendish, only in this century could gutter scum like you become a 'Lady,'" Julie emphasized the word.

Katherine exploded. "Thou be a witch's whore! Thou should have died in Salem! Thou art under Satan's protection to have survived my justice of thee!" She yelled angrily. "Escape this prison. I shall. Execute thee, I shall. Thou shalt die as I torture strangle, then hang thee to death. I know thou must be used to being hanged by now!" Katherine gave an evil smile.

"I didn't know how pathetic you were until now. I understand you spent a century pining over killing me. With all that time, planning, and the element of surprise, you still failed? That must be so frustrating." Julie gave a wry smile.

"I shall not fail next time."

"It's been 26 years for me since your husband tried to help Mr. Nash murder me in the woods. And even though it was justified, I have felt bad that entire time for killing him. But now, I no longer feel bad about it. He was a monster just like you."

"Lady Avalon, thou be fraudulent. Thy speech be altered. Thou left my life in ruins. I didst watch thee those five years in Boston. Strut around preening, deceiving people of thy nobility. A true witch thou art. Didst throw myself and my Lord asunder, across time. Thou didst ruin my life anew. Thy life be fair trade!"

"No one forced you to follow us that day." Micheal countered. "My guess is that both of you were upset that we were acquitted in the heresy trial. You decided to come try to kill us. Not knowing we were leaving that century. I saw Lord George on the edge of the drop zone at just the wrong time. And you, Lady Cavendish, must have been behind him. You were pulled through the portal on his wake wave. So it was both of your faults, not ours."

"Lord Avalon, so superior thou art to everyone else!" George began.

"You're right! Avalon is superior to all others, particularly Cavendish." Micheal smirked.

"Insolent peasant!" George attempted to lunge, but the shackles stopped him.

"I was originally planning on apologizing for insinuating at the trial that you suffered from a lack of mental clarity. But I see now you absolutely don't deserve such contrition. You are a lout. A name doesn't make you noble."

George was fuming, about to respond, when Katherine said, "George, calm thyself. These be meager serfs. We shall extinguish them very soon. I shall look joyfully into thy eyes." Katherine indicated her. "As thy life drains from thy body. How sweet the day shall be." Katherine grinned.

"I can see why you like each other. You have got to be the most pompous, arrogant people I have ever met. On top of being sadistic, cold-blooded killers. You are perfect for each other." Julie said.

"The cause of all was thee!" George said.

"You being on our ship was unfortunate. I was sorry that our actions affected you like that. But all you would've had to do was come to us. We may have been able to send you back! Did you ever consider that? My Lord!" Julie yelled in annoyance.

His reaction indicated he hadn't actually considered that.

"How's the neck, Katherine?" Micheal redirected. "I think I'm looking forward to round two. To see such an arrogant bitch turn into a terrified little girl. It was beautiful. You ready?" Micheal asked Julie.

Even as the Cavendishes burst into outrage, they simply ignored them and walked out.

-August 12, 2373 BC

"We have been out of the limelight for almost eight months now. During that time, we received so much love and well wishes from all over the world. I'm finally ready to return that love in the form of a new tour. All tickets will be free.

Even 26 years later, the nightmares of my execution have remained an unwelcome companion. And they returned to the forefront when I was nearly murdered again. Through his efforts to aid my recovery, both in body and soul, Micheal and I have now returned to our long-shared perfect harmony. And I love him now more than ever before. I would not have thought it possible."

PS: Happy 21st anniversary to us.

Lacking Faith

"Aphrodite, or should I call you Julie Hall?" MELINA asked as Aphrodite walked in.

"Melina, you can call me whatever you want. Just as long as you call me friend."

"Are we friends?" Melina asked sharply. "Are you really Aphrodite? Because Katherine says, you're a witch from her time period."

After what happened at the Atlas Awards, Melina had discovered that two of the closest 'people' to her, had a terrible history. 'Aphrodite' if that actually is who she was? Was Lady Avalon, who, during Katherine's time period had murdered Katherine's husband. Then against her will, threw her through a time portal.

Melina was still inclined to believe she was Aphrodite but that Aphrodite might have a darker side she had never shown Melina. She would callously kill the lesser 'humans' when it suited her. Melina had taken Katherine under her wing and taught her everything she knew. She was like a daughter to her.

"Is that what I saw you come out all those years ago? What you went into a few centuries ago?"

"Yes, those are temporal portals."

"So then, are you really Aphrodite?"

"I am," Aphrodite answered without hesitation.

"Did you murder Katherine's husband?"

"It was self-defense."

"Self-defense? A goddess needing to kill a human in self-defense? I've seen you fight off hundreds of assassins without killing any of them. I can't believe you would've had to kill him." Melina grit her teeth.

"That wasn't my intention. I was just trying to stop them. I nearly died in the process."

"The great Aphrodite! Almost killed multiple times? See why I'm skeptical?"

"Just because we are Gods doesn't mean we can't be killed. And our powers wane when no one believes in us." Aphrodite reminded her.

"Then why would you go to a time where no one believes in you? Wouldn't Koios know what times in which you would be more vulnerable?"

"We didn't go there by choice. We were expelled there against our will. It was an attempt to strand us there."

"Some of your points are valid. However, I don't know if I can trust you anymore. If it comes down to you or Katherine, I'll choose her. She's like a daughter to me. And I don't believe your protestations of self-defense. I will allow you to leave out of respect for our past friendship, but if we cross paths again, you should consider me an enemy."

"I don't know what there is between you and Katherine. But you do know what she is, don't you?" Aphrodite paused. "She's a cold-blooded killer."

"No, you are!" Melina shot back. "She was just seeking justice for her husband when she tried to kill you!"

"You know I'm right. You've been around her for a century. Someone as smart as you, and you don't know? I think not. But believe what you will. If we are no longer friends, then farewell." Aphrodite left the chamber.

Melina wasn't sure who she believed. She realized there probably was some truth to what Aphrodite was saying but was also certain Aphrodite was lying to her. She must choose Katherine over Aphrodite. Some might think it dangerous to cross the gods. But Aphrodite had freely admitted they were vulnerable due to a lack of faith in them.

"Melina! So good to see you again." Melina's train of thought was interrupted by Gabriel.

"Gabriel, it's been a while."

"You're not happy to see me? That hurts me right here." He pretended to grab his heart.

"That would require a heart." She shook her head.

"Anyways, I have been quite busy."

"Doing what?"

"Oh, a little of this, a little of that. You know, thinning the herd, so to speak."

Gabriel had always been a bit off-putting, even scary sometimes. But something about the way he was talking filled her with dread. She closed her eyes and focused. The voice? His voice reminded her. When the Imperial agents requested a viewing of The Phantom, His face was always blank, but she had heard his voice a few times. He sounded like Gabriel.

She considered the possibility for a moment. He was well-connected in all of the halls of power. He had spent centuries honing one skill after the next. And she knew he was obsessive. As well as psychologically unstable. He really could be the Phantom.

This line of thought brought her back to the memory of that day.

"You're dropping your arms too much." Gabriel pointed out as they continued sparring. They had done this periodically for centuries.

As he came around for his next attack, Melina raised her arms as he had instructed. But she had to react quickly to deflect an attempted takedown.

"Impressive reaction." Gabriel laughed. "I think it's time to work on weapons defense." He said, bringing a pause to the action. He pulled out a wire garrote. "See if you can stop me." He began circling around her.

As he moved in, she spun, redirecting his attack. She went on the offensive, landing a kick on his back. He went down. She attempted to stomp-kick on his head. He rolled away, then spun into a sweep, taking out her legs. He locked her legs with his. She flipped up on top of him, attempting to take the advantage. But he used her momentum to flip her over. She landed on her back. He sprung up on top of her.

She raised her arms in front of her neck to defend against the ligature. He wrapped it around her wrists. Then, he flipped head over feet in one motion, performing a 180° twist. As he came down, he forced her hands away from her neck. Then, he quickly looped the wire around her neck.

She tried to grab the wire, but it slipped past her fingers. Then he immediately yanked hard on the handles, dragging her across the ground by her neck. She attempted to flip up to free herself, but it didn't work. She fought to get her feet under her and finally succeeded. She felt them slam into a wall. She tried to twist her way out of it, but as she turned to face him, he wrapped the wire around her neck again. In the same motion, he reversed their positions, pinning her to the wall.

She attempted to knee him in the groin, but he avoided it and kneed her in the thigh in retaliation. He then raked the inside of her leg with his boot. It felt numb and wouldn't respond to her will. He then took both handles of the garrote in one hand and chopped her arms with the other, stunning them in the process.

Then, taking each handle of the garrote in his hands, he lifted her off the ground by her throat. Leveraged against the wall, she was defenseless to stop him. She looked into his eyes, and there was a terrifying darkness there. As she dangled helplessly for what felt like an eternity, he was looking right back at her. By the look on his face, he appeared to be enjoying this. She could feel her body begin to convulse as it went into shock. She realized he might actually kill her. Her fear was cut short as she lost consciousness.

Melina awoke in her bed. "There you are! I was worried there for a second. I have to go, but maybe next time you'll get the better of me." Gabriel laughed, and then he left her chamber.

Melina came out of the memory and rubbed her neck. The flashback was so vivid. She shook it off. She needed to look at the Phantom again with new eyes.

"Isn't that something? Katherine almost kills Aphrodite, and then Koios almost kills Katherine. The God's powers must have waned significantly." Gabriel laughed, snapping her back to the moment.

"No one believes in them anymore."

"That means they're vulnerable. Wouldn't it be a shame if someone were to kill Aphrodite?"

"Wouldn't it?" Melina's argument with Aphrodite was fresh in her mind.

"Melina, Priestess of the Gods, have you lost faith?" He raised a brow. "Well, nothing lasts forever, not even the gods. If someone knew that their power came from kinetic energy, and knew how to cut off their access to it. They might be very vulnerable, very vulnerable indeed." Gabriel left her with a chill down her spine.

CHAPTER XVI: THE PHANTOM MENACE

Spotlight

"Ladies and gentlemen, Bellatrix Buenavista." JULIE introduced her.

Bellatrix was one of the Delta originals. She was the very first winner of the Music Artist of the Year award over a century ago. They had encouraged her to perform as a featured guest artist on the revival tour. Her voice was amazing.

"So, Belle, what do you think now?" Julie asked backstage after the show.

"Thank you for making me do this," Belle said with satisfaction.

"Julie? What's wrong?" Julie was crying.

"Melina and I have... Had a falling out."

"Do you want to talk about it?" Belle replied sadly. When Julie didn't respond. "That's okay." Belle continued after a moment. "Let's go do something."

"Like what?"

"I think I know just the place."

An hour later, they arrived at the Piano Bar. They were nearly mobbed by the crowd waiting to get in.

"Zara! Corra! Rosalyn! It's so good to see all of you." Julie said.

"Your Highness!" Zara said, bowing.

"Oh, please!" Julie rolled her eyes.

"And you, Belle, are the queen maker," Zara added. "It's been too long, Julie. I know a lot has happened."

"I have given up trying to defend myself from this Phantom," Corra said in resigned defeat. "Nothing can stop him, if he comes for me I'm just dead."

"He's killed so many of my friends!" Rosalyn wiped tears from her eyes. "I hate him."

Julie hugged her. "I don't want to be sad right now. Let's celebrate with each other tonight, okay? I like what you've done with the place." Julie noticed the many changes Zara had made.

"It's a proper exclusive music venue again, thanks to you."

They sat at Zara's private booth and drank and chatted for several hours.

"I need to use the little girl's room." Julie excused herself.

It was karaoke night, and when Julie returned no one was singing. So, instead of going to the booth, she took the stage.

"Well, this brings back memories." She said with a smile, and the room erupted. "These next few songs go back over 50 years. They were written by my good friend Zara." She said in introduction. Julie sang a few of Zara's hits from decades earlier. "Now, I think I'm going to need some help with this last one... Zara! Will you join me on stage?" Julie extended her arm in Zara's direction. Zara shook her head. "I'm not going to take no for an answer."

Zara reluctantly came to the stage and joined her in singing *Across Emerald Skies*. "What do you think, Zara? Do we need some more help?" Julie said, indicating the rest of their friends.

"Absolutely!" Zara agreed, grinning from ear to ear.

The five of them harmonized on several random songs to the delight of everyone.

As the night wound down, Julie addressed her friends. "You are all my best friends. We all know what's happening right now, and thankfully, none of us has fallen so far. I will continue to pray for our safety. I love you all." Tears came as she bid farewell. "Please stay safe."

Julie arrived in the city of Babylon, their next tour stop; it was very late. MICHEAL was half-asleep.

"How were the girls?" he asked as she slid into bed.

"We made the news already?"

"Must've been quite the performance." He laughed.

"Do you ever consider how our decisions have led to so many horrible outcomes?"

"To what are you referring?"

"Well... When I decided to put us in the spotlight, to sort of pay you back for all the times you just went with it. I didn't consider some of the negatives. Now, a crazed killer is killing all of my friends. And, there's a good chance he will soon come after me. I know we joked early on that he would be stopped when he came after me. But going over all the things that he's done, I will likely just become his latest victim." She sounded truly fearful.

"We will stop him."

"Even if we do, I don't want him killing all of my friends." She began to cry.

Micheal had tried to figure out a plan to stop the Phantom. But the Phantom seemed unstoppable. So much had happened to Julie over the nearly 27 years since the fall. And due to the circumstances, she rarely had any real friends. Now, most of the friends she had made in the 24th century had been murdered. Melina had abandoned her. And the friends that remained would likely be killed any day now.

The Phantom had killed over 500 of the top singers, actresses, models, athletes, and media celebrities in the world over the past two and a half years or so.

He held Julie, sleeping so peacefully, trusting him to protect her from the demons of the night. But it was the demon of the day that was haunting his dreams. The Phantom had beaten every security system on the planet. He had found ways to evade all the cameras and leave no usable forensic evidence. And that was despite even better forensic technology than they had had in the 21st century.

None of the women who had tried to hide had succeeded either. There seemed to be nowhere to run. The Phantom appeared unstoppable. Julie was now the most famous woman in the world. So Micheal believed the Phantom might be saving her for last. And Micheal feared he wouldn't be able to protect her. The thought filled him with dread. He felt so helpless. He looked down at the angel in his arms and had a horrible feeling their time was running out.

Atlantis High-Tech

"So, how's it coming?" Micheal asked as he entered the labs.

"I think this formula might be pretty close," JULIE said. "The petroleum element I added, if it bonds, will allow the flexibility in the fabric I have been trying to achieve." She informed him.

She had spent years trying to adapt what was known as a tri-poly alloy into a flexible version that could be made into clothing. The closest thing to it she knew of in fiction was Black Panther's Vibranium weave suit from the Marvel comics. The tri-poly alloys still amazed her—elements that typically do not mix but in the right combinations, bond into a lattice structure. The most impressive one they had seen was ten times lighter than titanium but ten times stronger, with a melting point of around 10,000°F.

"If we can get this to work, we can make clothing as thin as a T-shirt that is bulletproof. How's it coming on your end?"

"I'm a few days from doing some real-world trials. The biggest sticking point is the antirejection coating. In the early tests, the body recognizes the nanos as a threat, so the immune system always reacts. That very thing is what has tripped up the Atlantean medical scientists so far. I have spent much of the last five years trying to perfect the nanos. So long as the body doesn't reject them, they can perform all kinds of beneficial tasks."

"What kinds of things again?"

"The first, and the most important, is helping mend wounds on the skin and on the inside. They could also target diseases, both viral and bacterial. Oh, and even parasites. They could break up blood clots or plaque buildup in your veins."

"Is the body's rejection protocol really that potent?" She looked up from her work.

"I'm quite optimistic," he said with obvious doubt. "And when do you think the tri-poly flex alloy might be ready?" He raised a brow.

"If this test is a success, perhaps by tomorrow."

"Good! Hopefully, we will have a few new toys by week's end." He walked out of the lab.

"You'll be interested to know that I'm fairly sure I have thoroughly studied every advanced technology Atlantis has that is unavailable in our time," Micheal said later that night at dinner.

"Studying up to potentially use as we go forward in time?" Julie asked.

"Of course. The more things we have at our disposal, the better our chances to survive the run."

"As if there's any chance of that." Her head dropped.

"Don't tell me you're giving up."

"It's just a matter of time." Tears came to her eyes.

"We could go to the moon."

"For three years? No. He'll come soon, and we won't be able to stop him." She shook her head.

"Use your rings. We can still say we're Aphrodite and Koios if necessary."

She considered that for a moment. "Okay. If the gods can't stop him, no one can." She felt a little better. Then she remembered. "Do we know why the rings didn't work at The Atlas Awards?"

"No, I think it was just a fluke."

A couple of days later, MICHEAL pressed the plunger of the syringe to remove the air. "Here goes nothing." He injected himself with the nanos. After waiting a few minutes, he handed Julie a knife. "Will you do the honors?"

She lightly cut into his arm. He watched as, within about a minute, the wound was closed. He wiped away the blood and could see the cut was there, but it was no longer bleeding. "Looks like a success to me. In a day or two, it should heal completely. Your turn." He handed her the syringe with a smile. She injected the nanos.

"The bonds took hold, and this is the result." Julie handed him a piece of fabric. It felt soft, almost like cotton. She had fabricated it into a shirt.

"Is it bulletproof?"

She removed her lab coat and handed him a gun. "Shoot me, but angle it a little, just in case."

He raised the gun, then he hesitated. He fired at her shoulder. The bullet ricocheted off and hit the wall. "Doesn't that still hurt?"

"Come look at this."

He came to the screen, and she had a scan of the test fire that demonstrated that the lattice bonds seemed to solidify with each other in reaction to the impact.

"Much of the energy is absorbed by the bond spacing. And the rest is distributed across a large area. You still feel it, but it feels like this." She slapped his shoulder with an open hand in the same place where he had shot her. It felt like a love tap.

"Are these high-velocity rounds?"

"Yes... Want to try?"

He donned the shirt she had given him. Then she shot him point blank in the chest. It really did feel like a love tap.

"Want to see something cool?" She raised a brow.

She led him to the roof, where she had a platform attached to one of the obelisks. "What is this? 100 feet?" he asked.

"Yes." She donned a beanie cap. "And what do you say? Geron-imo?!" She jumped. She landed on her back. A moment later, she stood up and calmly strolled back to the obelisk.

"Very cool. I think we're going to need a full wardrobe made of this material."

That evening they sat on the balcony overlooking the massive sea of light that was Atlantis.

"Are you thinking of trying to help protect Corra, Rose, and Belle from the Phantom?"

"I offered, but they refused. Corra convinced them that nothing can stop him, so they've resigned themselves to their fates." Her head dropped.

"But you're not."

"After Salem, I'm on borrowed time—"

"No! Your fate is what you decide it to be. You will not give up now. I won't let you. Have faith in us. Remember what Adam told us?... There's never been before, nor will there ever be again, two people capable of doing what we're doing. We will win this. You have my word."

"I am trying, but everywhere I look, I see the shadow of death shading everything."

"I told you once. The night is always darkest before the dawn. This night is dark, that's true, but the dawn will come. You will not die this night. You will live for many years to come." He turned her chin to look at him and decided to convince her without words.

Phantom Menace

They blew out their concert at The Garden of Light in Delta. JULIE had decided that they should continue their tour. A month had passed, and she was feeling much better.

"Thank you so much, Rose, for singing tonight. It was great!" Julie complimented.

"You know I always loved to sing with you guys."

"Hey, Corra just texted that she wants me to come by her place tonight," Julie said.

"Can I come?" Rose asked.

"We both know she would always welcome you."

Corra had told them just to come in. As they went through the door, it smelled like dinner.

"Corra, we're here!" Rose said loudly. But Corra wasn't in the kitchen.

A feeling of dread began forming in Julie's stomach as she approached the bedroom. Julie broke down as her worst fears were realized. "Don't come in here!" Julie tried to warn off Rose through the tears.

Corra was hanging nude from the rafter beam. Her hands were bound behind her back. Julie slowly approached and checked her pulse, but she already knew. Rosalyn was inconsolable. Julie called the police. Then she and Rose cried together.

"Maybe I should just kill myself before he does," Rose concluded bitterly.

"You can't do that. You have so much to live for."

"I've lived almost 700 years; Corra was my best friend, my truest sister for the last 300 years. We went to Delta together over a century ago. We were supposed to become famous, have amazing careers, then grow old together. But now I know I'm next."

"You don't know that."

"Yes, I do. And he's going to torture me and drag it out as long as possible. So I've decided I'm going to control my own destiny." Rose stated firmly. "And don't you try to stop me, Julie. If you're a true friend, you won't take this away from me."

Julie didn't know what to do. "How are you going to do it?"

"Pills, with a bag over my head. I just want to fall asleep and then go peacefully." Tears glistened on her cheek.

Early the next morning, Julie awoke to a text: "Julie... Go check on Rosalyn." She didn't recognize the number.

She and Micheal arrived at Rosalyn's penthouse. As they entered, she had the same butterflies in her stomach. She realized Rose was probably dead, but how did she die? Julie opened the door slowly. Then she ran out quickly.

Rosalyn was tied to the bed naked, with a plastic bag over her head. Julie was so overcome with grief that she barely heard Micheal reading a note.

" *'My dear Rose, unfortunately, you tried to cheat me out of my rights to you, so I had to take some extra time to ensure we both had the full experience.' - The Phantom.*" Micheal finished.

Inside the haze of misery, Julie was now in. She recognized that the note indicated the Phantom had caught Rose attempting to commit suicide. He stopped her and then tortured her even worse because of it. A mix of sorrow, hate, anger, and helplessness overwhelmed her.

The Phantom had taken two of her best friends in two days. The pain was more than she could bear. It was made worse by the fact that he had made her discover their bodies.

JULIE spent the next few days crying in bed until Belle came to visit.

"We want to record a song for the victims of the Phantom. I've asked Micheal to write it," Belle said tearfully.

Julie broke down again, and they cried together, holding each other.

Julie agreed to go to the studio. As she entered her office, seeking a moment of solitude.

"Eminence Aphrodite!" Gabriel said from behind her.

She turned to face him. "Gabriel, what are you doing here?"

"I am so sorry about your friends..." He paused. She didn't respond. "I understand you and Melina had a fight. I would like you to know that I'm here for you in these difficult times. My Goddess. If there's anything I can do."

"Thank you, Gabriel, for your sentiments. I have to go to the studio." She turned to go.

"Aphrodite!" She turned back. He came and threw his arms around her. She didn't know what to do, so she awkwardly hugged him back. "I am so sorry," he whispered.

"I really appreciate that; they're waiting on me."

"Of course, they are, your Eminence." He broke the hug.

Melina's words came to her mind as she gave Gabriel one last long look. "He's dangerous, he's obsessed with you." Could Gabriel be the Phantom? She realized that his background and history could potentially allow him to pull it off.

While they were in the middle of recording the song *Memories*, Bellatrix excused herself. Julie became worried when she hadn't returned by the time they had finished. And she thought Gabriel had been in the building earlier.

"Micheal? Will you come with me?"

"Where are we going?"

"Belle hasn't returned, and that was almost an hour ago."

"Let's check her office."

Micheal opened the outer door slowly. He cautiously peeked inside. "Bellatrix? Collette?" He yelled, but there was no response. He opened the door all the way. There didn't appear to be anyone there, which scared her because Belle's assistant, Collette, was almost always at her desk.

Micheal pushed open the door to Belle's inner office.

"No!" Julie screamed. Belle was lying naked on her desk with a thin wire wrapped tightly around her neck multiple times. Julie broke down. As she turned to leave, she saw Collette on the floor behind her desk in a puddle of blood with her throat cut. The last thought she could remember was: "Fucking Gabriel, evil bastard!"

Hot and Cold War

Following the murders of Corra and Rose, the murders of Bellatrix and Collette at the Sky Records Studios made Julie inconsolable. MICHEAL was becoming extra worried. Julie hadn't left their suite in the penthouse since Corra and Rose's funerals. She had barely spoken.

Micheal didn't know what to do, so he would work in the lab whenever she wanted to be alone. Julie told him that Rosalyn had been driven suicidal by a sense of hopelessness. He had begun to worry that she might be going the same way.

He redoubled his efforts in the labs to produce something that might stop the Phantom. It gave him the illusion that he might be able to take control of the situation. But inside, he knew that it was all a fantasy. Despite his best efforts to determine the identity of the Phantom, nothing worked. They'd use the sky-net to try to track this individual. But the scans always came up empty for some reason, even though the precise time and location were known. He truly was a Phantom.

"Micheal?" He heard Kelsie say.

"What are you doing here?"

"I need someone to talk to."

"You should find someone else."

"There is no one else. All my friends are dead. I know it's just a matter of time." Kelsie began to cry. "You used to be my friend." She turned to leave.

"Kelsie, come here." She came into his arms.

She cried on his shoulder for a while. "Micheal, I don't want to die."

"Sh..." He cooed in her ear. He didn't know what to say. Any reassurance he might offer would be a lie.

They sat, and he just listened to all of her fears. As they were talking, Julie suddenly entered the room.

"Julie!" Kelsie said in surprise, wiping the tears from her eyes. "I'm sorry, I will leave." She rose to leave.

"Kelsie." Julie stopped her. "Come here." Then they cried in each other's arms for a while.

Finally, Kelsie pulled back. "I'm sorry, Julie... For what I did..."

"It's okay. That's all in the past. And I forgive you. Our time is too short for there to be enmity between us."

"I'm sorry I ruined our friendship."

"You're still my friend." Micheal knew Julie was desperate for a friend.

It was late, so they put Kelsie up in one of their guest suites.

"How are you doing, Jules?" Micheal pulled her into his arms.

"I don't know, everything's been a blur for the last week or so..." She paused for a second. "I think the Phantom might be Gabriel."

"I know he's a little weird, but why?—"

"He's been obsessed with me for 900 years. Melina told me he was dangerous. With his family connections, he could go places and do things where few others could, and no one would ever suspect him."

"I mean, he's always been nice every time we've encountered him."

Over the centuries since they met Gabriel, his original obsession had seemed to fade. He had always been respectful. You might even say he was a friend.

"If you had 900 years to perfect your act? Couldn't you pretend to be whatever you wanted?"

As he was considering his response, there was a breaking news banner on the television.

"Sorry, Jules, I want to hear this."

They sat down, and he un-muted the TV.

The TV said: "... If you're just joining us, the world may be descending into a full-scale conflict... Following the destruction of a Babylonian battleship by a suspected Sumerian drone. Babylon has begun a massive invasion across the Straits of Sumar ... Now we go to Seria in Phoenicia with an update on what's happening there... Thank you, Turiel. We estimate that over one million Phoenician soldiers have entered Canaan. The Phoenician government said they were interceding in the five-year civil war that has raged there, claiming at least 10 million lives. Many foreign ministers are questioning the coincidental timing of this action with Babylon's moves in the Straits of Sumar, as well as India's action in Philistia... Many tensions have been bubbling just below the surface in many places for quite some time. And now those cold wars are turning red hot. Because the kettles begin boiling over around the world, these wars may embroil the entire world... Back to you, Turiel... Foreign ministers from all over the world have called an emergency meeting of the Global Counsel in Central City... The Atlantean ambassador to the Council, Nirissa Cass, had this to say... The Atlantean Empire and her alliance will remain neutral in these conflicts. We urge all world leaders to defer to diplomacy rather than war... Korilla is in Phillistia... Turiel, with the global population recently passing 38 billion the competition for resources has led to many disputes. When Phoenicia cut the flow of raw ore supplies drastically to India, India moved militaristically in an attempt to secure the mining interests in northern Phillistia...”

Micheal muted the TV.

“Do you think this is the beginning of the doomsday apocalypse that will end Atlantis?” Julie asked.

“I don't know, do you think a world war could completely destroy this civilization? To the point where it's lost to history? Let's get some sleep.”

The next morning Micheal found Julie and Kelsie having breakfast on the veranda.

“Morning, ladies.” He gave Julie a kiss.

“You would think it would get easier to go to funerals after so many.” Kelsie shook her head.

“It only gets worse, doesn't it?” Julie said.

“Every time I close my eyes, the only thing I see is my horrifying death and my depressingly sad funeral, attended by no one. Because all of my friends are dead.” Kelsie began to cry. Julie went and embraced her.

After a little while, Micheal broke the silence. “At Belle's funeral tomorrow, I will sing the song I wrote.”

“I know it will be beautiful,” Kelsie said.

“Whatever happens, Kelsie, you will be remembered,” Julie promised.

“Thank you both for being my friends,” Kelsie said, and then they shared a three-way hug.

The Funeral

Kelsie spent the night, then the next day, she joined Micheal and JULIE as they traveled to the Island of Iapetus. The island was to the east, in the Strait of Heroes, near the Pillars of Hercules. It was nearly perfectly round and two miles in diameter. It received its name because it has been a burial site for the aristocracy, going back to classical antiquity.

Their friend Bellatrix Bonaventure belonged to one of the oldest families in Atlantis. Following the coming of the age of the pyramids, they had been used as tombs for the nobility. So, she was being honored by having her funeral on the island, and she would be buried inside the central pyramid.

The attendees included nearly everyone of importance from Delta, as well as much of the aristocracy from Atlantis. Her father would give the imperial eulogy. And Zara Zepata would give the luminary eulogy. Zara was her best friend.

Julie, Micheal, and Kelsie sat in the front row, as Zarek Bonaventure, spoke for an hour about Belle's history and how she honored the Bonaventure name. Then it was time for them to sing tribute to the woman who had promoted their stardom.

Julie tried to channel her sorrow into the bow of her violin. She felt the spirits of all the friends she'd lost embracing her like a warm blanket. She felt like she wasn't consciously controlling her strokes. But the beautiful melancholy that Micheal had written, filled the air with emotion. In seamless harmony with Micheal's piano.

His satin voice carried the lamentation across the sky. An ode to the life of Bellatrix.

Julie allowed the emotions to permeate her soul. Her voice was muffled by sorrow. It was fortunate that Micheal could sing for both of them.

When the last note faded into the wind, those gathered sat in teary silence.

Zara spoke about Belle's career in Delta and the impact she had on the world of entertainment. Then it was time for the burial rites.

Belle's sarcophagus was stood on its end. The laser-cut encasement looked like a statue of Belle. The resemblance was striking. The image of her beauty was preserved perfection, for all time.

It was carried through the threshold as the sun slid below the horizon. And 781 Chinese-style lanterns were released into the sky, one for each year of Bellatrix.

Julie had no emotional energy left to attend the life celebration that followed. Micheal stayed, but she didn't want to be alone, so she caught a ride with the Aquarius twins, their tour friends.

As they entered the twin's palatial estate on the shores of the

Sea of Egypt, Julie felt something prick her neck, and everything went dark.

<hr>

She opened her eyes, and the haze began to clear. Aeliana was tied to a chair. And Ameliana was tied to the bed.

Julie tried to move but found herself restrained to a chair. She tried to activate her rings but found her fingers naked. Then she realized that the rest of her was as well. Neither of the twins had any clothing on either.

This had to be the Phantom. And with her rings missing, this was likely the end.

And then, he arrived.

"Kingu! You evil bastard!"

He spent a moment leering at each of the twins. Then his attention turned to her. His eyes traced her body, pausing when he looked between her legs.

"You are so disgusting." She wanted to hurl.

His eyes snapped up at that. "My apologies, Julie. Let me help you."

He stepped over and began untying her ropes.

"What kind of sick game is this?"

"We must hurry, before he comes back."

Her wrist was nearly free.

"Too late to play hero, Kingu." A sword thrust through his chest.

As his body fell away, Daniel Woods was standing behind him.

"The whore of Delta causes more trouble." He used a wet cloth to wipe the blood off her body. And tightened the knot Kingu had loosened.

"Of course, you're the Phantom."

He laughed. "Please, you thought your stalker here was the Phantom." He dragged Kingu's body to the side of the room.

"You were higher on the list. You've threatened me multiple times."

He stepped back to her. "And apparently, you couldn't wait to give me my justice. I meant to kill you last. But now will have to do. It's poetic that your last living appearance was a funeral." He squeezed her breasts hard, then grabbed between her legs. "But it's not quite your turn. The twin sluts first. They were my actual target tonight."

Daniel moved to the bed.

"Micheal will kill you."

"Your hapless husband? Even suspecting me, you could do nothing. I'll deal with him next. But first I want Aeliana to enjoy the show while I extinguish her other half."

Julie fought against her restraints. But time was against her. Aeliana cried and pleaded while Daniel raped and strangled Ameliana.

Julie continued her efforts, but the ropes were stubborn.

"Wasn't that fun? Bet you wish you'd said yes now, right?" He flared in Aeliana's face. She dropped her head in tears. "Now I'm going to show you mercy. You deserve equal treatment to your sister. But I need to save my reserve for "The Queen". And is one twin any different from the other? And besides, do you really want to live without your other half? Let's get this over with."

Daniel stepped behind her and pulled a plastic bag over her head, and fixed it in place with a zip tie. He pulled a chair up next to Julie. Aeliana was only about five feet away.

Julie struggled, as the plastic fixed itself to Aeliana's mouth and nose. Daniel was taunting her, and laughing like he was at a sporting event. He rose in celebration when her body went limp, and her head dropped back. Her death stare taunted Julie.

"Did you enjoy the show? Oh, my queen, perhaps you would rather participate? We'll need to move you to the bed."

He went and untied Ameliana, then dragged her body from the bed, using the handles of garrote around her throat. Laying her at her sister's feet. Then he retrieved a syringe.

As he moved to inject her, her fight against the rope was won. Julie caught his hand preventing the tranquilizer. She shook his hand and the syringe fell to the ground.

Daniel grabbed her throat with his free hand, trying to choke her out. She punished his nose with a headbutt, and he staggered back.

She flipped the chair back, shattering it to pieces. He pounced on her and again grabbed her throat. She bridge-roll reversed him and elbowed his face.

He kicked her off and she tumbled across the floor.

She remembered the syringe and dove for it. He tackled her and they rolled together. When the momentum stopped, he was dead weight on top of her.

Julie pushed him off and checked his pulse. He was still alive. She bound him and called the police.

As the scene was being processed, she gave her statement. Then Micheal came and brought her home, calming her delayed panic along the way.

In their private chambers at the penthouse, she felt her emotions pulling her in different directions. In one day, she'd buried one friend, lost two more, and stopped the Phantom. Her grief for her friends was juxtaposed with the lifting of the weight of her dread of the Phantom.

"How do you feel?"

"Exhausted. Like I've ridden the world's longest rollercoaster. My body and my heart are throbbing. And now having experienced yet another terrible situation, I keep thinking about what you said. He'll be stopped when he comes for me. And that leads to one conclusion. I wish he'd come for me sooner. Because while I would still face the trauma, all my friends wouldn't be dead."

She cried on his shoulder for a while. When she finally composed herself, she wanted to know what the news was saying about it.

She turned on the TV. The TV said. "... The Phantom serial killer has been captured. He is Daniel Woods, the partner of Parisa Maximus. She released a statement disavowing him. He was stopped by Julie Hall, of Avalon. But not before he murdered three more people. The Aquarius Twins, and Kingu Valor, a previous person of interest in the case. Investigators are trying to determine how he did this... The forensics teams have searched Mr. Woods' properties, as well as the crime scene, and have yet to discover his technological advantage..."

Julie shut off the TV.

"Even when he's caught, he's still a phantom."

"He's in prison. He'll likely be executed soon. Let's not waste any more time on this piece of human garbage."

Julie sighed. "You're right. I think the exhaustion is taking me." She laid her head on his shoulder and consciousness faded.

Betrayed by the Gods

The eruption of a potential world war renewed MELINA'S focus on the coming apocalypse. She needed to see Koios.

She sat on the balcony overlooking The Palace of the Gods. As she contemplated her life there centuries ago, a voice came from behind her.

"Quite the view," Koios said in his own words.

"I remember it like it was yesterday."

"You're upset with us." He seemed to read her mind.

"I believed in you, in both of you."

"How have we failed you?"

"Why, Eminence Koios, did you curse me with foresight?"

"Foresight is a gift. Only the most worthy would ever be endowed."

"Why me? My visions have haunted me for over a century."

"You know why, Melina Hellas. Only the strongest could bear this burden. But through this gift, you have been able to help innumerable people."

"I didn't ask for this! I didn't want this! The weight of the future is too much to bear." Tears flowed.

Koios came and touched her shoulder. "Every gift has its counterpoint. I know you, Melina; I know how strong you are. Your strength is one of the reasons I chose you. You are the most amazing human we've ever met."

"If I can't use it to stop the coming apocalypse then what was the point?"

"You have touched the lives of billions through this gift. The point wasn't to stop the apocalypse. It was to make the lives of people better. No one lives forever, whether it's one year or a thousand. It's about using the time given to you to help the people around you."

"You're the gods! You... Koios, knew this was coming, and you're letting it happen. And that's another thing. What exactly is coming? I have never been able to see it clearly. Not that it really matters at this point." She caught herself on the balcony rail.

He studied her with consideration, seeming to decide whether to tell her.

"You gave me this gift... Koios... Please, you owe me that."

"Let's sit." He directed her to a table on the veranda. After a moment, he looked her in the eye. "There will be a global flood. Three years from now."

"How is that possible?"

"They're the Gods."

"You and Aphrodite are part of this?" She rose and took a step back, horrified. Aphrodite really was evil.

"We did everything we could. Uranus felt the waning belief in us was a mortal threat. He decided to clean the slate. Start from scratch. Aphrodite and I led the resistance. There was a battle, but we lost. We were expelled from the heavens." Aphrodite was telling the truth about their expulsion. "Aphrodite and I care deeply about humanity. We fought for you and every other person."

"I trusted in the gods, and they betrayed me! Which of the gods other than Uranus have turned against us?"

"Gaia, Kronos, Hyperion, Oceanus, Mnemosyne, Themis and Tethys."

"Mother Earth has turned against us?" She was seething.

He touched her shoulder. "I'm sorry, Melina. I'm sorry we failed you."

"Where's Aphrodite?"

"She's asleep."

She was still angry with Aphrodite. She still didn't trust her. She no longer thought of Aphrodite as a friend. But if she was being honest, she had hoped to see her.

At this moment, she received an urgent phone call. "Koios, thank you for telling me. I need to get back to the temple. Can you fly me? For old time's sake."

He raised a brow for a second and then gave in. "Okay."

He took her in his arms, and they flew up into the twilight sky. As the wind blew through her hair, she sighed at the amazing sensation of soaring through the sky like the birds. It had been centuries since she had had the pleasure.

As they landed at the temple, they were greeted by most of the priestesses, who went to their knees at the sight of Koios.

"I appreciate the ride," She said, still using the words of the gods.

She and all the other priestesses watched in awe as Koios took flight.

She had come to think of Koios as a friend. He had always been kind to her. Although her visions of the past century had helped build up some resentment toward him. He explained his and Aphrodite's attempted defense of humanity and revealed the betrayal of the gods. She still felt ambivalent toward him.

Later that night. "It's always awe-inspiring to see the gods fly through the air isn't it?" Gabriel asked rhetorically. "And you got to fly with Koios." He shook his head. "Lucky you." He smiled.

"Gabriel, why are you here?"

"Ouch, sis, that hurts right here." He grabbed his chest, feigning pain.

"Gabriel!"

"You know that the gods are in a weakened state. You know that if someone were determined to take them down. They might actually succeed like they almost did at The Atlas Awards. But now I remember that you and Aphrodite are no longer friends, so I suppose you don't care." He shrugged. "It makes you wonder why they didn't fly, use super strength, or shoot lightning. I mean, Katherine very nearly killed Aphrodite on live television. I do have to admit that seeing Aphrodite's breasts on full display was quite enjoyable. It would've been a shame if Katherine finished those off. We'll have to discuss this further in a few days. I will see you later, Melina." Gabriel left her there alone, a chill down her spine.

The creep factor from Gabriel was stronger than ever before. Following their previous conversation a few weeks earlier, Melina had come to suspect that Gabriel was the Phantom. But she had been afraid to confirm her fears. Despite his creepy nature, she still thought of him as a brother. They had known each other for over 900 years. But now she needed to know for sure.

She went to the Oracle chamber and focused on the Phantom killer. Aphrodite passed randomly through her head. Melina closed her eyes.

Aphrodite was lying on a bed, bound at the wrists and ankles. Melina took a closer look. Aphrodite was naked, and there was a wire tight around her neck. There was an obvious death stare on her face. Melina turned and looked back the other way. Gabriel was there, then he said. "My goddess of love, my greatest conquest. You never saw this coming, did you?" He said proudly, holding some kind of device in his hand. He displayed it directly before

Aphrodite's lifeless eyes. "To kill a goddess, especially the Goddess of Love. Now your timeless beauty is mine forever."

Melina came out of the horrifying vision. Now she knew. Gabriel was the Phantom. And he intended to kill Aphrodite. The device in his hand must allow him to take down the gods. Should she attempt to warn Aphrodite? Or should she let him have her?

CHAPTER XVII: GABRIEL

The Gods, Down-To-Earth

AFTER SUCH A STRESSFUL experience, MICHEAL let Julie decompress. She'd slept for 36 hours straight. And he was eating lunch on the veranda.

"Micheal, that was Kelsie on the phone." Julie walked onto the terrace.

"Good morning, Jules." He rose and kissed her.

"Oh, sorry. Good morning." She kissed him again.

"What's going on?"

"Kelsie says someone's stalking her."

"Are we going to Delta then?" Micheal raised a brow.

"You are," she instructed. "I trust you both."

"You trust Kelsie?"

"Kelsie and I discussed everything. We are all good now. You go... I have to help with the twin's funeral... I love you, Micheal."

She kissed him.

"I love you." Then he kissed her again.

Upon his arrival in Delta, Micheal noticed that the door to Kelsie's place was cracked. He cautiously let himself in.

"Kelsie!" he yelled as he opened the bedroom door.

"Eminence Koios, nice of you to join us," Gabriel said with a smile.

Kelsie was fully naked and bound to the bed.

"Where's Aphrodite?"

"You son of a bitch!"

"Hey! Don't talk about my mother that way." Gabriel smiled. He turned to Kelsie for a moment. "I bet you didn't even know that your friend Micheal here is actually the God Koios. And his wife Julie is my one true love, Aphrodite, Goddess of Love and Beauty. Go ahead your Eminence, show Kelsie here some levitating lightning. I always loved that one."

As Kelsie looked at him, her look of fear was replaced by a look of interest.

He wasn't sure what Gabriel's angle was, but he thought, what the hell. He brought lightning to his hands. "Gabriel, give up now, or I will have to hurt you." He rose toward the ceiling in an attempt to be even more menacing.

"Isn't it impressive?" Gabriel asked Kelsie. She had a look of true fascination on her face. "Koios, my old friend. There's just one problem. I've studied you and Aphrodite for centuries. And you know what I've learned?" Gabriel didn't seem worried at all, which concerned Micheal.

He decided he should stun Gabriel and get it over with. Gabriel took cover momentarily and said, "The source of your power." He clicked the button on a device in his hand. The lightning sputtered and Micheal's hands. He fell hard to the floor. Gabriel stood over him as he struggled to breathe and said, "Now, Koios, I have the upper hand."

They fought fiercely for a few minutes. They were quite evenly matched.

"You're better at this than I expected," Gabriel said.

Gabriel went in for a takedown, but Micheal anticipated it. He reversed Gabriel into a choke hold. as Micheal was attempting to choke him out, Gabriel expertly reversed him. An elbow came down hard to his face, and everything went dark.

When he gained consciousness, Micheal realized he was naked, cuffed to the bed. Gabriel was washing the blood off his face.

"I gotta hand it to you, your Eminence. I thought you gods were mostly tricks and magic. You very nearly beat me, even without your special powers. I'm impressed. Despite my appreciation of your Eminence. I am still angry with you for betraying the goddess we both love with Miss Ambrose here." Kelsie was tied naked to a chair.

"So, what should I do as a way of punishment for the two of you?" Gabriel made his way over to Kelsie. He began fondling her all over her body.

"I bet you didn't know you were fucking a God?" Gabriel leaned over, staring Kelsie in the face.

"They're quite amazing, aren't they? I can't fault you for your attraction. I mean, look at that perfect ideal of a man. If I were the type, I couldn't help myself. And if only I were that well-endowed. It's good to be a God!"

"We never had sex!" Kelsie said.

Gabriel seemed temporarily taken aback. He had turned away from Kelsie in the process. He returned to Kelsie, staring her down again. "You're lying!"

"Not that I didn't try."

Gabriel pulled back; he looked at Micheal and then back to Kelsie. He seemed to believe her. But then he shook his head. "Well, I suppose we will have to change that, won't we?" He went and began to untie Kelsie.

"I bet you never thought you would get to fuck a God? Did you, Kelsie?" He finished untying her, grabbed her wrists, and turned to face her.

"Now, Kelsie, you will follow any instructions I give you. You will not attempt to flee; you will attempt no resistance to me. If you do anything other than what I tell you, I promise I will torture you one day for every violation, and then I will kill you. Do you understand?"

"Yes." Tears came to her eyes.

"Now, Koios, I will let your binds out. It will not allow you to leave the bed, but you can still perform. If you refuse, I will torture

Kelsie for a week. And I will ensure you have a front-row seat to the show."

"Your father would be ashamed of you!" Micheal said bitterly.

"Cato has been dead for four centuries. It's been a long time since I cared about his opinion. Kelsie, can you believe I've known the gods for over 900 years? And Koios..." He indicated Micheal. "And Aphrodite came down from the heavens to rule over the Atlantean Empire. It was a magical time. It was amazing how they built The Palace of the Gods in Atlantis. The crushing of the Babylonian hordes. A time of unmatched prosperity. It was an amazing time to witness." Gabriel seemed truthfully in awe. Kelsie once again gazed at Micheal in fascination. "All right, enough sentimentality. Kelsie, Koios, show me how a God fucks."

Micheal had been trying to calculate a way out of this. But it was evident that there was no way he could free himself. The device Gabriel had been holding earlier must be generating a dampening field because his rings were useless. Every ounce of him did not want to do this. But as he looked at Kelsie, he couldn't condemn her to such torture. Although Gabriel might do it anyway, he had to take the chance that Gabriel would be true to his word.

Gabriel began directing the show. And Micheal and Kelsie had no choice but to do as directed. Micheal couldn't stop a tear running down his cheek as he came the first time. Gabriel requested the use of every position in the book. At least what was possible with Micheal in shackles. This went on for a few hours.

The hate and anger had been building inside Micheal the entire time. Now he was on his back, and Kelsie was mounted on top of him. As he was nearing climax, a pulse of energy surged through his electric ring. The injection of electricity pushed them both over the top to Gabriel's obvious delight. Micheal thought maybe Gabriel might have paused the dampening. But his attempted activation failed.

"Now that is the sex of the gods I remember hearing about! And on top of that, nearly 3 hours Eminence Koios? Stamina befitting a God." Gabriel rose and bowed to him. A look of fear flashed across Kelsie's face as she realized it was likely time for her to die. "Now, Kelsie, you will remain in that position."

Gabriel pressed another button, and the cables tethering Micheal's arms and legs to the bed retracted, pulling his hands to the corners.

Gabriel withdrew a thin wire garrote and kneeled on the bed

behind Kelsie. "Now, Kelsie, you've done well; there's just one last thing you must do. I'm going to strangle you, and you will not fight me. Or I will drag out your death for hours. And Koios, you will not close your eyes or avert your eyes. You will watch the entire time. You will see the life drain out of her eyes. Or I promise I will drag Kelsie's death out for hours." Micheal's feelings of rage and anger were bubbling beneath the surface.

Gabriel drew the wire around Kelsie's neck multiple times, pulling it extremely tight, to Kelsie's horror. But she obediently took it. She was fiercely grabbing on the bed covers. Her face turned to an expression of disbelief. He was still inside of her, and she began to quiver. This stimulus, against his will, brought Micheal back to attention. As the minutes dragged on, Micheal's helplessness overwhelmed him. As he was forced to watch the life draining out of Kelsie, he thought, how could he have let this happen? He had been so close to beating Gabriel. Now, because of his failure, he had to watch her murder.

After what felt like an eternity, a look of acceptance came to Kelsie's face. Gabriel yanked as hard as he could on the garrote handles in an apparent attempt to finish her off. She quivered violently, and Micheal couldn't stop himself from coming. Perhaps a minute later, her stare became distant. He could feel her soul leave her body as her pupils dilated.

"You fucking bastard!" Micheal growled, tears coming to his eyes. Kelsie's lifeless eyes stared down at him while Gabriel held her up by the neck for another minute. Then he tied the wire off, as tight around her neck as he could. "Just to be sure," Gabriel said casually. He then dropped her on top of him.

There was a look of immense satisfaction on Gabriel's face as he admired his handiwork. "Koios, thank you for the great experience. I enjoyed it very much. Now, I will leave you with your whore. While I go claim my love. To kill a goddess. To possess Aphrodite," Gabriel said longingly. "I have dreamed of this day, since that day 909 years ago when I first laid eyes on the Goddess of Love and Beauty. Now that day is finally here," Gabriel said with glee.

As Gabriel rose to leave, Micheal let out a torrent of vitriolic rage. Gabriel stopped for a moment. He turned, and without a word, he smiled and bowed, then left Micheal to wallow in his failure and self-pity. Knowing he was helpless to save Julie from this monster. His life had ended this day, he thought in misery.

The Devil You Know

Following several sleepless nights, MELINA decided she had to do something. She wasn't sure she cared if Gabriel killed Aphrodite or not. But she knew if he wasn't stopped, he would undoubtedly kill many more women.

Particularly because Daniel Woods had been fingered as the Phantom. Following this revelation, she'd looked into both of them. Both had murdered multiple female celebrities.

Daniel had now openly claimed to be the Phantom. Admitting to all murders. Said this was all about punishing Delta. Their rejection had caused the suicide death of his wife. But Melina discovered this was only partially true. Gabriel was responsible for most of the Phantom's kills.

She didn't want to intercede directly; that would be too dangerous. Perhaps she could talk to Gabriel to better understand his plans so she could interfere with them.

"Gabriel?" Melina said through the phone.

"Melina? What's up?"

"Are you able to come by the temple?"

"I will be there in a few minutes." He hung up on her. She would have to tread carefully, not to let him know she was on to him.

Gabriel entered the chamber as Melina finished a reading. "My dear Melina, what's this about?"

"I'm worried about Aphrodite." His presence was skin crawling now that she knew what he had done.

"What for?"

She played ignorant. "The Phantom is out there. She's the most famous celebrity in the world, and she is vulnerable. He might kill her. And I know how much you care about her."

"Oh, sis, I realize you're sheltered up here on high. You didn't hear the Phantom is in custody. It's my prospective son-in-law, Daniel Woods. It's all over the news."

"My mistake. It must've been a misinterpretation. I guess I don't need to worry about Aphrodite, then. Could you go check on her for me? Protect her if she's in danger."

"And what am I supposed to do about it? If the gods can't protect themselves, how could I possibly do anything?"

"Gabriel, I've known you for nine centuries; I know what you're capable of."

Gabriel had begun to leave, but he stopped at that. He turned and walked directly up to her. She took a nervous step back. "You do, don't you?" He studied her face. "Melina, what have you seen?"

"Seen?" She played stupid.

"This misinterpreted vision?" He grabbed her by the arms. "You know, don't you?" He squeezed tighter. "What did you see?" He said sharply. She said nothing. "I swear, Melina, I will kill you right now—"

"All right! I have seen the Phantom kill many times, but it was only once I suspected you that I saw your face."

"I'm surprised it took you so long to find out. The great Oracle of Atlantis!" He mocked.

"Why? Why would you kill all those women?" Tears in her eyes. She was devastated. It was one thing to see it in a vision. It was a whole another to confirm it face-to-face. Despite everything, he was like a brother to her. She felt betrayed anew.

"Why? Because I enjoy it."

"You need to stop."

"Stop? I'm not going to stop. I've been doing this for 900 years. I will never stop."

"Nine hundred years?" Melina was stunned. "How many have you killed?"

He shrugged, then said, "When I killed Kelsie Ambrose today … That makes 81,281 women for my enjoyment and another 20,047 others for various reasons. So that would make a total of 101,328." He smiled.

"And now you're going to kill Aphrodite?" She was disgusted and horrified at the same time. How could someone she had known for so long be such a monster?

"Why yes. My first goddess, I've been planning this for centuries. I have desired her since that day in the Council chamber. I'm warning you, Melina. I love you like a sister, but if you interfere with my plans, I will kill you."

"Love? Love Gabriel? I've served love my whole life. You don't know what love is. And we are not family! Or friends anymore! I don't ever want to see you again!" she yelled through the pain and tears.

He stared at her for a moment. He looked dark, like a demon. Then he said, "if you interfere in any way. You will see me again. And it will be the last thing you ever see."

Melina stood defiantly, staring him down with ire. After he stormed out, she collapsed to the floor in anguish.

After stewing in her grief for a few minutes, she decided to do something. But what could she possibly do? She went to The Oracle Chamber and focused on Koios.

She saw Delta. She came to a door. She walked into the bedroom. Koios was shackled to the bed. The actress Kelsie Ambrose appeared to be dead, lying on top of him. Gabriel had said he had killed Kelsie Ambrose. He had also alluded to the fact that the gods were vulnerable. Just before she came out of the vision, she saw the same device that Gabriel had been taunting Aphrodite's body with. She thought that must be some kind of technology Gabriel had made to take down the gods. He had captured Koios. He really could kill Aphrodite. She needed to stop Gabriel. This wasn't about saving Aphrodite; it was about saving Gabriel's future victims. She needed to release Koios. The gods were likely the only ones who could stop Gabriel. If she let Gabriel kill them, he would never be stopped.

MICHEAL was determined to free himself, but after hours of trying, it was no use. To make matters worse, Kelsie was lying on top of him. Anytime he happened to look at her, her lifeless eyes stared at him unblinking. And she would remind him of his failure to protect her.

Even though Gabriel was nearly unstoppable, he had almost done it. Perhaps he had just been projecting, but on several occasions during their sex together, he thought he saw an accusing look in Kelsie's eyes because he had failed her. Then, as she was being strangled, she stared at him like he had betrayed her.

It was all true. If only he had been slightly better, Kelsie would be alive. He wouldn't have had to have sex with her. And Gabriel would've been stopped. And now Micheal was helpless to save Julie. All because he had failed.

Soon, Julie would be dead, and his life would be over. What's the use, he thought. He gave up on the pointless attempts to free himself and wallowed in self-pity.

As the tears flowed, there was a sudden movement in the hall. He wasn't sure what to do. He listened for a moment; he didn't hear anything else. When he was sure no one else was in the house, he closed his eyes and prayed that some miracle would save Julie.

After a few minutes, he drew out of his self-pity momentarily. While the definition of insanity is trying the same thing over and over and expecting a different result, he decided to give the rings one last try.

He tapped the silver ring, and a tiny spark came… They worked again?

He activated the copper rings. The polarized field pressed the magnetic shackles apart. His hands were free. He gently slid Kelsie off him. Then he slipped his feet out of the ankle shackles.

He quickly donned his clothes. He went to Kelsie for a moment. "I'm sorry." He shook his head through the tears and brushed her hair out of her face. "I will stop him. I will get justice for you. And all his other victims. Goodbye, Kelsie." He stroked her cheek with the back of his fingers. Then he hurried to the hover car.

As he flew to Atlantis, he contacted the authorities in Delta and told them about Kelsie and everything else he was forced to do. He was in a race against time. Would he get there in time to save Julie? He thought not. He would most likely fail. And Julie would pay the price. How pathetic was he?

Aphrodite

When Micheal hadn't returned and wasn't answering his phone, JULIE became terrified something terrible had happened. She was about to go to Delta to look for him when a report broke on the news.

The TV said: "Delta's brightest star, Kelsie Ambrose, was murdered today. It looks like the work of the Phantom, but the Phantom is in custody. Maybe it's a copycat, or someone else." She shut the TV off as she turned to leave.

"Aphrodite, my love." Gabriel startled her.

"Gabriel! I apologize; I really must go; it's an emergency." He grabbed her by the arm as she tried to step past him. "Let go of me, now!" He only squeezed tighter. She spun out of his grasp and brought lightning to her hands. As she attempted to shock him with it, the spark sputtered out.

"Is that any way to treat a devoted lover of your Eminence?"

Gabriel smiled. "I bet you didn't see this coming, my Goddess of Love," he said proudly.

She realized he must be doing something to counteract her rings. She thought there must be a range to this effect. She attacked with a torrent of kicks—the final one connected with force, sending him flying. She turned and ran full speed into the glass courtyard. She activated the black rings and flew up, attempting to escape.

The rings suddenly gave out. She had flown a few hundred feet above the penthouse. Now, she was in freefall back to the courtyard. If not for the tri-poly clothing she was wearing, the impact would've killed her. As she was about to get up, Gabriel took her in a chokehold. She tried to fight against him, but he was too strong. He pressed even harder on her neck, and she passed out.

⁎

As she opened her eyes.

"There you are." Gabriel smiled. "I apologize, Aphrodite. Are you okay?" He feigned concern.

"Like you care, you evil bastard!"

"But I do, my goddess. Do you remember the day we first met? Your beauty was hypnotizing. I fell in love with you that day."

"If it were love, I wouldn't be naked... And you were just a boy."

She was completely naked. She was shackled to the bed. He ran his fingers along the curve of her breast, stopping at her nipple. "Such perfect beauty shouldn't be hidden..." He circled her nipple with his finger, then squeezed her breast. "Flawless, in every way. The Goddess of Love and Beauty, sculpted by Uranus himself. The definition of beauty, against which to measure all else." He admired her body.

"Why would you attack me like this?"

"I didn't attack you. I came here to prove my love to you. And I was just a boy when we first met, but now, I'm a formidable man. I even defeated Koios in single combat. I am more worthy of you than he is. Now, I have defeated you. Defeating two Gods? That makes me a God, I think."

Was Micheal dead? She thought. She broke down in tears. Then she was filled with rage.

"Worthy? You're pathetic! Gabriel, Decima would be ashamed of you."

"Don't talk about my mother!"

"If she knew what a monster her son had become..."

"Shut up!" He swung the blade in his hand at her neck, then stopped just as it cut in. "No! You need to stay perfect. You're trying to provoke me." He accused. "This is supposed to be a joyous day. I finally possess Aphrodite ... I have loved you so long. I've dreamed of this day for 900 years." He ran his fingers down her cheek; he stopped when he reached the cut on her throat. "I'm sorry about that." He wiped the blood from the cut. "Would you look at that? Closed already. It is great to be a goddess, isn't it?" He gave a slight smile.

The medical nanos must've closed the wound already. He kissed the cut on her neck. "So clearly, you know, I'm the Phantom. I punished your cheating, God Koios. I forced him to watch as I strangled that bitch, Kelsie Ambrose. I did that for you."

"You killed Kelsie for me? Did you kill all my other friends for me also? Because Daniel says he's the Phantom."

"I killed most of your friends, but I didn't get them all. It was especially a shame he beat me to Adelaide. I must give him credit. He outsmarted me, and that's extremely difficult to do. I even outsmarted Elissa, kind of. She unfortunately discovered my secret, so I was forced to kill her." He shook his head.

Julie felt sick. Elissa was missing: presumed dead. Her body was never found. At least now she knew what happened. "Oh please, you did it because you got off on it."

"I won't deny that I enjoyed the act. But I never planned to kill her. The only person closer to me at the time was Melina. And I will only kill her if I have to."

"Don't try to pretend to have a soul. You'll kill her soon enough."

"She did just discover the truth. I let her live when she confronted me. But you talked me into it. Despite our brother-sister connection, she will expose me. So, once you're dead, I'll go take care of her."

"You would've anyway. Don't try to blame me."

"Whatever. As I was saying, Daniel planned his vengeance, against you no less. He forged a relationship with my daughter to access the halls of power to aid him. Through this relationship he discovered my secret. Then coopted my technology. His mistake was not knowing who you really are."

"If you 'love' me? Why didn't you just come for me? Why did you have to kill all my friends?"

"None of them were worthy of a goddess."

"And you are?... No. You're just that pathetic little boy I met all those years ago who could never be a true man to an actual woman. So you have to take them by force. How many have you killed? I remember ... The look in your eyes that day. I saw the signs. Then, you served me for five years, and I had no doubt about your potential to become this kind of a monster. I did hope Decima would steer you down the right path. But then she was murdered. And that was your trigger moment, wasn't it? From that day forward, you plotted your first kill. Then, when we returned to the heavens a few months later, that sent you over the edge, didn't it? So how many women have you murdered over the last 900 years?"

"81,281. But I've never killed a goddess before." He looked at her with hungry eyes. He leaned over and kissed her on the mouth. She head-butted him in response. He nearly hit her. Then he shook his head. "It's no matter. Once you're dead, my Aphrodite, all of this perfection belongs to me." He admired her body from head to toe as he ran his hands from her neck down over her breasts, then on down between her legs. As he caressed her down there, he said. "The softest, most beautiful flower." She shuddered.

He couldn't be any more revolting. "So now, what great expression of your love do you have for me? Rape?"

"I'm not going to make love to you like this. I'm not worthy." He bowed.

"We agree on that."

"You know, Aphrodite, you should be thanking me! I'm the one who saved you when Katherine almost killed you at The Atlas Awards!" He flared.

"Oh! So that's why my powers didn't work that night. Because of you!" she deduced. "So don't pat yourself on the back too hard, Gabriel. You only do things if they serve you! I wouldn't have needed saving if you weren't there!... And now that I think about it. You probably only stopped her because you wanted to kill me, and she nearly beat you to it!" She glared.

"Did you think that perhaps Katherine might also know how to stop you?"

She mock-laughed. "You're joking, right? She doesn't even know I'm a goddess. And she hasn't wanted to kill me as long as you have. You've spent the last nine centuries fantasizing about how you were going to do this, haven't you?" She was sick of his game. "I'm finished discussing your pathetic nature, Gabriel. You want to kill me? Then kill me already! Just get it over with!"

"You're right, even without knowing how to weaken you. I was so close to trying the last time you visited 450 years ago. Because I wasn't sure I would get another chance. But I'm glad I waited. During that time, I fantasized about this day over and over. So I'm sorry, Aphrodite, but I can't have it end that quickly. I must savor this. Oh, and also, there are so many ways I have imagined doing it. I do have to try a few of them, right?" He smiled.

With Micheal dead, she had decided to surrender to death. But the thought of a long, drawn-out, agonizing death was not what she had in mind. At that moment, it was like she was back in Salem. She was staring death in the face for the first time all over again. The same feelings of horror and helplessness flooded over her.

Gabriel injected her with two different syringes. "This first one will keep you alive longer, extending the fun. And it also monitors your vitals, so I know when you're approaching death. That way, I can stop just before. The second one will prevent the decomposition of your perfect, beautiful body. You will be mine, frozen in this perfect state forever. We will be together at last. Now, shall we begin?" He was grinning from ear to ear.

Using the magnetic shackles to control her. Gabriel moved Julie to a chair in front of a mirror. He withdrew a clear plastic bag from his pocket. "How about we start with an old favorite of mine." He slid the bag over her head and tightened the drawstring around her neck.

Whatever he had injected her with did apparently drag it out. The plastic was soon stuck to her mouth and nose. The terrible fire in her lungs from the suffocation, as well as the pressure in her chest, lasted for what felt like eons. To make matters worse, Gabriel's hands searched her body the entire time.

Why did all of her deaths always have to be so agonizingly long? If Gabriel was serious about trying multiple methods, this was going to take a lifetime. The walls finally closed in around her, and everything went dark.

When she came to, she was still shackled to the chair. "Welcome back!" Gabriel said with a smile. "How was round one? I know I certainly enjoyed it," he said excitedly. "I have never been able to truly test these nanos. You lasted 12 minutes! Very impressive, Aphrodite. Now for round two, an old classic. The thin wire garrote!" He quickly wrapped the wire around her neck a few times and wrenched it hard. It felt like multiple blades slicing into her neck. And her agony repeated.

"13 minutes for round two! Let's aim to improve on that with each round." He suggested. "I've decided to change it up for round three."

He forced her into the bathroom. There was a glass tank there. He locked her inside, and the tank began to fill with water. Just before it overtook her nose, she took a deep breath. The fear rose as the minutes passed. She was desperate for a breath, but also desperate not to take one. She couldn't hold out anymore. She took a deep breath of water. Drowning was even worse than strangulation. Utter helplessness consumed her as her lungs were about to burst.

Her mind went to Jessica. Was this what she went through? Julie's body went numb. A warm calm came over. Then suddenly Jessica was there.

"Hey, little sis." Jessica communicated telepathically.

"Are you here to take me to the other side?" Julie responded in kind.

"No, you reached out to me. I felt that you were scared. So I came to comfort you."

"I'm sorry I haven't reached out to you as much as I used to. It's been so crazy since I fell through time."

"That doesn't matter. All that matters is the love we share." Jessica reached out, and Julie felt her touch.

Julie instinctively moved to hug her, and the next thing she knew they were fully embraced. After a few minutes. "I have to go now. I'm so happy I got to see you again. I love you, little sis." Jessica pulled back.

"I love you, Jess." The tears came, and then Jessica disappeared in a flash.

Julie turned and looked back into her lifeless eyes. Then she suddenly felt the pain return with a vengeance.

As she was coughing up water, she heard Gabriel say. "I'm sorry, Aphrodite. I nearly waited too long. It would've been such a shame to cut the fun short." He smiled. "Are you having a good time? Cause I certainly am."

"You evil bastard! You will burn in the fires of Tartarus." She glared.

He just laughed. "I'm glad you've got your spirit back. I want you to experience this in full. The more pain and anguish you experience, the better. Now for round four."

He carried her to the bed. After setting her down on her hands and knees, he hadn't secured her; at least, she thought he hadn't. But when she attempted to move off the bed something held her there.

In the mirror, she saw him come up behind her. "I do love your slender, delicate neck." He stroked her neck, then he slipped a belt over her head and began throttling her from behind. After jolting her violently numerous times, he began exploring her body with his disgusting hand. She had to go through all the horrors and pains once again.

As the dark shadow closed in again, all the fight drained out of her. She prayed Gabriel would finally show an ounce of mercy and finish her for good.

But when she came to, the nightmare only continued. Now her hands and feet were constricted to the corners of the bed. Gabriel came and inspected her whole body by hand. Then he continued.

Over the next few hours, he cycled through over half a dozen different ligatures, including a thin rope, a cord, a zip tie, a shoelace, and a silk scarf. Strangling her to the point of death and then bringing her back repeatedly. In addition, two rounds of hanging, one with a cable and the other with an extension cord, were performed.

As he prepared for round 12, Gabriel spent a good deal of time inspecting her neck. "Well, this is unfortunate. Aphrodite, I have enjoyed our time together so much that I could go on for days. But I fear this will have to be the final time. The nanos have been doing a great job preventing any surface bruising. But, if I go much longer, I risk doing too much damage to this elegant neck. So, unfortunately for me, the time has come for me to finish you off. I just want you to know that the perfection of your body will remain in this immaculate state forever. So now you, Aphrodite, will be all mine." He smiled with glee.

Despite her intense repulsion, she didn't respond. She was ready to die. He was straddling on top of her stomach. He wrapped a nylon stocking around her throat, and the long, horrible process began. The only silver lining was that this would be the last time.

He pulled as hard as he could on the stocking. It bit so hard into her neck that she was nearly convinced that it must actually be a wire. While the intense pain cut through her badly bruised neck, the pressure in her chest became unbearable. The minutes dragged on agonizingly long. He periodically yanked on the ends of the stocking, attempting to strangle her even harder.

Eventually, she stopped reacting to such antics. Her whole body went numb. She was attempting to retract herself from the pain. When there was a sudden blur, and the pressure released dramatically. Then she realized Gabriel was gone.

She squeezed her eyes, attempting to help focus them. When the fog cleared, she turned to see Gabriel in combat with... Micheal? A rush of emotions flooded through her. She had been so despondent, believing Micheal was dead. Now she was filled with a new hope that they might survive.

Micheal and Gabriel went back and forth a few times, then Gabriel retreated to the balcony. Micheal pursued him. They exchanged volleys a few more times, and then Gabriel parlayed one of Micheal's attacks into a body toss. And Micheal went over the edge.

Gabriel lept up onto the guard rail of the balcony. He appeared to be intensely observing. He stared a minute longer and returned to the bed.

"Wow! While I did plan for this possibility, I was still rather surprised to have Koios show up. But it appears that my preplanned trap worked like a charm. Koios is now nicely skewered on the ledge below. I've got to admit it's quite thrilling to kill a God. And it will certainly be even more thrilling to kill a goddess. Now, where were we?" He sounded giddy.

As the nylon bit into her neck again, her newfound sorrow was soon replaced by horror.

MICHEAL came to in a massive amount of pain. Even wearing the tri-poly clothing, that hurt! He coughed up some blood. He saw that he was lying on some kind of overhang a couple hundred feet below the penthouse. Gabriel must have decided he was dead, so Micheal had one more chance to take him down.

He was in excruciating pain, but he knew Gabriel would kill Julie soon if he didn't hurry. The windows were unbreakable, and the building exterior was too smooth to climb. Then he had a crazy idea. He was unsure of the range of Gabriel's dampening fields, but he hoped they did not go all the way to the ground.

He made his way to the corner of the building; he took three quick steps and dove off the side. As he was falling, he desperately tried to activate his black rings. The building got wider as it approached the ground. He collided with the side of the building, causing him to go into a tumble. Finally, the rings activated, preventing him from hitting the ground.

He flew far out, away from the building and then shot straight up well above the building. He made sure he was above the roof and began to descend. When he reached approximately 200 feet above the roof, the rings sputtered out, and he went into freefall, hitting the courtyard with force.

JULIE had been throttled for what felt like an eternity. Her vision had narrowed. Then, through the static buzz in her ears, she heard Gabriel say. "Time to finish you." He wrapped the nylon around her neck another time and pulled as hard as he could. While she was nearly numb from head to toe, the pain flashed life back into her nerves. She couldn't help but react to Gabriel's obvious delight.

There was a sudden loud thud, startling Gabriel. He hesitated, staring into her eyes. He seemed to be deciding whether to finish her first. Then, clearly frustrated, he left to investigate what the noise was.

Julie took in air for the first time in five or 10 minutes. The nylon was still tight, but she could breathe a little.

As Gabriel was nearing the door to the courtyard, he was kicked hard in the face. As he stumbled backward, to Julie's shock, Micheal bolted through the door. Pouncing on top of Gabriel.

They scuffled for a minute. Then Gabriel threw Micheal across the floor. Micheal began an elusive tumble around the room, evading Gabriel's attempts to attack him. Finally, Micheal returned to the offensive, connecting with force to the buckle of Gabriel's belt.

Since Micheal returned from the dead, Julie had been attempting to activate her rings. Suddenly, she felt the power flow through them.

The copper rings came to life. She generated a limited polarized field, which she used to counteract the magnetic cuffs. They began to slip a little. With all her might, she was able to break the magnetic bonds, freeing her hands. She was then able to release her ankle shackles. She removed the nylon and breathed deeply, attempting to steady herself.

Julie saw that Micheal was losing. Gabriel was attempting to break Micheal's neck. She ran full speed and kicked Gabriel hard in the face. Gabriel went to the ground as her kick knocked him off Micheal. As he rose, they were on either side of him.

Both she and Micheal were seriously injured, which slowed them both down. Gabriel was matching them blow for blow. Gabriel knocked Micheal down hard, and she exchanged blows with Gabriel. He performed the same kind of pressure point attacks Katherine had used against her. Her legs gave out, and she went down.

Micheal plowed into Gabriel, and they began scuffling again. Then Gabriel tossed Micheal across the balcony.

Julie stumbled full speed into Gabriel, and they both went over the edge of the building. As they fell, Julie remembered she was still naked. Micheal had most likely survived because of the tri-poly he was wearing. So she thought, after all that, she was about to die anyway. She desperately attempted to activate her rings, to no avail. They hit hard, and everything went dark.

MICHEAL ran to the edge and looked down. Julie had landed on top of Gabriel. He needed to get to her as quickly as possible. He had to eliminate the kinetic dampeners. He ran full speed and dove off the top of the tower. Once his freefall reached the same point that the rings had worked before, he activated the black rings and flew out away from the building.

He circled the building quickly, locating what he was sure were the dampeners. He fired up his lightning, and from a distance, he systematically destroyed them all. When he was confident they were all destroyed, he quickly flew to Julie.

Gabriel was clearly dead, skewered by his own spikes. One of them had penetrated all the way through him and had impaled Julie in the stomach. With no time to lose he quickly flew her to the nearest hospital.

As he was waiting for word, Micheal's mind was filled with so many things. How was he going to face Julie? After what happened with Kelsie. And his failure to protect both her and Kelsie.

He should have taken the Phantom more seriously. He should've realized that if the Phantom, Gabriel Maximus, could elude the Atlantean investigators. As well as their own efforts to identify him using their sky-net. That he must be quite formidable.

Micheal had been too impressed with himself. Believing they could deal with whatever came their way. But he fooled himself. And now Kelsie was dead, Julie had been tortured, and he had had sex with another woman.

Julie had made him promise not to run again. So he would stay... For now. Despite how much he just wanted to leave. He was damaged goods. He would need to make Julie realize he was not good enough for her.

Aftermath

"Micheal?" JULIE opened her eyes. She could feel his hand on hers.

"Yes, Jules?" he replied softly, squeezing her hand.

"I'm so glad you're all right. When I thought you were dead..." She was overwhelmed with emotion.

"Sh... It's okay."

"How come so many horrible things always happen to me? Is it because of me somehow? Do I deserve..." She was feeling so terrible, but Micheal stopped her.

"No, Jules!" He shook his head. "This was primarily the work of one man, who was obsessed with you... Because of me."

"Because of you?"

"I... Go with it... Us being Gods. And look at all the consequences that have come of it." He had tears in his eyes.

"It's not your fault."

"No! It's true. And now you have been brutalized again. All our friends are dead, and I was forced to have sex with Kelsie." He said through the tears.

"What? Forced to have sex with Kelsie?" It was like a punch to the stomach.

"It's all my fault. I couldn't protect either of you. I nearly stopped Gabriel when he came for Kelsie. If I could've held on a few seconds longer, but he escaped my grasp and knocked me out. When I woke, I was shackled to the bed naked. He had Kelsie there, also. She was naked. He threatened to torture Kelsie for a week if we didn't perform for him. He told me afterward that he wanted to sully me for you. And he succeeded. Then I was forced to watch him strangle Kelsie while she was still on top of me." He broke down again. She was devastated. "I'm sorry, Jules. If I had put my foot down with Kelsie years ago, Gabriel would not have desired to punish my infidelity to you. I understand why you can't look at me ..." She had only just become aware that she hadn't looked at him since he told her. "I need a minute." He walked out of the room. It was all too much. She cried herself to sleep.

MICHEAL went to an empty room to be alone. Many of the negative thoughts he had buried at the bottom of his memory files were filtering to the top. He recognized the truth of many of them. The most glaring was how selfish he was. He would usually make decisions for his own sake at any given moment without considering the consequences to himself or those around him. He was a terrible person.

Now, those chickens were coming home to roost. Nearly everything bad that had happened to Julie since they met was his fault. All that pain and anguish. Why was she with him? As he went through all of it in his head, he only became more and more confused. There were, of course, some good things between them, but there were so many more bad things. The cause of which, was mostly him.

For Julie's sake, he needed to find a way to convince her of the truth.

To his shame, he realized that part of him had enjoyed the encounter with Kelsie. Which only made the guilt that much worse.

Micheal needed something to take his mind off everything. He turned on the TV.

The TV said: "... Our top story, The Phantom serial killer, is now confirmed dead. Authorities confirm that the world's second-oldest man and third-oldest person, Gabriel Maximus, was indeed the Phantom. Daniel Woods has admitted he imitated Gabriel. Here's Fabiana Helton, Deputy Director of investigations. "A search of Mr. Maximus's property holdings uncovered a secret underground facility filled with files on every victim he had murdered, including his final victim, Kelsie Ambrose, who was killed the night before Mr. Maximus met his own demise. All 581 victims of the Phantom have been accounted for. Gabriel killed all but 23 of them, who were killed by Daniel. This vault contained files on more than 100,000 people going back over 900 years. Mr. Maximus was among the richest people in the world and had connections in government and business worldwide. He was also in regular attendance at gala events in Delta. He was killed last night by Julie Hall of Avalon, who was defending herself against his murderous attack..." Okay, we are going to leave director Helton to discuss a related story. This video captured the scene outside the God's Plaza, where Phantom Gabriel Maximus met his end. This figure is clearly flying on his own without aid of any kind. And he is also firing lightning out of his hands. Some claim he is a God ... Lilia?... "While the religion has gone out of style over the last few centuries. A good number of people still believe in the gods of old. While many now believe them to be just a myth. There is one true believer who claims she has actually met them. Here is Gallia Karallis, the world's fifth-oldest person. You say you've met these gods? Yes, I am 917 years old. When I was eight, the God Koios and the Goddess Aphrodite came to rule over Atlantis. It was incredible. They built The Palace of the Gods practically overnight with their magical power. They ended wars and plagues. Their rule was peaceful and prosperous for all. When I was 12, I had the greatest honor of my life. Koios and Aphrodite visited me. I was sick, and I was going to die. They used their magic to heal me. For the last 900 years, I've thanked the gods daily for my life. Then, five years ago, they returned to Atlantis. They were calling themselves Micheal and Julie Hall of Avalon. The one featured in the video is Koios, the God of Wisdom and Knowledge. And Aphrodite was the one who stopped Gabriel. Who I am ashamed to say I have known for centuries. Are you sure they are the gods? I am. If you don't believe me, ask Melina Hellas. She was Aphrodite's personal handmaiden during their rule. She was the one who heralded their coming nine centuries ago. I idolized Melina. I wanted to be just like her. Not like Aphrodite? I could never be like her..." Here is Melina Hellas. "Can I confirm that the gods of old are real? They are absolutely real. Did I serve Aphrodite and Koios? Yes." "Melina, are Micheal and Julie Hall, Koios and Aphrodite?" It doesn't matter. The gods have abandoned us. The world will end in three years. I suggest everyone use that time wisely." That was Melina Hellas, the Oracle of Atlantis..." Micheal shut off the TV.

"Great, one more headache to deal with; that is, of course, my fault." He shook his head.

JULIE woke up, and Micheal was still gone. She didn't know how to feel.

She tried not to think of him differently, but the revelation that he had essentially experienced rape had stirred a torrent of emotions within her.

It was made that much worse because it had been with Kelsie. A part of her did blame him. But at the very least, she believed it wasn't intentional. And personally speaking, she was dealing with the fact that Gabriel had violated her sexually. While he had never penetrated her. He had done nearly everything else. She shuddered again at the thought.

"Jules?" Micheal appeared at the door.

"Yes, Micheal?"

"Are you sure you want to make us work?"

"Why wouldn't we?"

"There's something I didn't tell you."

"Okay?" She was even more nervous.

"When Kelsie and I were forced to have sex." He stalled for a moment. "Part of me enjoyed it... I hate myself for that. But..." It was like a knife to her heart.

"Why would you tell me that?" Tears came to her eyes.

"I just want to be honest with you."

She suppressed her anger. "It's okay. We will work through all this together."

"Because I will leave if you want me to."

Damn him. He wanted to run again. His promise was likely the only thing keeping him here. And despite her current ambivalence toward him. She had lost so many people so fast; she didn't think she could survive losing him as well.

"No... We will find each other again, just like last time." He seemed a bit surprised by her decision. Despite his efforts to hide it, she caught a hint of disappointment in his face. He had told her about Kelsie in an attempt to get her to send him away.

"Well, on a different note. When I flew to rescue you from the ledge and bring you here, it was caught on video. Now Gallia Karallis shows up talking about how I'm Koios, and you're Aphrodite. She even told them to talk to Melina. At least she didn't confirm anything. But now we have yet another problem that I caused." He shook his head.

"What are we going to do about it?"

"I don't know. Avoid answering any questions. And I need to go and talk to Gallia." He shrugged his shoulders.

"Isn't Gallia the sick girl from Carthage we treated personally? For bacterial infection?"

"Yes."

"Be kind to her, won't you?"

"Of course I will. Now, get some rest. I love you, Jules." He kissed her.

"I love you, Micheal." He left the room.

* * *

MICHEAL arrived at the Sunset Beach Retirement Village on the west side of Atlantis's outer ring island. He knocked on the door. Gallia opened the door and immediately went to her knees. "Eminence Koios?"

"Gallia, you may rise. May I come in?"

She rose. "Of course, Your Eminence."

When he entered, there were pictures of them as Avalon all over her walls. She also had a shrine to each of them. They sat in her living room, and she poured a drink for both of them.

"My God, how may I serve you?"

"How are you, Gallia?" She seemed surprised by his interest.

"Oh! I am so well, your Eminence." Tears came to her eyes. "I have paid tribute to you and Aphrodite every day for the last 905 years, for my long healthy life... Never did I think I would be before you again." She looked at him with a sense of awe.

They discussed her life for a while. Then he pivoted to the reason he had come. "Now, Gallia, there is one thing I ask of you."

"Anything, Your Eminence!"

"We very much appreciate your devotion, but we ask that you not talk to the media about us, about our true identities."

"My apologies, Eminence Koios. I was just so excited."

"It's okay. We're not angry with you. You may discuss us with your friends and family. But no media, okay Gallia?"

"You can count on me."

"Thank you, Gallia. Aphrodite and I very much appreciate it." As he was about to leave, she asked. "May I hug you?"

He embraced her tenderly. "Farewell, Gallia."

Now there was something else he needed to do.

Honoring Heroes

MICHEAL arrived to find Gabriel's vault cordoned off. With police standing watch. But since he'd heard about Elissa's fate, he needed to honor her. Reports said the centuries-old bodies, with no claimant family, would be mass interred. Elissa deserved better than that.

He flew up into the clouds and then dove like a rocket past the cordon and inside the vault. He found her body on display in the furthest corner. Because she was his first preserved victim.

The conversation that Julie had with Gabriel, which she related to him, indicated that Elissa likely invented the technology.

He scanned the chamber, and no authorities were around. He opened her display case and looked into her eyes. It was as if she just passed.

He shook his head at the destruction of life that Gabriel left in his wake. He unwound the garrote from her neck, then gently closed her eyes.

Micheal levitated up to the ceiling of the vault. Investigators entered and began walking the aisles marking the cases. He slowly flew to the exit, then accelerated out and up into the sky.

He stopped at the penthouse. He brought Elissa into the labs.

He scanned her body and fed the pattern into a fabricator to mold a sarcophagus out of gold. It was going to take some time, so he sat next to Elissa to wait.

"Eminence Koios." Melina entered the labs.

"Come sit with me."

She came and hugged him. He felt tears on his shoulder. Then she sat with him.

"You followed me here?"

"I went to try and claim her body, but they rejected me. While I was trying to come up with a different plan, I saw you fly out with her."

"I wanted to thank you."

"For what?"

"It was you who came to Kelsie's penthouse in Delta."

Melina averted her eyes. He knew she had conflicting feelings about Gabriel.

"I finally discovered Gabriel was the Phantom. I tried to convince him to stop and all he did was threaten me. Without hard evidence, I couldn't go to the authorities, but I needed to stop him. I'm a skilled fighter but he was better. I knew you were the only ones who could stop him. I saw where you were and came to shut down his technology. If I'd gotten there sooner, Kelsie would still be alive."

"Why didn't you come into the room?"

She shook her head and tears came to her eyes. "I was ashamed. I should've discovered the truth sooner."

Micheal took her hand. "You did well. Aphrodite only survived because of you."

"How's she doing?"

"She's damaged in more ways than one. I hope she can be made whole."

"I hope so also." She stood up next to Elissa. Micheal joined her.

Melina touched her forehead. "I was there when she was helping Gabriel develop this technology. She seems to be only sleeping, for 300 years, and soon she'll wake up."

"Perfection in life, perfection in death."

An indicator dinged. "It's ready."

The sarcophagus was an inch thick solid gold, true to life image of Elissa. It weighed more than a ton. He activated his rings and carried it out to the courtyard.

He returned and carried Elissa out to her coffin. Melina followed.

Melina conducted internment ceremonies, then Micheal laid Elissa to rest.

Then he gave a dedication.

"What is a hero? Do they battle through dozens of foes? Or do they utilize their gifts to make the world a better place? That is what you did, Elissa. You were the greatest mind of a millennium. And you selflessly used your time to improve the lives of people everywhere. At great sacrifice to your own personal happiness. This modern world wouldn't be here if you hadn't cared about others before yourself. That is your legacy. And that is the essence of a true hero. Your life was a testament to the purpose of knowledge and wisdom. You are a most worthy representative of me. I miss you, my dearest friend, and I will see you again when I return to the heavens."

After a moment of silence, they transported Elissa's sarcophagus to the Temple of the Gods, where they placed it in a standing position in a private memorial, only accessible to the priestesses.

Micheal looked at Elissa through the glass cover of the sarcophagus. Even after 300 years, she looked perfect, as if she were only sleeping. Now she was safe among her family, no longer Gabriel's trophy.

"So, she's in Elysium? She earned exaltation?"

"Yes. And she's been reunited with her family."

"You've seen her since she died?"

"I'm not going to divulge details of the hereafter. But I will tell you she's found her happiness."

Melina went and touched the glass. "I'm glad. She was always a little sad. She deserves happiness."

Micheal touched her shoulder. "So do you. I know I burdened you with future knowledge. But you've proved that foresight combined with purity of heart is a most powerful combination. Remain fastidious and you will find exaltation as well. And Elissa will be there to welcome you."

Melina hugged him. "This brings that terrible time back like it was yesterday. I should've found her before Gabriel did this. I failed as an oracle. Why couldn't I see it was him?"

"Love clouds our vision."

Melina pulled back. "I didn't love Gabriel."

"Yes, you did. You knew each other for 900 years. It wouldn't be possible not to care for each other. He was truly evil, but everyone has good and bad qualities, even him."

"How can you not be filled with rage over what he did to you, and Elissa, and Aphrodite?"

Micheal had a flash of all the terrible memories Gabriel created. As well as the vision Melina shared about what he did to Elissa. He sighed to quell his anger.

"This moment is about you, not me. Losing so many people who mattered to you. And this was a double hit. Gabriel's betrayal of your trust cost you both him and Elissa. I know this will try your resilience, but persist in your gift, and you'll find exaltation. In Elysium, you'll dwell in joy with Elissa and your family."

Melina laid her head on his chest. He laid his head on hers, and just held her. He knew she needed caring contact. She silently embraced him for a good while. He knew she was going back to the time she lost Elissa, in her head.

Whenever he returned to the loss of Amanda, it was always a raw experience. So, he would allow her to lean on him.

She finally sniffled and pulled back. "Thank you, Koios. I didn't mean to impose." She wiped her face.

"It's no trouble. If you ever need to talk, or someone to lean on, don't hesitate to come to me. Now, I must get back."

Melina bowed. Micheal touched the glass of Elissa, then returned to the hospital.

CHAPTER XVIII: MYSTIQUE

Separate Ways

A WEEK LATER, THEY left the hospital in a media frenzy. They had expected it. As a large portion of news coverage kept playing the video of MICHEAL taking out the kinetic dampeners. Along with endless discussions about the gods of old. And numerous profiles of Aphrodite and Koios.

With everything they had suffered, the extra glare of the gods opened the cracks in their relationship to the breaking point.

"You're leaving?" He found Julie in her room, packing her bags.

"I can't stay here... In this situation anymore." There was a quiver in her voice. "I thought we could work through this together, but it isn't working." She shook her head as she closed her suitcase.

"You mean with me, don't you?"

"I need some time alone."

"For how long?"

"I don't know." Tears came to her eyes.

"22 years ago today, we were married."

Although he wasn't really trying to dissuade her, ever since that day, he couldn't get past his shame and failures. He still knew he was no good for her.

"I don't know if we can get through this... I still love you, but maybe 22 years has been two years too long." She took her bags and walked out.

This was what he thought was best, right? He had been with her in some way, shape, or form for more than half his life. But their relationship had been circumstantial from the beginning. He knew that even now, under any other circumstance, she wouldn't give him the time of day. He had always had a thought nagging at him from the start, saying this dream would never last. Typically, in that scenario, it was always he who ran away. And Julie would realize he was right. Then she would move on.

However, that never happened. The few times he had run away, she had always come and found him, or like the last time, he had eventually returned. And for some strange reason that he still didn't understand, she always took him back.

As he watched her disappear from sight, he knew it was for the last time.

Their anniversary only emphasized the problems they were having. JULIE had realized that Gabriel had succeeded in what he had intended. Ever since Micheal had told her what happened with Kelsie that day in the hospital, she couldn't look at him the same.

Now that she had finally fully recovered, physically at least. She had nothing left to give. She needed time to think through everything she was feeling. So she was going to Amazon, a mega-city on the most western coast of the Empire, to get as far away from everything as possible. Would she ever return to Micheal? She didn't know.

Julie moved into Mystique. It was a privately owned, special suburban beachside city near Amazon. It was an exclusive place where famous people could go to just feel normal. And she needed that right now.

A week had passed since Julie had left, and MICHEAL couldn't stay in the penthouse any longer. He didn't know where Julie had gone but knew where she wouldn't go.

He arrived at The Frozen Sea port city of Tyre in the northeast of the Empire. He bought a large, isolated mansion next to the sea where he would try to forget his problems. If only that were possible.

He was 90% sure that she was gone for good. The thought sent him deeper into a depressive state of mourning. Even though he knew it was best for her. His mind couldn't comprehend not being with her. How could he live without her?

A month after JULIE arrived at Mystique, she called the penthouse in a moment of weakness and discovered that Michael had left a week after she did and had not been heard from since. She decided to take a break from worrying. She began going to clubs and parties.

"Hey everybody, this is my new friend Aphrodite." Gaia introduced her to a dozen other women.

"You must be new to Mystique." One of the women seemed particularly interested in her. "I'm Valentina, by the way."

"Not really; I've been here for about a month."

"Oh, I'm surprised I haven't seen you before." Valentina raised a brow.

"Hi, I'm Harley, and Valentina here is the Social Queen of Mystique. She knows everyone."

"So, Aphrodite? Like the goddess?" Valentina asked with a smile.

"If only, right?" Julie joked. Everyone laughed.

Drinks were served, and they proceeded to talk and laugh.

Later that evening. "Is everything all right?" Gaia asked.

"I thought we weren't supposed to say things like that about our identities."

"Oh, you mean the goddess comment by Valentina? It's not what you think. May we have a sidebar?"

"Okay."

Gaia led her to a private area. "That was completely unintentional on Valentina's part. You did use Aphrodite. And with all the talk that you really are. Well. Valentina has been here since the beginning, almost 100 years ago. She never exposes herself to the outside world. Intentional or unprovoked rule-breaking is very rare. I promise you this Aphrodite. It's likely the rest of the women here know who you really are. But outside of this kind of agreed sidebar, they will all pretend otherwise."

"Okay, thank you, Gaia."

"Want to go back?"

"Let's go!"

"Let's dance!"

***

MICHEAL spent about a month mostly meditating, focusing on himself. Usually, this extra-critical view of himself caused him to think poorly of himself. So, he focused on the times when Julie would give him compliments or advice. He wanted to see himself through her eyes. If he could accomplish that, and he still felt like damaged goods, then he would let her go.

As the days passed, his self-focused mind began to turn towards empathy for Julie. He thought for the first time he understood her view of him. And while he had pushed hard to run her off. He realized that to her, he was everything. In her eyes he was far better than he could ever think of himself to be.

While he still didn't fully understand it, he felt she needed him. And while Gabriel had damaged him. He came to see that all she was trying to do was help him heal his wounds. But in this situation, her wounds were still too raw.

Through all this self-reflection, he realized, beyond a shadow of a doubt, that he needed her. And he wouldn't spend one more day than necessary outside of her presence. He would go find her.

***

JULIE was feeling much better. She felt normal again, probably for the first time since they had arrived in the 24th century BC. Now, she spent her days hanging out on the beach with her new friends. Or she would go to a party at a different beach house. She would go shopping with her friends. Or they would go to clubs.

Now, when she said "normal" she meant, no expectations. None of her new friends had any of the ridiculous expectations she was used to. They all treated her like just another party-girl socialite, which was how all of them, including her, were acting. It was like they were the real-life version of "The Hills."

The only area she had resisted participating in, was hooking up with any of the countless men who had pursued her. She had danced with many of them and got to know a few reasonably well. But no matter how nice or great they were. They weren't Micheal.

Now Micheal had clearly been broken by everything that had happened. And he had made a clear and concerted effort to push her away. When she woke up on their 22nd anniversary, she finally decided to give him what he wanted. It was true she had some anger and resentment towards him. But not enough for them to go their separate ways.

In the first month at Mystique, she had suffered through severe heartbreak. Even now, whenever she was alone, she thought of him. Was he well? Would he be able to find the peace he was looking for? She wondered, especially, if she would ever see him again. She desperately wanted to. How could she live without him? But he had chosen solitude. She only wanted him to be happy, even if it wasn't with her.

MICHEAL returned to the penthouse. "Bernice, any word from Julie?"

"Mrs. Hall called here a little over a week ago looking for you."

"Did she say where she was?"

"I'm sorry Mr. Hall."

"Thank you, Bernice." He left the penthouse.

He stopped at the Emperor's Palace.

"Mr. Hall, we're so glad you're back." Empress Regina Seneca said as he entered her office. "I just want to give my deepest condolences for all that has happened to you and Julie." The Empress shook her head. "Now, how may I help you?"

"It's Julie, we had sort of a disagreement and she left. And now I can't find her."

"Do you think something bad has happened to her?"

"No... Well, at least it's not likely." His stomach twisted.

"I will make a few calls."

"Thank you, Empress Regina."

"Good luck Micheal, and if you need anything else, don't hesitate to ask."

Over the next few weeks, with help from the Empress and all aspects of the administration. All efforts to help him came to nothing. That did start to worry him. Either she didn't want him to find her. Or something terrible had happened to her. Neither one was a good option.

"So we have to celebrate your birthday, Aphrodite." Valentina implored JULIE.

"Oh, all right."

Over the past week, Valentina had been hounding her about a birthday party.

"Great! I will take care of everything. We'll do it at your beach house. And I promise you Aphrodite, it will be the social event of the month. Everyone will be there!"

"Great!" She wasn't sure she wanted such a celebration, not without Micheal.

"And also Aphrodite, I will find you the perfect man to wish you a happy birthday." Valentina gave a wink.

"I already told you. I don't need a man right now."

"Now Aphrodite, this sad sorry state you're in, just won't do. Trust me, I'm a great judge of who's perfect for who. I promise I will find someone who is your ideal... At least promise me you'll give this one a chance."

For the last month, Valentina had put forward numerous matches for her, but she couldn't move on from Micheal, even if he could move on from her.

MICHEAL had moved heaven and earth with nothing to show for it. There was only one thing he hadn't done. Go talk to Melina.

While she and Julie were no longer friends, there was still a chance Melina would know something. If nothing else, he could perhaps test her Oracle skills. Melina had blamed him for her curse of foresight. And while initially, he had scoffed. On further consideration, Melina had attended three of their comings and goings. He wondered what kind of an effect being exposed to that much temporal energy could potentially have on someone.

He didn't think it was a coincidence that Melina had gained the sight following her third exposure at their previous departure.

In the circumstance where she had placed him on the spot regarding her visions of the future, Michael had to support her belief in him as Koios actively. He spun an adapted version of The Flood of Noah, as an Atlantean apocalypse brought on by the gods of Atlantis. Now he wasn't sure if that was what was coming. But what he did know was that Atlantis was more or less lost to history.

As he flew from the penthouse in central Atlantis to The Temple of the Gods, he couldn't help but wonder how such a mega-city, home to more than 300 million people. And a world of nearly 40 billion that was more advanced than they were in the 21st century could possibly be destroyed. But clearly, it had.

Based on his understanding of the biblical timeline, the Flood of Noah could happen at any time. According to the tachyon readings, an event of unbelievable magnitude was approximately three years away. Could that be the Flood of Noah? Was that the apocalypse that Melina had spoken of? The one that would end Atlantis?

On a more personal note, that event coincided with the day they were to depart the 24th century BC. So they better not miss their jump. That was one more reason he needed to find Julie.

"Melina?" Micheal said as he entered the chamber.

"Koios?! What are you doing here?"

"I need your help."

"How's Aphrodite doing?"

"That's why I'm here. Gabriel caused a rift between us. She left and I'm trying to find her."

"He hurt me as well. The great Oracle of Atlantis was fooled." She squeezed her fists.

"You're too hard on yourself, Melina, which is why I'm here. Our foresight gets clouded by love."

"You need my help to see?"

"I realize you and Aphrodite are in a bad place. That is why you're the last person I came to."

"Let's see what I can see." She began leading him to The Oracle Chamber.

"Thank you, Melina."

"You may not like what I see."

"I just need to know."

Melina entered The Oracle Chamber. Then she relayed what she saw.

"I see her... Aphrodite is alive... She appears to be in some kind of a dance club. I can't see the name... She appears to be living up to her name..."

"What does that mean?"

She hesitated for a moment. "She's... Loving many men..." Micheal's heart sank. Melina continued. "She's loving them at clubs... At the beach... At parties..."

"I get it!"

"Sorry! I'm sorry, I can't pin down a location for you... I can tell you she is well... And she's near a beach somewhere."

Tears came to his eyes. Julie had apparently moved on. It was no more than he deserved.

"I'm sorry Koios." Melina gave him a hug.

"Thank you, Melina, you're a good friend." He left the chamber.

Julie had moved on, perhaps he should as well. But he wasn't sure if he could.

Mystique

JULIE was feeling nervous. She had begrudgingly agreed to give Valentina's birthday man a chance. But she wasn't sure how to feel. She had been kissed a few times by some of the men that Valentina had introduced her to. She still felt guilty about it. Despite the fact that she was convinced Micheal had moved on, she had trouble letting go.

If ever, even for a moment, she had considered any of these men. She knew they could never measure up to Micheal. So what could she do?

"Aphrodite, all the girls are going kite surfing, want to come?" Gaia asked excitedly.

They all went to the beach, dressed in their bikinis. Then one by one they each took a turn on the kite. They would all watch and would chat about anything and everything. Everyone was just enjoying the sun. Then was her turn.

As the wind blew through her hair, her memory went back to the time she flew as Aphrodite. She had always loved flying and she longed for the days of her goddess flights.

The boat changed direction, and at that moment the buckle of her harness broke. She began trying to signal that she was in trouble. But a large gust of wind hit the parachute, shaking her violently. She was pulled over a rocky outcropping at the end of the beach. Then another gust hit the sail hard and she lost her grip.

As she went into freefall from around 500 feet, she didn't know what to do. The jagged rocks were coming up fast, then she reacted. She activated her black rings stopping herself about 20 feet above the rocks. As she turned herself vertical, she saw her friends gaping at her in shock. She did the only thing she could think of. She flew over and landed next to them.

"Aphrodite!" Gaia exclaimed wide-eyed. "You really are... Aren't you?"

They all stared at her in amazement. Julie shook her head in resignation.

"You're the actual Goddess of Love and Beauty?" Valentina was studying her.

"I am." Julie hung her head.

Valentina touched her shoulder. "It's okay Aphrodite, the rules of Mystique apply to all, even a goddess." The rest of her friends all agreed. "Now Aphrodite, I promised you the perfect man. And tomorrow I will deliver him."

"And just who might you be?" A beautiful woman randomly asked MICHEAL, while he was shopping in the produce section of the grocery store.

"Are you talking to me?" She was smiling at him.

"Is there another handsomely tall man that I could be talking to?" The woman looked him up and down.

"My name is Koios, and yours?"

"Valentina... Koios? As in The God of Wisdom?" She raised a

brow.

"Indeed." He kissed her hand.

She scanned him from head to toe again. "So Koios, there's a new art exhibit at The Pier Gallery. Would you like to accompany me? I hear it's amazing."

Valentina was about five-foot-six, she had light brown hair, glowing amber eyes, and a tan complexion. She was quite beautiful. And while he wasn't sure he could move on from Julie, he would've felt bad turning down yet another woman who had approached him. It happened about once a day since he came to Mystique, about two weeks ago.

He had spent the week following his viewing by Melina, trying to decide what to do now. But the glaring spotlight was only getting worse, so he needed to get away. He decided to go to the celebrity retreat city of Mystique. He knew Julie would never come here. When he first told her about this place, she had been appalled that everyone could be so fake. She had never understood what the whole concept was meant to do. It was to be a retreat from fame.

"What time should I pick you up?"

"... This piece speaks to me," Valentina said, holding his elbow as they walked the gallery.

"Very fine detailing... The texturing is amazing."

They paused, admiring the next canvas.

"Koios, a friend of mine is having a party at her beach house tomorrow. You should come."

"Why not?"

Valentina sat him down on a bench. "I have to be honest with you, Koios."

"Okay?" He raised a brow.

"I was looking for someone for my friend. And you seemed perfect. But I wanted to be sure."

"So you took me for a test ride?" He wasn't sure how to feel about that.

"You're not mad, are you?"

"It's okay. Who's your friend?"

"Her name is Aphrodite. And you're Koios. Isn't it perfect?

Koios and Aphrodite shared eternal love in the old mythologies."

"Indeed they did..." He stared longingly, thinking of Julie. "I would love to meet your friend."

"Great! Though I do have to admit that I was almost tempted to keep you for myself." She stroked his shoulder.

JULIE was a bit nervous. While hundreds of people attended her beach house birthday party, Valentina was bringing her perfect man. And she had promised to give him a chance.

"So, are you excited to meet Mr. Perfect?" Gaia gave a smile.

"Of course."

"You have nothing to worry about. If Valentina picks him for you, he will be perfect."

Julie spent the next hour making the rounds. Then, as she was sitting on the couch surrounded by her friends, she suddenly heard Valentina say. "Aphrodite!"

She looked up and was shocked to see Micheal standing there looking as shocked as she felt.

Upon their fashionably late arrival at the party, MICHEAL felt it was a birthday party. It was at a very large mansion on the beach. Valentina escorted him through the crowded, wall-to-wall party. They entered a large entertainment room with floor-to-ceiling windows overlooking the beach.

Valentina guided him over to a large sitting area. Then she said, "Aphrodite!"

The woman in the center of the couch looked up, and Micheal was stunned to see that it was Julie in the middle of about a dozen other women.

When her apparent shock wore off, she stood up, and Valentina said. "Aphrodite. I would like you to meet Koios."

He wasn't sure how to proceed, so he followed Mystique's protocol. "Aphrodite, a pleasure." He kissed her hand.

"Charmed." She smiled.

He introduced himself to all the ladies. Then, they invited him to sit down. After a moment, Gaia said. "Good job, Valentina. If Aphrodite is not interested, I am *so* available," to the surprise of much of the couch.

"Gaia!" several of the women said in concert.

"What? He's sexy."

All he could do was laugh. After chatting with the ladies for little while, he stood and said, "Ladies, may I borrow the birthday girl for a dance." Aphrodite took his hand to the swoon of the couch.

JULIE was surprised that Micheal had played it so cool. So she decided to play along. "So, Koios, how long have you been in Mystique?" Aphrodite asked as they started to slow dance.

"Almost two weeks. And how about you, Aphrodite?"

"About three months now. So what brought you here?"

"Well, first, I pushed my wife away and spent a month celebrating a pity party. While I worked to heal myself. Then I searched the world high and low to find her. But I failed. So, I returned to the pity party for another week. But then the spotlight around my penthouse became too bright, so I sought refuge here. I know, it's a long, boring story. My apologies."

"Did you come here expecting your wife to be here?"

"No, my wife said this place was the ultimate sham. And completely ridiculous. It's the last place in the world I would ever expect to find her."

"Well, I don't think your wife knows what she's talking about. No offense." She gave a sly smile.

"So, you came here with Valentina? How long have you known each other?"

"Yesterday, in the grocery store. She approached me and invited me to the art exhibit at The Pier Gallery."

"Did you come to Mystique to move on from your wife?" She raised a brow.

"I came to get out of the spotlight and just relax. Maybe make some new friends."

"How did your 'date' go with Valentina?"

"The exhibit was quite interesting, and Valentina definitely knew how to make conversation."

"No good night kiss?"

"No, I was still pining over my wife. I don't think I can ever get over her. So, if you're looking for something serious here, it probably won't work. But I digress. Valentina decided to invite me to one of her friends' parties. She did not specify birthday, by the way. She said our date was to affirm her impressions of me before she introduced me to her friend." He shook his head.

"So you were just looking for friends."

"Well... I was fresh out."

"I know what you mean." She shook her head.

"I'm sorry, I'm a party pooper. It's your birthday, you shouldn't worry about all this stuff. Stay here for just a moment..." He left the room for a moment.

Valentina came over. "Isn't he great? He's smart and funny and obviously..." She smiled. "So you seem to be getting along very well."

"You did well, Val."

Then Koios returned. "Valentina, want to see some real dancing?" The tempo of the music picked up. "Aphrodite?" He held out his hand. Aphrodite smiled and followed his lead.

At first, the floor was cleared, and everybody watched as they performed a series of dance styles. To match the pace of the music, they danced the likes of the jive, the quickstep, the tango, and the samba. They put on a show, complete with lifts. Then they took a break. And everybody else joined in the dancing.

"Wow! You were great out there. Both of you." Gaia looked back and forth between them.

The rest of her friends joined the conversation. And they all talked for a few hours then it was time for the presentation of the lifespan—the Atlantean birthday tradition of presenting an item representing the length of longevity of life.

Valentina stepped forward. "Attention everyone!" She quieted the room and unveiled a chain full of gems. "I present this lifespan of 58 gems representing the 58 beautiful years of my friend Aphrodite!" Everyone cheered as Valentina draped it over her shoulders.

The party was nearing its end. Koios stood. "Ladies, a divine pleasure to meet you all. And especially the lovely Aphrodite. But before I go. I can't leave without giving the birthday girl a gift." He said elaborately. "Aphrodite... For you." He bowed, handing her an orb.

"Koios... Thank you very much... What is it?" She was fascinated as she inspected it. It appeared as if it were made out of liquid.

"It's a memory orb. It displays whatever memory you desire to see as either a photo or a moving picture."

"Really? Will you show me?" She would have to ask how it worked later.

He took it in his hand and then seemed to focus for a moment. Then he handed it to her. There was a woman who appeared to be floating ethereally in water. Then Aphrodite recognized her. It was Jessica. She looked up at Koios. She had to fight back the tears. He touched it again. And it transitioned to a white horse; it was Angel.

She smiled. He took his hand back. She focused for a moment. Suddenly, her parents, Jason and Jennifer, were there. "Thank you so much!" She threw her arms around him.

He finally pulled back. "I must go... Happy birthday, Aphrodite." He left her, remembering why she had fallen in love with him.

Aphrodite & Koios

-APHRODITE- November 12, 2372 BC

"I have suffered so much. And it nearly destroyed me. I didn't think I could go on. I was this close to ending it all at the end of a rope. It would have been fitting, as I've been there so many times. I had lost everything. So what did it matter? Right? I had come to Mystique with that in mind. No one outside of Mystique would have known—a quiet end to a life in the spotlight.

As I stood on the chair with the cable noose around my neck. I closed my eyes and imagined my life if I stayed. I still saw nothing worthwhile, so I began to step off when the doorbell rang. I considered ignoring it, but even in that dark moment, I thought it would be rude. And that is when I met Gaia.

She said she was going to go surfing with some friends, but they all bailed on her. She asked if perhaps I might like to join her. As odd as it seemed I felt bad for her, so I agreed. Those unusual circumstances pulled me back from the brink. And now two months later, I feel completely alive again. And I received the most amazing birthday gift.

I met a new man. His name is Koios. Although he's not exactly a man. He's a God! The ideal match for a Goddess.

*We've only just met. By looking into his crystal ball gift I can
already see our future together."*
   PS: I can't believe I'm 58 already.

KOIOS woke to a fresh sea breeze coming off the ocean. As he
walked out onto the balcony overlooking the beach, he marveled
that one day, this tropical paradise would be the city of San Francisco. Mystique was located on the north half of the north end of
the peninsula. And it was essentially the same size as the city of
San Francisco. The primary difference was that in the Atlantean
era the bay area was located at 18° north latitude instead of 38°
north latitude.

   Koios sighed deeply, taking in the sea breeze. He thought about
how crazy it was that a random person, Valentina, would inadvertently bring him and Aphrodite together. On her birthday, no less.

   Aphrodite was his ideal match, but courtship was a delicate
game. He would have to play this just right. But as he considered
how to proceed, he realized he was 54 and had never been on an
actual date before. He would need to get some expert advice.

   "... I understand," Valentina said. "The Gods don't usually date,
do they?"

   "No, we don't."

   "Well, the most important thing is to be confident. Confidence
is attractive. And focus on her. We can have a tendency to talk
about ourselves too much. You're trying to learn about her. Do
something interactive, you know, something fun. And finally, just
be yourself."

   "Something fun... How about horse riding on the beach?"

   "That's perfect! Now, my God of Knowledge, go win the heart
of The Goddess of Beauty."

Koios picked up APHRODITE in an Odyssey, a fancy sports car
brand. They drove to Oceanus Park, in the southwest quarter of
Mystique.

   "So, Aphrodite, have you ever ridden a horse before?"

"It's been a few years. Hey girl!" She patted the big white mare on the neck. Koios' horse was a giant white stallion. "Race you to the end?"

"Yah!" She commanded, and the race was on.

As they raced, the wind blew through her hair. It reminded her of her rides with Angel at Bostonian a lifetime ago.

"So. Koios? What kinds of things are you interested in?" she asked as he pulled up next to her.

"I love long walks on the beach." He smiled. She laughed.

"You mean as long as the horse does the walking."

"How did you know?" He jested. Then he sobered up. "But seriously, I have loved the stars for as long as I can remember. I remember my mother was holding me in her arms. I was not quite one yet. I remember because there were Fall leaves on the trees. The stars were so beautiful. I was fascinated. Then, a year or so later, my mom saw me lying on the lawn outside, staring up at the stars. She pointed out Polaris. She told me that was the North Star, that it showed true north. A guardian in the night to show you the way home. And I've loved the stars ever since."

She was touched by his waxing poetic. She couldn't help herself. "You never told me that story before." She broke protocol.

"You never asked." He pointed out. "It's not like I think of that story on a regular basis. Now, Aphrodite, what's your story?"

"The earliest memory I remember was when I said my first word... Cookie... I was not quite one. I wanted a cookie, and so I asked for one."

"Were you walking yet?"

"Yes. My parents said that I walked for the first time when I was eight months old. And I was running around at ten months. But anyway, that cookie started it all. I learned pretty quickly that all of those packages in the kitchen had things in them. And I wanted to know what. My dad always read me a bedtime story. By the time I was perhaps 18 months old, I had begun to understand what many of the words meant. So, I quickly learned how to read by age two. With the power of new knowledge, I proceeded to go through the pantry on my own and take whatever treats I wanted. When my mom found out what I was doing, she put a stop to it and told me that until I was buying the treats, I had to get permission first. Now, my dad would always watch the news at night, and one day, there was a report about a girl with a lemonade stand. And I thought I could do that. Now it was the summer of '82; I wasn't quite three yet. But Jessica helped me. While Dad was at work and Mom was watching TV, we snuck outside and set up the stand. It was a hot day, and we sold out the pitcher in less than an hour. And at a nickel a cup, we made about two dollars. A dollar each..."

"You made that off of one gallon?"

"Oh yeah... We took the bathroom rinse cups. They were 3 ounces a piece... Now, when we were taking down the stand. My mother found us. She was trying to decide if we would get to keep our ill-gotten gains because we took the lemonade and cups without permission. My dad's solution was that we would have to pay back what we took, or we would keep the money, but we could never do that again. We paid back my parents, which was around a dollar. Then we used the rest of our profits to do it all over again. But only under my mother's supervision.

"Jessica and I ran the stand in the neighborhood all summer. We had treats like cookies and brownies. Over the summer, we averaged $20 a day and brought in a total of about $2000 to split between us. I ran that lemonade stand like a well-oiled machine. It costs an average of around four dollars a day to operate. That meant Jessica and I each pocketed $800 in profits. It taught me that I could make my own money and buy my own treats. That experience gave me my love for business. We even made the news.

"After that, every summer I would come up with something to sell. Then, after I graduated high school at 12, I founded Bucking-ham Investments."

"A true business maven with ten years' experience." Koios joked. "I think it's time for dinner." They stopped to set up a picnic.

"Beautiful sunset." She said with a sigh. "I love the way the light reflects off the water, like a path of gold running through the green."

"You're beautiful."

She looked at him. Their eyes connected for a moment, then he looked away. She continued to look at him.

"I'm sorry, that was a bit forward." He rose to his feet. She stood and grabbed his arm to stop him from leaving. "It's okay." He turned back and looked at her. He was searching her face in consideration.

"Aphrodite, may I kiss you?"

"You may."

He cupped her face in his hands and gently kissed her on the lips. She had to fight to control herself. This was a first date.

KOIOS took Aphrodite home. Then he got a second good night kiss. Although, in reality, he knew her well. He felt like he was getting to know her for the first time.

They went to the zoo on their second date a few days later.

"Look at the size of that thing!" Koios commented.

"What is it?"

"It's a glyptodon. Like a giant armadillo." It was about 10 feet long and weighed about two tons.

"This is the first time I've been to a zoo since I arrived."

"Me too."

They stopped for lunch between the Smilodon exhibit, which was a sabertoothed cat. And the woolly mammoths. It was surreal to have two of the most famous Ice Age animals right there.

"What do you want out of life?" Koios asked Aphrodite.

She considered for a moment. "To live a life of meaning." She began, then paused, still pondering. "To help people less fortunate than myself—to be a good friend to my friends. To do something great for humanity." She had been averting her eyes, and then she looked at him. "I was given a rare gift. I knew from when I was quite young that I was different. And when I realized how different I was, I felt an enormous responsibility not to waste the genius I had been given. So, I worked hard to get an education. And then I came up with a plan to make enough money that I could make a difference in the lives of others."

"And do you think you've had success to that end?"

"For the most part. Particularly when I was young, but some-times life chooses for you." There was a hint of sadness in her voice. "And what about you, Koios?"

"I had a similar interest in helping other people, but I didn't feel like I owed anyone anything. I grew up in poverty, and my parents didn't really know how to work the school system, so I had to wait until I was five to start my education. By then, everything in school was so rudimentary that I had little interest. My one constant desire in life was knowledge and understanding. And the place that was supposed to facilitate that, kept attempting to force me into the box they thought I should be in. I had nothing in common with kids my own age. And for someone who was naturally, severely introverted. It made me feel like even more of an outcast. I only had one friend.

"The feeling that the school system had failed me built up severe resentment. That, along with being bullied on a daily basis. Caused me to sink into a deep depression. And depression is a very self-centered thought condition. Most of my thoughts made me angry at society. So, I didn't have a whole lot of concern for helping society.

"I wasted the first three decades of my life, my potential, wallowing in self-pity."

"So you were able to leave your pity party? How?"

"Well... There was this life-changing moment where I was forced to step up or die. And for whatever reason, I chose to step up. But that wasn't the real reason. I only realized later that that decision brought someone into my life who made me want to be a better person. They encouraged me to reach for my potential. Not my genius potential. No... my human potential." Aphrodite had tears in her eyes.

"Sounds like quite a person."

"She is. She is the best person I've ever met." Tears came to his eyes. "She is such a genuine good person. She taught me everything I know about life, about what's important. She made me the man I am today."

"What happened to her?"

"I lost her. I pushed her away. I wasn't good enough for her... As I stood on the chair with the rope around my neck. I thought about this woman. And how much she meant to me. I was at a crossroads. I could end it all, and no one would care. Or I could do the hard thing. I could work on myself with even more determination and try to become good enough." He closed his eyes.

"Did you succeed?"

"I don't know. She's the only one in this world that I trust. And I lost her."

"You haven't lost her. As the Goddess of Love, I know something about it. You have everything to live for. She loves you more than you could know, and she needs you very much. As Aphrodite, I know her heart. You are good enough for her. She wanted me to give you this." She pulled him up and kissed him deeply.

They continued their way around the Atlantean zoo. Seeing things like Gigantopithecus, the largest ape ever. Giant dire wolves and the short-faced bear. Along with Mastodons, the giant beaver, as well as a Megalania, a giant monitor lizard 25 feet long and weighing almost a ton.

"Want to come in?" she asked as he dropped her off.

"Quite tempting, but I want to wait a little longer."

"Just don't keep a girl waiting so long this time!" She implored him, and they locked lips.

Renewal

"So, APHRODITE, how's it going with Koios?" Valentina raised a brow.

"It's going great. You certainly found the perfect man."

"Don't you mean the perfect God?" Lynexa asked.

"Who knew knowledge was so sexy?" Kartilia added.

"Ladies!" Aphrodite said loudly.

"You know, Aphrodite. You haven't shown us anything since the beach. I'm not saying you have to. I'm saying, we're your friends, and it would be so cool if you did, at least once." Gaia prodded.

"Oh, all right, you talked me into it." Aphrodite shook her head. "I'll start with the easiest one. Take that knife and stab me with it. I promise it's okay."

Gaia grabbed the knife and stabbed it at her arm. The knife stopped right at her skin, to the amazement of all.

"Lynexa, hit me over the head with that sledgehammer." Lynexa did, and it bounced off.

"Now for a fun one." Aphrodite opened her hands, and lightning sparked between them, mesmerizing them all. She built up a large ball of light in her hands and then sent it into the clouds. She reached her hand up, and the bolt came back down. She caught it to the delight of all her friends.

"Watch this!" She was on a roll now. She walked over and picked up a car. She was holding it above her head like Wonder Woman. All of a sudden, she realized her friends were looking past her. She turned around and saw Koios standing right there. "Koios!" She was startled and accidentally threw the car at him.

He caught it by the bumper in his hand.

"Nice catch!" Gaia said in amazement.

As Koios set the car down, he said. "Aphrodite. Putting on quite the show, are you?" He raised a brow.

"Just satisfying the ladies' curiosity."

"And how are you ladies today?" He smiled at them.

"We were just enjoying the show, Eminence Koios." Valentina smiled back.

"Ladies, if you don't mind, may I borrow Aphrodite for the evening?" Koios gave them a bow.

"You take care of our girl now," Gaia said playfully.

"So, Aphrodite, what should we do? Your choice."

Aphrodite considered for a moment. "Follow my lead." She turned to her friends. "Now, for my final demonstration." She floated up about 50 feet above the ground.

"Ladies." Koios bowed, then floated up to join her.

"Up, up, and away!" she shouted as she flew up to the first cloud deck. Then Koios followed her.

"So you decided to go full goddess?"

"They already knew. There was a... Kite sailing incident about a week ago. My harness malfunctioned, and I fell about 500 feet to the ground. Just before I was going to be impaled by the sharp rocks, I reacted. Stopping me around 20 feet above the ground. All the ladies saw this happen... I'm sorry."

"Don't worry about it." He shook his head.

"The ladies all agreed that the protocols cover God's as well... Here in Mystique, at least."

"All right. Want to take a walk in the clouds?" He gave a smile.

"Micheal? Can I have a sidebar?"

"Of course, what's up?"

"Well first, before I say anything else, I just wanted you to know how much I'm enjoying this dating game. But I digress... Something you said the other day hit close to home. So, I was afraid to address it at the time. But I really need to know."

"Okay." He furrowed his brow.

"When you said you stood on a chair with a rope around your neck, that was figurative, wasn't it?" Her stomach tickled.

He turned away slightly. "No... By the time I settled in, in Tyre, I truly felt I had nothing left to live for. I had successfully pushed away the only person who meant anything to me in this life. And the demons from my youth came back with a vengeance, telling me to end it all." He turned back quickly to face her. "How did this hit close to home?" He studied her.

She averted her eyes. "After I left, I knew you had been trying to get me to leave, so I finally decided to give you what you wanted. But then, nothing had any meaning anymore. So I decided to end it all. As I was about to step off the chair. The doorbell rang. I almost ignored it. But then my manners got the better of me. And that's when I met Gaia. She pulled me back from the ledge. She saved my life." She looked back at him, and he was crying.

He flew over and embraced her. "I am so sorry." He held her for a moment. Then he pulled back and kissed her. He looked into her eyes, wiping away the tears. "I will never push you away again. I will never leave you again. My life is meaningless without you." He kissed her again. It was exactly what she needed to hear. She threw her arms around him and got lost in his loving embrace.

The weight of the emotions that had been clouding her for the last few months began to lift. She felt newly refreshed.

"So Koios. Want to do the Superman." Aphrodite smiled. She dove for the beach below. It was like skydiving from the cloud deck. Just before hitting the ground, they jettisoned out over the ocean, flying just above the surface. After a few miles, they shot straight up through the clouds with an outstretched arm, of course. She readied herself for the cold.

While the temperature in Mystique was about 90°F. At 30,000 feet, it would be -10 Fahrenheit. Luckily, the polarized magnetic field around her would buffer the wind.

The thin, cold air was well worth it. Floating high in the clear green sky. The sun was low toward the horizon. The clouds were far below. And she could hear the Superman theme song in her head the whole time.

"This is my favorite part about being a goddess."

They returned to her beach house. As they shut the door, APHRODITE said. "I'm not waiting any longer." She ripped his shirt open and began exploring his rock-hard abs with her mouth. Then she removed his pants and took him with her mouth. He, of course, returned the favor.

He was a bit rough, grabbing hard on her breasts and tweaking her nipples between his fingers. All her pent-up frustration was released in a multi-orgasmic explosion. When she had recovered from her first trip to ecstasy, she was ready for more.

She forced Koios on his back and rode him toward oblivion. As she climbed towards the top, she added an electric spark to the mix, pushing them simultaneously to the climax.

They spent the rest of the night having sex like the gods they were. Or at least they were pretending to be.

They continued to "date" in Mystique. And as the months passed Aphrodite and Koios helped them find each other again.

"You know what tomorrow is right?" Koios asked.

"Of course I do."

He dropped figuratively to one knee as they walked in the clouds. "Aphrodite, will you be my goddess?"

"My God, I will."

The next day was a flurry of activity as Valentina made all the arrangements. With help from the priestesses at The Temple of the Gods. It had been there since their reign a millennium earlier.

"They did a very good job, didn't they?" APHRODITE said, looking at her likeness. Her statue and the statue of Koios were facing each other across the chamber. They were both about 100 feet tall. The temple was the only pre-Mystique building in Mystique.

"It is certainly a little weird."

The priestesses bent over, hand and foot, to serve them. It reminded Aphrodite that they all still worshiped her.

"Aphrodite, your love inspires my wisdom and encourages me to share love with the world. You are my goddess of love for the millennia that have gone before and will be for the millennia to come. I love you for eternity." He slid the nano ring on her right ring finger.

"Koios, your knowledge encourages my love for the whole of the world. And your love restored my love within. You are my God of wisdom, always showing me the way through the darkest nights. Our love is timeless." She slid the nano ring on his right ring finger.

"By the declaration of the God Koios and Goddess Aphrodite, they be wed." Altairis, the chief priestess proclaimed.

They floated up above the stairs of the temple to the full view of everyone. And as the lightning pulsed over their bodies, they kissed, sending sparks out of their lips.

Nearly everyone in Mystique came for the party. And it was epic. They showed off their God powers and even took some of their friends for flights.

"It's been 28 years since I fell in love with you. I've loved you for more than half my life." Micheal said wistfully. "But it feels like my whole life."

"There is so much love between us, and I am eternally grateful for you, for your love." Julie sighed.

Following the celebrations of her 59th birthday and his 56th, and just over 29 years since they fell through time. They finally left Mystique.

CHAPTER XIX: NOAH

World at War

"*Mystique was exactly what we needed. It allowed us to just be us. I have accepted that Aphrodite is a part of who I am. I may not really be the goddess of love. But now, I'm relatively sure the Aphrodite from history is based on me.*

By the time we returned to the real world, the secret of our identities was out. Gabriel had stalked me through the centuries. He had all kinds of shrines devoted to me. He also had true-to-life paintings of me. They had been authenticated as centuries old and looked exactly like me. All of that evidence combined with Gallia's proclamations. Along with Melina's non-denials and the video of Micheal. The world is now convinced beyond a shadow of a doubt that we are the gods of old.

We are the second most talked about subject in the media. The world war being the first. Over the past 18 months, every country except Atlantis and its allies, are now at war. Babylon and its allies have conquered half of the world outside of the Atlantean alliance. I hope, for our sake, no one tries to get us involved in this war. I wish we could just live relatively quietly for the next two years, then move on to the next time stop. But when has that ever happened? Perhaps we should have stayed in Mystique."

They returned to Atlantis. MICHEAL was happy they could avoid the paparazzi in the penthouse.

"Did we really have to leave Mystique?" Julie sighed.

"We have much to do before we leave this time stop. We have to find out if the forthcoming apocalypse is The Flood of Noah as I suspect. We also need to solidify our financial assets for storage."

"Why do we need to worry about this apocalypse?"

"The biblical timeline is not exact. The Flood could happen at any time. If Melina's visions are accurate, then the timing of this apocalypse is close to our departure date."

"And you think this apocalypse is The Flood of Noah?"

"That's the only kind of event I can imagine that could destroy all of this." He indicated the megacity of Atlantis, which had nearly as many people as the entire United States in 2010. And the Atlantean Empire, at 8 billion, was home to more people than the whole world in 2010.

"And what about our 'gods' problem?" She shook her head.

"I don't know. Do you think the no comment or plausible deniability will work?"

"No, that absolutely won't work." She rolled her eyes. "I'm more worried that everybody is going to expect us to fix every problem."

"Regina!" Micheal said as Empress Regina Seneca entered the veranda.

"I am pleased you've returned. There is much to discuss." Micheal noticed she had come alone, with no escort.

"I'm surprised you never came to see us after the Phantom situation," Julie said.

"I was busy with the war. And the controversy surrounding the

Maximus clan, and the Council. I needed to keep my distance."

Julie cried. "So many of my friends were gone. It would've been nice to see you."

"I'm sorry Julie. About everything you've been through."

"Thank you, Regina." Micheal took a seat and indicated she should sit. "So why have you come now?"

They sat on the veranda with a great view of Mount Atlas. Bernice brought refreshments.

"To begin with, I will state firmly that this conversation is off the record." Regina began. "First, I will say I have never believed in the gods of old. But, the preponderance of evidence presented has convinced me that you are not exactly... Human." Regina was searching for words.

"It's true, I am Aphrodite, and he is Koios." Regina's wide eyes searched them. "You've known us for years, Regina."

"Will you... Show me... Show me your powers."

"Okay." Julie stood. Then she floated up in the air, bringing lightning between her hands.

Then Micheal stood and took the table's edge between his thumb and index finger. It was metal; he effortlessly lifted it above his head. He set it back down. "I know you carry a gun. Fire it at me."

She drew her gun. She took aim but hesitated for a moment. Then she fired. She still seemed surprised that the bullet was stopped. Then it just fell to the ground. She picked the bullet up and was inspecting it. "This war is... Wait, you have these powers... How did Gabriel almost kill you, both of you?"

"Gabriel had known us since he was 18; he was obsessed with Aphrodite. He studied us for centuries in a desire to possess her. He discovered a way to short-circuit our power. Which has already been weakened by an internal dispute with our father..."

"You mean with Uranus, right?"

"Yes, that's why we are here to begin with. We have also been weakened by the general lack of faith in us. The video of me flying around the building was when I was destroying the dampeners that Gabriel had set up."

"Didn't Katherine Cavendish almost kill you, Aphrodite?"

"Yes... Gabriel told me that he had discovered the Cavendish's plot against us. He had apparently decided to use the chance to test his dampeners. So without our powers and their element of surprise, they ambushed us... And well." She shrugged.

"Okay... That answers that... Many people think you should intercede in this war."

"Of course they do." Julie rolled her eyes.

"In the last year and a half, over a billion people have died because of this war. Billions more are suffering. I'm being criticized for my decision to remain neutral. And now, we have two gods living amongst us. How can we do nothing?"

"Everyone is afraid of Atlantis, which is why Babylon has not provoked us. If we enter this conflict, whoever we side with will win. But it will cost many Atlantean lives. Babylon has always considered us as some form of an enemy. But our relationship with them before this war began was probably at its best point in centuries. I know it's difficult but doing nothing is the best strategy. There is one caveat, however. Babylon must possess some new secret weapon." Micheal said.

"What do you mean?"

"They had to think that at some point Atlantis would get involved. And, as previously stated, they would lose that fight. So why would they start this now?" He paused a second to let her consider that. "Sometime in the last three years, they completed a new super weapon. I would advise you to put much covert effort toward discovering what it is. Then perhaps you can stop it."

"You are the God of Wisdom. You have foresight, correct?"

"While I am here, my sight is limited. However, I am certain of the Babylonian threat. For better assistance, I would suggest talking to Melina. She has a direct connection to the quantum stream."

"Melina was too busy to receive me... The last time I talked to her, she was clearly upset about something. She seemed despondent, almost like she had given up on the world... I have known Melina for a long time. I will attempt to reach out to her again. In the meantime, there are many atrocities taking place in this war. You might consider at least putting a stop to those." Regina rose to leave. "And I know I can count on your discretion. Once again, I'm glad you're back." She left the veranda.

"It's a good thing Regina is a friend. Otherwise, she would probably demand that we do those things." Julie said after Regina was gone.

"I think we should probably intercede to stop the atrocities."

"Seriously? Do you think we could even do anything? Micheal, you're not actually Koios. When we pulled off our portrayal of the gods, it was against Romanesque technology."

"We have several things we can use to shut down some of these horrors. And if we play it right, we won't have to do very much to end the war crimes. Obviously, I know I'm not Koios. But they don't know that."

"Why do we always have to be the heroes? How come it always has to be us?" Julie shook her head.

"Because we can... As Uncle Ben told Peter Parker. 'With great power comes great responsibility'. Now, we don't have the true power of the gods. But we do possess a form of great power."

"And what is that?" She rolled her eyes.

"Our genius."

"There are many geniuses in the world, especially in Atlantis with the thousand-year lifespan."

"When one of these normal people acquires genius through elevating IQ based on age. They still do not have the innate genius mind like we do." He paused for a second. "I know we can do this. And I don't think I can live with myself if I do nothing."

"Okay, So what's your plan?"

"Well, first, we need to look the part. Now, originally, I made these for fun." He pulled out modern-style versions of their warrior God battle suits. "Try-poly... Along with some kinetic energy additions."

"I suppose we should try these on." Aphrodite inspected the jumpsuit. It was white, with gold trim. And it featured multiple symbols of Aphrodite. Micheal thought she would look simply divine.

Arks

-March 12, 2369 BC

"I was initially opposed to being a superhero. But after Micheal talked me into it I've found it very empowering, and I have done much good in the process. After everything Gabriel took from me, it has become a way for me to get some of that back. This last year and a half has me feeling almost whole again.

In that time, Micheal and I have become closer than ever. After nearly 25 years of marriage, we are in love anew. We realized that while our trials have changed us. Our love is evergreen."

-PS: this is a banner day for me. Today marks my crossing of the temporal threshold. After this day, I have lived in the timeline longer than before the fall.

JULIE arrived at the scene of a hostage standoff. "Aphrodite! Thank goodness you're here," Agent Gillam said with relief.

"What's the situation?"

"The leader of The Children of Kronos, a doomsday cult. Hundreds of people, mostly women and children, are held hostage. He's threatening to kill them all."

"I'll go talk to him."

As she entered the compound, she was greeted by a hail of bullets.

"Hold your fire!" She heard someone yell, and all the shooting stopped.

She just waited there for a moment.

"Your Eminence!" A woman said, and then she bowed. "Geb would like to speak to you." The woman indicated she should follow.

As they made their way through the compound, everyone who saw her bowed to her. They finally came to a great hall. The room was filled with hundreds of people, primarily women and children, being held at gunpoint.

The man in the middle, Geb, she supposed. Stood bowed, then stood again and said, "Eminence Aphrodite, we are honored by your presence. My deepest and most sincere apologies that my men fired upon you." He bowed again.

"What is going on here?"

"The Apocalypse is upon us. We must make an offering to Kronos."

"Kronos would not be pleased by such an offering."

"A sacrifice of time, he would desire of us."

"You misunderstand; I know Kronos. A sacrifice of time for a productive purpose is what honors him. The sacrificing of lives is the ultimate waste of time. And wasting time is what Kronos despises most." She paused to see how he would react.

"But the Apocalypse is upon us!"

"Yes... It is." She confirmed. "Kronos gave you the gift of time.

All people have their time. But that is not for you to decide. All you have to decide is what to do with the time that is given to you." She quoted Gandalf from "Lord of the Rings."

Geb stared at her for a moment. She could tell he believed her. Then he said, "They're going to send me to prison, aren't they?"

She ambled up to him. "You swear to me, on Kronos, that nothing like this will ever happen again. And that you will honor Kronos with your time. You will use it in the service of others for the betterment of the world. If you so swear, then you will not go to prison."

Geb went to his knees at her feet. "Your holy Eminence, Aphrodite. On his holy Eminence Kronos, I so swear."

"And the rest of you?"

"I so swear." They all echoed in unison.

"I take you at your oaths... We will be watching."

She led them all out of the compound. "Agent Gillam, Mr. Geb Makeras has sworn an oath to follow the law faithfully. They have surrendered their weapons. No further retribution shall be delivered."

"Your Eminence, we are going to arrest the leaders."

"Regina, the Empress has empowered me to make such decisions... Unless you would like to answer to her?"

Agent Gillam stared at her for a moment, obviously stewing. "As you command your Eminence."

***

"So, how was your day, my dear?" Micheal asked as JULIE entered the penthouse. He was typing on the computer.

"I went down to Tycho to put an end to the hostage standoff." She unzipped her bodysuit.

"And how did that go?"

"I talked them out of a suicide pact... I'm surprised you haven't heard yet."

"I'm sorry, Jules. I was busy researching something... And that reminds me. You're going to have to put the superhero on pause for a little while..." He closed the computer.

"I don't think so. In the last year, I've done so much good." Her suit dropped to the ground.

"I know, but we have less than six months before we leave. And

I thought we should see if we can find Noah and his ark."

"Oh yeah, that is supposed to be in this time, isn't it." She considered a moment. "Okay, so where do we start?" She slipped into her comfy clothes.

The next day, they went to a place west of Central City on the coast. As they approached the ark, it was massive. Perhaps 500 feet long and 100 feet wide. It was constructed of wood and was sitting in a drydock. A man came to greet them.

"What can I do?... You're them!" He went to his knees. JULIE rolled her eyes in exasperation.

"Rise," she commanded. "What is your name?"

"Noah, your Eminence, Noah Mensah. How may I serve you?" He groveled.

"May we have a tour of your ark?" Micheal asked.

They were taken deck by deck. It was mostly empty, and the interior matched the exterior in construction and style.

"How long have you worked on this?" Julie asked.

"About 100 years, your Eminence." Mr. Mensah responded proudly.

"Why did you build it?" Micheal asked.

"There's going to be a flood."

"And how did you know there was going to be a flood?" Julie asked.

"Because God said there would be."

"I'm curious. How did God tell you this?" Julie asked.

"Well..." Mr. Mensah stammered.

"He didn't, did he?" Micheal deduced. "And where are all the animals?"

"I am gathering as many as I can. To get me, my family, and friends, through this flood."

"One final question. How old are you?" Micheal asked.

"I'm 569, why?"

"Thank you, Mr. Mensah." Micheal led Julie away.

"So you don't think this is the Noah from the Bible?"

"I don't think so. He would've said he had a dream or vision. And there would be no 'friends'."

"Maybe the Bible got some things wrong."

"I doubt that. And the wood was not correct."

"Then how does he know so much?" She raised a brow.

"He must've heard the real Noah preaching."

During the next month, they visited ten other arks of various shapes and sizes. All but one were made of metal.

"So that's it, I guess," Julie said as they left ark number 11.

"Actually, there is one more."

"Where?"

"Eden."

Noah El

"Not exactly the picture painted in Sunday school," Julie commented as they waited for 'Noah'.

MICHEAL felt similar to when they were about to meet Adam and Eve. Could this be the Noah from the Bible? Micheal had used the tachyon scanner to try to project when the flood would come. He had discovered an ominous truth. The flood would begin on August 12, 2369 BC. That was about three months from now. It was also the same day they were to leave this time stop.

"Not exactly... But then we do have a much clearer picture of the real history."

The door opened, and a woman entered. She had deep red hair, piercing green eyes, and an olive complexion. "Eminence Koios, Aphrodite, I am Jessalyn El; my father has been delayed. I, however, am curious about your interest in my father's work. Don't the gods have more important things to do than bother simple people like us?"

"Mrs. El, we are but simple people. Your father's mission is the most important one since Adam and Eve." She seemed surprised by the mention of Adam and Eve. But before she could reply, they were interrupted by a man entering the room.

"Jess, this is the final list of specimens for the project." The man said, handing her a stack of papers. "I apologize, I didn't mean to interrupt... Wait, you're the gods, right?" The man raised a brow.

"David, this is their Eminences, Aphrodite and Koios... And this is David Angelos, our animal expert on this project."

David came and shook their hands. Then paused a moment with an odd expression on his face. "It's amazing to meet the gods of old." He smiled. "Eminence Aphrodite, you are so much more beautiful in person."

"Thank you. You're an animal expert?"

"Oh yeah, I've loved animals as long as I can remember," David said in consideration.

"Must have been quite the task tracking down all those animals?" Micheal said.

"It was a labor of love—"

"Mrs. El, Empress Seneca is here." A secretary announced.

"Koios, Aphrodite, I urgently need your assistance."

"Regina, what's going on?" Julie asked.

"You warned me Babylon was developing some covert weapon. I asked Melina to look into it. The only thing she could see was that it was in space. We've spent months analyzing Babylon's space infrastructure using our satellite network. And have found nothing. Koios, I was hoping you could look again."

"Okay, give me a minute," Micheal said as he left the room. He indicated for Julie to stay. He went into an office down the hall. And connected to the sky-net. He scanned the Babylonian space network. None of the surveillance or scientific infrastructure appeared to show anything amiss. He scanned the farming platforms and detected an anomaly. He did a thorough analysis of all the data. He recognized a magnetic signature on the support rings of the support rods of the farming platforms. After doing the structural analysis, he realized the rods were unnecessary.

"Oh, my goodness!" These were kinetic rods. They could be dropped from space, and it would be like dropping an asteroid on a target.

He returned to the other office.

"So what did you find out?" Regina asked.

"On their farming platforms, they have built kinetic rods into the support structure." Micheal shook his head.

"Kinetic rods?"

"Large solid metal rods that you drop from space, and they can destroy an entire city in an instant," Julie replied for him.

"These rods are a thousand feet long and 50 feet in diameter. Depending on the impact velocity, they can each obliterate an area 15 to 20 miles across. And they have over a thousand of these."

Micheal said with alarm.

"I will order their destruction immediately."

"That would be a mistake," Micheal warned.

"How so?"

"They are at-the-ready. If Babylon feels threatened, they will drop them immediately."

"We have to do something!"

"I have an idea. Regina, you return to Atlantis and warn the Council. And within a few days, I will come and detail my idea, okay?" Julie said.

"Thank you, Aphrodite, Koios." Regina walked to the door. "Mrs. El," she said, then left.

"That sounds bad," Jessalyn said.

"It is... But it was inevitable." Micheal said with resignation.

"Do you still wish to see my father?" Jessalyn raised a brow.

"Yes, is he going to be much longer?" Julie said.

"I will go check." Jessalyn opened the door and nearly ran straight into a man. "Dad!... Dad, this is Aphrodite and Koios."

"And what do the gods of old want from me?" Noah raised a brow.

He was almost as tall as Micheal, perhaps six-foot-two. He had black hair, blue eyes, and a light complexion.

"You have built an ark?" Micheal said.

"I have... What about it?"

"Why did you build it?" Julie asked.

"God, the real God..." Noah laughed. "Told me to."

"God told you to? How?" Micheal asked.

"A little over a century ago, I had a vision from God. He told me to build an ark. He told me how big to make it. And which materials to use."

"What is the ark for?" Julie asked.

"The world is evil. It needs to be cleansed. There is going to be a flood. And only my family will survive."

"Everyone else is evil?" Micheal asked.

"I spent a century trying to bring people back to the teachings of God. It's a lost cause." Noah shook his head.

"How old are you? If you don't mind my asking?" Julie asked.

"600... What difference does it?..." Noah broke off. "What is that around your neck?" He was staring intently.

"It's an amulet. Why?" Julie said.

"Where did you get it?"

Julie looked at Micheal and then back to Noah. "It was a gift."

"From who?" Jessalyn, who had been sitting quietly, cut in.

"Everyone called them the elders. We knew them as Adam and Eve." Julie said.

Jessalyn and Noah shared a look. "You're the ones?" Jessalyn asked.

"Why would they have given them to you?" Noah furrowed his brow. "The gods of old?" He laughed.

Micheal put his hand to his face. "We are not actually the gods—"

"Not the real one, at least." Jessalyn laughed.

"Of course not" Micheal snapped. "There's only one true God! I would've never thought the great Noah, would have been so flippant!" Micheal shook his head. "But I guess they didn't really include a whole lot of detail about what you were like, did they?"

That seemed to sober Noah up. "What they said about me? Who is they?" Noah was looking back and forth between them.

"We are not from this time period." Julie began. "In our time, there is a scripture called the Bible. In the Book of Genesis, it talks about a global flood. And tells of Noah and his ark. Where he preserves everything so the world can be renewed, it tells how big the ark is. About all the animals. It even says you were 600 at the time of the flood."

"Adam and Eve gave the amulets to false gods?" Jessalyn seemed horrified.

"For goodness sake! We are not gods!" Julie said in frustration.

"I've seen all the videos. I've seen everything you can do, Aphrodite. To my shame, I had come to greatly admire you. And I love your music." Jessalyn admitted.

"I'm sorry if I'm ruining your opinion of me, but it's just technology that we invented. These rings. The silver one channels lightning." Julie brought up some lightning. "The black one makes us fly and makes us able to lift heavy objects with magnetic properties. And the copper ring generates a magnetic force field around us." She demonstrated both of them. "But without these." She indicated the rings. "I'm just Julie Hall, a normal person. And he's my husband, Micheal Hall. We are time travelers from 4300 years in the future."

"So, the amulets?" Noah inquired of Micheal.

"We've been jumping through the timeline. Nine hundred years ago, about 16 by our experience. We were here in Eden when

Adam sent for us. We were given a quest. They took us into The Garden of Eden, and we harvested materials from the trees of Life and Knowledge. Adam and Eve made these amulets from both of the trees."

Noah's demeanor changed drastically. Jessalyn seemed curious. "In the histories, Aphrodite and Koios ruled Atlantis for five years... Did you actually rule?" Jessalyn asked.

"Yes!" Julie looked sidelong at Micheal.

"It was an honest mistake that they thought we were gods," Micheal said defensively.

"He just decided to go along with it... Without even consulting me!"

"I think I'm even more impressed than when I thought you were really some kind of aberration," Jessalyn admitted.

"Wow... This is a lot to take in... All right, Julie, Micheal..." Noah cut in. "Do you want to see my ark?" He returned to the original discussion.

"Indeed!" Micheal agreed.

"Well then, let's go."

Noah's Ark

It was a familiar sight as they approached The Island of the Elders.

"This looks familiar," JULIE said.

"It does?" Ariella asked with surprise.

"Micheal and I spent six months here about 900 years ago."

"Really?"

"They were the ones Methuselah told us about," Noah informed her. "The ones who visited Adam and Eve."

As the boat pulled into the pier, there was a rare sight in Atlantis.

"Julie Hall, just as beautiful as last time I saw you nearly 500 years ago." A much-aged Methuselah said in greeting.

"Time has distinguished you, Methuselah." She kissed his cheek.

"I am sorry for all you've suffered these last few years." Methuselah touched her shoulder.

"You knew they were here?" Noah asked in annoyance.

"Of course, I've kept tabs on the two of you since you became the golden couple of Delta."

"And you didn't tell me?"

"That's not how this works, son. They had to find you on their own... I wish I would've been able to tell that Gabriel was what he was." Methuselah turned back to them.

"You knew Gabriel?" Micheal asked.

"Of course, everyone in The 900 Club knows each other. I am the oldest man. Gabriel was the second oldest. And I obviously know your friend Melina Hellas. An impressive woman. We have never seen eye to eye on religion, but she was equally passionate about the two of you as I am about God." Methuselah waxed nostalgic.

"I am sorry about that, by the way." Micheal apologized.

"For what?"

"I was the one who decided we would play Gods." Micheal shook his head.

"I know you have never talked to me about the five years you reigned over Atlantis. But Adam did... He said it was the most peaceful, prosperous time in the Empire's history, and the world as well. And then, in the past year or so, your superhero act of playing Gods has bettered the lives of countless people. In lesser hands, those rings would've been used to take over the world... The God of Wisdom and Goddess of Love and Beauty indeed." Methuselah bowed to each of them.

"Thank you, Methuselah." Julie bowed back.

"Well now, I suppose you're here to see the ark?" Methuselah returned to the purpose of their visit.

They walked through the woods. As they entered a clearing, the ark was there.

"300 cubits, by 50 cubits, by 30 cubits," Noah explained.

The Atlantean cubit was about 20 inches. So, the ark was 500 feet long, 83 feet wide, and 50 feet tall. It was a wooden rectangle tapering slightly as it approached the ground. There was an access tower next to it.

As they neared the access tower, all the people loading things stopped what they were doing and came to greet them. They all lined up.

Noah stepped forward and declared, "I want to introduce my family to you. This is my wife, Namia, and my sons: Japheth and his wife, Aresia; Shem and his wife, Pandora; Ham and his wife, Zeptah. You've already met my daughter Ariella and her husband, Garrit. This is my daughter Xenia and her husband, Tiberius, as well as my daughter Godiva and her husband, Kale. You've already met my daughter Jessalyn and her husband, Lykos. Lastly, my daughter Kallisto and her husband, Zane. These are the individuals who will be saved on the ark."

"Everyone! This is Micheal and Julie Hall!" Noah announced loudly.

"No Dad... We had no idea!" Kallisto feigned surprise, which brought laughter from the group.

The line broke down, and everyone came and gathered around them.

"I love Avalon! It's an amazing honor to meet you!" Kallisto gushed.

Everyone fawned over them for a few minutes.

"Okay, children. This isn't why they're here!" Methuselah interrupted.

"Leave it to Grandpa to spoil all the fun." Godiva chided.

They took an elevator up to the deck level, 40 feet above the ground.

"Now, I know it looks old-fashioned, but God said to use this specific type of wood," Noah explained.

Once inside, they were guided into an elevator, which took them to the bottom deck, deck one.

Deck one was general storage and the power station. Deck two was more general storage. Then, they came to deck three.

"This is where we are storing all the embryos." Noah guided them through a large, refrigerated deck. "God said to gather two of some animals and seven of others. I've spent decades gathering these animals for preservation. That is why I set up El Biological in the first place."

Julie had always wondered how Noah could fit all the animals into such a small ark. It had always challenged her faith because the logic of her mind could never conceive how two of every animal could fit in a 500 x 80 x 50 box. But of course, she had never considered that the world had been more advanced 4300 years in the past than it was in 2010. Or that the myth of Atlantis could have been the pre-flood civilization. It finally made sense as she stared at the endless rows of embryonic cold storage.

"The back half of the lab deck is cryo-storage. The front half is the incubation labs." Noah explained. "Over the last 50 years, we have collected around 10 million embryos from approximately 1 million different species."

"Sounds like a lot of work." Micheal's eyes went wide.

"We had the assistance of God who sent us David, who without his assistance we would not have succeeded at this task."

As they boarded the elevator, Julie had to laugh.

"What's so funny?" Micheal asked.

"Not exactly the picture that was shown to me in Sunday school." She laughed again.

"What? It's not the pitched boat overflowing with wild animals from your childhood?" Micheal chuckled.

"Yeah, none of the pictures had an elevator either." Julie was still smiling.

"And here we are," Noah said as they exited on deck four. "This is the garden and the farm." Noah showed them where the livestock would be. And the hydroponics garden, which was already in full bloom. "These are almost self-sustaining," Noah explained of the bounty on deck four.

The tour continued on the top deck, deck five. They exited out the opposite side from which they had entered. After walking on the outside deck to the back of the ark, they entered the end of the deck housing.

"A swimming pool?" Julie was surprised as they walked past the edge of a 40 by 20 foot swimming pool.

"Yes," Noah confirmed. "We don't know how long we will have to live on the ark. Recreational options will be vital for our sanity."

The next room was a multi-use sports court. And that was linked to a fitness gym. "And finally, the general recreation room." Noah described a large room filled with nearly every entertainment or games table known to man. "This is the general lounge," Noah said as they passed through the entry lounge. "Over here on the left is a 20-seat movie theater."

A large kitchen and dining room were on the opposite side of a long hallway. The whole of the top deck had a rustic yet comfortable feel to it. The only thing they had yet to see was the sleeping quarters. Upon leaving the kitchen, they headed to the end of the hall.

"This is where you will stay for as long as you choose to visit." Noah led them into a private suite. "You can explore the rest of the suite on your own from here." Then he left them alone together.

MICHEAL could tell the first room of the suite was a sitting room, perhaps 20 by 10 feet.

"This looks rather comfortable," Julie said as they explored the bed chamber. Which was also about 20 by 10 feet.

"When I was a kid, the image of Noah and his family on the ark was of them huddling together in a damp, dank, miserable dark ark. This is more like being on a cruise ship." Micheal said. "Although I've never actually been on a cruise before."

"Look at this Jacuzzi tub," Julie said happily as they entered the bathroom. "We'll have to test that out later." She gave a sly smile. "And, of course, a walk-through closet."

"Noah's luxury ark." Micheal chuckled.

"An amazing day... So cool to see the ark. But now we need to focus. We have to present our plan to counter the kinetic rods before the Council tomorrow." Julie informed him.

"Okay... What's your plan?"

"A polarized shield. To divert the rods back out to space."

"Good idea. We'll worry about the details tomorrow. But for the moment... Come here, Jules."

Julie went over and threw her arms over his shoulders. "Can you believe we are here?" She shook her head, scanning the room.

"It's been quite a day."

Julie kissed his cheek, then turned away. She slipped out of her clothes and walked toward the tub. "I need some relaxation, want to join me."

Micheal dropped his clothes and followed her into the churning bubbles. He sank into the warmth, and she slid up next to him. He wrapped his arm around her and sighed. "Just what we needed."

"I know we've said it before, but..." Julie took in the setting. "Hell of a life." She smiled.

"Hell of a life."

CHAPTER XX: PRISON BREAK

Gods of War

MELINA BEGRUDGINGLY SAW EMPRESS Regina. "What do you want Regina?"

"Is that any way to greet a friend?" Regina scowled.

"Are we friends?"

"We've known each other for centuries." Regina pointed out. "I've always considered us friends... I don't understand what has changed."

"That's because you're not the Oracle. You haven't spent the last century with visions of apocalypse."

"No, I haven't, and while I'm sure that would be tough, it's something else isn't it?" Regina seemed to deduce.

Melina considered for a minute. "Fine... I found out what's

coming."

"Is it the war?"

"No, but about that... Now you have Aphrodite and Koios running around like superheroes trying to stop the atrocities?" Melina laughed.

"How is that funny? In the last year or so, they've put an end to the rampant war crimes that were being perpetrated by all sides. And in the process, they are likely responsible for turning the tide against the aggressors."

"Oh, and let's not forget how you've used them to take down most organized crime throughout the Empire... They look so perfect in their pretty little battle suits." Melina laughed again.

"I still don't see the humor."

"It's all meaningless!" Melina finally snapped back. "The apocalypse will be here soon. And there's no stopping it. Within the year, the whole world will be wiped out!"

"That's not possible!" Regina shook her head.

"Oh, what, Koios didn't tell you?" Melina laughed snidely. "The gods are playing you for a fool."

"What do you mean?"

"Koios told me that Uranus, his and Aphrodite's father, and King of the Gods. He was angry that his creations no longer believed in the gods. Uranus means to wipe the slate clean and start over."

"I know Aphrodite and Koios; they won't let that happen." Regina seemed uncertain.

"I didn't think you believed all this gods nonsense?"

"It's hard not to believe. When you see them firsthand... I also know Aphrodite and Koios will protect us." Regina tried to convince herself.

"They can't! Why do you think they're here? They did fight Uranus for us, but they lost! They were expelled from the heavens as punishment. They're weak! Why do you think Gabriel nearly killed them? They might die with the rest of us."

"You say you know now what is coming? I thought there was a wall you couldn't penetrate?"

"There still is, but Koios told me about the war between the gods. He said Uranus intends to drown the whole world in a flood. And based on his statement, the timing is less than a year away. So that's why I say... It doesn't matter!"

"What possible mechanism could Uranus use to do such a thing?" Regina's eyes went wide.

"They are the gods."

"You truly believe this will happen?" Regina's shoulders dropped.

"I do, if you think there's any way to stop it. I would say your only hope would be other gods."

Regina stood in silence for a moment, seemingly lost in thought. Then she asked, "Will you look at Babylon for me? I need to know about their weapons programs... And I mean secret weapons."

"Okay." Melina went into the Oracle chamber. She connected to the quantum stream.

"Emperor Egino Rainard is discussing a covert construction project... They are in outer space... The Babylonians have doubled their astro mining frequency over the last three years. The focus of the construction is... This doesn't make any sense... I just keep seeing their farming platforms and other research stations. I don't see anything that is of a specific military nature... But then you did say covert. So, if I had to guess, I would say they are hiding the weapons in plain sight... If they exist."

"Thank you, Melina."

"Perhaps Koios could give you better insight."

"Thank you again," Regina said in parting.

Melina rarely watched the news, but she decided to get an update.

The TV said: "... The Cult of Hyperion is about to launch their latest mission to Tartarus, the fourth planet from the sun. Here's the cult's leader Camilla Salenius... Praise be to Iapetus. Who has welcomed us with open arms. His grace has aided in our successful construction of Monument City near The Face of Iapetus. I would also like to thank the priestess of the gods, Melina Hellas, who foretold of our glory... And that was Camilla Salenius..."

Melina thought about her visions of Tartarus. She had only viewed their first mission years earlier. She decided she would look again. But then the news changed.

The TV was saying: "... The war has taken a sharp turn. Over the last two weeks, The Southern Alliance's offensive in Northern Phillistia has broken through the border defenses and pushed into India... In Canaan, the Phoenicians began attacking civilians in a desperate attempt to reassert themselves. This provoked the gods of war, Koios and Aphrodite, who crippled the Phoenician frontlines. Which allowed the Eastern Alliance to push the rest of them out of Canaan... And the Babylonian offensives in Sumeria and Mesopotamia suffered major defeats... So now, the original allies of Babylon are under invasion. And Babylon is on the retreat. This has led many to believe the war, which has claimed nearly 3 billion lives, could end within the year...”

'The gods of war' Melina thought to herself snidely. Then the report turned to Aphrodite and Koios specifically.

The TV continued: “... Aphrodite was captured on surveillance taking down the leadership of The Underworld Gang. The most powerful gang on the west coast...”

“That sanctimonious bitch!” Melina said to herself. She had become annoyed by Aphrodite’s superhero act. While Koios had done some of the same, Aphrodite was out there all the time. Melina decided it was time to take her down a peg. But she would need some help.

Prison Break

The TV was saying: “... One of the physical attributes confirming Aphrodite’s identity is her eyes. They are the color of the sea. And of course, she was born of the sea... Many may not know the story... Uranus, the primordial father. Was not only a fighter, he was a lover as well. He had a rabid affair with Selene, The Goddess of the Night. When Gaia found out she castrated Uranus’ love implement and tossed it into the sea. He was so potent with love that the foam of the sea manifested that love in the form of a woman, The Goddess of Love, Aphrodite. That is how she was created... The book is *The Gods amongst Us* and it chronicles the visitations of the Atlantean gods of old... Thank you Dr. Savas...”

KATHERINE shut the TV off in disgust.

“Does thou believe Lord and Lady Avalon are indeed these gods of old?” Lord George asked in English.

“I know not. Melina did say as they were. Why then did not they use these... Powers against us?” Katherine responded in kind.

“Because of Gabriel,” Melina said in English as she entered their cell.

“Melina!” Katherine was surprised.

“There isn’t much time,” Melina said as she picked the lock to their cell. “This way.” Melina led them out and down the hallway to the right.

Melina snuck up behind a guard and choked them out. She took his card and opened the next door. Melina was wearing a full-body black catsuit. Now she pulled the mask down over her face. "Stay here." She went and disabled three more guards. She then signaled for them to advance. They went into a supply room and Melina had them put on black catsuits.

From there, they swept systematically section by section. And the three of them laid waste to all that were in front of them. In one of the outermost sections, they faced off against about two dozen guards. Katherine cut through the group. She did it in a nonlethal fashion, per Melina's edict.

Melina went to the control room and opened all the doors. Then she set up some kind of device. It sent out a shockwave and everything went dark. In the cover of darkness, they slipped out into the yard. They came under immediate sniper fire.

After taking cover, Melina gave them wristbands. "These will thwart their night vision."

With only starlight to illuminate the area, they began to fight their way through the army of guards between them and freedom. As she neutralized one after the other, Katherine had to resist the urge to kill any of them.

They broke through the final line of defense and quickly scaled the inner fence. They had to dodge a hail of sniper fire. That was being fired randomly due to their cloak of darkness. Then, they climbed the outer fence.

As they landed outside the final gate Melina yelled. "200 cubits ahead!" They reached a vehicle that was waiting for them. They quickly boarded and made their escape.

Once they were safely in the air. Katherine turned to Melina. "Melina, it did take thee long enough to free us from that wretched place."

"You had to know breaking you out of that place is nearly impossible."

"My understanding of thy connections. Would have believed, charges be dismissed." George raised a brow.

"You idiots tried to kill the most famous people in the world on live television. Even I can't sweep that under the rug."

"It still remains, how then now?" Katherine inquired.

"Gabriel was the Phantom—"

"Know this, we do." George cut in.

Melina stared down George in irritation. "He developed some technology that was necessary for this endeavor."

"Two years dead, Gabriel has been." Katherine protested.

"It took that long to figure out and adapt all of his contraptions."

"Thou did indicate as, Gabriel was why we were able to take on Gods?" Katherine returned to the original question.

"Yes, Gabriel was obsessed with Aphrodite. I had known this since we both served Aphrodite 900 years ago. His obsession led him to study her and Koios over the centuries. He was able to determine the secret of their power. He developed a dampening device to neutralize their powers so they would be vulnerable to him. When he found out about your plot to kill them at The Atlas Awards, he decided to use the opportunity as a test to see if it would actually work. He enjoyed your show until Aphrodite was nearly dead. Then he swooped in and saved the day. He certainly wasn't about to let you kill his ultimate prize. Only he had the right to do that."

"Ultimately, he failed. That, at the very least, allows me another chance. How much sweeter it shall be to know, a goddess she is. Explain that does, their apparent witchcraft."

"I don't think you should kill them."

"Deny me justice, thou wouldst?"

"I am no longer convinced of Aphrodite's guilt." Melina retorted bluntly. "I believe she was defending herself."

"The gods of old. Do needs kill a simple human in defense of self? Have not we seen such exploits as they do combat against entire armies? Demonstrate resistance they do to bullets. Could not, she have stunned them with lightning. Or have simply flown away?" Katherine was incensed.

"They didn't have their powers, they were vulnerable. In the time you come from no one believes in them anymore. Do they?" Melina challenged. "Their powers come from the beliefs of simple people. If no one believes in them they are powerless."

"Why then wouldst they go to such a time?!"

"They were expelled to your time by the primordial father Uranus. Because they fought against him... For us!" Melina flared.

"What dost thou mean?"

"Uranus believes that humanity's waning belief in the gods is a mortal threat to them. So he decided he's going to wipe everyone out and start from scratch... The apocalypse that's coming... Koios says Uranus intends to flood the entire world. He says that it's only a few months from now." Melina explained sadly. "Because of their experience ruling over humanity, Aphrodite and Koios have developed a care for us. They were able to convince half of the gods to rebel against Uranus. There was a war, but they lost. In punishment, they were expelled from the heavens to a point in time where they would be powerless. Where they would be vulnerable."

"Thou hast seen this... Flood?" George asked.

"I have... And by the way, my foresight is a gift from Koios."

"Thou always deemed it a curse." Katherine countered.

"I had thought that it was. Koios showed me why he chose me to bear this burden. All the good I have been able to accomplish." Melina clearly admired Koios.

Katherine considered everything she had heard of the Greek gods. Of course, she had dismissed them as mythology. Even after she had learned that the Atlantean Gods were the Greek Titans, her faith had taken a hit when she first arrived in Atlantis. The Bible never said there was any of this before.

Now she had indisputable evidence that her mortal enemy is Aphrodite, The Goddess of Love and Beauty. God or no, she and George would kill them... As soon as they got some answers about this apocalypse.

To Catch the Gods

Knowing that Koios, Lord Avalon, had failed humanity only emphasized to GEORGE that they should still take down Lord and Lady Avalon. If they genuinely were Greek titans, of which George was still skeptical. They would need Gabriel's devices to nullify their powers.

"How? Might I inquire, shall we acquire these devices?" Lord George asked Katherine.

"Melina does have said devices. We shall borrow them."

"Borrow them, quite right. Melina will simply allow such to occur." George was an excellent judge of character. He knew Melina would try to stop them if she knew their plan.

"Luv, Melina be as mother to me, understand our actions, she would not."

They flew to The Temple of the Gods.

"Rania, is Melina here?" Katherine inquired.

"No, she went to visit with the Council. She should return in an hour or so."

"We will wait in her chambers."

"We only have half an hour to search." George pointed out as they entered the chambers.

"Then get moving!"

After they searched Melina's entire quarters, they found nothing.

"So what now?" George asked in frustration.

"I have an idea."

They came to the end of the hall that accessed The Oracle Chamber.

"You distract Rania while I search the chamber," Katherine instructed.

"Rania, can I talk to you for a moment?" Lord George would have no trouble distracting Rania. Of course, women were drawn to his magnetic personality and his debonair good looks. It was obvious that no man could measure up.

"What do you want to talk to me about?"

"I've always wondered what made a woman such as yourself devote her life to the gods?"

"A woman such as myself?"

"Yeah, an intelligent, beautiful woman." George smiled.

"You think I'm beautiful?" Rania demurred.

"Obviously... You'd have to be blind not to see." He touched her arm. She began to blush. "So why the gods?"

"Because of Aphrodite, I first encountered her at this temple nearly 500 years ago. She was truly astounding—her beauty and loving kindness were unparalleled. She embodied the perfect image of a woman. I realized I could never emulate her, so I dedicated myself to serving her." It was evident that Rania was deeply enamored with Aphrodite.

"I've met Aphrodite. And you're even more beautiful than she is... in my opinion, at least." George smiled.

He saw Katherine coming. "Let's just keep this between us." He put his finger to his lips.

"We have to go."

"Thank you, Rania." As they began walking away, he looked back at Rania and winked at her. She smiled.

"So, did you get it?" George asked.

"And then some... These make you invisible to cameras." Katherine said, handing him a bracelet. "And these shots of nanos deconstruct DNA evidence if it falls off of you... If I understand correctly. No wonder Gabriel was the Phantom." She seemed impressed.

"Now we will be the Phantoms." George smiled.

MELINA returned to the temple. As she entered her quarters, she noticed a couple of items were slightly out of place. Her first thought was that George and Katherine might have come looking for the dampeners. She had already expected they would still try to kill Aphrodite and Koios.

She had hidden Gabriel's special technology in a most unusual place. She was fairly certain Katherine wouldn't think to look there. She had a secret stash location under a tile in The Oracle Chamber. She decided to ask Rania if anyone had been in the chamber.

"Rania, has anyone been in the chamber?"

"No... Melina, Camilla Salenius is here for you."

"Send her in." She would need to check the hiding place later.

"Mrs. Salenius, how was Tartarus?" Mrs. Salenius entered The Oracle Chamber.

"Quite incredible, a vision of the underworld. The brownish red everywhere. The glory of seeing the face of Iapetus, 15 stadion long by 10 stadion wide. There were already monuments to the God of the underworld on an adjacent artificial plateau. It must have been built a long time ago by other pilgrims or perhaps by Iapetus himself. There is a five-sided pyramid and a conical tower. We have built dozens of pinnacles to honor Iapetus. And with all of that, we still found time to visit Mount Othrys as well as her counter The Canyon of Hades. We also visited the ice cap Crown of Theia."

"That is indeed incredible. So how can I help you now?"

"Great Oracle of the Gods, I come to request another viewing. Will I see Iapetus again? Does he receive our offerings?"

Melina focused on her current mission. She was on a spaceship, flying to Tartarus. "You will see Iapetus again. You will build a special pinnacle. He will accept your offering. You will be satisfied. You will find what you seek."

"Thank you, Oracle. Please give my regards to Koios. Thank him for bestowing upon you the fortune of foresight." Mrs. Salenius bowed and then departed.

Melina decided against telling Mrs. Salenius that the effects of the apocalypse would still reach them. Even on Tartarus.

Now, she needed to check the stash. She went to the secret tile and removed it.

"Dammit Katherine!" Melina said aloud. Most of the stash was gone. And she berated herself for underestimating Katherine.

CHAPTER XXI: THE RAIN OF BABYLON

Downfall

JUNE 28, 2369 BC

"Over the past month and a half, we have lived on Noah's Ark. And we didn't just eat for free. It was our honor to assist in the final preparations for the flood. The ark is now ready for the deluge. To show appreciation for our contributions, Noah removed a panel plank from the side of the ark and gave it to us as a gift. With the work done, we decided to leave the Els the remainder of the time to spend together.

We leave to make our final plans. We now know the precise moment the flood will begin. We can't afford to be late. Our departure is on flood day, a little less than an hour after the flood commences. If we miss this jump, there will be no second chances."

PS: Flood Day is our 26th wedding anniversary! I love you, Micheal! :)

LORD GEORGE was impressed with his own genius. He had designed the perfect trap for the Gods of Avalon. He rolled his eyes at the thought. As lords, they were already insufferable. But as Gods, they were beyond words to describe them. He couldn't wait to look them in the eye, with them knowing that the Cavendishes had defeated them.

"My Lord, dost thou believe they shall fall prey to such scheme?" Katherine gave him a side-eye.

"Read, I have exploits of heroes, in whose style they portray themselves. When the challenge of protecting innocence lay before them, come they will... Priestesses of Koios, shall we take to bait trap. On Mount Atlas, at The Temple of Koios." George laughed, seeing a picture of it in his mind.

"Might I kill them? A small few to indicate we are serious?"

"Thou may, with reason."

She laughed deviously. "Gods, witches, or demons. Whichever they be, on the morrow, kill them, we shall." They both laughed excitedly.

Being in a celebratory mood, Lord George picked up Katherine and carried her to the bed. She ripped off her clothes and threw the tattered threads to the floor. He cuffed her to the bed. He pulled off one of her thigh highs and wrapped it tightly around her neck. As he thrust deeper and deeper, he pulled ever harder on the nylon. She no longer made a sound. And she was meeting him thrust for thrust. A minute later, she came, violently pulling him over the top with her.

He released the stocking, and she breathed deeply in pleasure. She loved erotic asphyxiation. And using one of the nano shots she had taken from Gabriel's stash, she could go twice as long as normal.

George had initially resisted strangling Katherine. But once he finally did, he had found it rather exciting. So, it had become a regular enhancement during sex. Katherine had told George she had originally discovered the enhancement aspect during her special agent training. All agents were required to develop resistance to the fear of being strangled since it is the most frequently employed lethal attack in their line of work. If you panic, you die.

George had been through the training himself, and he still hated being strangled. But being the one to do the strangling did have some appeal.

⁂

JULIE and Micheal had spent two weeks since their return from Eden finalizing all preparations for their impending departure. And now everything was set to go. All they had to do now was show up at the appointed place and time. They had just a couple of loose ends to tie up.

"We have to move quickly to build your deflector array to defend Atlantis from the kinetic rods," Empress Regina said gratefully. "Thank you again, Aphrodite and Koios... We are hopeful this may be able to thwart the forthcoming apocalypse... Phoenicia and India have surrendered. And we believe Babylon will fall any day now."

"That sounds great... Regina, it has been a pleasure knowing you." Julie embraced her.

"Why does this sound like goodbye?"

"Our time here is coming to an end. We will be returning to the heavens within the month. And it's likely we may not see you again before then."

"It's because of the flood, isn't it?" Regina said sharply. "Melina told me."

"Regina... That's why we're leaving." Micheal said.

"Cowards! Melina told me about your failure, and now you're running away!"

"No, Regina, we have found a way to go back. We are going to try one last time to stop this." Micheal explained.

Tears came to Regina's eyes. "I knew it; I knew you wouldn't abandon us." She hugged Micheal. "Thank you. Thank you so much, Aphrodite!" Regina hugged her.

Julie felt bad deceiving her like that. But the flood would come, no matter what. So why should they crush Regina's hope?

"So this is farewell. It has been a particular honor to know you.

I will pray for your success. So goodbye." Regina bowed to them.

"Farewell, Regina." They both replied. After one final hug from each of them, they parted ways with the Empress.

They went to The Piano Bar. Zara was singing on stage to a packed house. When she finished her song, she signaled for them to join her.

"Ladies and gentlemen, give a big welcome to Avalon. My personal friends Micheal and Julie Hall... Or should I say... Aphrodite and Koios!" Zara said as they took the stage beside her.

The music for *Endless Love* by Diana Ross and Lionel Ritchie began playing. They sang to the delight of the crowd. Following an extended set, they exited stage left with Zara in tow.

"Zara, we came because we are leaving... This time and place," Julie said truthfully. She had been nearly tempted to try to bring Zara with them. Zara was their only close friend. But Micheal had convinced her that they couldn't save everybody or solve every problem. They were destined to make friends throughout the timeline. Julie knew this would be her most challenging path through history.

"I knew this day would come. As soon as I knew who you were, it was only a matter of time."

"After everyone we lost, you have been my truest friend." A tear came to Julie's eye.

"My Gods... You reminded me why music means so much to me. I will never forget you." Zara began to cry.

Micheal embraced her. "We will miss you greatly."

"I shall pray to you both."

As Julie was embracing her, Zara pulled back abruptly. She wiped the tears from her cheeks.

"I think you are needed elsewhere." She indicated the TV.

Julie looked, and there was a hostage situation at The Temple of Koios on Mount Atlas.

"We don't do that anymore," Julie said.

"We could... Just this once?" Micheal said.

"But you said—" Julie began.

"I know what I said. One last time?" He raised a brow.

"For old time's sake."

"This is farewell, Zara; thank you for your friendship," Micheal said. All three of them hugged, then it was once again into the breach.

KATHERINE cut the next priestess' throat. She held her up by her hair for the camera as she bled out, gurgling. "Much time this is taking," Katherine complained in English.

"Come, they will, I assure you. They have been absent of late. A bit more time, will it take."

"Kill more whores I will, as consolation." She had already killed 12 of the Koios whores.

"Dost thou think authorities may again try a raid?"

"After last failed attempt? Unlikely."

While they were suiting up in their formidable battle gear for the last time, MICHEAL switched on the news.

The TV said: "... The standoff in central Atlantis continues... Approximately two hours ago, Babylonian terrorists took over The Temple of Koios. They have demanded that the Empress stand down the Atlantean military. They gave a one-hour deadline. When it passed without a response from the Empress, they began executing hostages every 10 minutes or so... Following the third execution, Central Intelligence agents attempted to move in and end it. They were repelled by unimaginable firepower... Half of the raid squad were shot, a full 24 agents. As a penalty for the attempt, the assailants immediately executed five more priestesses of Koios. They have executed 12 of the priestesses so far... Central News' own Salencia Asellus had been doing a feature on The Cult of Koios at the temple when the assailants stormed in. She is being held with the rest of the hostages... Wait, something is happening..."

"I told you to shut up!" The woman said. The female assailant forced a woman in front of the camera, likely Salencia Asellus because she was wearing clothes. The priestesses of Koios didn't wear clothing. The assailant dressed all in black stepped up behind her and promptly slashed her throat...

"Julie! We need to go!"

They flew from the penthouse down to the temple across the way.

Just when GEORGE was beginning to worry his plan was failing, the gods arrived in all their glory. They flew in through an upper window of the temple with lightning in their hands.

"Now!" He yelled, hitting the switch. The lightning in their hands sputtered and then went out. And they fell the remaining 20 feet to the ground.

Lord George immediately pounced on Koios. After a couple of firm strikes. Koios threw him off.

"Unbelievable... The fucking Cavendishes!" Koios said in English. Then came straight at him.

JULIE had been caught off guard after hitting the ground hard. She had taken several hard blows to her head. While she was slightly dazed, she was able to counter with a flurry of attacks. All of which were countered. One of those counter strikes connected to the base of her neck where it meets the shoulder. It made her left arm go numb. It reminded her of the time Katherine had hit her pressure points.

She threw her attacker off. "Katherine?!"

Katherine removed her mask. "Goddess or no, you're going to lose!" Katherine came at her again.

MICHEAL had taken a few hits but was holding his own against George. He looked over, and Katherine had Julie in a chokehold. Earlier, George had tried to attack him with a knife. He had disarmed him. Now, he dove to the knife, grabbed it, and threw it at Katherine. It stuck in her arm, and she released Julie, who fell limp.

Katherine pulled out the knife and charged at him. He redirected her into George. George was now bleeding. But they attacked him at the same time. He could fend them off at first, but then they overwhelmed him. He took a few bad hits to the face. Then Katherine clamped onto his neck. He tried to throw her off, to no avail. Then George tackled them both to the ground.

KATHERINE was able to get a death grip on Koios' neck. And with George's help, she knew he would succumb very shortly. Suddenly George was lifted off of Koios and body slammed to the ground. Then Aphrodite was on top of her.

She had to fend off a knife attack. Then she was locked in furious hand-to-hand combat. Just as she felt she was on her heels, she was struck from behind and everything went dark.

When MELINA heard about the attack on The Temple of Koios, she feared the worst. Her fears were confirmed upon her arrival—this was Katherine and George's plan to entrap the gods. Melina was furious at all four of them.

Wearing her full-body catsuit, she slid in and struck Katherine in the back of her head. After Katherine fell unconscious, Melina turned her attention to Aphrodite. Knowing Katherine had crippled the gods' powers, Melina knew she had the upper hand.

After exchanging a few attacks, Melina swept Aphrodite to the ground and pounced. She was able to get her arms around Aphrodite's throat and choked her out.

Melina ran over to where George and Koios were locked in battle. Although Koios definitely had the upper hand. Melina chopped George in the pressure point at the base of his neck, and he dropped like a rock.

Then Koios was the last one standing. Melina attacked, and they traded blows back and forth. Koios countered her and got her in a chokehold. She pretended to go limp. He continued to strangle her for another minute, apparently trying to be sure. Just when she thought she was going to pass out, Koios released her to the ground. After a moment of pretense, she sprung up and climbed Koios in an instant. She wrapped her legs around his neck and dropped him to the ground. Then she kicked him in the head, and he was down for the count.

She quickly bound them all, then gathered them onto a maglev platform. Then, using her knowledge of the temple and its connection to The Palace of the Gods, she snuck them out past the authorities.

Captive State

MELINA took them all to a secret underground facility she had built underneath The Temple of the Gods.

Melina slapped Katherine hard on the cheek. "Katherine! Wake up!"

"You didn't have to wallop me."

"Yes! I did." Melina glared. "How could you so callously kill all those people? You're almost as bad as Gabriel." She felt betrayed all over again by someone she cared about.

"Oh please, Melina, you know I'm a top spy for Atlantis."

"So that makes you a cold-blooded killer?" Melina was appalled.

"You have to kill in my line of work." Katherine shrugged.

"But it doesn't teach you to murder innocent people!" Melina was heartbroken by the revelation.

"No one is innocent." Katherine scowled.

"Aphrodite was right. You're just a monster." Tears came to her eyes.

"So now you're on her side?"

"How could I possibly believe anything you say anymore?" Melina glared.

Katherine seemed to soften. "I'm sorry, Melina, this quest for vengeance has consumed me."

Melina closed her eyes. She was ambivalent. She had known Katherine as a daughter for over a century. Therefore, she felt some responsibility because she had trained Katherine. And she had never discouraged her desire for vengeance. Katherine's use of her new skills to become a secret agent of Atlantis had apparently been the catalyst to make her into a sociopath.

JULIE started to become conscious. She was lying on a bed, and there were magnetic shackles on her wrists. The same kind Gabriel had used. She looked over, and Micheal was lying on the bed next to her. Julie had a headache.

"Micheal?"

"Yes?" He groaned. She saw that his left eye was swollen.

Julie tried her rings, and of course, they didn't work.

"You were right." Julie heard Melina say.

"I was? About what?"

"About Katherine. She is exactly what you said she was. I just didn't want to believe it. How come everyone has to betray me?" Melina shook her head.

"Do you still think I betrayed you?"

Melina considered for a second. "All the gods did."

"I'm sorry we failed you... You devoted your life to me, and I couldn't protect you." Julie's guilt and sorrow about the forthcoming flood and the loss of Melina's friendship brought tears to her eyes. "Some Goddess of Love I turned out to be." Julie shook her head. "You were right... I'm not worthy of your devotion or your friendship." The tears were streaming.

Melina came and embraced her. She returned the embrace.

"'Twas Melina, who did take us down?" LORD GEORGE asked in English, he was annoyed.

"Such public display, surely would attract Melina's attention."

"My fault then it be? No reproach didst thou make!"

"Thou were losing, as it were."

"I did see as thou were losing as well!"

"Lose, I do not!" Katherine flared.

"You were both losing!" Melina cut in as she entered the room. "You should be glad I stepped in when I did."

"If so evil we art? Why then didst thou intercede on our behalf?" Katherine scowled at Melina.

"You're still my daughter. I am saddened by what you have

become, but it's partly my fault." Melina averted her eyes.

"How so?" George asked.

Melina looked up. "I taught Katherine how to fight. When she told me about her husband, I never discouraged her desire for revenge. I should have encouraged a better path." She looked away again.

"Mother, please, I'm 134 years old; I am no child."

"And I'm 930. You're still a child to me."

"Melina, didst thou let the gods go?" George asked.

"No, they're here; I haven't decided what to do with them yet."

"Talk to them, we shall," George suggested.

"Only to talk, understand? Anything else, and you will not like my response."

———————

MICHEAL awoke to Julie dabbing his eye with a wet rag.

"How do you feel?" Julie asked in English.

"Aside from my eye, I feel all right."

"Melina got you pretty good."

"That was Melina?" Micheal was surprised. "Why would she attack us?"

"I needed to stop any of you from killing the other," Melina replied as she entered the room.

"Okay, but why are we shackled?" Micheal asked.

"I wanted to be able to control you." Melina shrugged.

"What are you afraid of?" Julie asked.

"I'm not afraid. I'm deciding whether to punish you."

"For what?" Micheal was incensed.

"For the betrayal of the gods," Melina said sharply. "You, Koios, made me your Oracle. I never asked for this."

"No, you didn't. And whether you believe us or not, we did fight for you and everyone else, but we failed. If you want to punish us, we won't fight you." Micheal said.

Melina looked away, then looked back with tears in her eyes. "Koios... I'm so sorry about your priestesses." She left the room.

"The shackles prevent us from leaving the room, don't they?" Micheal asked.

"Yes," Julie replied. "But we do have full run of this suite."

Micheal turned on the TV.

The TV said: "... Our top story. The attack on The Temple of Koios in central Atlantis... 12 priestesses and our own reporter, Salencia Asellus, were slaughtered by the hostage takers. Koios and Aphrodite attempted to stop the monsters, but it appears, it was a trap. As we know, Gabriel Maximus, the Phantom, developed a technology to neutralize the gods. The assailants must've used similar technology. So, the gods are missing. Many people are praying to them in hopes of giving them more power..."

KATHERINE shut off the TV. "Monsters?" She laughed as they entered the chamber where the gods were being held. "They pray for thee. How lovely."

"Katherine!" Melina interjected. "I must go for the moment. The four of you will just talk if anything else happens. You will answer to me," she threatened, and then she left the room.

"What fools the people are to see thee as heroes." Katherine and George sat down at the table.

"Please sit," George instructed them.

"What's there to talk about?" Aphrodite glared.

"Thou thinks thou art so superior." George accused.

"The only thing that made me feel superior to you and your family was the inferiority complex you put on display during the trial." Koios jabbed at George.

"Thou lied about what happened that day!"

"Of course I did... Do you think I could possibly tell those puritanical morons the truth? All they wanted was blood."

"As did I!" George retorted. "Thou ruined my life! Then thou threw us through time."

"You followed us. No one forced you to." Aphrodite pointed out.

"Thou murdered my husband!" Katherine sneered.

"Your husband was a monster. As are you. The way you slaughtered all those innocent women." Aphrodite glared back.

"Irrelevant, that is," George cut in. "Apocalypse be upon us. Is it not?" He returned to the reason for this meeting.

"Discuss this Apocalypse we must," Katherine stated firmly.

The Rain of Babylon

"And why would we talk to you?" Koios asked dismissively.

"For five years, did we attempt identification of Apocalypse," KATHERINE said.

"Fault of the gods, it is!" George scowled.

"Now you believe in the gods? I thought you were Christians?" Aphrodite chided.

"Christians? Our Savior won't be born for over 2000 years." Katherine scoffed.

"So you think the true religion of God doesn't exist until the birth of Jesus Christ?" Koios laughed.

"The gods of old believe in God?" George asked.

"The creation of the universe is more complicated than you know." Koios pointed out.

"No more talk of religion." Katherine was annoyed. "What does thou know of Apocalypse?" She went back to the reason for her to tolerate the bitch.

"Didn't Melina tell you all about it?" Aphrodite asked.

"Melina did tell us of a flood. Details, however, were limited." George said.

"Koios... If thou indeed are?... Would know more." Katherine said.

Koios seemed to be considering something. He looked at Aphrodite and then back at her. "If we tell you what you want to know, you'll likely just kill us after that."

"Much desired that outcome would be. Promised Melina, we have. No danger is thee presently in."

JULIE didn't feel like being very cooperative. But she also felt bad about not doing more to try and stop the apocalypse.

"The forthcoming Apocalypse is indeed a flood. You would likely know it as The Flood of Noah." Julie said.

"Great global flood from Genesis?" George's eyes went wide.

"If it be Noah's flood, would not there be an ark?" Katherine asked.

"Indeed, there is. We were there only a few weeks ago." Micheal said.

"Curious I am, why dost thou sound so different now when thou speak English?" George raised a brow.

"We speak many languages. We conform to the speech patterns of our surroundings. English is one of the most adaptive languages of all time. So it sounds different depending on the place and time in which it is spoken."

"So thou did portray false, in our time, when thou was in Boston?" Katherine scowled.

"Familiar portrayal, necessary for assimilation. Had I done so, no witch trial would I have faced," Julie replied in Colonial English.

"Impressed of Lord from Avalon, all were. Had it been known thou were fraudulent portrayal. By Gods no less, despise Avalon, all would." George's jealousy was obviously rising.

"You, my Lord, are just jealous that people seem to acclaim us no matter what time and place we happened to be in," Micheal said.

"Compared to gods! 'Tis not fair!" George roared.

"George!" Katherine yelled. "Unproductive this be!"

LORD GEORGE had to calm himself. He thought of how they still planned to kill these arrogant, holier-than-thou, exiled gods.

"What does thou know of this flood? Of Noah's Ark?" Katherine returned to the original topic of discussion.

"The flood will begin Seleday, Tethysel, the 22nd day, at around the 18th hour. Approximately three weeks from now." Koios said with certainty.

"No such flood is possible." Katherine looked at him.

"The volume of the continental aquifer, combined with the aquatic shield bubble, makes it possible." Koios pointed out.

"If it be true, of what could possibly disturb such from stable state?" Lord George worried.

"It has not yet become clear to me."

"What of Noah and his ark?" Katherine asked.

"The ark is ready to go. We assisted Noah and his family with final preparations a few weeks ago." Aphrodite explained.

"What of the location?" George asked.

"It's in Eden," Aphrodite said.

"The mad Noah El?" Katherine asked.

"He is not mad," Aphrodite said.

George had noticed that Koios had his eyes shut. "Koios?"

Koios opened his eyes. "I have just seen the catalyst."

"What is it?" Aphrodite looked at him.

"The Rain of Babylon." Koios returned her gaze. At that moment, the door swung open.

MELINA had decided to allow the gods and the Cavendishes to have time to discuss some things. She had also decided to look at the apocalypse again. She sat in the Oracle Chamber and focused. She felt a surge of energy flow through her. Then, the images began to come.

She saw Babylonian Emperor Egino Rainard in an emergency meeting with his war council.

"We must surrender." One advisor admonished.

"There is one final option." The emperor's chief advisor declared.

"And what is that?" A different advisor asked in confusion.

"Emperor... Bring the rain." His chief said. Most of the room seemed confused.

"Do it." The Emperor ordered.

Suddenly she was pulled into outer space. She saw the Babylonian farming platforms. Large metal rods detached from beneath them and began floating toward the earth. Her perspective was drawn back, and she could see hundreds of them.

The last image that crossed before her was of a clock. As she came out of the vision, she checked the time. That time was now!

Melina hurried to the secret location where the gods were being held. As she rushed through the door.

"Melina?!" Katherine said in surprise.

"You all have to see this!" She turned on the TV.

The TV said: "... The alliance ground forces have surrounded the capital of Babylon. The surrender is anticipated any time now... Wait, we have an emergency press conference from Empress Regina Seneca... "People of Gaia, the Babylonian Empire has unleashed an apocalypse on the world. Less than one hour ago, they released a doomsday weapon from space. It's called The Rain of Babylon. This weapon is like dropping a thousand asteroids on every major city in the world. If you are in any city, evacuate the central zones as quickly as possible!"... We cut back to Babylon to notify you that something major is happening..."

Melina saw a bright streak flash through the screen, and then there was a massive explosion in the city of Babylon, followed by a bright flash, and the screen went dark. The news channel changed to another camera.

All five of them watched in stunned silence.

The TV said: "... This video just came in from The Global Counsel in Central City..." The video's perspective was from a great distance, covering the entire city. A large streak crossed the sky. There was an impact generating an incredible explosion.

The horrifying hits just kept coming. Less than an hour later, the whole room began to shake.

"Have we been hit?" Lord George asked.

"No! These are seismic waves!" Koios explained.

The Rain of Babylon had certainly sent shockwaves all around Gaia.

CHAPTER XXII: THE FLOOD

The End of Days

T HREE WEEKS LATER, THE seismic tremors continued reverber-
ating around where they were being kept.

"Why do these tremors keep going?" Julie asked MICHEAL.

"Remember the aquifer? In my analysis of the superstructure
that holds the continents up, I discovered giant crystalline structures in a latticed network. The combined kinetic energy from
The Rain of Babylon likely destroyed much of the support network. I believe these tremors are indicating the breakdown of the
remaining structures. At some point, the whole network will fail,
and then..."

"... The Flood of Noah," Julie finished for him, shaking her head.
"We need to find a way out of here."

"I doubt Melina will leave us here to die."

"Yes, she will. She's not the woman we used to know... She's angry. She feels completely betrayed."

"I think you're wrong. She will come." He tried to convince both of them.

"What's she waiting for? She could have released us anytime in the past weeks."

"I don't know."

He was now doubting his own conviction.

"Weeks have we spent." LORD GEORGE began. "If Koios speaks true, this flood shall come, day after next. Kill them, we should!"

"Promise, did we make to Melina." Katherine reminded him.

"It matters not. All shall die day after next."

"Melina does control all dampeners."

"No more!" He pulled out a few devices. He smiled, then took a moment to consider his superior ability to achieve whatever he set out to do. He was every bit the man Lord Avalon was and then some. And this was despite not having the cheap fraudulence of being Koios, God of Wisdom and Knowledge. When they killed the gods on the morrow, they would be happy to die, safe in the knowledge that they were superior to Avalon. Superior to the gods.

With only two days left on death row, JULIE decided to write her thoughts.

-August 10, 2369 BC

"In two days, I will die... In The Flood of Noah... When I read Genesis as a child, I never could've imagined that I was part of it. I am also ambivalent about my impending doom. I don't want to die. But I also feel, to some degree at least, that I deserve it. Why should I survive when 30 billion other people won't? That includes some people I care deeply for: Zara, Regina, and even Melina. While we had a falling out, she has been my most special friend since we arrived in Atlantis. From my perspective, it has

been 25 years.

I'm 60 years old, but my reflection says I'm 20. And I have lived one amazing life. So, I die with no regrets. And I will be in the arms of my one true love, my soulmate.

Having visited the other side, I no longer fear what comes next. But I do wish I could continue this incredible journey with Micheal."

PS – In two days, we will celebrate our 26th anniversary. This is not exactly what we had in mind for a celebration.

Julie put down the pen. "Micheal?"

"Yes, Jules?"

"Are you prepared to die?"

He considered for a moment. "No, I love my life and will never stop fighting for it... But, if you're asking if I have any regrets, I have none. Because I got to spend this life with you." He touched her cheek. "All these trials we have faced together have only made me love you that much more." He kissed her deeply. Then, they expressed their love with more than words.

KATHERINE was watching TV, stewing over these evil gods and the impending doom they had perpetrated upon humanity.

The TV said: "... The death toll in Jericho is around 50 million. And it's nearly 100 million in Carthage, the other Atlantean city that took a hit... It has been estimated that worldwide, 5 billion people died when The Rain of Babylon fell. That, combined with the 3 billion other casualties, and the Babylonian war has claimed over 8 billion lives. That has cut the current world population to approximately 30 billion... In related news, scientists are still trying to assess the fallout from The Rain. It is estimated that the combined size of the 1000 kinetic rods is the equivalent of a 750-cubit asteroid impact. The dust from the impacts has now circled the globe... Then the earthquakes, which have become constant, are only getting worse. There have been tsunamis on nearly every coastline..."

Katherine shut the TV off. "My Lord George, it is time." She grinned.

They snuck inside through the secret passages. All they needed was an hour. The flood was supposed to begin in a few hours. So long as Melina didn't interfere, they would finally get the pleasure of killing the gods.

Katherine cracked the door open. The gods were having sex. She opened the door wide enough for George to see. They enjoyed the show for a few minutes until the gods had finished.

"How typical!" Katherine said as they entered the room." One last time, before the end?"

"What do you want?" Aphrodite said.

"Melina may be content to let thee die in Noah's Flood. However, it being all the same. Our preference, kill thee ourselves." Katherine smiled.

"Satisfaction shall be ours, at last," George said.

Aphrodite glared at them. "Come now, Aphrodite, little difference does it make." Katherine unfurled her favorite weapon, a thin wire garrote.

"You're sick!" Aphrodite snarled. "And you're a coward! Take these shackles off and face me woman to woman!"

"I think not." Katherine shook her head as she constricted the shackles. "Look thou in thy eyes, I shall, as I strangle thy life out of thee... Appreciate that, I believe, as so many a time before... Koios shall watch. After which, Lord George shall beat him to death. And all shall be done with time to spare before apocalypse cometh." She and George laughed.

Katherine proceeded to wrap the wire around Aphrodite's delicate, slender neck many times, then began to throttle her. As the minutes went on Katherine thoroughly enjoyed the expressions of pain, terror, disbelief, and finally, acceptance, which all ran across Aphrodite's face.

The wire was biting deep into Aphrodite's throat. The arteries in Aphrodite's neck were bulging beautifully. Her face was turning slightly purple. And her mouth and eyes were fixed open.

Aphrodite had been kicking and squirming. But she had calmed significantly. Katherine began yanking hard on the garrote to evoke a response to her utter enjoyment. Then the reactions died off, and Katherine knew the moment was near. She looked deeply into those deep-sea eyes, preparing to see the moment the last breath of life drained from her.

Just when it seemed the moment would arrive. Melina was in the doorway.

Melina struck Katherine in the side of the head. When her

vision cleared, George was lying unconscious on the floor. The next thing Katherine knew, Melina kicked her hard in the face and everything went dark.

Farewell

MELINA was outraged that Katherine broke her promise and once again was trying to murder Aphrodite. This time, she was also angry with herself. She had allowed her anger with the gods in general. To cause her to punish Aphrodite and Koios by proxy. She should have let them go sooner.

"I am so sorry, Aphrodite. Can you forgive me?"

Aphrodite coughed violently. "I thought we were friends. I can't understand why you've treated me so horribly." Aphrodite looked despondent. Melina looked at Koios. He raised his hands, indicating that this was between her and Aphrodite.

Melina's guilt and regret hit her like a punch to the stomach. Everyone close to her had betrayed her. And now she realized how much she missed Aphrodite's friendship. Knowing that death would come any time, Melina desperately wanted Aphrodite's forgiveness.

She fell to Aphrodite's feet. "Please, Aphrodite! Please forgive me?" Melina pleaded, the tears streaming. "I know I don't deserve your forgiveness. I'm a terrible person, a terrible servant, and worst of all, a terrible friend! I threw away our friendship! I'm not worthy of your friendship. Aphrodite! I would give anything for your forgiveness!" She began sobbing at Aphrodite's feet.

She felt Aphrodite wrap her in a loving embrace. "Melina, I forgive you," Aphrodite finally said, pulling Melina to her feet. Melina just cried on her chest.

"I was so stupid—"

"Sh..." Aphrodite stopped her. "None of that matters now. We entities of love can sometimes allow our passions to cloud our minds. All this time, you have remained my most special friend."

"I love you, Aphrodite."

"I love you, Melina... We need to go. Time is short. We must leave this time period... Come with us, Melina."

"No, Aphrodite, I have had my time. 930 years of it. My life ends with this temple." Melina embraced Aphrodite. "Thank you for your friendship. For giving meaning to my life... Please remember me, Aphrodite!"

"I could never forget you, Melina. You are a part of me." Aphrodite stroked her cheek.

Melina then turned to Koios. "I have always treasured your friendship, Koios." She threw her arms around him.

"You have been very special to me."

"I do honestly feel honored that you chose me as Oracle. I was able to help so many people. And while I can't stop the apocalypse, I realized recently that it's not the end that matters; it's how we live." Melina stared up at Koios, an actual God.

"There is no one more worthy of greatness. And great is what you are, Melina." Koios was about to break their embrace.

Melina stopped him. "Koios, Aphrodite, if I might make one final request," she asked nervously.

"Anything!" Aphrodite said.

"I have long desired to experience the kiss of God. And I would be lying if I said I hadn't fantasized about you, Koios. You are utterly mesmerizing." Melina averted her eyes in embarrassment at the admission. "That's okay... I shouldn't have said anything." She began to pull away.

Aphrodite stopped her. "Melina, I did absolutely mean anything."

Koios touched her cheek, turning her face him. They had remained locked in an embrace. His soft eyes hypnotized her. He slowly leaned down, and his lips met hers. She closed her eyes and was enraptured by the waves of energy flowing from him right through her. It was as if her most erotic fantasies were caressing her whole body. Then, all of a sudden, his kiss became electric, literally. As the sparks pulsed through her entire body, all her senses became overwhelmed. The sensations between her legs were pushed toward climax. And she couldn't stop herself from coming.

Melina's legs turned to jelly. Koios held her up. As he steadied her, he pulled back from the kiss. She was still trying to catch her breath and was looking down in embarrassment. Koios stroked her cheek. She met his kind eyes. "Are you satisfied, Melina?" He gave her a wink.

She looked over at Aphrodite, who met her gaze with a slight grin. Then Aphrodite stepped over and they all embraced in a three-way hug.

"We will miss you always," Aphrodite said as the tears returned to her eyes.

"This life ends. But Elysium awaits. I am ready."

"And I promise you, Melina, you will be welcomed by the ones you love," Aphrodite assured her.

They quickly made their way to the overlook gardens. She had one final embrace with each of them. Then they majestically took flight one last time. She watched till they were nearly out of sight. Then the ground shook violently, and a sudden jet of water ripped out The Atlantic Passage. It shot all the way to the heavens.

Deluge

JULIE heard a deafening sound crack in the sky as they flew southwest toward the jump point. A wall of water shot up to their left. The rushing jet of water began to roar like the loudest waterfall ever. She looked down below and was grateful she wasn't in the chaos. Buildings were shaking and swaying and collapsing. The ground was moving in waves, like water.

She suddenly felt the power drain from her rings, and they went into freefall. The ground was coming up fast. Then, the rings reactivated, mitigating the force of the impact. A wave rolled through the ground beneath them, and when they reached the crest they were thrown into the air. The rings channeled enough energy to keep them in the air.

LORD GEORGE and Lady Katherine got their wits about them. As they exited the tunnels to the overlook gardens. They saw the gods take flight, leaving Melina standing there.

"Follow them, we must!" Katherine yelled. "A way out, might they have!"

They quickly climbed into their hover car and pursued the gods down the coast to the southwest. George looked to his left. The massive skyline of Atlantis began to disappear behind a rising wall of water.

"Certain is thee of a way out?" George worried.

"Flying with purpose, are they. No other reason would they have."

The airspace ahead of them was a swarm of chaos. George manually steered the car, dodging other vehicles and debris being thrown into the sky by the waves of earth. The magnetic fields fluctuated, and the vehicle went into freefall. George skillfully angled the car toward a magnetic rail and was able to ride it back into the air.

Upon his arrival in Atlantis, Lord George had become a quick study at piloting, which came as no surprise to him. His superior capabilities always proved he was a cut above the lowly masses of people—a true Cavendish Lord.

MICHEAL realized that the magnetic fields must be fluctuating. Which was why the rings had become unreliable. They were getting close to the jump point when the rings gave out again. And they fell hard to the ground. However, they both implemented a break-fall to minimize the impact.

They didn't have time to linger; the waves of the earth continued to roll beneath them. After multiple attempts to reactivate the rings, Micheal realized they were about a mile from the jump point. Now, they would test their parkour skills.

They began running full speed, jumping over some obstacles, and diving through others. Micheal checked the time. They had just over five minutes. Spray started raining down on them in torrents. They were dodging debris left and right. Then they saw a big problem. A literal big problem. A building had tipped on its side and blocked the path for a thousand feet.

They paused momentarily, trying to figure out what to do. And time was literally running out.

"I have an idea!" Julie yelled. "If we time a wave correctly, we may be able to use it to catapult over the building!"

They looked back, waiting for the precise moment. "Now!" She yelled.

They started building up a head of steam. As they approached the building, they propelled themselves off the cresting wave of earth. They didn't clear the building entirely; instead, they landed on the side of the building. They repeated the same process, running at full bore and propelling off the edge of the building as the next wave crest.

They landed hard but rolled right back to their feet. "100 yards to go!" Micheal yelled. Ten seconds later, they arrived at the jump site. "We have 10 seconds!" Micheal yelled as they quickly worked to pinpoint their positions.

Micheal looked at Julie as the green vortex burst between them. A flash split the air as a wave of water slammed into them.

KATHERINE tried to keep the gods in sight as George skillfully maneuvered through the chaos and explosions. Then she thought to herself that this truly is what the apocalypse looks like.

The gods went to the ground, and she lost sight of them. George brought the car to a stable hover while they scanned the area for the gods. Katherine feared she would never find them amongst the chaos. But then she saw them. They were doing their superhuman act. And she was genuinely impressed by what she saw.

They jumped over a building that had fallen on its side in two leaps. At that moment, another car careened into them, sending the vehicle crashing to the ground. As they pulled themselves from the rubble, they saw it.

"Run!" she yelled. The gods had opened one of their green temporal portals.

"'Tis our only hope!" George yelled.

They sprinted through the undulating and rolling fields. Katherine took George's hand, and they jumped toward the portal. There was a bright flash, and they were sucked in.

MELINA spent a few hours walking through the temple and its grounds. She was the only one left. Everyone else had fled. She sat down in the gazebo on Heaven's Point. It was the highest spot in the overlook. It would provide decent shelter from the ongoing deluge. But it was open, so she had a perfect view of the end of the world.

She went into her memories, starting in her youth. She had plenty to run through after nearly a millennium of life.

She relived the day the gods had arrived. She reveled in the memory of the day Aphrodite had made her Chief Priestess.

She went back as she often had to see her one true love, Darius. It was centuries ago. And she felt a pang of regret that she had allowed her children to drift away over the centuries. Most of them couldn't handle her Oracle status. Her son Maximus and daughter Iris had fallen away after a few hundred years. They said they were desirous of being their own people. Then, about 200 years ago when Darius died. The fallout had caused her son Eros and her daughter Echo to drift away. When the doomsday visions began, Melina's obsession with the apocalypse drove her final daughter, Talia, away.

So, 20 years later, when Katherine arrived, she had filled the void in Melina's heart.

She then relived the highlights of her relationships with Aphrodite and Koios. In the end, they were the only ones who hadn't truly betrayed her. All of her children, Gabriel, Katherine and George, had all betrayed her. And then there were the gods, led by Uranus. They had all turned on her.

Aphrodite had been a true friend. Who became as a mother to her. Aphrodite's unconditional love, through which she had so easily forgiven Melina's betrayal, had restored some of Melina's broken heart.

Then, her friend and mentor, Koios, gifted her with the sight. She closed her eyes and relived the kiss. The kiss of a God was everything she had dreamed it would be.

In final reflection, Melina said aloud to herself. "What a life I have lived!"

Melina had made peace with her fate. Now, she would witness the awesome power of the gods firsthand.

She looked south, and the jet wall of water stretched from one end of the horizon to the other. She remained in that place as the dark of night passed by, and she dwelled in her thoughts.

As night turned to day, the wall of water had begun to spray more horizontally. Literal rivers were cascading down the sides of the overlook pinnacle. The gazebo had shaken throughout the night.

All of a sudden, the fountain wall began to die off. As it did, there was a deafening crack and the entire overlook began to sink quickly into the sea.

Melina was sucked violently into a maelstrom. It was utter chaos. She opened her eyes and saw nothing in the murky darkness. She made no effort to fight the ripping currents. She was being whipped around like a ragdoll. She had instinctively held her breath. Now, her body was screaming for air. As she took a deep breath, her lungs filled with water. The agonizing pain seemed like it would last forever. Then, it faded away and was replaced by a warm, comforting feeling. Then she saw it.

Aphrodite was there, with blonde hair. She gently pulled Melina's soul from her body and led her toward Elysium, where Darius and Elissa were waiting.

PART III: ATLANTIS REBORN

Atlantis Reborn

- August 12, 2176 BC

"Today, I reflect on a significant milestone. Micheal and I celebrate our 30th wedding anniversary. Over 35 years ago, when we fell through time. I had just turned 30. And now we have been married for approximately the same amount of time. Most of that time has been wedded bliss, but the last few years in the 24th century really tested the fortitude of our relationship.

So after barely surviving The Flood of Noah, the last five years of peace and quiet in the 22nd century BC have been tonic for our souls and our love. We have spent those years in a newly rebuilt Atlantis.

Upon our arrival in this time period we checked the sky-net. And it revealed the once-familiar face of the earth. There was no more pangea. The sky is now blue instead of green. And I saw my first rainbow in 25 years. We could also see that most of the islands that made up the city of Atlantis had survived the flood. So we made our way 800 miles south from our arrival on the French coast to see what it looked like now.

We arrived to find Noah's daughter Jessalyn as the Queen of Atlantis. It was good to see a familiar face, so we decided to stay and live full-time. There was no spotlight, no Gods of Atlantis. Just a quiet, white picket fence life.

We restored The Investment Hall, then spent most of our time pursuing leisure. Just enjoying each other."

PS: I'm 65 years old. If I were still in the 21st century, I would be a senior citizen. :)

As JULIE set down her journal, the doorbell rang. She went to see Micheal open the door to Noah and Namia. Noah still looked like he was in his 20s, nearly 200 years after the flood at 795 years old.

"Namia, Noah, it's so good to see you." Julie kissed them both on the cheek.

"Welcome to Avalon," Micheal said.

It was the first time Noah and his wife had visited their estate in the Strait of Hercules, which was modern-day Gibraltar.

"Namia, let me show you to the gardens," Julie suggested, and they headed out back.

"So, how's the quiet life?" Noah asked with a smile.

"It's much more relaxing than playing Gods or rock stars," MICHEAL admitted as they sat down in the lounge. "So I never really got to discuss your plan of restoration."

"What about it?"

"Sending all your children off to different areas of the world must've been difficult."

"It was difficult, but there was so much to do. We began preparing them from their youth. They were each to be their own versions of Adam and Eve. They were tasked with repopulating the world of both animals and people. We had to organize stable food chains with the proper predator and prey balance. We had to determine which animals complemented each other. Then, we were committed to following the first edict to Adam and Eve. To be fruitful and multiply. That included Namia and me. The plan has been a roaring success. In the 200 years since the flood, the world's population today is approximately 100 million. And the animal populations have reached healthy levels of stability. We've also been able to nearly restore the technological level that we had before the flood." He paused. "My only regret is that so many people have already turned their backs on God." He shook his head.

"How so?"

"The most glaring example is this tower they are building in Babylon. The last time we visited Japheth, one of the richest people in Babylon declared that he would build a tower that could reach Heaven." Noah rolled his eyes in disgust.

"What are you boys talking about?" Namia asked as she and Julie returned from the gardens.

"God's Tower in Babylon."

"Oh! That horrible thing." Namia shook her head.

"The Tower of Babel?" Julie said.

"No, it's the God's Tower." Noah tried to correct her.

"No... It does sound like the Tower of Babel," Micheal said.

"What's the Tower of Babel?" Namia asked.

"Our Scriptures tell of a situation believed to be around this time..." Micheal indicated the time they were in. "... The people had become prideful again, so they built a tower in an effort to reach heaven. So God punishes them by confusing their tongues so they can't communicate with each other. It caused everyone to Babel. Which is why it became known as the Tower of Babel."

"You mean people speak differently?" Noah seemed shocked.

"Yes, the language we are speaking right now has been nearly lost to history," Julie said.

"This is our original speech pattern," Micheal added, then said in English. "Our native language is called English." Then he repeated the statement in Atlantean.

"The words we are speaking we call Atlantean. But Micheal and I can speak dozens of languages."

They proceeded to demonstrate many of the languages which they could speak. And they detailed the places of origin which were related to the same.

Once Noah and Namia retired for the evening. Micheal and JULIE did the same.

"What do you think happens to this civilization?" she asked. "Obviously, the flood explained the original version of Atlantis's demise, but then Noah and his family did an amazing job repopulating the world and restoring the technological level. It is similar to what it was before."

"I don't know, but whatever it is has to be nearly as bad as the flood."

"Like what? An asteroid impact or a supervolcano? Or perhaps something like a nuclear war?"

"We will definitely have to try to figure that out because we don't have the same potential foresight that the flood provided." Micheal pondered nervously. "The only thing we may be able to determine for certain is when it will happen."

"You believe it will leave a similar mark on the temporal stream like the flood did?"

"Indeed... On a different note, Noah gave me an update on everybody." Micheal sat down on the bed.

"Of course, Jessalyn and Lykos are ruling Western Europe and the western part of Africa out of Atlantis," Julie said.

"The city of Atlantis now has over a million people. And the Atlantis region has surpassed 12 million ... Noah and Namia still lead New Eden Out of Turkey, which covers Eastern Europe to the Ural Mountains and the Caucasus region. Approximately 10 million people live there, and they are based near modern-day Istanbul. The nine governed regions have roughly 10 to 12 million people."

"So what are the nine regions again? I can never keep them straight."

"So I've mentioned two already. The others are Ham and Zeptah, who run the rest of Africa, which they call Egypt, out of Giza.

Shem and Pandora run the Middle East south of Turkey and west of Mesopotamia, extending through the Arabian Peninsula out of a city on the Israeli coast. They call their domain Judea. Japheth and Aresia rule Babylon, encompassing central Asia from Russia down to India. And they are based near Baghdad. Then, Xenia and Tiberius rule China which is the rest of Asia from Siberia to Vietnam. And they are located near Xian. Kallisto and Zane have been running Oceana out of Singapore. And that includes Australia and New Zealand. And finally, the daughters who went to the Americas were Godiva and Kale. They went to South America and are based in the Amazon Delta. And Ariella and Garrit are running North America out of the Chesapeake."

"So they're all doing well?"

"Yes, they're mostly just disappointed that so many of their people have moved away from their core principles... And apparently, they're also disappointed that we haven't visited them since our arrival."

"Maybe we should take a world tour and visit everyone... It would also allow us to see this 'Tower of Babel.'" Julie raised her brow.

"Sounds like it's time for another adventure." Micheal pulled her into his lap.

"Our first since we arrived in the 22nd century BC."

"I wouldn't say that." He kissed the side of her neck, and they shared a more personal adventure.

The Tower of Babel

MICHEAL and Julie began a world tour, spending one week in each region governed by one of Noah's children. They started in Eden (North America) with Ariella and Gerrit. They then proceeded south and then west across the Pacific. Now, nearly six weeks into their tour, they were staring at the pyramids in Giza. They had been restored to their pre-flood glory.

"Well, at least the historians got a couple of things right," Julie said as she admired The Great Pyramid.

"What do you mean?" Micheal asked.

"While the purpose of the pyramids is not what historians thought it was, they did accurately date their construction around 2550 BC, during the early development phase of the Atlantean

Industrial Revolution, and The Pharaoh Khufu built the Great Pyramid. His science advisor and vizier Hemiunu had conceptualized the concept of kinetic energy extraction."

"He was basically their Nikola Tesla."

"Yes, but he was successful, and it became the principal energy source that powered Atlantis."

"And the Pyramids of Giza are some of the only ones that survived the flood. And now they have been restored to working order." Micheal was impressed.

"Remember, back before the flood, we nearly didn't recognize them because the area was a tropical rain forest... Now, it certainly looks more like we would have expected."

"With the exception of the perfect casing stones and the beam of light coming out of the top." Micheal laughed.

"I was talking about the desert." Julie rolled her eyes.

"Well, they haven't repaired the Sphinx." Micheal indicated the monument.

"And I don't think they will."

"You two seem awfully interested in these pyramids. Is there something special about them?" Zeptah inquired.

"They are the most famous pyramids in our time, one of the seven wonders of the ancient world," Julie replied.

"They are the oldest pyramids in the world. We were glad they survived the flood more or less intact." Ham added.

"So Julie, you two really must perform for us before you leave," Zeptah stated fervently.

"Why not." Julie shook her head.

"Great!" Zeptah smiled.

Two weeks later, they stared at the tallest building they had ever seen.

"How tall is it?" Micheal asked Japheth.

"8000 cubits." Japheth sighed in exasperation.

JULIE did the calculations in her head. The building was 13,332 feet or approximately two and a half miles tall. "So what is it supposed to do? Obviously, you can't climb it to Heaven."

"It is supposed to utilize a special frequency to penetrate the holy veil and contact the other side. So they can communicate directly with God." Aresia told her.

As Julie stared at it, she wondered if the so-called confusion of the tongues from Genesis might have something to do with this 'special frequency'.

Over the next week, they traveled around Babylon, visiting with Japheth and Aresia. They were in the middle of their farewell dinner when some new people arrived at the Japheth estate.

"Micheal and Julie Hall, I want you to meet Felix and Drusilla Costa. They're the architects of The Tower of God," Aresia said.

"You designed the tower?" Julie raised a brow.

"Absolutely!" Drusilla said proudly.

"Japheth and Aresia don't approve." Felix lamented.

"It's antithetical to God to presume to communicate through the veil. But I don't want to argue about this tonight, if you will excuse me?" Aresia walked away.

"The official opening of the tower is the day after tomorrow. Would the two of you like to join us for a tour in the morning?" Drusilla asked.

"That would be amazing." How could they pass up a chance to see the tower?

They messaged Noah and Namia to let them know they would be a few days later than planned.

The next day, they headed 50 miles west of Babylon to the area that would become Ramadi in modern-day Iraq. Right next to the Euphrates River was the massive Tower of God.

"A generation ago, the Shinari built this ziggurat in an attempt to reach Heaven." Felix began their tour of the tower. "They used brick and mortar as an ode to the ancient tradition. But brick has its limits." Felix was describing a circular brick ziggurat. It was seven levels high and perhaps slightly over a quarter of a mile wide. It was 350 feet tall. "So we upgraded it... As you can see, 8000 cubits high. When activated, we will be able to talk to God directly. Just like our forefathers did." Felix indicated a staggeringly tall spiral metal needle tower rising from the center of the ziggurat.

It was about 600 feet wide at the base, with spiraling staircases twisting into the heavens. There was some kind of orb near the pinnacle of the tower. The whole thing was genuinely awe-inspiring. JULIE could almost believe you really could reach Heaven, if you climbed all those stairs.

Luckily for them, they took the elevator. "Welcome to the Eye of God," Drusilla said as they exited the elevator. They were on the top floor of the orb, at the top of the tower. "This way." Drusilla led them up a staircase. They emerged onto an open-air sky deck atop The Eye of God.

Julie crossed her arms against the chill. The air temperature was around 50°F with a wind chill near freezing. But you couldn't beat the view from two and a half miles up.

"Can you see eternity?" Micheal asked as he wrapped his jacket around her.

"Thank you," she said gratefully. "It's so beautiful." The sun was setting on the horizon, and the endless desert stretched as far as the eye could see to the West.

As they walked the circle around the top of the tower, Julie could see the mountains to the north and east. She could also see the fertile valley running to the southeast.

"Every time I come up here, I feel closer to God already." Felix interrupted the silence as the last sliver of the sun slipped out of sight.

"You don't feel it's wrong to try to communicate across the veil?" Julie asked.

"Before the flood, they were able to do it," Drusilla said.

"We have devoted our lives to God. It's only right we should be able to talk to him directly," Felix said.

"I hope you find what you're looking for," Micheal said.

"Come, we will show you to your suite." Drusilla guided them to a luxury suite near the top of the eye.

Once they were alone. "Do you think it's wise to be here?" Julie's stomach was turning.

"I highly doubt the main events in the Genesis story will happen the next day." Micheal tried to assure her.

"With our luck?" She sighed.

"Everything is going to be all right." Micheal wrapped his arms around her waist and proceeded to take her mind off her worries.

Around noon the next day, they were out taking in the view

again.

"It's just about time for the ceremony," Drusilla said. They began to head to the staircase when there was a loud succession of booms. The tower started to shake violently. Before they realized what was happening, the tower dropped out from underneath them, and they went into freefall.

Julie activated her rings and flew toward Drusilla. She saw Micheal diving after Felix. They were able to catch up to them just before they reached the massive cloud spreading out from the collapsing building. As they were flying the Costas from the chaos, a bright flash split the sky, and an enormous shock wave knocked them out of the air. Then everything went dark.

Confusion

MICHEAL awoke to a pounding headache. The light hurt his eyes as it pierced through the dust cloud. He remembered the tower collapsing after multiple explosions had shaken it. The tower had fallen out from under them, and they had literally gone skydiving without a parachute. Luckily for them, they had their rings.

Micheal began searching through the dust and debris for Julie. He found her unconscious, covered in dust. "Julie! Julie!" He shook her. As she began to rouse, he began wiping the dust off her face.

She opened her eyes and said, "$#?@&!" She continued talking, but it sounded like gibberish.

"Julie, can you understand me?" He pulled her to her feet.

She held her arms open with a confused look on her face. He remembered the shockwave that had knocked them out of the air and thought of the confusion.

JULIE woke to Micheal wiping dust off her face. "Micheal, thank goodness you're all right."

"&#%$@!" He said something as he helped her up, but it just sounded like blathering. She shrugged in confusion. Then she realized the confusion of the tongues must've happened. She tried to think through her skull-splitting headache. She went through the various languages she knew fluently; perhaps some of those were still intact. It was all jumbled up in her head.

There was a modicum of French, which was one of the few names of languages with which she was confident about. When she attempted to speak, what came out of her mouth seemed to be correct, but Micheal was clearly still confused about what she was trying to say. Following several more attempts, the frustration began to set in. She became overwhelmed, and the tears started flowing. Micheal embraced her and began whispering sweet nothings, literally, in her ear.

MICHEAL at least understood how Julie was feeling. Even if he didn't understand anything else. He thought it might be possible for him to focus his mind and reorganize his linguistic memories. He would be able to retrieve his ability to speak the multiple languages he knew he had, even if he couldn't remember any of their names. This would just be a blip; then they would be back to normal in no time.

He guided Julie to an oasis west of the tower debris. He sat down and began the meditation process.

He found himself at school, sitting in a classroom. He looked around and determined it was his seventh-grade French class. That's right, he thought, he should know this. But as he tried to make out what was being said it was all "French" to him. Trying to associate any of it was proving difficult.

He came out of that memory and then focused again.

He was in another classroom. One scan of the room told him it was 10th-grade Spanish. He tried to determine what they were saying, but no matter how much effort he gave it was all nonsense. All the words just looked like chicken scratch.

In frustration, he decided to take a break.

Clearly, Micheal's meditation session didn't go as he hoped. And JULIE'S confidence in them overcoming this took a hit. She closed her eyes and tried to remember the list of languages she knew. But it was also jumbled together, and nothing made any sense.

Julie went and found some paper and a writing implement. She thought that if she tried writing something, it would start to make sense. She began attempting to write an alphabet, any alphabet. She drew a blank. She just started moving her hand to see if anything would spark a memory. She got nothing. It was all just scribbling. She thought that if perhaps she focused harder, she could break through the clutter. The harder she focused, the more her head hurt. Eventually, the pounding drowned out everything else.

The pounding headache and frustration were exhausting. So she closed her eyes to calm her mind and fell asleep.

After Julie fell asleep, MICHEAL decided to try again. He went into his head and tried to think of their time in the 17th century when he was learning many more languages. But of course, in his memories, everyone was speaking nonsense.

He changed tactics. He went through his memories of phonetic learning. As he began sounding out the instructor's words, he realized the flaw in this idea. The phonetic references were mainly in a different language and they still had no meaning.

After considering for a while, he thought of one more idea. He went back to when he was a newborn and began from scratch. He began to try to relearn his original language. He went through years of memories, cherry-picking all the learning moments from them. When he had exhausted himself, he understood rudimentary English. But how long would it take to teach Julie so they could converse? He was growing frustrated. Julie had just woken up, so he decided to sleep on it.

JULIE had awakened to Micheal meditating again. After some time, she wasn't sure how long, he opened his eyes. He looked at her in consideration, then shook his head in apparent frustration. He indicated he was tired, and he took his turn sleeping.

She was now alone with only her thoughts. That struck her. How come she knew what she was thinking but not how to connect that with what her lips were saying?

She began trying to practice what she wanted to say vocally. No matter what she tried, the words were disconnected from her intentions. She changed tactics. She started trying to verbalize individual sounds of speech. But no matter how she verbalized it, it still wouldn't connect.

The frustration began to overwhelm her. She could feel the tears behind her eyes. She started humming a tune to try and calm herself. And that gave her an idea: music. Following several hours of effort, she began to gain some Association. But it was slow. She became frustrated again and fell asleep.

Frustration

They had spent three days in the oasis attempting to solve this confusion. MICHEAL had decided it was time to return home. When he awakened, Julie was making her own efforts to solve this. He went and gave her a hug and a kiss. Then, he indicated he would be right back.

He went and acquired a hovercar. When he returned, Julie was asleep. He loaded her into the car and headed for home. With the course locked in and the autopilot engaged, he returned to his memories and continued his effort to relearn English.

***

JULIE woke to the familiar sight of her bed. She had hoped that the last three days were just some kind of nightmare. And now that she was awake, everything would return to normal. But the situation was all too real. She sat up to find Micheal meditating by the window. She went over and touched his shoulder. He turned and looked at her as he touched her hand.

She was comforted by his touch and was confident that they would solve this.

***

As the days turned to weeks and months, the frustration grew daily. MICHEAL had re-taught himself basic English. But teaching Julie was proving far more challenging than he had expected.

"The pilot flew too low to avoid the storm." He indicated for her to repeat it.

"The pi-lot...f-loo too low too...a..." She ran her hand over her face in frustration.

"It's okay..." He tried to be soothing, but she exploded into an incoherent rant and then ran out of the room. She was clearly becoming more and more upset the longer this went on.

They had begun to have rambling arguments of nonsense. It was starting to put a strain on their relationship. They had only been intimate a couple of times since this happened. And now it had been nearly two months.

Julie was apparently never in the mood, so Micheal had given up trying to persuade her.

He was now sexually frustrated, to add to his general frustration. He didn't know what to do. They were just over one month from jumping out of the 22nd century BC. But would they even be able to pull that off without communication?

The English lessons were too slow to be viable anymore.

Micheal's efforts to teach JULIE a language she believed was English progressed agonizingly slowly. Throughout most of her life, solving problems has been nearly effortless. Now, her mind was betraying her. The continuous failures had engendered a never-ending sense of frustration. She had been venting her anger at Micheal, and he had become withdrawn from her.

She headed out to the shores of the Mediterranean. It was the only refuge she had. Atlantis and everywhere else had been affected by whatever happened at Babel. Atlantis was rampant with riots and violence. The entirety of the Atlantean region had ground to a halt. Society couldn't function without communication.

And it seemed her and Micheal's relationship suffered from the same deficit. And Julie wasn't sure what to do to fix it.

MICHEAL had never felt like such a failure; months of meditation and deep thought had failed to yield any tangible results. In the past 30 years, he had never faced a challenge he couldn't overcome. But now, he was an abject failure. And he wasn't only letting himself down. He was letting Julie down as well.

When all of this first happened, he was confident his superior mind would be able to fix it in no time. And he saw the same belief in Julie's trusting eyes. But as the days dragged on, he saw that trust slowly being betrayed in her eyes. And that had caused a rift to begin to form between them.

Whenever something came between them, Julie admonished him not to run away from the situation. That they should talk it out, but that avenue was not available. He didn't want to run but didn't know what else to do.

⸻ ◆ ⸻

JULIE began to spend her days thinking in circles. All her mental efforts were not producing any meaningful new ideas. Micheal had tried again to find a way forward, but she was in a nasty mood and had exploded on him. He had left, and she hadn't seen him since. And that was three days ago.

Her frustration and confusion of emotions had had her crying constantly. It had been 81 days since she had been able to talk to anyone. But especially to Micheal. Being around him but feeling a million miles away was the worst thing of all.

The separation and isolation were driving her insane. She pondered desperately for a solution. She was trying to fight through the personal hell of her own mind. And then it hit her. She had become so consumed by her selfish thoughts that she failed to recognize how terribly this must be affecting Micheal.

She had rebuffed most of his physical advances. Perhaps he had taken that as a sign of her resentment of his inability to fix this. And it was true that she did harbor a bit of resentment. But that had blinded her to his need of her. She decided to stop thinking and just be with him.

CHAPTER XXIV: THE QUEST

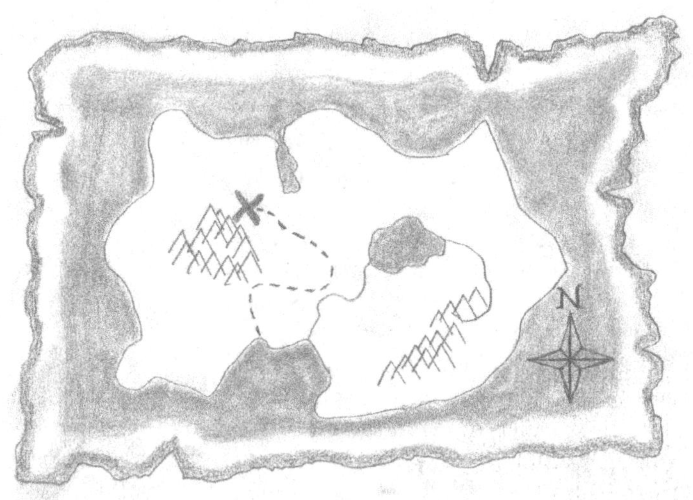

The Universal Language

MICHEAL HAD SPENT THE last three days out in the gazebo on the pier. He was now almost completely lost in his own mind. It was driving him crazy, going in useless circles. And if he wasn't doing that, he was losing himself in despair.

He was currently doing just that, staring at the waves below the pier. He closed his eyes and listened to the waves. He suddenly felt Julie embrace him from behind as she kissed him on the side of the neck.

In his surprise, he didn't know how to react. So he was frozen in place for a moment. She proceeded to kiss the other side of his neck. He grabbed her hands. He turned halfway, but his uncertainty stopped him.

She came around to face him. He turned his head away. She took his chin and turned him to look at her. She ran her fingers through his hair and stroked his cheek at the same time. He closed his eyes to the sensation. Her tenderness was amazing. When he opened his eyes, she was staring from the depths of her soul right through him.

The power of her love spoke more than words ever could. He let his lips do the talking, and he lost himself in her.

Their souls let their bodies speak for them. And JULIE let all her frustration and anger dissipate in the heat of their love. The 'conversation' continued until they had run themselves ragged. In exhaustion, they fell asleep.

When she woke, their connection was strong again. She felt no fear or trepidation. She knew she was safe, and everything would be all right. So long as they were together.

As she was taking in the pleasant smell of him, he began to slowly caress her body with his eyes closed. She closed her eyes and got lost in the sensation. Tendrils of warmth ran through her body until she finally needed a release. She mounted up and brought the connection deep inside her until her senses overflowed.

Her love for him chased away the storms that clouded MICHEAL'S mind. Then, one thought led to another. First, he thought about languages like Ancient Egyptian. Languages that were pictogram based. And that led to an idea about a similar communication system from the 21st century. Emojis, picture-icons that were new on smartphones in 2009.

Using a pen and paper, he demonstrated his idea to Julie. She picked up the concept quickly, and they were then able to converse on a fundamental level. Being able to communicate at all was a major relief.

Following a day of relaxing casual conversation, they turned to the problem at hand.

JULIE had limited exposure to emojis, but the concept was so universal. She was kicking herself for not thinking of it sooner. Over the next week, they were able to exchange ideas about the best way to try to solve this challenge. That was a small challenge in and of itself, proving that this was only a temporary solution.

They discussed many possible ideas but finally decided that, barring anything else, Micheal would continue to re-learn English and then teach it to her. But she couldn't help thinking there had to be another way to fix this.

Julie sat in the pier gazebo and took her turn meditating. After sorting through any possible ideas she could think of. She had an epiphany. "The Nectar of Knowledge," if it could give her total recall, perhaps it could fix this. There was only one problem. It had been lost in their jump from the flood. They had spent years trying to find the case that contained The Nectars of Eden. What possible chance did they have under these circumstances? But she decided they had to try.

The Quest

MICHEAL was irritated that he had overlooked this idea. But years of searching had yielded nothing, unless? Something occurred to Micheal. What if the container didn't go through the time portal? Would it be possible to find it following the flood and 200 years of time? The only way to find out was to go to North America.

They would have to go by sea. The M-pulse aircraft had been knocked out by the shockwave from the tower. And the magnetic hover cars could not fly over large empty areas like an ocean. They required magnetic rails.

They packed up everything and locked down Avalon. They had built it following their arrival in the 22nd century BC. And they intended to live in it in the 20th century BC as well. The manor house was a square approximately 200 feet in each direction with a 120-foot courtyard in the middle. Four corner towers reached five floors high, while the rest was three stories high. There was a large basement vault below ground. The entry hall protruded from the middle of the front of the mansion. The entire estate came in at a rather modest 100,000 square feet and was situated on a 1200-acre property on the Gibraltar Peninsula.

The lockdown was necessary as they wouldn't likely return during this time stop. They boarded the Melina, named in honor of their first great friend of their crazy adventure, and sailed into the open seas. Five days later, they reached the coast of Nova Scotia.

Micheal had guided them to the coordinates that lined up with where they had jumped out of the 24th century BC. It definitely looked different. But after a thorough analysis, he was sure it was the right place. They began a grid search of the area, attempting to find the capsule. As the third day was drawing to a close, they finally found it. Part of it, at least. While it was still recognizable after 200 years, it had clearly been pilfered.

He looked at Julie. She indicated they should continue the search. They were on the clock. There were only about three weeks to jump day. That meant they only had two weeks to find it. As he turned the other way, he was hit in the face, and everything went dark.

He could hear sounds all around him. Suddenly, he felt a hard slap on his cheek. He opened his eyes to see he was in a fancy house. And he was tied to a chair. He looked to his left, and Julie was also tied to a chair.

The men yelled at them incoherently. He noticed that the rings were gone from his fingers. At that moment, a man who was clearly in charge stepped forward and displayed a handful of rings. He then opened his arms in a questioning gesture, saying, where's the rest?

As he was trying to think of what to do, he noticed several things in the room that had come from the capsule. The man gave a signal, and another man showed them a picture of the Melina. The leader indicated again.

Micheal knew this wasn't good. Most of their riches had already been stowed in preparation for the jump. Whatever they had on the Melina was now gone. But it clearly wasn't enough for this wannabe king.

The entire time, he had been working at the ropes. And he was confident Julie was as well. The man demanded a response. The man became angry when Micheal indicated they didn't have anything else. After considering for a moment, a smile came over his face as he approached Julie.

The man began groping Julie's breasts. After this had gone on for about a minute, she headbutted him. The man became angry for a moment, but then he began laughing. He then signaled for several of his men to restrain her. Then he proceeded to reach down her pants.

He utilized the distraction to make his move. He had loosened his bindings enough that he was able, in one motion, to flip himself over in the chair. As he landed, the chair broke into pieces. And he instantly went on the attack.

With his attack as a distraction, JULIE revealed that her hands were free, and she began to assist him in the fight. Julie grabbed the man's arm, which was down her pants. She fell back in the chair and flipped the man over, breaking his arm at the elbow in the process. She then used pieces of the broken chair as weapons.

Micheal and Julie sequentially went through the room, neutralizing the leader's henchmen. Most were armed with guns, and they redirected their attempted shots, inadvertently shooting many of the men. A minute later, they had taken the room.

They quickly searched the room as well as the men. Julie found both sets of their wedding rings along with Micheal's family ring. But she failed to find the Gods' rings. Before they could search any further, she heard what sounded like reinforcements.

They ran through the compound until they found an exit. It opened up to the waterfront. They quickly found the Melina, boarded it and got underway as quickly as possible. As they headed out to sea, they came under fire. But they were able to reach a safe distance within minutes.

Micheal unrolled a map and indicated what appeared to be Prince Edward Island north of Nova Scotia. Then, he indicated Virginia as their next destination.

The next evening, they arrived in familiar waters. They were passing through the mouth of the Chesapeake, north of Virginia Beach—the location of the restored city of Eden. It was founded by Noah's daughter Ariella and her husband Gerrit.

Instead of stopping in the likely volatile city of Eden, Julie guided the Melina up the James River, the river of her youth. It would eventually flow through her childhood hometown of Richmond, Virginia. With that in mind, she continued to the familiar bend in the river that flowed past her childhood home.

Julie indicated the location's importance to Micheal after she moored the Melina for the night. She and Micheal sat together on the back deck and watched the sunset. The early December night was cool, but Micheal supplied plenty of heat to keep her warm.

The following day, they prepared for the next challenge. During their journey from Prince Edward Island to Virginia, Micheal showed her a map he had taken from the compound. He indicated that he was able to determine that it was a coded map detailing the location of some of the more special treasures from the capsule. It specified a location somewhere in the Chesapeake.

The first site was in the Norfolk area, within the city of Eden. As they walked the streets, they had their guard up. There were obvious signs of recent violence. But it did appear that some semblance of order had been restored. Much of the city had been burned out by riots since the last time they were here visiting Ariella and Gerrit.

Suddenly, they were ambushed. Julie utilized a metal rod as a staff and rapidly tore through the onslaught. She and Micheal coordinated well together. But soon, the numbers became overwhelming. Perhaps 30 or 40 men finally surrounded them. At that moment, a familiar face appeared.

It was Ariella's son, Cassius. He signaled for his men to stand down. After conferring for a few minutes, he indicated he would lead them to Ariella and Gerrit.

Ariella greeted them with hugs and kisses. Then, she expressed surprise that they hadn't avoided the confusion. She pointed out that she and Gerrit could still communicate. They had received a warning from Noah and had taken cover.

They showed Ariella the map, and she directed them to her granddaughter. Who told them about a cave in the North Chesapeake. And indicated a complex of traps and other challenges. She and Micheal looked at each other. Julie realized they would need to get their Lara Croft and Indiana Jones on.

The Cave

The next day, they traveled up the Chesapeake to a secret cave about 20 miles south of modern-day Annapolis, Maryland. Ariella and her grandson Hakon went with them. Through pictures, Hakon explained that over a century ago, his father had found the special case and recognized the symbol for the Garden of Eden.

He realized the vials contained the nectars from The Fountain of Life and Knowledge. He knew it must have belonged to the chosen ones. So, he built a gauntlet that only the chosen ones could conquer. It was an effort to protect the sacred nectars from everyone except them.

MICHEAL indicated that they were the chosen ones. He looked at Julie, and she rolled her eyes and shook her head. But now it was time for them to prove their worth.

The first test was opening the entrance. There were what appeared to be gems in a scattered random pattern embedded in the stone door; there was every color of the rainbow. There was a sign beside the entrance promising death to anyone trying to steal the gems. A few skeletons and some old bloodstains were proof that some had tried.

After studying the array of gems, something began to become apparent. Some were precisely the same color as the stone in his Ring of Destiny. He indicated to Julie, and she began to analyze the patterns.

She hesitantly approached the door, touched one of the stones, and then turned it. The stone began to glow. She sequentially turned all those same-colored stones, and they lit up in a pattern. After she turned the final one, the whole pattern became linked together, and the door slid open.

The door cleared away to reveal eight different entry points to what appeared to be tube slides. There was a sign above the middle showing two people holding hands. All eight openings looked the same. However, Micheal noticed that they were very slightly different sizes.

Micheal studied the opening and determined that all the openings were different sizes except two. He decided those two must be the correct ones. He hesitated as, once again, there was a sign indicating that a wrong choice would be fatal.

His analysis determined that entry points one and six were the only identical ports. He went and kissed Julie deeply. He touched his heart, then touched hers, indicating he loved her. She reciprocated. Following one final deep kiss, he climbed into port one, and she was in port six. On the count of three, they let go.

JULIE slid through the tube until it suddenly ended. She fell onto a stone surface. Micheal had landed opposite of her. The floor seemed to be moving. And she noticed she was at the edge of an abyss. She and Micheal quickly adjusted to maintain a balance of the flat rock upon whatever it was balancing on. But it seemed they had chosen wisely as several other openings dropped straight into the abyss. And the others must have other terrible ends as well.

They shifted in sequence, moving closer to each other. They stopped when they could take each other's hand. Suddenly, they had to move as the rock began tilting backward. They ran the last few steps hand-in-hand and jumped to a slightly higher stone. As the first fell into the abyss.

They repeated the process five more times to reach the top, which was stable ground. The landing was relatively small. Perhaps twenty by twenty feet. And there was a cable leading in the direction they would have to go. It was about an inch thick.

With no other options, Julie indicated to Micheal. She kissed him, then began balancing across the wire. With each step very carefully placed. After about 100 feet, she reached a sheer wall. A sign indicated up, so she started climbing.

As she neared the top, she was able to look down and see Micheal was right behind her. They both reached the top and celebrated with a hug. Now, there were two ropes. They appeared to allow you to swing across another abyss. Except the angle from the anchor point indicated it was a single-use rope. That meant you had to swing perfectly through the small opening in the wall. Or else you would hit the wall, and there were various spikes and other unpleasant dangers.

Micheal went first and landed perfectly. As Julie was swinging the rope began to abrade. It broke as she reached the wall. She was barely able to grab the edge of the opening. The edge rock gave way, and she began to fall, but Micheal caught her and helped pull her up.

They proceeded down the tunnel, and it came to a fork. There was a puzzle in the junction with three potential answers that all looked remarkably similar—one for each tunnel. Julie, of course, assumed that a wrong answer would mean death. After some consultation, they decided on the tunnel to the right.

They carefully walked down the tunnel. When they reached the end, the tunnel closed off behind them. There was a slide puzzle on the wall in front of them and an hourglass next to it.

Micheal stepped up and began shifting the pieces as quickly as he could. Just before time ran out, he seemed to solve the puzzle. The door slid open, and they stepped through as the ground fell away behind them.

They followed the tunnel until they came to a large cavern. There was a ledge in front of them. As they walked out onto it, it began to crumble in their direction. Julie saw a puzzle station and began working on it as quickly as possible. When she finished, there was only about one-fourth of the ledge left. Micheal was working the opposite puzzle. He finished with just a few feet to spare.

Another ledge began to extend out in front of them, so they followed it to another station, where they repeated the process. They had to go through one more cycle, with creeping oblivion chasing them the entire way. After completing the bridge, they were on a platform surrounded by pillars. The pillars were all at foot level, perhaps one foot thick.

The case containing The Nectars of Eden was sitting on a pedestal in the middle of the platform. Julie cautiously went and picked it up. The pedestal began to sink. As it did, a rumble began to come from her left. Then she saw that the pillars on that side were collapsing toward them.

She looked to Micheal, then turned and began running on top of the pillars to her right in the direction of a light that had appeared. She was so laser-focused on the tops of the pillars that she wasn't sure if Micheal was behind her. But the rumble was getting louder. When she knew she was in range, she jumped toward the light. She landed on a rock ledge with the Chesapeake in front of her. Then Micheal suddenly came tumbling out of the opening. He rolled toward the cliff. Julie dropped the case and dove, grabbing his arm as he went over the edge. She pulled him back up in time to see the cave superstructure collapse in on itself. Then, she and Micheal collapsed together in relief.

Total Recall

When they had finally caught their breath, MICHEAL sat up, and so did Julie. He opened the case and pulled out two vials of The Nectar of Knowledge. He handed one to Julie, then looked deep into her eyes, searching her soul. It had been four months since they could actually talk to each other, but their souls had been able to bypass that unspoken barrier. She kissed him deeply, then pulled back and after one last long look, she raised her vial. He toasted her, and they drank simultaneously.

A rush of images raced through his head, and he became overwhelmed, and then everything went dark.

When he came around, he felt just as he had before. But he thought about one of his childhood memories, and he could understand it. He sat up and saw Julie in a meditative position.

"Julie?" Micheal tried.

"Micheal. Oh, it's so good to understand you again!"

"It is so beautiful to understand your voice again. How do you feel?" He knew she was experiencing total recall again.

"I tried to prepare myself this time, but 22 years is a long time. However, I did remember your advice."

"I can't believe I've had to wait so long to say what I have been dying to tell you... I love you, Jules."

Julie rose from her meditation. "I love you, Micheal." They passionately locked lips for a good long time. When they finally separated, she said, "I think Ariella and Hakon are waiting on us."

Micheal had to laugh. "I'm sorry, there was only one thing on my mind."

She laughed at that. "There will be plenty of time for that... Let's go."

As they rounded the corner of the rock, Ariella and Hakon were waiting patiently.

"Ariella, Hakon, it's so good to speak to you again." Micheal switched from English to Atlantean.

"So, obviously, you were successful," Ariella said.

"Thanks to you," Julie said.

"May I?" Ariella asked about the box.

"Of course." Julie displayed it open for her.

"It is so amazing to actually touch something from The Garden." Ariella's eyes were wide.

<hr>

That evening, they headed off full steam to ensure they wouldn't be late.

"I guess now you'll have to hear all my nagging." JULIE quipped, only half joking.

"I will gladly take that over the alternative. But seriously. It drove me crazy not being able to tell you how beautiful you are every day. Like when you wore that pink dress a couple of months ago. Or how incredible you were in helping to solve that crazy situation. Or how much it meant to me that day when you came to the gazebo... I love you, Julie Hall, nagging and all." Micheal was clearly emotional. She almost thought he might cry.

"Now, about that thought that's been clouding your mind," she said seductively. "We have plenty of time now." She began to undress him.

Three days later, they were nearing the French coast, pushing the limits on getting to the jump point in time.

-December 21, 2175 BC

"It's been four months since I wrote in this journal. After The Confusion of the Tongues at the Tower of Babel, I finally got my language back.

When I was a girl and I first heard about The Confusion, I thought it was just a story. There was no way I could believe that was how all of the different languages in the world came to be. But then it happened to us.

We have been able to use the sky-net to analyze what happened at Babel. The Tower was a massive antenna. When it collapsed, which we discovered was due to sabotage, it sent a shockwave that knocked us out of the air. That shockwave was an energy wave that affected the language center of the brain. Anyone hit by that wave had whatever language was already in their heads jumbled into an incomprehensible mess. That wave circled the entire globe. We learned that the only people who weren't affected by it were Noah and his children.

Noah received a vision about it. He warned his children so they could take cover. That is what Ariella told us.

Micheal and I were able to endure one of the most challenging periods of our marriage. And now, we have learned through this experience that our connections are far more profound than I would have imagined. Over the past 31 years, we've had our ups and downs. And we have also been able to experience some of the most incredible things from history. As difficult as the last four months have been, it has shown me that if we can overcome this, we can overcome anything.

Total recall has been rough the past few days. All the horrors of these past ten years came back to the surface. It has been an emotional roller coaster. But after all these years, I still try to follow Jessica's advice. To focus on the good. And I do have so much good to focus on.

Now it's off to the 20th century... BC, that is. We have no idea what to expect. But it will always be me and Micheal, so it will be okay."

"I'm Julie Hall, and this is The Book of Avalon, Volume 5, signing off..."

CHAPTER XXV: AMANDA HALL

Crossfire

MICHEAL BEGAN TO COME around. There were loud bangs and sharp whizzing noises all around him. It made him think about World War II. They were jumping into the 20th century... BC, that is. But they were also jumping into the beaches of Normandy in northern France. Omaha Beach, no less. And now it sounded like a war was raging around him. He wondered if they had made a mistake; it was 1944 rather than 1960 BC.

He became concerned about Julie. He cautiously looked in the direction that she should be. She was lying on the ground about 80 feet away. She did not appear to be awake yet. He began making his way to her, going from cover to cover as the bullets were whizzing past him. He was not overly concerned as they both wore their bulletproof tri-poly clothes. However, their heads were still vulnerable. None of it would've been any problem if they hadn't lost their gods' rings on Prince Edward Island.

The bullets were coming from both sides, so it was apparent that they had fallen into the crossfire of a battle. He continued his way across the beach. Now, he was about 50 feet from Julie. She began to stir. He quickly closed to about 30 feet away. She sat up and was looking around.

"Micheal!" she yelled over the noise in his direction.

A bullet ripped through her left shoulder. Blood sprayed everywhere.

"Julie!"

He felt shock and horror. He ran toward her; suddenly, he felt fire burning in his left side, then his right. He looked down in shocked surprise as the blood poured out of his stomach. Then, another one ripped through his chest. He looked up at Julie, who had a look of horror on her face as a tear streamed down her cheek.

"Julie..." he could barely wheeze as everything faded to black.

* * *

JULIE watched in shock and horror as Micheal was shot three times, including one through the heart. He fell backward to the ground. He had a look of death in his eyes as a puddle of blood pooled around him. She needed to work quickly if she had any chance to save him. But as she tried to pull him out of the line of fire, a bullet cut through her side to go with the wound in her shoulder. She began to try again, but another bullet grazed her thigh. This wasn't going to work.

Julie turned to the West, which was the closer side of the beach. She ran full speed, dodging and weaving a hail of bullets. She reached the beach's edge. Several of the soldiers moved to meet her at the crest. She immediately went on the attack. She quickly disarmed the first soldier and then shot down the first four.

She examined the weapon for a moment, then thought. No wonder the bullets cut through their tri-poly clothing; it was a railgun. Now armed with the railgun, she systematically wiped out the entire squadron on the west side of the beach.

She assessed the situation and noticed the opposing squadron crossing the beach from the East toward Micheal. She wasted no time moving quickly along the crest, circling the beach's edge to the south. Intermittently firing cover shots as she went until the second squadron was directly to her north.

She quickly ran from her cover, diving off the crest of the beach. As she landed, she rolled up to her feet and unleashed a hail of rail pellets, mowing most of them down. A few of them were able to take cover and returned fire. She sprinted toward them and jumped over one of the mounds on the beach. She landed her flip and eliminated one of the soldiers.

Then, she quickly dodged the enemy fire and eliminated the last two soldiers. She took cover and cautiously did a final scan of the entire beach. There didn't appear to be anyone else.

When she was sure it was clear, she ran to Micheal. Julie could see death in his eyes. He had no pulse and wasn't breathing. One of the pellets had clearly ripped through his heart. Julie was overwhelmed with grief. After they had escaped death so many times, she couldn't believe this was how it would end.

She felt as though she existed outside her body as if she were trapped in a dreadful nightmare. This couldn't be real; she had to wake up.

"Wake up!" she yelled. "Wake up!" she repeated. She tried to force herself awake by sheer will. She closed her eyes, trying to calm herself with deep breaths. But when she finally opened them, it was all too real.

"Micheal!" she screamed. "Micheal!" she demanded as if she could order him back to life by sheer will alone. But the reality of the situation was starkly real. Overwhelmed with grief, she collapsed on top of him.

It felt like time was slowing down as she relived in her mind every moment she and Micheal had ever shared. Every moment of love, every tender touch, every expression of affection. All of their stimulating conversations.

One of these came to the forefront, and suddenly, she was there:

"What would I ever do if you were to die?" Julie asked.

"You don't have to worry about that. Together, we are immortal. There is no challenge we can't overcome... I promise that so long as we are together, we will abide... I promise that we will die together, in love, at the end of a very long life."

She took a deep breath. "I know you're a man of your word."

She came out of the memory. "You promised me!" she accused through the tears. Then she thought. There had to be something she could do, but what?... After a long moment of contemplation, she thought... The Nectar of Life... But would it work?

Amanda Hall

MICHEAL found himself outside his body. One look at the massive hole in his chest and puddle of blood, he realized he was dead. He wasn't sure what to do next. He saw Julie crying over him. He could still hear the bullets flying. He wanted to protect her, but he didn't know if there was anything he could do.

All of his attempts to assist her as she made her way around the beach, eliminating the enemy soldiers who had killed him, failed. He watched as their spirits left their bodies one by one and quickly disappeared.

When she had finished, she returned to mourn over him. All he wanted to do was comfort her, but he was utterly helpless. Suddenly, a light in the sky drew his attention. It felt like he was being pulled to it by some kind of tractor beam. He looked back at Julie one final time and wondered. Would he ever see her again? He didn't know.

He entered the light, and it became a tunnel. As the conduit raced past, he thought the light would have been brighter. The light at the end of the tunnel was a mellow blue. He passed through the end of the tunnel, and his vision blurred.

As it cleared, an incredible scene was before him. It looked almost like night. He was in an icy field. And a giant blue orb was floating over the horizon. It was a deep shade of blue with a giant dark blue spot, like an eye... Then he realized it was Neptune. He scanned his surroundings and decided he must be on Triton, the largest moon of Neptune.

He was trying to figure out why he was here, when he heard a voice call his name.

"Micheal?" While it was slightly different, he recognized it.

"Amanda?!" He turned to the voice. And she was there. Even all grown up, she was unmistakable.

Amanda was his kid sister who died of cancer when she was 12. As her big brother, and a supposed genius, he was supposed to protect her. One of the few times in his life he had tried to use his intelligence, he had failed to find a cure, and she died as a result of his failure.

He had blamed himself. He was supposed to be the big brother, he was supposed to protect her, but he had failed. When she died, he had sunk even deeper into his depression. He had dropped out of high school. He didn't care about anything anymore. He almost killed himself.

She had talked him back from the brink that day on Mount Olympus. But he dwelt in misery for years. He tried to lock his memories of Amanda deep in the recesses of his mind. So deep in fact, that in the 37 years he had known Julie, he had never mentioned her, not even once.

Amanda looked like she was in her early 20s. She was all grown up. Perhaps five-foot-ten. Her piercing green eyes perfectly complemented her shoulder-length strawberry-blonde hair. Her whole countenance was glowing.

"You are so beautiful." Tears ran down his cheeks. "Look at you, all grown up!" He smiled. "It's so good to see you."

"My big brother Mike. I am so proud of the man you have become." Amanda hugged him.

They embraced each other for a very long time. Then something came to his mind. "How do you know what kind of man I've become? I was an abject failure. I couldn't save you..."

"Micheal... You're my big brother, but it wasn't possible for you to save me. You need to forgive yourself. You were the best big brother a girl could have ever had."

"I was supposed to protect you..." He broke off as the tears streamed.

"I'm okay... And Jessica told me about you. Told me how you have become the best kind of man."

"Jessica?"

"Yes, your wife Julie's sister. We've become great friends. She looks out for both of you." Before he could react, she asked, "How is everyone?"

"Everyone is doing great... At least they were the last time I knew... But it's been almost 40 years since I've seen them. Father took your death very hard. I don't think he was ever the same after that."

"Tell me about Julie. Jessica has told me some things. But I'm sure you have a different perspective of her."

"Well, where should I begin? She's just so amazing. I still don't understand what she sees in me. Even in our unique circumstances, it baffles me that such a perfect angel could love me like she does." He broke off in wonder.

"You always told me you knew you would never get married. But what did I always say to you?" Amanda raised a brow.

"You said I was an amazing person and that when the time was right, I would marry an equally amazing woman."

"And now you have. Tell me more about her."

"Julie... She has such a generous heart and a genius mind. And obviously, her beauty outshines the sun, moon, and stars combined... Would you believe we've been married for over 31 years?" He was beginning to ramble. He paused for a moment.

"No one deserves love more than you do." Amanda smiled.

"But I guess not anymore, being that I'm dead and all. This whole time, I've had a question burning in the back of my mind."

"How am I here?"

"Exactly; technically, you won't be born for nearly 4000 years."

"Time, as I'm sure you now know, is fluid. It can change based on many factors. Anyone in your situation always remains tethered to your original time. When you die, you transition to your original temporal counterpart in the afterlife. So you returned to the temporal equivalent of 2010 because that is where your physical register lies."

"I guess that makes sense, but why are we here... On Triton?" As if acknowledging him, the moon erupted a geyser.

"It is beautiful, isn't it?" Amanda extended her arm, looking toward Neptune. She paused for a second as if taking in the view. "The way it works is that your transition to the other side is always the place in your subconscious where you are most comfortable. So this is the place you thought of in your mind, the place you most wanted to go. You always loved space. And I know that Neptune was your favorite planet."

"So that really is Neptune?" He stared in wonder. "How many times have you seen it?"

"This is the first time. While we can move at the speed of thought and have no atmospheric restrictions, we are all very busy. And we rarely have time for recreation."

They sat down on a mound of ice. He looked over at a very bright star. "Is that the..."

"The sun? Yes." She finished for him.

"So what happens now? You are my guide, right?"

"So now we wait." Amanda wrapped her arm around him, leaning her head on his shoulder.

"What are we waiting for?"

"Julie…"

"You mean she's about to die also?!" Micheal felt butterflies in his stomach.

"No… Julie will try to bring you back from the dead. But even I am not told everything. It may be possible, or it may not. And, of course, if it becomes possible, you still must choose to return," Amanda said in his ear as she embraced him.

"Why wouldn't I return?"

"Very few ever choose to go back. To most people, life is pain. The longer you are here, in the light of love, the harder it becomes to go back."

"What's taking so long?"

"Time works differently here than it does down there. Look at me," she ordered. When he did, she messed up his hair with a smile. "Don't worry, big brother. The decision is completely up to you."

It felt like days began to pass. When suddenly a voice spoke from behind him.

"Is my sister taking her dear sweet time?" He turned at the question.

"Jessica?"

"It's good to see you again, Micheal. I wanted to thank you for taking such good care of Julie for me." Jessica bowed.

"Come to check on me?" Amanda asked.

"Not technically. I couldn't pass up the chance to meet Julie's soulmate… Properly, I should clarify. After our brief encounter in the sea, I became curious if there was anyone related to you that I could talk to. And that's when I found Amanda. She told me all about her big brother Micheal." Jessica smiled.

"I still don't know why Julie loves me."

"We do; Amanda told me about every memory she had with you. About your generosity, your kindness, your brilliance. And so much more… You suffer from total recall. In the mortal dimension, it's rare. Everyone here has it, but it's meant for this world. Very few in the mortal realm ever experience it. It makes you skew everything to the negative. It's quite impressive that you're as normal as you are. It drives most mortals crazy. They usually either go insane or kill themselves. You are the ideal man for any woman." She came and embraced him in a hug. He wasn't sure what to do, so he hugged her back. After a minute, she pulled back. "I have to go now. It was a pleasure to meet my brother-in-law. I am so grateful that Julie has you looking out for her." She kissed his cheek. "See you later, Amanda. Goodbye, Micheal!" Jessica smiled at him and disappeared in a flash.

She was everything Julie had described. A peppy ray of sunshine. Seemingly carefree and fun-loving. The quintessential opposite of Julie's mellow, calm demeanor. But she certainly looked like Julie's twin, only with the blonde hair and the sky-blue eyes.

"Isn't she great?"

All he could do was laugh. "She certainly has spirit." He sat down next to Amanda. A tear came to his eye as he touched her cheek with the back of his hand. "You're so perfect. You had so much to live for... Why didn't I save you?"

Amanda embraced him. After a few minutes, she pulled back. She wiped the tears from his cheeks and said, "You did. It was you who got me through so many tough times. You never pitied me. You made me feel normal. To everyone else, I was already dead—a ghost in a shell. But to you, I was just me. You have no idea how much that meant to me. You fought for me till the end. You gave my life meaning. You gave me a life. And I lived every second of it. As short as my life was, I regret nothing. Thanks to you. So you see, you did save me." She smiled through her tears.

He pulled her into him. He felt like he was being enveloped by love. And the feeling was only getting stronger. It was so amazing. It was becoming intoxicating. He could see why she had said he might choose to say. Everyday life was so much harder.

<hr>

After what felt like hours, Amanda looked up at him. "It's time, Micheal."

"Time for what?"

"You can choose to go back."

"What am I supposed to do?"

"You have to choose whether to stay or go."

"My life seems so long ago. As if it was long past... Complete." He was confused.

"It was long past, 3900 years in the mortal realm."

"I'm feeling drawn to the light. Am I supposed to stay with you?" His mind was clouded. He didn't know what was real. All he knew was the feeling. The feeling of complete and total unconditional love was all around him. It had become part of him.

"I would love you to stay with me. But it's for you to decide... If you decide to stay with me, I will help with what comes next. Or you simply need to think of the mortal realm, and you will return to Julie." Amanda wiped the tear from his cheek.

"Julie!" He thought. He closed his eyes, and he could see her. Draped over him, crying. She kept yelling, "Come back!" All the force of love pulling him toward the light began shifting to Julie. "I have to go back!"

"I knew you would. I've missed you all this time. It was amazing to see you again, and in this place." She indicated Neptune.

"It really is amazing, isn't it?" he asked rhetorically. "It was so good to see you, Mandy. I love you so much, you have no idea."

"Yes, I do, I love you Micheal. Now go take care of our girl." Amanda stepped back, smiling.

He ran his thumb around her cheek and then tapped her nose. "I will see you later; I love you."

"I love you." She waved farewell.

He focused on Julie, and Neptune disappeared in a flash. The next thing he knew, he was on the beach next to himself and Julie. She looked like such a wreck. He wrapped her in a blanket of his love. She took a deep breath, as if in reaction. She rose from his body. She looked back at him.

"Micheal?!" As if summoned by her voice, he took one long last look into her loving eyes, then he drifted into his body, and everything faded to black.

Nectar of Life

JULIE began searching for The Case of Eden. It had apparently been thrown asunder in the chaos of the battle after they had jumped into the crossfire. After inspecting the first two canisters, she realized it must be in the third canister, mostly submerged in the surf.

The canisters were large, about 10 to 15 feet in diameter, and around 20 feet tall. She took a deep breath and dove under the waves. She swam straight to the access port about 15 feet below the surface. After trying for a few minutes, she had to come up for air. She dove down again and worked at it for another few minutes, but she realized it must be stuck.

She repeated the process five more times while precious time was slipping away. The access port finally wrenched open. She searched quickly and found the case. She swam to the surface, then back to shore.

The whole process took way longer than she had expected. By the time she reached Micheal again, he must've been dead for one and a half to two hours. Now, she just prayed that the Nectar of Life could work miracles. She poured about two-thirds of the vial into his wounds and then the final third into his mouth.

As the minutes passed, she began to worry that she was too late. At least 15 minutes had passed. She didn't want to give up, but how long does a miracle take? She looked at his face. His lifeless eyes were staring back at her. She couldn't take it anymore. She was too late. She closed his eyes and collapsed on his chest. She was overcome with grief; what was she going to do now?

All of these memories came rushing through her mind. She was becoming inconsolable. "Come back." The tears streamed. "Come back!" she tried again. "Come back!" she repeated, but it was no use. She collapsed in the ocean of her tears.

Her whole body went numb. She started to feel like she was outside of her body. Just then, a warm feeling came over. It felt like a warm blanket of love. She got the feeling that Micheal was looking at her from behind. "Micheal!" She turned to look, but it was an empty beach. She still had a strong sense that he was there. She thought she might see his spirit if she stared hard enough.

No matter how much she willed it, there was no one there. Then, she heard a deep breath behind her. She turned quickly, and Micheal was breathing. "Micheal!" She screamed as she took him up in her arms. He wasn't conscious, but he was breathing, and she was overjoyed.

Over the next three days, Julie watched over him as his wounds closed up. And then completely disappeared. On the third day, she wondered when he would finally wake up. And then.

"Water?" Micheal finally asked.

She gave him a few sips from the bottle. "How do you feel?"

"Thirsty." He sat up. "How long was I out?"

"Three days."

"I was dead... The Nectar of Life?"

"Yes... Thank goodness! I don't know what I would've done if I had lost you." She closed her eyes.

"It was pretty close there." His eyes shifted to the distance.

"How do you know?... Wait, that was you, wasn't it?... On the beach?"

"Yes, you looked so sad. All I wanted in that moment was to wrap you in my love." There was a most tender look on his face.

"Wait... What do you mean, pretty close?"

"They said I had to wait to see if you would make it in time. Or if I would stay dead."

"Who said?"

"Well, Jessica wanted to know what took you so long." He smiled. "She is exactly as you described her." He shook his head.

"Jessica was there to greet you?... Why wasn't anyone from your family there?"

He sobered up. "Julie... There's something I need to tell you..." He broke off.

She was becoming worried. "Okay?"

"My sister was there also." Tears welled behind his eyes.

She was horrified. Had one of his sisters died since they had fallen? "Vanessa or Kim were there?"

Micheal paused a good long moment. "No... My sister Amanda." He averted his eyes.

"Amanda? I thought your sisters' names were Vanessa and Kimberly?"

"I had a third sister, Amanda... Is my youngest sister."

"Youngest sister?" She furled her eyebrows.

"I meant to tell you sooner... I just..." He looked away as the tears streamed down his cheeks.

"A sister you meant to tell me about?" She was both hurt and angry. "We've been married 31 years, and you never told me about another sister?..." Then she realized. "Wait, how did she die?"

He looked up at her. "Cancer..." She went and threw her arms around him. "She was eight when she was diagnosed. I spent the next four years trying to find a cure... All my supposed genius and I couldn't save her..." he explained through the tears.

"How old were you?"

"13... When she was diagnosed. I was her big brother; I was supposed to protect her. But I failed... After that, I wouldn't try to prove my genius anymore. I dropped out of school. Nothing mattered, for a long time... She told me I didn't fail her. She said I saved her. But if I had, she would still be living in the mortal realm. And when I saw her all grown up. The woman she would have become. It only emphasized my failure." He was rambling.

"You were just a kid. You can't blame yourself for not finding a cure for cancer." She rubbed his back. "So this is the reason you dropped out of school? And why you shut down your potential?" It brought new light to his struggles in his youth. He had never gone into detail about the cause of his depression. Other than his perfect memory.

"I was filled with such guilt. I was already sinking into my depression, because of all my problems, particularly my appearance. Then, this was a situation where I believed that my intelligence could save my sister. But my one good quality failed me... And Amanda." She could tell he was reliving those memories.

He just cried on her shoulder for a while. Finally, he pulled back. "Goodness, your beautiful... In so many ways." He was studying her face. "That's why I came back. Your beauty outshone the light."

"What do you mean?"

"On the other side. It felt like I was there for days. Amanda said I may not want to go back. Because the longer you're there, the more enraptured you become with the light. So, it becomes difficult to pull yourself away. Amanda and I spent most of the time just talking. Enjoying the view."

"Can you describe it for me?"

"We were on Triton, the largest moon of Neptune. And, of course, Neptune loomed large in the sky."

"You were out by Neptune? How is that possible?"

"Amanda said that your mind unconsciously takes you to a place where you will feel most comfortable. In the afterlife, you move at the speed of thought. And you don't feel the effects of the environment the same way we do. So you could literally go anywhere in the universe." Micheal looked away, lost in thought. "Triton was a dim ice ball of a world. You could feel the low gravity and the cold, but it didn't bother you. And the view was incredible. Neptune was the most stark color of blue you have ever seen. It felt like it was always night, except there was a very bright star in the sky. It took a bit to recognize that it was the Sun... The whole scene was just amazing... Then Amanda informed me that it was time to make my choice. The feeling of love surrounding me was intoxicating. I didn't think I could pull myself away. Then I thought of you... I could see you on the beach trying to will me back to life. That's when your love overcame the light, and I had to return. I said farewell to Amanda. I focused on you, and then I was there standing next to you on the beach."

"I understand why, but I still wish you would have told me about Amanda." She felt conflicted. She could understand, in one sense. But 30 years of marriage, and her loss of Jessica?

"You're right; it was wrong not to tell you something like that. I should have told you after you told me about Jessica, but it felt presumptuous. I have betrayed our marriage again."

"I forgive you; I love you." They would have to work through this, but not right now. Right now, she was happy to have him back.

"I love you, Jules." They kissed as the sun set on Normandy.

CHAPTER XXVI: THE BRITISH EMPIRE

King George

"**Y**OUR MAJESTIES, HOW SHALT we honor thy magnificent 100-year reign?" Lord Pontius asked KING GEORGE and Queen Katherine.

"What of the palace at Devon?" King George asked.

"Completion shall be two months hence." Lord Tarrek informed them.

"Upon completion of the new palace, festivities shalt we host," George said.

"That will be all!" Katherine dismissed the Council.

George couldn't believe he had been King of England for 100 years. It had been more than a century since they landed on the coast of Normandy. In the Atlantean year of 1968. Two hundred ninety-nine years after The Flood of Noah. In all that time, they had been unable to find the gods, Lord and Lady Avalon. Perhaps they had returned to the heavens. He decided it didn't matter. He and Katherine had made more than the most of the situation the Lords of Avalon had put them in. The civilization had been reborn. Highly advanced, but in a limited scope geographically.

They had crossed The Channel from Normandy to find a lawless British Isles run by many heathen warlords. While it took about ten years, his obviously superior noble stature was able to bring order out of the chaos. And it was only fitting that they should spread that order across Europe.

They expanded the empire every decade, first in Ireland and then in the low countries, followed by a grueling conquest of the Norse lands to the edge of Russia. And that was all in the first 30 years of their reign. They took a 30-year break to have children.

In the beginning, George worried he had inherited the Tudor curse. They had five straight daughters, followed by a string of stillbirths and miscarriages. Finally, he got his son. With his long-awaited heir, they returned to expansion.

The next 30 years of conquest saw the expansion take the Holy Roman Empire, Austria-Hungary, The Commonwealth, Russia, and finally Italy. Their empire was now more extensive than Rome. They had nearly conquered the continent. From the Ural Mountains in the east of Russia, the border ran Southwest along the coasts of the Caspian and Black seas and the Caucasus Mountains. The only holdouts were the Ottomans and the Greeks in the East, and Celtic which was France, and Atlantis which was the Iberian Peninsula in the West.

Several wars with Celtic didn't go as planned, and Atlantis was negotiating an alliance with Celtic. Britain would need to strike soon before that alliance was solidified.

They had sent a test incursion raid into the frontier of Normandy. But the entire squadron was wiped out. And these were some of Britain's best special forces, using the most advanced rail guns in the world. They knew a third party had perpetrated it because the Celtic special force squadron had also been eliminated.

"Who dost thou believe couldst have committed such act?" King George asked Katherine.

"Apart from us, thou mean?" She raised a brow.

"Quite obvious that would be."

"Our children, perhaps?" She stated the obvious.

"None would so cross us... Remind me that does. All shall attend festivities."

"And what of thy 147th day of birth?"

"Remind me not of such things." He didn't like being reminded of his age.

She laughed. "Hast thou forgotten that I am 245?"

"Thee looks not a day over 25."

"Flatter me not. Celebrate thy birth, we shall." She gave a stare to broach further argument. "A gift I have for thee." Katherine indicated the bedroom.

———————

King George entered the room to find a beautiful young woman wearing next to nothing. This had been a compromise he had had to make. Early in his reign, he felt like he and Katherine had become a bit stale after 20 years of marriage. So, thinking like the King he was, he had taken on multiple mistresses.

However, Katherine had been corrupted after living a century in Atlantis. She would only accept co-equal rule. When she found out about his mistresses, she brought them into their bedroom, lined them up in front of him, and then killed them one by one. Afterward, she threatened to kill him if he did it again.

He proposed a compromise: She could sleep with other men. However, she protested vehemently, declaring that she would never entertain such an idea. In response, she offered a counter-proposal: He could have sex with any other women he desired, but with a unique condition – she would kill them afterward.

Her decades in the spy game had made her a cold-blooded killer. She had come to enjoy killing. During their early years on the throne, he had been able to rein her in. However, he had agreed to her terms.

"Juliet... His Majesty the King," Katherine introduced her. She was tall with raven hair and deep blue eyes. She dropped into a curtsy.

Katherine watched as usual while he had his way with Juliet multiple times. He always made the most of these opportunities. Katherine would join in some of the time. Other times, she would just sit and watch, then go in for the kill, like this time.

He indicated he had finished with Juliet. Katherine intercepted her as she rose to depart, striking several of her pressure points. Most of her body ceased to function, and she collapsed into Katherine's arms.

Katherine proceeded to torture-strangle Juliet. She picked her up off the ground several times. Juliet was helpless to resist at all. George did feel a little bad about it. But what was he going to do? Give up his rights as King to unlimited extracurricular sex? Not a chance.

"Didst thou enjoy my King?" Katherine asked.

"Very gracious, my Queen. Didst thou find pleasure?" George asked seductively.

"Ready for more I am!" She climbed on top of him.

They always had wild sex after Katherine got her kill. They were lying in bed, exhausted from their joyful exertion. George watched as the cleanup crew removed Juliet's body, and he wondered how many women Katherine had killed over the years. He did a quick calculation in his head and determined that over the past 90 years, she had killed more than a thousand women. That meant he had bedded over a thousand women. And he thought to himself. "It's good to be the king!"

Queen Katherine

"Beautiful, highness. End of shoot, it is." The photographer said with a bow. "Thou shalt have final say, your Majesty."

"Dismissed." QUEEN KATHERINE ordered. She had just finished a photo shoot for the Atlantic. It proclaimed her the most beautiful woman in the world. And, of course, that was obvious. Now and then, Katherine would think about what her life would have been had she stayed in Boston.

She knew she was beautiful. She would have easily remarried. She would have had children and grown old in an insignificant fashion in the 17th century. She would've never seen her 252 years. And she certainly would have never ruled Europe, as the British Empire, for nearly a century. She was a cut above everyone else. Which was why she was Queen. She knew now... She was born for this.

The next day, Katherine and George were traveling in a processional through the streets of London. Millions came out to celebrate their 105th year on the throne.

"Envy of the world are we," George said as they took in the adoration. The festivities were being covered by media from around the world.

"Rule Atlantis we should have before the flood," she said with annoyance.

"Correct that we shall, soon enough."

"Only if our George finally completes French conquest." Katherine shook her head. Their son had been leading the French campaign in Celtic, which stood in the way of any conquest of Atlantis.

"Through subversion have our forces softened Celtic's capability of response. They know not; war has begun."

"Our son shall win the day." Katherine feigned confidence. She had been disappointed in her son. He was the only one of their children who had failed to win a successful military campaign. While she had raised all five of her daughters to be just like her. George had been a doting father. He was too soft on them. But she had ensured they would all be a force to be reckoned with.

"China and Eden both have moved to ready. Upon our word, they shall commence." George turned toward the bigger global picture. China was their ally in the East. And Eden was their ally across the Atlantic, in the Americas. Together, their alliance would run the world. Of course, she and George would command the coalition. She would then be Queen of the World. She liked the sound of that.

They arrived at the Tower of London. George had insisted on using the names they were familiar with.

The royal purple carpet was lined with all the high-class lords and ladies as they walked. Later that evening, they sat down for an interview with Skylar Varus. She was the world's most famous journalist, out of Egypt. It was to discuss their reign as the world's longest-serving rulers.

"95 years, to what dost thou attribute such longevity?" Skylar asked in English.

"Prosperity and justice do mark our reign," Katherine replied proudly.

"There are some who make that claim; others, however, say thou art conquerors."

"Long has our goal been such promotion of the values we hold dear. Our intentions have been to establish order out of chaos. On occasion, such transitions have had their difficulties." George said.

"Perhaps thee declare that Celtic and Greece remain in chaos?" Skylar said a little sharply for Katherine's taste.

"Violations of our sovereignty shall never go unpunished. And should thee cross us, a price shalt thou pay," Katherine said in warning.

Skylar changed the subject. "Thy children's profiles have risen over the years. All have children of their own. Wilt thou step aside at some point, making way for a new generation?" Katherine disliked Skylar's suggestion.

"No intention do we have. Many years still do we possess."

"Thy age becomes apparent. Does not thee desire a quiet retirement?" Skylar's backhanded insult stung Katherine, but she maintained her composure.

"Retire? No intent do we possess." She replied pleasantly. Skylar Varus was clearly jealous. She had recently finished second to Katherine in the survey of the most beautiful women in the world.

Skylar was beautiful with her brown hair, amber eyes, and olive complexion. Katherine understood her jealousy. But the sharpness of her insults would not go unpunished.

Katherine patiently waited a few months to exact revenge so as not to arouse suspicion.

As she entered the room, the TV said: "... Police still have not found Skylar Varus's body. But the sheer volume of her blood found at the scene has led to the conclusion that she is dead. The bloody knife and some of her blood-soaked clothes are more than enough evidence to put her boyfriend, Leonidas Tacitus, away for a long time..." Katherine shut the TV off.

"Thou are now dead," she said to Skylar, whom she had tied to a chair.

"Thou shall not escape justice for this!" Skylar yelled in anger.

"Justice have I just achieved, presently. Now, how shalt thou die?"

"If I have wronged thee—" She cut Skylar off.

"Thy jealousy was thy undoing. High toleration did I have for thy insults. However, thy implication regarding the apparent nature of my age? That is unforgivable. Did I not say, of those who cross me, all shall pay?" Katherine grabbed the garrote. She sat on Skylar's lap, facing her.

"My apologies, Your High—" Katherine cut the apology short. With the wire tight around Skylar's neck, it was too little, too late.

The French Conquest

KING GEORGE and Queen Katherine arrived in the area that would become Paris. They were visiting their troops who were about to deploy to the front lines near the foothills of the Pyrenees. It was for the final push to end the last bastion of resistance.

"Perhaps little George has finally earned his conquest," Katherine said with mild vigor.

"Too harsh, thou art, my Queen." George felt defensive of his only son.

"Not did it take five times for any of our daughters."

They attended, as their son gave an inspirational speech to rally the troops. George was very proud of his namesake. And now his son was general of the French conquest. They just had one final push. The Celtic leadership were holed up in a fortified bunker near the Atlantic end of the Pyrenees.

"Your Majesties, Dr. Varinia Helton, has returned. A new grand weapon does Atlantis pursue." Chief advisor Thais Cran informed them.

"Of which grand weapon dost thou speak?" George asked.

"'Tis called a nuclear bomb. Destroy a city with but one bomb."

"Spare no expense; provide Dr. Helton all she requires." King George ordered. "My Prince, my Queen, complete this conquest now we must. Atlantis does seek a new grand weapon. Wage war against them presently, we must."

"This very moment, do our best special forces converge on the bunker. Cut off the head of this Celtic snake, we will." Prince George surprised them.

An hour later, they oversaw the final offensive.

"The autonomous-maglev-military-operatives are in place." Prince George said. "The A.M.M.O. shall move on my command."

"What of thy preparations for counterstrike?" Katherine asked.

"Magnetic guns stand at ready. Eye in the sky, does keep us apprised of enemy movements. Operations commence, presently." Prince George gave the signal, and the entire operations began.

By the evening, word of their special forces was in.

"General, a near complete failure of operation. All men are dead." Prince George was clearly irritated by this report.

"If a task needs completing, one must make effort themselves!" Prince George snarled. "Prepare Gamma and Delta units presently!"

"My son, what dost thou intend?" Katherine demanded.

"I shall lead this operation directly." Prince George said.

"Thou shalt not go alone." Queen Katherine stated firmly. Prince George considered arguing but obviously knew better.

A couple of hours later, King George, his son, and the Queen, were leading the special forces toward the bunker. A.M.M.O. units cleared the immediate area. George could see the sun setting over the Bay of Biscay. And he thought. *The sun sets this night for Celtic, for France.*

They gained access to the first level of the bunker and immediately took fire. They began to clear the level. King George knew he was the second-best martial artist in the world. Katherine was significantly better. They were also being aided by the new technology they had taken from Atlantis' research agency. They wore flexible tri-poly alloy metal suits. They were specially made for this type of situation. They were impervious to stabbing weapons, most bullets, and fire. It also made the impact of taking a physical strike meaningless. As a result, they were like machines, just cutting through the defenses of the bunker.

By level 10, the special forces who had accompanied them were all injured or dead. So now it was just the three of them with three levels to go.

"Escape hatch, my Prince. My Queen and I do have this."

George and Katherine neutralized over a dozen guards on level 10. Then, nearly two dozen guards on level 11. Now, they were on the final level. They paused some 20 feet apart as about 50 guards moved to intercept them. They dropped their guns, and George smiled at his Queen. It was rare for them to have such a challenge. So they were going to enjoy this.

George scanned the small army, and there was an odd silence. There were around 20 female guards and 30 male guards. He knew they were all well-trained. But he also knew they couldn't use high-velocity rail guns. So he and Katherine would be impervious to the pellets.

George began running full speed at the guards. He slid into a sweep, taking down a few of them. On his hands, he kicked two more in the face. One of the female guards attacked low. He sidestepped and caught her head in his arm, and in one motion, he broke her neck. He continued in his flow to hit a male guard in the nose with the heel of his hand, killing him instantly.

By the time he met Katherine in the middle, they had left the dozens of guards a mess in their wake. At that moment, Queen Anastasia Ivy of Celtic along with her advisors, came running out of the escape hatch with Prince George in pursuit.

"Your Majesty!" King George thundered, stopping them in their tracks. Queen Anastasia looked around the room. She appeared to be calculating an escape plan.

"Make no attempt, for it be futile," Katherine said.

"My dear Ana, what shall I do with thee?" Prince George gave a grin.

"Do what thou will; thou art a sick bastard!" Anastasia glared.

"'Twas this attitude which hath my mercy at its end." Prince George was obviously irritated. "Thou should have agreed to marriage all those years ago."

"Surrender, thou means... Never!" Anastasia flared.

"Yet here we are." Prince George gloated. "And thy children?" He indicated the teens in the group.

King George had both of them not two years earlier at a global summit in Atlantis. Anastasia's daughter Florentina, who was 19 years old, was her heir apparent, and her son Cenric, who was 17 years old, was training to be her next general.

"My Prince, 'tis thy conquest, it be thy decision." Katherine pressed him.

Prince George gave a signal, and King George and Queen Katherine quickly executed the five ministers. Queen Anastasia and her children attempted to flee. Prince George subdued Anastasia. Then King George and Katherine restrained the children.

Anastasia was now bound with her hands behind her back. "Your Majesty, 'tis unfortunate that thou must now meet thy end." Prince George announced her sentence. He then took his repelling cable and fashioned a noose. He threw it over a rafter. He slid the loop around her neck and lifted her off the ground.

Anastasia had been dangling for about three minutes when Prince George gave the signal. King George and Queen Katherine proceeded to cut the Prince and Princess' throats. It became apparent to King George that his son had harshly taken her rejection all those years ago. King George saw the reaction of horror on Anastasia's face. He did feel a little bad. He had known Anastasia for the entirety of her 25-year reign. And even before that, a total of about 40 years.

The first time he met her was at a summit with her father. She was a precocious three-year-old. His son was seven at the time. And the two of them were very gracious to each other. That was the first time he had entertained the idea of them becoming betrothed.

The topic was under negotiation when Anastasia's parents and her older brother died in an accident, placing Anastasia on the throne at just 17 years old. She ended the discussions. When she remained unwed five years later, the subject was broached again. Then Anastasia became worried they were trying to steal her throne.

She and Prince George had been doing unofficial courting, testing the waters. His son had admitted to him that he had fallen for her. She abruptly changed course. His son remained persistent. She became very nasty, attempting to push him away.

King George watched as the last breath of life left Anastasia. The following day, they publicly displayed the bodies of the royal family. As a result, the last elements of the Celtic military surrendered.

As his son took the throne of Celtic, he renamed it France.

CHAPTER XXVII: SLAVES IN TIME

Research and Development

IT TOOK A LITTLE while for MICHEAL to fully learn Celtic, which is what the area of France was currently known as. They learned that Celtic was in a soft conflict with Britain. It was actually called Britain or the British Empire. They originally thought it strange until they discovered that the Cavendishes had taken over the British Isles and then conquered most of Europe.

"King George, can you imagine?" Micheal asked Julie.

"Queen Katherine? Now, there's a scary thought. How are they still alive?"

"They must've followed us... When the flood was beginning."

"That was two stops ago."

"Precisely. They had followed us out of 1697 and ended up two stops ahead of us in the 24th century BC. They must be catching our wake wave. They skipped over the 22nd century and landed a century before our arrival."

"And now they're far more powerful than the last time we dealt with them. Plus, we lost our Gods rings."

"We'll just have to make more. That's why we're going to Atlantis. I'm sure Jessalyn will help us."

"You think she's still alive? She would have to be over 400 by now."

"According to the Bible, Shem lived longer than that. And he's older than her."

They arrived at Atlantis and it was far bigger than it was in the 22nd century. There were perhaps 35 million people in the city alone—nearly 350 million in the Empire.

"Micheal, Julie, how good of you to come visit again," Jessalyn said in greeting. "It's been what 200 years or so?"

"More or less," Micheal said.

"You don't rule Atlantis anymore?" Julie asked.

"I gave that up after Lykos died."

"I am so sorry, Lyn; how did that happen?" Julie asked.

"He was murdered ten years ago. During the coup that gave Atlantis to the despots," Jessalyn said with hints of sadness and anger. "They kept me alive because I'm Noah's daughter. For a while, they coerced me to play figurehead. Finally, I said they would have to kill me. So they let me 'retire' here."

"The Confusion really hit hard, didn't it?" Micheal asked.

"I had meant to mention how you seem to have fixed your confusion."

"We were able to find The Nectars of Eden," Micheal said.

"Do you want us to help you take back Atlantis?" Julie asked.

Jessalyn shook her head. "I've been responsible for Atlantis for 400 years... Their fate is no longer in my hands. A reckoning is coming I can feel it. I'm content to live out the rest of my days here in peace and quiet. What will you do?"

"We will reacquire Avalon and just focus on research and development," Micheal said.

They once again put their collective heads together, and at this point, JULIE was no longer surprised they were able to achieve seemingly tricky things. They had quickly used the mining bores to gather the resources to reacquire Avalon. And now, they were to focus on technological development in the laboratory.

"So what should we focus on this time?" she asked Micheal.

"I think you should focus on improving the tri-poly alloys. Obviously, it couldn't stop a railgun. And I need to build a rocket so we can service the sky-net. And perhaps we can upgrade it. It's been up there for nearly 1500 years."

"Okay, let's get started."

-July 24, 1954 BC

"Five years have passed so quickly. Today is the fifth anniversary since we reacquired Avalon. My primary focus has been upgrading the tri-poly alloys. It's been quite the challenge. But I have become fully in love with the labs. Micheal has been putting most of his efforts into nanotechnology. To scale everything down to such a degree that the processors in the sky-net will be far more efficient. Soon, we will return to space for the first time in 20 years.

Wow... Has it been that long since we went to the moon? Where does the time go? We have been in the temporal ether for over 40 years. We are nearly a third of the way home. And so much has happened.

Micheal and I have been so many different things over the years. We've faced incredible challenges in our relationship, from Gabriel Maximus to The Confusion. But we have endured. Most people don't stay married for over 35 years and there are many years still to endure. And many looming obstacles. Such as George and Katherine. But hopefully, they will remain blissfully unaware of our presence.

The Age of Atlantis will end soon. I agree with Jessalyn. A reckoning is coming. But what could possibly end a civilization that is as advanced or more advanced than the one I fell from in the 21st century? I just hope we will leave this time before we find out.

There's just over a year before we jump out of the 20th century BC. We will bide our time here in Avalon(on the Gibraltar Peninsula). In quiet obscurity and maybe we will invent a few new things along the way."

PS: I'm certainly looking forward to our anniversary in space. And the perfect gift of Zero-G sex.

Julie set down her quill. "It sure looks peaceful from up here," Julie said as Europe passed beneath her window view.

"Anything looks peaceful from 20,000 miles." Micheal chuckled.

"Really... Ferris Bueller?" She couldn't help but laugh.

"But anyway, now we can see that it's the familiar map we are used to... Except, Atlantis, that is."

"So you're thinking that whatever is coming is going to sink Atlantis, just like Homer describes?"

"It has to. Where else did Atlantis go? And what else could destroy this civilization?" He opened his arms. "Okay, we're approaching the sky-net."

"The distribution of the nano pods is complete." She informed him.

"Let's go out there."

"So it looks like your spacesuits are working perfectly," Micheal commented as they began their spacewalk.

"You sound surprised." Julie was annoyed by his implication.

"Not surprised, impressed. These are far superior to anything NASA has ever made and probably better than the Atlantis Space Agency had in the 24th century."

"The entire thing is a mix of different tri-polys. These suits can withstand reentry. We can return right now if you want?" She laughed.

"That sounds fun. Perhaps once we've serviced the sky-net." There was a smile in his voice. "Bring up the link to the sky-net."

"Link complete. Running diagnostics."

"Isolating malfunctions. Initiate expulsion on my mark."

"Standing by." Her finger was at the ready.

"Mark..."

"Preparing for nano graft."

"I'm going to test it on one of them." He grabbed one of the nano-sats. Julie watched as he placed the upgraded coating over the satellite. "Initializing."

"The diagnostics says the graft isn't taking."

"What does it say is the reason?"

"The magnetic resonance of the network."

They spent hours trying many different cohesion formulas until finally.

"The graft finally took!" Micheal said.

After diagnostics confirmed the link, they upgraded the network.

"It's incredible, isn't it?" Julie said, referencing the nightside view of Earth from their geosynchronous orbit above Europe.

"Indeed, it is."

About a month later, they touched down at Avalon.

"It will get easier," Micheal said as they entered the mansion.

"How was space?" A woman was sitting in the lounge.

"Who are you?" Micheal asked.

Then Julie asked. "What do you mean space?"

"I am Calypso Kosta, science advisor to the Empress. And we have been watching your progress for a while. It is an honor to meet you. Atlantis needs you." Julie exchanged a look with Micheal. This wasn't good.

Slaves in Time

"Our apologies, but we aren't going to be around much longer. I don't think we will be of much help." JULIE waved her hand.

"Well, actually, you have plenty of time."

"We have a prior commitment, so we will have to regretfully decline," Micheal said.

"We know all about your 'prior commitment'... Time travel always did fascinate me. But I never imagined I would actually meet real time travelers!" Calypso said with excitement.

The words hit like a gut punch to Julie's stomach.

"Now you will work for the government. And if you produce certain things within our time parameters, we may allow you to keep your prior commitment," Calypso said casually.

"You can't stop us," Julie said.

"On the contrary, we most definitely can." Calypso pressed a button on some object she had in her hand, and Micheal collapsed, writhing in pain. She hit the button again, and he stopped.

"No!" Calypso said as Julie moved toward her. "We know of your martial skills as well. We are also aware of the history that exists between the two of you and the King and Queen of Britain. Our spies inside the British government tell us the Cavendishes believe you to be some kind of gods. I don't see it myself, but who knows?

Now I need to go over our arrangement..." She explained how the relationship was to work.

The arrangement would allow them to live normally. Except they would do research for the government. And they would be on a need-to-know basis. So, about half the time, they didn't know what exactly they were working on.

As the months passed, they endeavored to devise an escape plan. They dutifully solved problem after problem. Calypso gave them positive feedback in response to their work. Julie wasn't sure that was a good thing.

"Do you think there's any way to get out of this?" she asked when she was sure they couldn't be heard.

"I'm sure we'll eventually figure something out. But will it be in time?"

"It's already too late, in one sense anyway," Julie said.

"How's that?" Micheal asked.

"You know, all these problems they're asking us to solve are to make weapons." She shook her head.

"That was obvious from the start."

"And that doesn't bother you?" She was annoyed by his passive acceptance.

"It does, but what are we supposed to do? Every nation has a program, We have more affinity for Atlantis."

"I think we should just refuse to help them."

"I'm pretty sure they'll kill us."

"That's okay. It's better than assisting in the deaths of who knows how many!" She was certain of her decision.

"I agree; we've had an amazing life together."

The next day, they refused to go to the labs.

"Are you both sick or something?" Calypso asked when they opened the door.

"No, we won't be a part of this anymore. If you're going to kill us, then just get it over with." Julie said.

"Kill our two most genius scientists. We wouldn't dream of it." Julie was both relieved and confused by Calypso's statement. "I'd like you to meet a few of your less accomplished colleagues. This is Chloe Franco, she's the team leader. Then there's Rufus Asker, Marilla Lasco, Antonius Markos, and Vita Galanos. They were our worst-performing science team." Calypso gave a signal, and some kind of SWAT team came in and surrounded everybody. As they quickly bound all five of the team, Julie became filled with dread. "Chloe, you and your team have produced no tangible results in the past six months. Do you accept responsibility?"

"I am the team leader," Chloe said, a look of worry on her face.

"I like a leader who accepts responsibility, but I'm afraid that an example must be made." Calypso pulled a thin razor wire garrote out of her pocket and wrapped it around Chloe's throat. It quickly cut deep into her neck, and blood sprayed everywhere. Micheal moved to intercede, and Calypso quickly hit the remote, and Micheal fell. Calypso then proceeded to continue the effort until Chloe's head was severed. Once Micheal regained his feet, Calypso said. "Mr. and Mrs. Hall! You need to learn obedience." She pulled out a small railgun and shot the other four members of the team in the forehead. "Don't worry, a team will arrive shortly to clean up this mess. Now, this unfortunate circumstance is over. I will see you both tomorrow? Or did you have such a good time today that you want to do it again tomorrow? Any more disobedience will incur additional restrictions on your lifestyle as well," Calypso finished. Then, she and the SWAT team left.

Julie broke down in tears when they were gone, racked with guilt. Those people were horribly murdered because of her decision. And she knew those lifeless eyes from Chloe's severed head staring back at her would haunt her forever. So, it was back to work after that. They were building weapons that would be used to kill thousands of more people.

They remained focused on the problems at hand because they knew that any sign of slow walking would result in punishment. They were always kept in the dark about the true nature of their work. They received hypothetical problems they were supposed to solve. Eventually, they usually managed to figure out what they had contributed to. The latest problem they were assigned had her concerned about the potential consequences of their actions. It was a troubling situation, given the unsettling nature of their work.

"What do you think it's for?" Julie asked Micheal.

"We recently deduced that your challenge was related to creating an isotope. And I'm fairly certain that it was to make plutonium 240."

"You mean nuclear?"

"Yes, and now mine makes sense. It's the design for an H-bomb."

"For a long time, I have tried to figure out what could end this version of Atlantis. And now I think we know." She was dejected. "We handed them nuclear weapons!"

"You think that's enough? This civilization is more advanced than our 2010."

"Yes... I quote Oppenheimer... Who quoted the Hindus... 'Now I am become death, destroyer of worlds'." And once again, it was her fault.

A Double Agent

After thoroughly discussing the ins and outs and ramifications, Julie thought they should discuss the situation with Calypso.

"You don't think we should use our new super weapon?" Calypso laughed.

"These bombs can destroy civilization as we know it!" MICHEAL said.

"We're not that reckless. We will only use these weapons in a limited fashion."

"Limited? You speak ignorance. In the time we came from, our world was nearly destroyed by these weapons. Every major country raced to build as many as possible, until there were tens of thousands. Then, everyone was on a hair-trigger. If one were to fire then everyone else would. And the concept of mutually assured destruction was born. Atlantis may be the only one with these weapons for the moment, but what happens when someone else gets them?" Micheal demanded.

Calypso went silent and averted her eyes. "You already lost them?!" Julie was appalled.

"Dr. Varinia Helton was a British spy."

"British?! That crazy bitch is about to have a nuke?!" Julie was incredulous.

"Dr. Helton may be a spy—"

"Not Dr. Helton. Queen Katherine is a psychopath. I promise you she will use these weapons," Julie said.

"You need to make every effort to get them back," Micheal said.

"Our first two attempts were a disaster. We are making every effort. But it is the Cavendishes. And after what they did to the Celtic royal family..." Calypso trailed off.

"What did they do?" Julie asked.

"King George, Queen Katherine, and the Prince, personally went to Queen Anastasia's security bunker on the Atlantic coast and tore through over 100 personal bodyguards of the Queen. Then they proceeded to execute her entire cabinet and then the entire royal family. Including Anastasia's teenage children..." Calypso seemed more afraid than sad. It was mildly humorous to Micheal to see a cold-blooded killer like Calypso fearful of anyone. "Then they display their bodies as proof that the longest ruling dynasty in the world was now gone—" Calypso was interrupted.

"Dr. Kosta?" Empress Selia said.

"Your Eminence?" Calypso bowed, and Micheal and Julie followed suit. "Empress, may I introduce Drs. Micheal and Julie Hall."

"Oh yes, of course, the time travelers." Empress Selia smiled.

The Empress appeared to be around 30 years old. She was blonde with brown eyes, perhaps five-foot-six. "At ease." She released them from their bows. "Stellar work, the both of you."

"Your Eminence, if I can speak plainly?" Julie said.

"Bold, I like you." Empress Selia said then altered course. "Hold your thought... There is something I would like to know first... Our surveillance told us you were from another time. But some other things were more confusing. We understand you have some kind of a history with Katherine Cavendish?"

"Yes."

"Over the years I have known Katherine, she told me stories about a Lady Avalon, who might also be the Goddess Aphrodite. She claimed this individual attempted to ruin her life on numerous occasions. Is this who you are?"

Julie looked at Micheal. He just shrugged. "I have been known as such."

"If you are indeed Gods, how were we able to covertly tag the both of you? Why do you not use your God powers to escape?" The Empress raised a brow.

"No one in this time believes in us anymore. So aside from superior intellect and skill, we are just like humans." Micheal explained.

"Exiled by Uranus." The Empress was considering. "Katherine said that as well."

"We need to discuss the nuclear program," Julie said.

"In a moment." The Empress said dismissively. "You also have a friendship with Jessalyn El? She and I were friends long ago until we disagreed on how Atlantis should be ruled." The Empress shook her head.

"Our visits to Jessalyn put us on your radar?" Micheal deduced.

"Indeed, I have to say I'm impressed with the both of you, whatever you happen to be. Now more than ever, we need people, or Gods like you, to help us. After what they did to Anastasia and her children..." She looked like she would almost cry. "You know, long ago, Anastasia, Katherine, and I were friends. We were going to rule the world together. But now Anastasia's dead, and Katherine and I are enemies." She was clearly upset.

"Which brings me to the nuclear program secrets!" Julie was annoyed. "We need to take back what Dr. Helton stole."

"That's not going to be possible, Dr. Hall. We have already lost some of our best teams in the attempt. Dr. Helton is now firmly under the protection of Princess Arabella in Rome. I will not sacrifice any more of my special forces on a lost cause." Empress Selia was firm.

"What? Does Princess Arabella have better special forces than you?" Julie seemed confused.

The Empress laughed. "Princess Arabella is the special force. Queen Katherine is by far the deadliest fighter in the world. She has no qualms about killing anyone. And she has made her daughters as much like her as possible. They are all formidable. Everyone is afraid of them. For good reason." The Empress was afraid.

"We'll go!" Julie blurted out. She looked at him. He understood her feelings about the situation.

"There is no use. They were all going to get these weapons eventually."

"I don't think you fully grasp the situation. If the Cavendishes get the nuke first, it's game over." Micheal said. "These weapons can destroy entire cities in seconds. All George and Katherine would have to do is use just one, and everyone would surrender. You have to let us go. We are the only ones who can match the Cavendishes' martial skills."

The Empress looked back and forth at them, then said. "While I would hate to lose you, I bow to your insistence." She turned to go.

"Your Eminence!" Julie stopped her. "I admonish you, do not use these bombs."

The Empress gave a long look then said, "You'd better get going." Then she left.

Julie looked at Micheal and said, "We better stop this nuclear age, or this will be the end of this civilization."

CHAPTER XXVIII: MISSION IMPOSSIBLE

-December 12, 1953 BC

"Once again, today we dive into the abyss. While there have been quiet times over our 45 years in the timeline. We have also had some significant ups and downs, some pretty crazy experiences, and some unbelievable ones.

I fear this mission we are about to embark on. While I'm confident in my training, having trained most days for the last five decades. We are about to poke the beast. The Cavendishes are currently unaware of our presence. Katherine and George have had centuries of training. I doubt we can match up with them. And how many times can we tempt fate? Eventually either we will kill them, or more likely they will kill us. But we must try to stop the proliferation of nuclear weapons.

I have still not figured out what we're going to do about Varinia. I had failed to consider that situation when I volunteered for this. But she must be neutralized in some fashion. We did get to know her over the past few months. I did like her. How far am I willing to go?

And then there's our other problem. Our time jump is fast approaching. And we have yet to formulate a real plan to escape from Atlantis and this time period. We have efforted to be prepared. I know we will find a way. We always do."

PS: it's 12 days till Christmas.

"This is everything we have on the Cavendishes. And a particular focus on Princess Arabella. As she rules Italy out of Rome." The Director of Atlantean intelligence was saying. "We suspect that to be Dr. Helton's destination."

"You don't have confirmation?" JULIE asked.

"It's not possible. All of our assets have been pulled out, or have been found out. The war is about to begin. They are purging all intelligence operatives. And one final thing. Due to our multiple attempts over the past few days. They'll be expecting you. It's not too late to withdraw." She prodded. Both Julie and Micheal shook their heads in unison. "Then farewell, and good luck... You're going to need it." The director departed.

"Not exactly the eternal city," Julie said as they arrived in Rome.

"I never had the pleasure in our time," Micheal commented. "Now we need to put on our colonial accents."

As they entered the main square downtown, it felt odd to hear English being spoken en masse, so casually. There had only been three other English speakers that she had heard in the past 40 years.

"I beg your pardon; of where might we find Club Boodle?" Julie asked pleasantly.

"Not but two streets down, make to thy left, then another some hundred feet or so." The woman directed them.

They arrived at the unassuming door. After a moment it opened. "State thy business." The man demanded. "God save the Queen, her most beautiful Majesty." Julie had to grit her teeth. Micheal handed the man a pouch with 100,000 British pounds. The man indicated for them to enter.

Once inside the first area resembled a modern dance club. "Shall we?" Julie took Micheal's hand. She thought it was a good idea to keep up appearances. Plus, she thought, it had been too long since they had been able to dance like this.

They spent a good amount of time extravagantly tearing up the dance floor. She thoroughly enjoyed herself. As they were coming off the floor. "Quite the moves." A woman said.

"Many thanks," Julie said.

"Not have I had the pleasure before."

"New to Rome, are we," Micheal said.

"I bid thee welcome, Iona, be my name. Might I interest thee in a game of chess? 'tis a royal game, imagined by their majesties."

They feigned ignorance as chess was explained to them.

"I do understand, I think." Julie sat down to play.

From her youth, Julie had enjoyed chess. She had become quite good at it. And while she hadn't played in years, it was like riding a bike.

"Thou art a quick study. Might thou be interested in tournament? To purchase in, a cost of 1 million pounds."

A couple of hours later. Julie was in the final match for 50 million pounds. "Move knight to Queen seven, Checkmate," she said calmly.

"Impressed, am I." A woman who appeared reminiscent of Katherine stepped forward. Julie knew instantly it was Princess Arabella.

"Many thanks Your Highness." She gave a curtsy.

"Might I have the pleasure of thy name? Mysterious champion," Princess Arabella asked.

"Alexandra Buckingham, and my husband William." She introduced Micheal.

"Quite an unusual name." Arabella raised a brow.

"A great English name, of which we are most proud," Micheal said.

"Most loyal of patriots thou must be. Would be an honor if thou would attend me at the palace on the eve of the morrow." Arabella invited them. "A night in honor of a new advantage we possess, and those who made it possible. And once again, I congratulate thee on thy victory." She departed.

"Dr. Helton will most definitely be there tomorrow. Have you figured out yet how you're going to deal with her?" Micheal asked when they were in their hotel room.

"What do you mean me?" Julie was annoyed.

"Do you really want me to do something? She's a woman." He tried to reason.

"So it's better if I do something to her?" She rolled her eyes.

"I'm not sure I could."

"Fine! I'm not going to worry about that right now. The chip with the nuclear designs will be on hand for the ball tomorrow, so we can reacquire those and neutralize Dr. Helton in one fell swoop."

Julie went over the plan. "We will send our mini drones in to disable the security field around the chip display. And I will finagle my way into close proximity. Then using a diversion, I will exchange the real chip for the decoy. Meanwhile, you will execute a break-in to the vault which contains the copies of the chip. Then we will use a ruse of being double agents. We will separate Dr. Helton into an isolated area and neutralize her."

***

The next day, it was all going to plan.

"Dr. Hall, not would I have expected thee here." Dr. Helton looked surprised and suspicious.

"Dr. Helton, our allegiance lies with Cavendish." Julie tried to convince Varinia.

"'Twas not informed," Varinia said skeptically. "I shall discuss with Arabella." As Varinia turned to go, Julie tripped her.

"Dear me!" Julie feigned surprise. The punch bowl spilled all over Varinia. It served as the perfect distraction to switch the chips. When she looked back up Varinia was heading to the back rooms where Micheal was breaking into the vault. But she was unable to follow because Princess Arabella came inquiring about the situation.

MICHEAL had been pushed to his limit, attempting to access the vault. Only one challenge remained. It all took much longer than he had expected, but finally, the vault opened.

He went and quickly exchanged the chips. As he was exiting the vault, he heard Varinia Helton say. "I might have known."

"Not does thee understand such circumstances."

"Indeed, I do... Come for the secret, have thee... Thou shalt get none." Varinia attacked him. The ferocity of her attack put him on the defensive.

After fighting for a minute, he recognized that she was definitely a match for him. They grappled for a moment. Then they both sprang to their feet.

"What is the meaning of this?!" Princess Arabella demanded.

"Mr. and Mrs. Hall, be Atlantean spies!" Varinia yelled then she came back at him.

"Ms. Hall!" He heard Arabella scream. And out of the corner of his eye, he saw her attack Julie. But he had problems of his own.

"Thou art quite skilled for a scientist." Varinia seemed impressed.

"As does thee." He returned the compliment. Then she attacked him again.

After a few spars, Varinia grabbed a knife and began slicing at him. She drew blood a couple of times. He attempted to draw her close enough that he could neutralize the knife, but she efforted to remain at a safe distance. So he pretended to lose his balance. She went for the kill, but he caught the knife hand, rolling her over. When she rose to her knees, the knife was stuck in her neck, but it had missed the carotid arteries.

As she grabbed the handle of the knife, the look of determination on her face told him she still intended to kill him. So he grabbed her wrist and yanked it hard, opening a large gash in her throat. Blood sprayed on his face and she collapsed on top of him. He rolled her off of him and a pool of blood was growing around her.

At that moment Arabella attacked him with the sword that she had just stabbed Julie with. He parried her with the knife. On her next pass, he blocked her and then tried to sweep her leg. She countered, then kicked him in the stomach. As they came apart, the tip of her blade etched a gash down the side of his neck.

She then went on the attack with a furious melee of strikes.

He was able to block the sword every time. But she took the advantage. He parried then spun around and got a direct stab in her chest. But it failed to penetrate. That meant it could only be one thing. She was wearing a tri-poly alloy.

Micheal's surprise at the discovery left him open to her counter. But her attempt to penetrate the gap in the seams of his clothes failed.

"Been stealing our work for some time, I see," he said, during a momentary pause.

"Had I known, 'twas thee. Would have efforted thy destruction, far sooner. For the ruin thou have brought upon my parents." Arabella said angrily.

"You are certainly a chip off the old block." He met her next attack.

She spun past and tried to skewer him. It failed to break the fabric. He kicked her in the back. She came again, this time disavowing him of his knife. He was able to parry several strokes with his arms. But she was able to get past his defenses and swung for his head. Her stroke was blocked by Julie with a sword.

Julie and Arabella took turns attacking and countering each other. The entire battle was taking place up high where their exposed skin was vulnerable.

Micheal rose to his feet, intent on assisting Julie. In that instant, Arabella parried Julie's attack and in one movement pierced Julie's left shoulder. At that exact moment, Julie slashed at Arabella's head. Micheal was certain that the blow should have struck home but was confused about how she missed.

Arabella slowly drew her sword out of Julie's shoulder. That's when Micheal saw it. A thin red line appeared across the middle of Arabella's neck. She leaned slightly toward him and her head rolled off right to his feet. When he picked it up a look of shock was still on her face.

Her headless body fell over, blood gushed out of her neck. Then they were surrounded.

"Make no attempt to flee... And if thou would kindly lay my sister's head down." Micheal wondered which sister this was.

"Lord and Lady Avalon, I presume, I am Princess Diana. Thou art quite impressive... My dear Lady Avalon, mother shalt be very cross with thee." Diana picked up her sister's head. "Bella was always my favorite sister." A tear came to her eye. "Execute thee here and now, should I." Diana gently grabbed Julie around the neck. Then with her other hand, she shoved Julie away and both she and Micheal were escorted off to what he thought had to be the guest house.

Enemy Spies

QUEEN KATHERINE couldn't believe it. That bitch of a goddess just wouldn't leave her alone. And now her beautiful Bella was dead.

She slapped Lady Avalon as hard as she could. Over and over. "How could thee? Thou hast murdered my baby!" The tears rolled down as her anger built.

"She wouldn't stop—" Katherine hit Lady Avalon in the stomach ending her attempt at justification.

"Thou could not leave be!"

"We had to stop the apocalypse." Lord Avalon said.

"Apocalypse? Thou hast killed my Bella!"

"All we came to do was to take back the nuclear secrets you stole!" Lady Avalon yelled.

"The great weapon?" Princess Diana deduced.

"At least we were able to destroy all of that." Lord Avalon appeared self-satisfied.

"Dost thou mean these secrets?" Diana held up a data chip. "Thou hast failed." She gave a smirk.

"You have no idea the danger of those weapons." Lord Avalon warned.

"Understanding I do have... 'tis the power of the gods!" Katherine felt even more proud of Arabella and her friend Varinia. They had brought them the weapons of the gods.

"These weapons will spell doom for all humans," JULIE said in frustration. She knew Katherine felt even more self-important than ever.

"Finished I am, I shalt no longer bide thy whore's voice! Of what shalt I do with thee?"

"Of that which they sow, so shalt they reap," King George declared. Which apparently meant Julie would be beheaded and

Micheal would have his throat cut.

Katherine stepped forward with a sword preparing to strike the killer blow. While Princess Diana put a knife to Micheal's neck. At that moment Julie's binds came loose. She had already known that the nano-drones had been cutting through them.

Julie rolled out of the way. She felt the wind of the sword stroke breeze past her head. She parlayed that action to sweep the legs of one of the guards. She commandeered a railgun in the process. She let loose a spinning spray of pellets mowing down all of the guards in the process.

KATHERINE and George dove for cover, narrowly escaping the slice of the rail pellets. As they popped back up to assess the situation, Katherine was concerned to find that Princess Diana was in a struggle with Lord Avalon. But she had trained her well. She knew that Diana would prevail.

So now she and George were attempting to disavow Lady Avalon of the railgun. But once again they had to dive for cover from the next volley of pellets. When the hail stopped, they moved quickly to try and pick up their own railguns. As Katherine turned to reach for the gun, she saw that Diana was on top of Lord Avalon. But then he suddenly reversed her. He was straddling her, pressing the knife down toward her neck. Katherine knew she didn't have much time.

She finally got the gun. As she raised it to fire, she had to duck another volley from Lady Avalon. When the hail stopped Katherine rose just-in-time to see Lord Avalon open a large gash across Diana's throat.

Katherine let loose a spray of pellets but Lord and Lady Avalon were able to dive through the exit. She and George ran to Diana. She tried to put pressure on the wound while George called for emergency assistance. But it was no use. She had to watch the look of horror slowly fade from her firstborn's face. The pool of blood ever-expanding around her. Diana gurgled one last time and Katherine saw the life drain from her eyes.

She was overcome by grief. Her sorrow slowly morphed into rage. Lord and Lady Avalon had murdered two of her daughters. They would feel her wrath soon, very soon.

Hunters and Prey

"This has all gone so terribly wrong!" Julie was clearly horrified by how their mission had gone. Not only had they personally killed two of the Cavendish daughters, as well as Dr. Helton, but worse they had failed to retrieve and destroy the stolen secrets.

"Why couldn't they just let us go? No one had to die." MICHEAL shared in Julie's regret. But he also had seen no other way out of it. "I'm sorry Jules, we were so close to succeeding. And now I have no doubt that George and Katherine have a blood debt against us. And we are still behind enemy lines."

They had escaped the Italian peninsula, but the British special forces were in hot pursuit. Everything was locked down, so their escape options were extremely limited. Their goal was to reach the Greek border. They were currently in what would become Croatia.

Micheal had to react to avoid getting shot. Then they were pursued by the assassin. They coordinated, using sign language. Micheal rolled out of the way and Julie grabbed the gun, knocking it away. Micheal threw a knife, forcing a second assassin to drop his gun. The new arrival charged at him. They rolled around on the ground for a moment. When he looked at Julie, she was on the floor, and the assassin had a ligature around her throat, throttling her from behind.

He was now in a strike, counterstrike, foray. They were both using whatever they could get their hands on as weapons. He caught a glimpse of Julie going limp. He knew he had to finish his fight now. He quickly rotated and caused the assassin to miscalculate his defense. The makeshift club connected to the man's face and blood sprayed everywhere. The man fell down clearly dead.

Micheal turned back to see the other assassin shoving his knee into Julie's back, viciously throttling Julie's limp body. As Micheal moved to intercede, Julie suddenly came to life and in one movement reversed the assassin getting her legs around his head. Then she snapped his neck in one quick motion.

A few hours later they reached the Greek border. But all they found was a burned-out city. Suddenly there was an announcement on a loudspeaker.

"Lord and Lady Avalon, I do welcome thee to hell. I shalt be thy host, Princess Selina. Thou hast murdered my sisters. Justice shall be paid, presently. All the Empire as witness."

"Great! Our very own version of the running man." Micheal shook his head.

The first hunters arrived on the playing field.

"What weapons do you have?" he asked Julie.

"None, since I ran out of ammunition."

So just like in *The Running Man,* they would be weaponless.

The first hunters were three women, they appeared to be triplets. They all wore full-body suits from head to toe. One was in white and she carried two swords. Another wore black and was holding two mini chain maces with blades on the ends. And the third was in red. She had a staff with sharp ends that sparked with electricity, perhaps to use as a Taser.

Micheal and Julie ran to the cover of a burned-out building and prepared for the onslaught. A few minutes later Micheal had to duck a chain blade. He used a full scramble to avoid the rampage of blades. He was finally able to catch one of the chains. He used it to pull her to him, then he kicked her hard.

In that instant, he felt a staff strike shock him from behind. He rolled away, then back to his feet. He pulled Julie out of range as the sword blades sliced through the air. With a quick signal, Julie understood.

They locked hands and he swung her around in a circle, connecting with all three attackers. Their positions were reversed. Micheal tried to dodge the swords. But the second one cut his cheek. As he dove to avoid the next sword stroke, he saw Julie yank the staff into the assassin in black, stunning her.

Micheal caught the assassin in white's sword hand and spun her around, while Julie turned the assassin in red straight into the sword. It pierced through the left side of her neck and out the other side.

The white kicked Julie in the stomach and then began a furious effort to kill her. Meanwhile for Micheal chain blades were back. And he was on the defensive. He reversed quickly catching one blade around his body. He pulled black to him eliminating her reach advantage. He jumped up over her wrapping one of the chains around her neck in the process. He flipped her by her neck to the ground. He began strangling her but that failed to slow the viciousness of her assault. He kept a firm grip on the chain and ran it up over a support beam exposed by the utter destruction. He lifted her off the ground. She was fighting like mad to extricate herself from the situation so he climbed on her back wrapping his legs around her preventing any chance of escape and expediting her death by hanging.

As she squirmed within his death grip, they slowly spun in time for him to see Julie drive a sword right into the V at the base of the white's neck.

A couple of minutes later Julie walked over to him. He dropped down from black's back. He looked into her eyes and saw the last bit of life drain out of them. Satisfied she was dead he said. "Grab those swords." Julie went and retrieved them as he picked up the staff.

"A well-deserved reputation, my Lord and Lady, the triplets were some of my best." Princess Selina said over the loudspeaker. "Thou shalt however, be crushed by Jack and Jill."

A few minutes later they got their first look at Jack and Jill. Micheal estimated Jack to be around seven and a half feet tall and bulky with muscle. Jill was approximately seven feet tall and of a similar build. They both wore some kind of body armor. Jack had a club mace. And Jill had iron fists.

The pair attacked in a headlong rush. Micheal dodged and connected with a sidekick. But Jack barely budged. Then with stunningly fast lightning quick reflexes retaliated with a strike from the mace dislodging the staff. Even with the tri-poly clothes he felt a shock of pain shoot up his side. He had to duck another strike. His attempt to sweep the legs was expertly evaded. Then he couldn't avoid a grazing blow that knocked him off balance. Then he took another punishing blow to his stomach.

This wasn't working. He needed a new strategy. At that moment he saw that Julie was taking a similar beating. He danced into a rotating Capoeira kick hitting Jack's arm. Once he was off balance, he used an upswinging roundhouse to disarm him. Then he aimed a kick at Jack's armpit, a weak spot in the armor. But Jack caught his leg and threw him into a wall.

Micheal came back quickly. But Jack caught him in a death grip. The tri-poly would only protect him so much. Every ounce of him was being crushed. He head-butted Jack a couple of times.

The second one appeared to break his nose. Jack seemed dazed. Micheal kneed him in the groin and Jack released him, so he pressed the advantage. He did a cartwheel reacquiring the staff in the process. He used it to Taser shock Jack. The effect was minimal, but enough. He then kicked the side of Jack's knee and he collapsed to the ground. Micheal grabbed Jack's mace. Jack was too slow to defend himself. And Micheal's swing, while partially blocked, connected. He knew he had damaged Jack's arm. He spun and connected again to the side of Jack's head. Then he brought it down one final time on Jack's face. Jack collapsed completely to the ground. The pool of blood growing around Jack told him he was dead.

Micheal turned in time to see Julie jab a broken sword between Jill's armor. She staggered, then Julie put the other sword through the eye slot in Jill's helmet. And Jill fell to the ground dead. Julie, while bruised and battered was victorious.

"How are you holding up?" Julie asked.

"I have been better." He admitted. "How about you?"

"I don't think I can take much more of this." She said wincing. She pulled the unbroken sword out of Jill's head.

"Well, we are most of the way through the city, and Selina might be running low on assassins."

They continued through the burned-out streets for perhaps another hour. As they approached some kind of stadium, they were attacked by a flamethrower. They dove through one of the portals into the stadium.

"People of Britain, the most treacherous of murderers have entered the arena. Now we will see if they can survive... The elements." Princess Selina announced.

The flames pushed them to centerfield. In front of them, a cloud of swirling dust emerged from another field entrance. Then on the flanks appeared spirals of water and wind coming at them from opposite sides. They were clearly surrounded by the four elements: Fire, Earth, Water and Air.

They decided it was best to go on the offensive. They ran headlong into the dust devil. They were immediately pelted by a hail of stones. They shielded their heads with their arms. Then they were hit by a sandblast.

Micheal dove at the spot he estimated would be where Earth was standing. He guessed right, tackling Earth to the ground. But the onslaught continued. He was being battered by clubs of stone.

His attempted kicks were ineffective against the sand. He saw Julie get sent flying in a dust devil.

Micheal was sure they were using kinetic energy to channel the elements. He searched in the murky haze for his staff. He finally found it and activated the electricity. After several attempts, he was able to strike Earth with the Taser. The dust cloud exploded from the shock. Earth waved his hand and Micheal instinctively ducked. When he turned around Earth was impaled with a stone spear.

Micheal turned back and saw Julie being thrown around by the wind. And he was suddenly hit by a blast of water, sending him flying. Then, he was hit by an explosion of flame. The heat was mostly shielded by his suit. He used sign language to signal Julie about the kinetic energy.

He charged Water and she hit him with a spinning vortex of water. He couldn't activate the staff or it might electrocute him as well as her. Fire whipped some flames in his direction. He noticed another woman entering the arena and making toward Julie.

At that moment Julie targeted the ion rings that Air was using to funnel the wind. She used magnetically charged pellets from Earth. The rings reversed polarization and Air was propelled several hundred feet into the sky. She flipped over and was driven hard into the ground. Julie seized the moment and quickly snapped Air's neck.

The newest attacker shrieked in evident dismay. Micheal's temporary distraction caused him to take a blast of fire full-on. It caught his hair on fire. He dove to the ground quickly smothering it with sand. But he could tell most of his hair was gone.

He got to his feet and ran full-bore at Water. She tried to hit him with her water whips, but he evaded them, drawing them toward Fire. One column of water hit Fire full on, just as Micheal had planned.

With Fire temporarily short-circuited, he charged right at him before he could ignite a spark. Micheal struck him in the chest with the stun staff. Then, a quick rotation strike connected to the actual target, the gas line on Fire's fuel tank. Fire attempted to blast him, and the tank ignited. Fire, went out with a bang.

Micheal was suddenly blasted with a water pulse that knocked him into the middle of the arena. He looked over and saw that Julie was in an intense battle with the new attacker who he then realized must be Princess Selina.

Julie ran to him, they locked arms, and he swung her into Water, sending her flying. Then he spun her back around, laying a severe kick into Selina, then he swung her back toward Water and let her go.

He turned and met the oncoming attack from Selina.

"Thou hast murdered my children!" Selina screamed, swinging a bladed staff.

"All of you Cavendishes are psychos!" he retorted while he parried her strikes with the staff. Selina looked very much like her other sisters. But she was nearly six feet tall and to him seemed to be the most formidable fighter of the bunch. So far at least.

"Thou murderer my sisters!" She continued her attack.

"Your sisters tried to kill us! And we never touched any children!"

"The elements, be my children!"

Now he went on the offensive, finally connecting.

"Fiona!" Princess Selina screamed, looking past him.

He glanced back quickly to see Water being drowned in her own water whips. Julie had apparently entangled her.

"Princess Selina!" Micheal yelled, causing her to hesitate. "Let us leave in peace... And we will save her."

"Never!" She ran at Julie. He slid and tripped her.

She immediately turned on him. They grappled for a moment. Then she was on top of him. Julie pulled her off and the two of them began wrestling.

As Micheal charged an attack, Selina rolled away from Julie and Micheal traded blows with her.

Suddenly one of the air whips cracked around Selina's neck. Julie dragged her across the ground with it. Then before Selina could find her balance, Julie pulled the whip up over a support beam at the edge of the playing field, hanging her.

At that moment they came under gunfire from a squad of British forces. Julie ran toward him and he knew what she was thinking. They locked arms and he swung her around letting her go for the oncoming squad. She landed on one of them and quickly disarmed him. Using that distraction Micheal ran and slid into another one deflecting his attempt to shoot Julie. He wrested the gun away and he then systematically eliminated all the foes in their path to the bleachers.

While under constant fire they reached the top of the seating. Luckily the clothes had stopped most of the bullets, but he could see that Julie had been hit a couple of times and he felt the sting as well. They dove off the top of the stadium, landing on more British forces. They were terribly outnumbered. Things looked bleak.

Then suddenly, a different squadron of forces appeared, massacring the British troops. "Doctors Hall! The Empress sent us!" The squad leader yelled, in Atlantean. They quickly boarded the hovercraft and were flown south to the safety of Greece.

Weapon of the Gods

KATHERINE stared at the lifeless body of yet another daughter. Three of her five daughters were now dead. She would make Lord and Lady Avalon pay. She wanted nothing more than to capture them intact. After which she would take them apart piece by piece, nice and slow.

Tears streamed down her cheeks. She rarely cried. She hated crying. It was weakness. Why had they come back? It had been over a century. Now they return, and the first thing they do is start killing her daughters?

"Mother?" Princess Camilla interrupted her thoughts.

"My darling princesses," Katherine said, embracing Princess Olivia and Camilla.

"Mother, we shalt hunt down Lord and Lady Avalon, then we shalt execute them," Olivia promised.

"Thou shalt not!" Katherine implored them. "No more of my daughters, can I lose!"

"What of this new grand weapon?" Camilla asked.

"'Tis of the gods."

"The gods? Oh, Lord and Lady Avalon? Thou does not believe such fairytales?" Olivia protested.

"If thou had seen what I have seen, thou wouldst believe also," Katherine said sharply. "Great power did they have. State of current power, we know not. Therefore, I implore thee both, seek not reckless vengeance." They both nodded in agreement.

"Now then... A grand weapon, design made of the gods. Harness, a most elemental power, it does. Our scientists do say, as it might destroy an entire city with a single bomb." Katherine informed them. "We shalt lay Selina to rest, then we shalt witness such power firsthand."

Two days later, they arrived in the desolate lands of Northern Russia.

"Majesties, I give unto thee, Aries, weapon of the gods!" The head of the weapons program said proudly.

The bomb was about the size of a horse-drawn coach. Katherine was skeptical that such a small thing could destroy a city.

They were taken to an observation bunker some miles away. And then the countdown began. "Three... Two... One..." When the countdown ended there was an amazingly bright flash, it was blinding. As her eyes began to adjust, Katherine heard a thunderous sound. It was the loudest thing she had ever heard. And it was accompanied by a trembling of the earth. The light began to dim. Then, she saw a large cloud rising from the horizon. It looked like a mushroom climbing into the heavens. It was truly a weapon of the gods. And she knew they would fear her. Soon enough.

The next day, they went and inspected the damage firsthand. The high-speed camera footage of the detonation was unbelievable. But nothing could have prepared them for the sheer destruction seen up close.

The town of Archangelo was selected because the city of nearly a million people had mostly been abandoned after the Russian conquest 20 years earlier. So it was the perfect place to truly witness the awe and power of the gods. While most of the town had been damaged during the battles, most of the structures had remained standing. Now the city had pretty much been wiped off the map. All that was left was melted and disfigured rubble. It was a wasteland, the very picture of hell.

When they returned to Moscow, they were met by their chief Intel advisor. "Majesties! Dire news do I bring... Atlantis has exploded a great weapon. Egypt also prepares a test." She informed them.

"What of our allies?" King George asked.

"They near full readiness. However, others have programs as well."

"Power of the gods in the hands of humans?" Katherine asked

rhetorically. "Afraid the gods shalt be... Terrified indeed." She closed her eyes, and she could see Lord and Lady Avalon. They were terrified of her.

Too Late

JULIE awoke in her bed in Avalon.

"Welcome back, my sleeping beauty." Micheal kissed her on the forehead.

"How long have I been asleep?"

"About three days. Here... Drink this." She gratefully gulped down the water. "When you're ready, there are some things I must tell you."

She sat up. "I'm ready now."

"Okay... Well, first, the world is at war. The burned-out city in Greece, in which we had our showdown. Was the first city the British had ransacked on their invasion of Greece."

"What's next?" Julie shook her head.

"Princess Selina died. I know you had hoped otherwise."

Despite everything, Julie really didn't want to kill anyone. And every time she did, she felt like a piece of her went with them. She had felt that way since the day in 1692 when she had killed for the first time. Those three men in the woods who were attempting to lynch her. Including Peter Talmage, Katherine's husband. That incident was the one that set off this whole vendetta that Katherine has against her. Now, she was responsible for killing three of Katherine's daughters. When she looked at it from Katherine's point of view, she could understand her hatred.

"Any more bad news?" She sighed.

"Britain tested a nuclear bomb in Northern Russia... Two days ago... And then Atlantis tested theirs in the Sahara Desert yesterday." Micheal sighed. "And at least 12 other countries are believed to be within about a week of completion as well." He shook his head.

"So we truly are responsible for ending The Age of Atlantis?"

"The Age of Atlantis?" He raised a brow.

"I think it sounds fitting... And once we leave this time period in a few days, this age of human civilization will get lost in history." A feeling of sadness overcame her.

"The history is already written."

"I just thought of something... We don't even know if we haven't already altered history by our many actions. How do we even know if this is the same timeline?"

"Unless our temporal readings from the 17th century were incorrect. Or our actions had already altered the timeline before we made the tachyon scanner. Then, based on the current readings, we are at the very least in the same temporal continuum we were in when we built the tachyon scanner."

"How fascinating..." Empress Selia interrupted in English. They both bowed. "At ease."

"Your Eminence speaks English?" Julie asked.

"But of course, many years ago Queen Katherine was quite close to me. 'twas she which taught me... Proudly did she proclaim it to be the words of the gods. Fascinated did I become upon thy arrival. Thou hast not failed to disappoint." Julie looked at her with surprise. "My Gods, Aphrodite and Koios, how magnificent thou art in aspect. A gift has also been of thy brilliant minds. And also, thy ill-fated mission did eliminate three of the Princesses of Britain. To which I do owe much appreciation. Therefore, I do declare, no escape shalt thou require. I grant thee leave to meet thy timely appointment." The Empress met her eye with a smile.

-February 21, 1952 BC

"Today we leave Atlantis... Probably for good. We may now finally get the ancient world we had anticipated nearly 40 years ago. Micheal assures me that the history of the 15th century BC is well documented. So I have no doubt that the destruction of Atlantis is inevitable, at some point, likely soon. Dozens of countries now have nuclear bombs. In the midst of a truly world war. And despite the fact that for the history we know to come to fruition, Atlantis must end. I have yet to reconcile the unmistakable fact that we are likely directly responsible. It is little consolation that at the very least we don't have to live through those terrible consequences.

There is another aspect of my life that gets emphasized every time we leave. That is saying goodbye to everyone I know. I have to do this over and over again. So many friends left behind. So many still to come and go. Up to this point that aspect has been mitigated by the centuries-long life spans that have allowed for some continuity of friendships across time stops. However, that aspect is coming to an end.

I look into the mirror and the young vibrant face staring back at me does not seem to reflect the reality of my nearly 75 years. So much has happened. I have had so many amazing and terrible experiences. 40 years ago, before we left Boston, I questioned who I would be when we returned to the 21st century. 150 years in the timeline would certainly change me. We are now only 30% of the way home and I already don't recognize myself.

Micheal and I have had our ups and downs, but I would never survive this journey without him. He is my best friend, my partner on this journey. And my great lover. He has helped me maintain my sanity through it all.

We must now go one more time into the breach. Our departure point is far behind enemy lines near Dunkirk in France. As such we have buried most of our most important items here in Avalon, on Gibraltar. Now we just need to avoid the Cavendishes."

"This is going to work, right?" Julie worried. They were at the edge of space, at approximately 50 miles altitude.

"It's going to work. We drop on the coast at Dunkirk, and after a few minutes set up, we are on our way to the 15th century BC." Micheal tried to assure her. "Even if they detect us. They won't be able to react fast enough." He pointed out, then they began their descent.

From such an altitude, Julie could see the entire British Isles to her left and Norway and Denmark to her right.

They began a rapid dive toward the coast. A few minutes later they touched down on the beach. As they exited the car, Julie scanned all 360° around them and there was no one.

"Five minutes!" Micheal informed her.

Julie used the tachyon scanner to locate their individual positions. Micheal came over and took her by the hands.

"This is farewell to Atlantis. It's been an amazing run. And through all of it, I love you that much more." He kissed her.

"I love you," she said, as he pulled back. They just looked at each other for a moment.

"I will see you on the other side." He kissed her again.

"30 seconds!"

"I love you, Jules." He moved into position.

"I love you, Micheal." The portal began to open. She prepared herself for the transition. "We made it." She whispered to herself as she felt the vortex begin to draw her in. She closed her eyes.

A moment later nothing had happened. She opened her eyes and the vortex was gone. It was replaced by a fist coming right at her face. It was too late to move. The force of the impact knocked her on her back. She had to roll away from Katherine's next attack.

"Time has ended for thee!" Katherine scowled. "Justice shall be mine!" She pressed the attack.

Julie retreated toward the car. A team of special forces surrounded the vehicle. She targeted one of them and quickly relieved him of his railgun. She received a powerful blow to her back from Katherine. As she fell to the ground, she unleashed a spray of pellets. Katherine dove for cover. They exchanged fire a few times as Julie made for the protection of the car. She closed the door just in time to shield her from Katherine's latest volley.

As she took off, she saw that Micheal was on the ground. George was about to deliver a potentially killer blow. She turned the vehicle's guns on George. The spray of pellets found their mark. As George fell to the ground bleeding, she swooped in and quickly retrieved Micheal from the beach.

Julie launched to the sky under a hail of fire from the British forces. The craft was designed to take it. It was reinforced with a potent tri-poly alloy. They were immediately pursued by several unmanned aerial military drones. She skillfully outmaneuvered them and destroyed them one by one.

A short while later, as they landed at Avalon, the reality of the situation hit Julie. She climbed out tears streaming down her cheeks. "What are we going to do now?"

Micheal wrapped her in his loving arms. "Everything will be all right."

She wanted to be comforted but all she could think about was that in that instant the road home just got decades longer.

Global War

MICHEAL HAD TO RUN the numbers, and it wasn't good. Missing the jump not only made them have to wait another six years in the 20th century BC. It added seven more stops and 63 years to their course home.

That reality had caused Julie to sink into a deep melancholy. Micheal had taken to the labs to distract himself from the ever-escalating global conflict.

The TV said: "... The latest full-scale attack on the British capital of London has been repelled. There was even less damage than Atlantis sustained in the last attempt by the British... Britain has also sustained enormous losses at The Battle of Canaan. The Egyptian-led alliance succeeded in ambushing the attack. They destroyed nearly every drone in the armada... On the Western front, Eden has been making major gains. Half of the southern continent has been conquered...

In contrast, China has suffered one defeat after another. The last time was at the hands of Babylon. They have begun the first invasion of China... In related news, Sumeria is the latest country to demonstrate The Weapon of the Gods. So that makes 32 countries with such power... In other news..." Micheal shut the TV off.

"That sounds bad," Julie stated from behind him.

"Jules? How do you feel?"

"All those memories from so long ago all came rushing back." She closed her eyes. "It almost felt like I was separated from myself. I mean, another 63 years? That's literally a lifetime." She shook her head.

"The Empress informed me that the Cavendishes had spies keeping tabs on us. That's how they learned our departure time and location... They did it on purpose!" Micheal was angry all over again.

"So now what?"

"We prepare."

"For what?" She looked at him sidelong.

"The apocalypse."

"And when is it going to happen?"

"I don't know. It could be any time in the next 10 years."

"Don't the temporal waves show us when?"

"There's far too much temporal turbulence. The energy is spiking already. And it goes on for at least a decade."

"So what do we need to do first?" She felt a new resolve.

"We need something to shield us from a nuclear detonation."

Over the next five months, the war intensified. Nearly every country in the world now had nukes. And the British invasion of the Iberian Peninsula was drawing closer to Avalon.

"Activate the nuclear reactor," Micheal said.

"100 Sieverts per hour."

"Bring it up to a thousand."

They ran the exposure test for several hours. When it was complete Micheal said, "Shut it down... And decontaminate."

They put on their clean suits and went to see if the capsule had withstood the final test.

"Readings are normal. Our nuclear-safe pod is finished. Now all we need to do is stock it with supplies and we are ready for Armageddon."

"My gods..." Empress Selia interrupted in English. "Disappointed to hear of thy failure, I was. However, this war has made a turn for the worse. The Empire dost need thy assistance once more. It can only but help to have the gods behind us." She feigned a bow.

"Well, your Eminence—" Micheal began.

"Splendid! A place have we established for thee."

The capsule was loaded up and they were taken to Atlantis. Then they were given a tour of their new penthouse as well as the laboratories in which they were to work. Then the Empress said she had a special task for them.

"You want us to go back to London? To steal their defense network codes?" Julie seemed annoyed.

"All of our assets have been neutralized. We are losing this war. Without those codes, this war is lost." Empress Selia seemed certain.

"You should send someone else," Julie suggested.

"The two of you shall do this. That is final. Eden has nearly conquered the hemisphere. China has begun to make gains. And Britain has taken Anatolia, Greece and Canaan. Thou art our only hope... So, I shall not discuss this further." The Empress was firm, stemming any further argument.

Gods and Women

"I don't know if I'm ready for this," JULIE stated definitively as she looked over the edge of the space platform. They were 300 miles up in orbit.

"It's just like skydiving, for five minutes." Micheal tried to assure her.

"No, it's space diving, without a parachute." She was a bit scared, which was unusual. She had learned to fear almost nothing. But now their lives depended upon the tri-poly suits she had designed, withstanding reentry and landing without a parachute.

"It will be okay." He took her hand. "In five seconds." His confidence was reassuring. And while she feared the end, it gave her the courage.

They dove off and initiated their M-Pulse deceleration system. They were aiming directly for London, near the mouth of the Thames. They were jumping at night and she could see all of the cities lit up like sparkling gems.

A couple of minutes after jumping off, they made contact with the upper atmosphere. Flames were raging all around her. The whole experience was exhilarating. And she was lazer focused, to maintain her form. It was like being in a cocoon of fire. Eventually, they slowed down enough that they were now just freefalling.

"We are off target by 1.2°, altitude 80,000 feet," Julie announced.

"Compensating." Micheal tucked into a dive pulling ahead of her.

A few minutes later they were right on target. The British defense headquarters was coming up fast. The target was tiny, perhaps 30 feet across. Micheal hit first and rolled to a stop near the edge. She hit slightly closer to the middle and tumbled toward the edge. As she slid off Micheal caught her, arm to arm. He then pulled her back up.

They slipped out of their suits and proceeded to repel down to the 101st floor. Julie used a glass cutter to gain access. They silently made their way through the maze of floors and secure rooms to the vault which contained the defense access codes.

Despite a few close calls they successfully retrieved the codes and exited the way they came in. They resealed the window, climbed back up to the roof, and retrieved their suits. They dove off leaving no trace they had ever been there.

They bought their way onto a transport before dawn. Just when Julie thought they had made a clean break. The craft was escorted to the ground by the police.

"Identification?!" The officer demanded of everyone. They presented their forged documents. They had to wait a few tense minutes while they were being checked. The officers were visually scanning the crowd the entire time. Finally, the officer in charge said. "We thank thee for thy cooperation." Then they left.

The transport continued onward, and they arrived in Rome as the first light of dawn illuminated the horizon, upon their exit.

"Thy day of reckoning is at hand." A woman declared, clearly one of the Cavendish Princesses.

"You don't want to do this," Julie warned.

"Lady Avalon, Aphrodite, whoever thee may be. Thy end is at hand." Another Princess said.

"You should just let us leave, no one has to die today." Micheal tried to reason with them.

"Wrong Koios, thou hast murdered our sisters. Justice shall be served." The first Princess retorted.

The second princess attacked. The battle raged for several minutes. Micheal and Julie exchanged adversaries several times. Until Julie noticed that Micheal had been crippled by a pressure point attack. She moved to protect him and found herself outmatched two to one.

Julie was on the defensive, retreating, until they had her cornered. Just when all hope seemed lost, a ray of sun burst over the horizon blinding one of the princesses. Julie used the momentary distraction to divert her attack into her sister. The blade sliced the princess' neck open. The other princess ran to her sister's side.

Julie began making her way over to Micheal, who was still struggling to find his feet. She was attempting to lift him when she had to duck an attack from behind. The blade made a glancing blow to her cheek, opening up a bloody gash. Then she dove on top of Micheal shielding him from an attempted kill shot. She proceeded to roll into the princess' legs tripping her. But more importantly, it drew her away from Micheal.

The ferocity of the Princess' attack had Julie on her heels. She was having trouble fending her off. In one quick stroke, the princess was able to push Julie's shirt up, separating it from her pants. In the next stroke, the blade came up through the gap. Pain shot through her side and up into her abdomen. The princess seemed to be savoring the moment.

The Princess was swept to the ground by Micheal. Then in one quick motion, he removed the staff blade out of Julie's side and beheaded the Princess.

They quickly absconded with the Princess' vehicle, while they came under fire from the police who had just arrived.

Their return to Atlantis was greeted by Empress Selia. "Didst thou find success, my gods." She asked in English.

"Here are your precious codes!" Micheal said sharply, handing them to her.

"I do apologize for thy injuries, Aphrodite." She did seem genuine. "No detection was there, I do hope?"

"None," Micheal said shortly. They had used some of Gabriel's stealth technology to bypass any surveillance.

"We can now win this war, thanks to thee." She paused a moment. "Thou didst deliver quite the bonus. Thou hast eliminated Princess Olivia and Princess Camilla." The Empress had a slight smile. "I shalt call on thee again... Soon." Then she left.

Stonehenge

Tears mixed with rage as KATHERINE looked down at the bodies of her last two daughters. Despite no surveillance video showing what happened, she knew exactly who was responsible. She decided it was time to get her revenge once and for all. But in the interim, proxies would have to serve.

She walked into the next room where a dozen women who greatly resembled Aphrodite were waiting. She then proceeded to practice her vengeance, killing her nemesis, over and over again. It was a cathartic release.

Now she needed to come up with a plan. But what would draw them into her trap? After she thought about it, she remembered that her intelligence sources had told her that Empress Selia had put some kind of reins on the gods. So that meant she was also responsible.

Katherine was filled with a whole another dose of rage. Many years ago, Selia was a friend to her. Back then they along with Queen Anastasia were going to rule the world together. But now Anastasia was dead and Selia was her mortal enemy. Then a plan came to mind. She would kidnap Princess Fabia, Selia's precious youngest daughter. She knew Selia would send her dogs running after her.

Over the next week, the effect of their mission became clear to MICHEAL. In a true case of shock and awe, the Atlantean drone Army laid waste to London, Paris, Rome, and nearly every other major city in the British Empire. It had taken that long for the British to realize what had happened. But he knew it was now likely too late for them to recover.

Egypt and Atlantis' other allies were moving to secure gains in Russia, Anatolia, and Eastern Europe. At the same time, Atlantis moved in to secure France and Italy.

"How do you feel?" Micheal asked Julie.

"I almost feel myself again. Just a few more days. Thank goodness for nanos." She referenced the nanobots they had been injecting into themselves. That aided in her recovery from the stabbing.

"Well, on a different note, the war has taken a turn in Atlantis's favor." He shook his head.

"Oh great, more death and destruction on my account. I almost think the next time Katherine tries to kill me, I'll just let her." She seemed depressed.

"It's not your fault."

"I can't help but feel that it is," Julie said through the tears. "I was just a normal person. I never wanted to hurt anyone. And I certainly would've never dreamed of killing anyone. But now I've killed more people than I want to think about." She broke into a full sob. He wrapped her in his embrace, trying to console her.

He had considered all of those factors. He had never thought he would ever kill anyone. But he had also felt comfortable that he had always acted in a proper moral fashion. His conscience was clean. He did still regret how many people he had had to kill in self-defense.

"I see their faces at night. Then when I think of how dangerous time is. I have to wonder how many more people I will kill, defending myself?" She cried on his shoulder for a long while.

All he could do was hold her. He wished he could take away her sorrow. Give her back the innocence she had had in her other life, before all this had happened, so many years ago. And that thought brought to the forefront of his mind, the fault he shared in her suffering.

He was the one who had to play Lord. He had to play God. If he had just played normal, none of these situations would've happened. So all of her guilt lay at his feet.

"I'm sorry." He apologized to her.

"Sorry? For what?" Her confusion momentarily snapped her out of her sorrow.

"I made you what you are. My—"

"No!"

"Yes! It was my decisions that brought all of this upon us. Playing lords and gods. Can you ever forgive me?" Micheal asked desperately as a tear came to his eye.

"There's nothing to forgive." Julie pulled him into her.

A moment later. "Am I interrupting?" Calypso interjected. "Your presence is requested."

They arrived at the palace where a summit of the allies was taking place.

"Drs. Hall, or should I address you your holy eminences? How nice to see you again." The Egyptian Pharaoh Sesostris said in greeting. They had met him several times at various socials.

"Your Majesty." Micheal and Julie both bowed.

"How have you been?" Micheal asked.

"Your retrieval of the British defense codes has been invaluable. You single-handedly won this war for us. It does always help to have the gods on your side." Sesostris smiled.

"My Gods!" Empress Selia yelled, interrupting them. "They've taken Fabia! Our Intel says she's being held outside the City of London in Southern England."

"How terrible for you," Julie said sharply.

"You will go! And I will hear no arguments!"

"Very well." Micheal agreed.

"You will bring her safely back to me... Or else!"

"Or what?!" Julie scoffed.

"Go!" Empress Selia yelled, and then they left.

In rare moments alone, KING GEORGE allowed himself to shed tears. To mourn his little girls. Lord and Lady Avalon had proceeded to murder all five of his daughters. Then they had apparently spent the rest of their time since they arrived in this time period, working to destroy his life and tear down everything he and Katherine had built.

Most of the time, he had to be strong for Katherine. And for all of Britain. Their Empire was on the verge of collapse, thanks to Avalon. At least he still had his son. And after today, they would rid the world of the scourge of the gods. Once and for all!

They had set everything up at Stonehenge, on the Salisbury Plain. The thousand-year-old monument had only recently been completed. When he was a boy, his father had taken him to visit the monolith. At that time, it was nearly 5000 years old. Although he didn't know that at the time. All he knew was that it was very ancient. The experience had filled him with awe and wonder. Even today it did. The mystery of it. What better place to kill the Gods?

As they arrived at Stonehenge, JULIE knew there would be some kind of a trap.

"Lady Avalon, how wonderful it is to see thee again." King George sneered. "It shalt be the last time. My Lord Avalon, thy days of havoc, be at their end."

"Give us Princess Fabia and no one has to get hurt." Julie tried.

The sun was low near the horizon. It burst between two of the vertical standing stones. She had visited Stonehenge in 1997, her final year at Harvard. It looked diametrically different, now compared to then. It looked new, pristine. The outer circle was complete.

"Oh, dost thou mean the daughter of that bitch Empress?" Katherine glared. "Come and take her."

Julie ran a circle around Micheal. They linked arms and Micheal tossed her up and over the outer circle of giant stones. She sprinted towards Fabia who was bound to the center stone. Just before she reached her, she had to duck Katherine's oncoming attack. Then once again it was a battle of skill.

They each took turns on the attack. She took a quick moment to see how Micheal was doing. He was attempting to fight off multiple drones attacking from all sides. The last one fired a net that entangled Micheal.

With him momentarily neutralized, George suddenly attacked her from the other side. It was two-on-one. She could only hold them off for so long—finally, one of Katherine's strikes connected with force to the side of her head. Julie was momentarily disoriented. George jumped on her back, wrapping his arms around her upper body and his legs around hers, squeezing her in a death grip. They fell backward to the ground. Katherine pounced on her lap, straddling her.

"What memories dost this bring?" Katherine unfurled a piano wire. She wrapped it around Julie's neck multiple times. The thin wire bit deep into her throat.

It did in fact bring back memories. From the Atlas Awards in the 24th century to Salem in the 17th century. It all came flooding back. Through the searing pain, she saw the look of glee on Katherine's face staring into her eyes. It was a determined look of satisfaction. Then Katherine began naming off all of her daughters one by one. Julie's guilt sapped the fight out of her.

Julie stopped fighting and resigned herself to her fate. Although she still had to brace herself against the agonizing pain. The minutes dragged on like hours, followed by the numbness. The world was closing in.

KATHERINE was thoroughly enjoying the sweet taste of vengeance. Her eyes were fixated on Aphrodite's. She saw surrender in those deep-sea eyes. The thrill was that much more incredible because she was killing a goddess. She loved how the wire was so tight around the bitch's neck. Her face was turning a bluish-purple. Her eyes were now fixed open, staring into the distance. This was the point where Katherine liked to pull as hard as she could to finish the bitch. As she pulled hard on the handles of the garrote, Aphrodite's eyes went wide in response.

There was a sudden blur to her left, coupled with a hard jolt. Then Katherine felt something tighten around her throat. She was ripped off of Aphrodite. It was Koios. He had apparently escaped the net. Which momentarily impressed her because the best escape artists in Britain had all failed.

But now she was focused on the fight. She tried to break his grip on the draw cable from the net, which he had wrapped around her neck. It only worked for a second, then he reestablished his grip. She kicked and punched him a couple of times with minimal effect. Then he lifted her off the ground by the cable around her neck. He proceeded to swing her legs up and slam her down on her back. Her head hit the ground hard, and the pain blinded her for a moment.

By the time her wits had returned, he was straddling her. Her arms were pinned beneath him. He then wrapped the cable around her neck a few more times. His mass and sheer strength overwhelmed her futile attempts to dislodge him. The minutes dragged on for what felt like hours of agonizing pain. The walls were closing in around her. There was a flash, and the pressure released.

MICHEAL had to MacGyver his way out of the drone net. The Cavendishes had tag-teamed Julie and he knew she was near death. He was surprised that neither George or Katherine had reacted to his approach.

Wielding the draw cable from the net, he rushed up and kicked George hard in the head. And in the same motion, he ripped Katherine off of Julie by her neck with the cable. Following a short fight he had her pinned. He wrapped the cable around her neck a few more times to make sure.

All of the horrors that had been visited upon Julie at Katherine's hand ran through his mind as he felt the life draining out of her. He would be lying if he said he didn't want her dead. Suddenly he was plowed off of her. Then it was a struggle with George.

JULIE had accepted her fate. But she was suddenly released from the Cavendish sandwich of death. The fight came back into her. And she desperately fought to remain conscious. She slowly unwound the wire from around her neck.

She took her first breath in an eternity. She sucked in oxygen through her painfully bruised throat. And once again, she had to maintain consciousness, as the blood drained from her head. She focused on her breathing. She knew she needed to move soon. Her first two attempts to sit up had failed. She thought. *Third time's the charm.*

She forced herself up. As she rose to her feet, she saw Micheal in a struggle with George. At that moment Katherine fired a shot at Micheal grazing his arm. She was looking for another try, but the chaos of the battle made it difficult.

Julie decided she couldn't allow that. She rushed Katherine from behind wrapping the wire around her neck, taking her to the ground, and the gun tumbled away.

She needed to finish this once and for all. The only way to end this was kill or be killed. If Katherine died the battle would be over.

They rolled on the ground for a moment, then Julie was on top, and brought an elbow down dead-arming Katherine. She repeated the action, and straddled Katherine, pinning her arms.

Julie pulled hard and time became a blur. Then she saw Katherine's pupils dilate, and her body went limp. A quick check found no pulse. She didn't know how to feel. But she still needed to focus on helping Micheal.

⁂

KATHERINE threw off the garrote and saw George in a mortal struggle with Lord Avalon. She collected a rail gun and found an opening. Her shot caught Lord Avalon in the shoulder. She needed a better one. Their movement made it difficult. She was about to make an attempt, when a wire around her neck jolted her to the ground.

Lady Avalon was on top of her. The bitch never stopped. The fight was a blur, then Katherine was on bottom. The witch's whore stunned her arms, then pinned her.

The wire bit deep and the throttling began. She tried to fight but the bitch overpowered her.

Her whole body was on fire. The flames of hatred gave way to frustration. Centuries of vengeance were wasted. So many times she should have murdered this bitch had failed. The evil Lords had killed her daughters. She had become Queen of an empire, and this was how it was going to end. The whore was going to win? By killing her with the implement, she'd hand-picked to finish the bitch?

Her whole body went numb. And her narrow vision only saw that bitch's face. 253 years rushed past her, then everything faded to black.

GEORGE saw Lord Avalon strangling Katherine. He tackled him off of her. He needed to finish Lord Avalon. He needed to end this feud, once and for all. He drew a blade and tried to plunge it into the bastard's eye. Avalon was trying to force the knife into his neck. He wrenched it away and then it was punch for punch.

They separated for a moment and George saw Lady Avalon on top of Katherine. As he moved to assist her, he was hit from the side by Lord Avalon. They rolled around numerous times. On multiple occasions he attempted to go to Katherine's aid, but Lord Avalon repeatedly hindered his efforts.

He decided his only chance was to finish off Lord Avalon as quickly as possible, then he couldn't stop him from helping Katherine.

They went back and forth for what felt like an eternity. How long did Katherine have? He finally got the upper hand when he was pulled away by Lady Avalon. Following a brief scuffle, he drew back and realized Katherine must be dead.

Katherine lay still, staring blankly at him. They had taken everything from him. They destroyed his empire, they murdered his daughters, and now they had murdered his wife of over a century. There was no way he would allow them to leave with a complete victory. He stepped over and following a short statement, he jabbed his knife into Fabia's neck, then he opened a gash so deep he knew they would never be able to stem the bleeding, guaranteeing her death.

He walked over to Katherine and collapsed to his knees. Through his tears, his mind was filled with rage and vengeance. They would pay. They would all pay. He promised himself.

MICHEAL was plowed to the ground by George. After a tumble, a blade flashed toward his neck. He forced it around and George was on the defensive. The knife was sent flying and shortly they came apart.

They both saw that Julie had the upper hand on Katherine.

George's focus became helping Katherine. He hindered his attempts to help. He needed to give Julie time to finish this. A part of him felt bad as he saw George's desperation grow. He knew how he would feel if that was Julie. But he knew that this life-and-death struggle would only end with a death.

Eventually, George finally turned his full focus on him. It was a fierce, desperate fight. George got a clean hit to Micheal's temple, dazing him. George grabbed his head, attempting to break his neck. There was a blur and George was gone.

Micheal stood up and looked over at Katherine. The blank stare on her face confirmed her death. A feeling of mild satisfaction came at that fact. Then he immediately felt guilty for the thought.

George's scream snapped him out of his thoughts. He retreated about 10 feet toward the center of the stones. He looked over at Katherine's lifeless body. Tears came to his eyes. And then he said. "My Lady Avalon, my Lord, thou hast killed my family... And the world with them."

He stepped over to Princess Fabia and, in one quick motion, slashed her throat. A look of horror appeared on her face, clearly illuminated by the last ray of the setting sun. Then he walked off toward Katherine.

Micheal and Aphrodite ran to Fabia's aid but there was no use. Her head was nearly severed. They cut her down and boarded their car. They flew top speed back to Atlantis.

"So Katherine's dead? You killed her?" Micheal asked JULIE.

"I made sure." She covered her face. Her words sounded like someone else.

"You had no choice," he tried to console her.

She looked him in the eyes. "After everything she's done to me, I should be glad." She looked away. "But that makes me feel like a bad person?" She looked back.

"You're a good person, the best I know." He touched her shoulder.

Out of all the people she'd killed, this was the only one that felt personal. So many years of enmity. So many ways they'd wronged each other. Now Katherine was dead, at her hand. The fact that she didn't feel completely bad, made her feel even more terrible.

But at least it was over.

"So what about George? What do you think he will do?" She wondered if they made a mistake leaving George alive.

"I'm afraid to think about that. The more pressing concern is what will Selia do?"

She considered Selia's dead daughter. He looked away toward the twilight horizon. "I think we have one more fight on our hands."

Apocalypse Now

King George walked through the palace halls like a ghost. There were certainly many haunting him. He saw the faces of his five little girls, beautiful and sweet, all gone now. His incredible wife of 120 years had gone to join them.

He sat in his private chamber stewing in grief and rage. He had been a king for over a century and he was still no match for the gods.

"Your Majesty?" The Defense Minister intruded upon his solitude.

"What is it?"

"The Norse lands have fallen." The minister informed him.

"Leave me!"

It had taken a week or so. But Britain had determined that when Lord and Lady Avalon had had their showdown with princesses Olivia and Camilla in Rome. They had somehow secretly stolen their defense system codes. That allowed Atlantis and their allies to invade the Empire nearly unimpeded. So Avalon was responsible for the destruction of his family and his empire. If they really were Gods, they didn't play fair. He would have to get them back somehow.

"Your eminence, we are truly sorry," MICHEAL said, bowing.

"Fabia!... Fabia!" Empress Selia shrieked. She looked at them with fire in her eyes.

"Remove them from my sight!"

They were locked in a lounge.

"So what do you think she'll do with us?" Julie worried.

"I don't know. But she blames us for Fabia's death. So she'll probably throw us in some kind of gulag." He paused. "How's your neck?"

Her neck was terribly bruised. "It only hurts when I breathe, swallow, talk or move." She joked.

"I am so sorry. I'm sure you're exhausted." He gently caressed her neck.

She leaned into him, and they laid down on the sofa. "I suppose we find out our fate in the morning." She fell asleep in his arms.

"Wake up! My gods!" Empress Selia yelled, awakening them from their slumber.

"Your eminence," Micheal said.

"Your failure caused my daughter's death. Before I decide what to do with you, I want to know precisely what happened."

They told the story blow-by-blow.

"So you let George kill her?"

"There was nothing we could do." Micheal tried to argue.

"When you escaped from the net, you could have let them kill her..." She indicated Julie. "And you could've saved my daughter. And even if you hadn't come to your husband's aid after you killed Katherine, Fabia wouldn't have been vulnerable. And I would still have a daughter!" Selia turned that toward them, tears streaming down her cheeks. "You chose your wife over my daughter! So I will remedy that right now!" She hit the button and Julie fell to the ground spasming in pain.

Micheal moved immediately to try and stop her. She hit the other button, and he fell down, writhing in pain. He efforted to fight through it. He knew if Selia sustained the shock, it would kill them. He fought to his feet. The pain was blinding, but he forced his way through it.

Selia tried to run to the door. Micheal dove at her feet, tripping her. She kicked him in the face, then regained her feet. As she reached the door, Micheal sprang into a handstand, bringing his legs up around her neck. He dropped her to the ground, breaking her neck in the process. The pain died away with her. Micheal checked her, and she was undoubtedly dead. He took the remote and permanently deactivated their implant chips.

"Thou shalt do as I ask." KING GEORGE ordered his son to take shelter in the royal bunker.

"Mother has yet to be buried!" Prince George protested.

"I shalt not say it again!"

"Yes, father."

"I love thee, my son," he said goodbye as the door closed.

King George hadn't slept since Katherine's murder. After more than a century together they were like two halves of a whole. He felt lost without her. Like he was already half dead.

As he thought through everything. Lord and Lady Avalon had ripped both he and Katherine from their own time periods. They had killed Katherine's first husband. Then they find that the Lords of Avalon are actually the God Koios and Goddess Aphrodite. It's little wonder that they became so legendary. They had the God's edge.

Then they along with the other gods, tried to wipe out humanity in The Flood of Noah. And then they returned to torment him and his family once again. They murdered all of his daughters and destroyed his empire. And now they had murdered his other half, Katherine. They and the gods had constantly ruined his life.

Now it was his time to turn the tables with the weapons of the gods in the palm of his hand. All he had to do was press the button.

He sat on the palace roof, pressed the button, and waited for the world to end. A couple of minutes later, there was a flash far more brilliant than the sun, and a second later, he was blown to oblivion.

With the Empress dead, JULIE knew they had to move before security found out.

"The Empress needs you," she told the guards as they exited the room.

They barred the door and made a run for it. They sprinted through the palace halls and into the room at the end of the hall. They were on the third floor but jumped out the window to the gardens below.

The alarm had clearly been raised, and they were met by several dozen guards. At that moment, the air raid siren began to blare. It signaled one minute to attack. Julie saw that their shelter pod was perhaps 100 yards away, near the Long Pond in the gardens.

They wasted no time engaging the security, fighting them as quickly as possible. They broke through the mob and made for the pod.

As they reached the hatch, they were tackled by several guards. She knew time was short. Micheal moved to take them all on to give her time to open the hatch. She stepped inside, and then Micheal broke free of the guards. He jumped through the hatch behind her. As she attempted to seal the door, a hand grabbed her. She had to kick the hand away. Just as she pulled the door shut, a blinding flash enveloped the view through the porthole. She turned the seal as the pod was hit by some kind of shockwave.

When the pod came to a stop, they could clearly see two mushroom clouds rising from Atlantis. They checked their sky-net scans. And the full scope of the horror became clear. Several thousand high-yield nuclear detonations had been detected on every continent of the world.

Most countries had evidently placed their arsenals in orbit. And so when Britain initiated the first launch, every other government launched in response. Within a few minutes, Julie knew The Age of Atlantis was coming to an end.

At that moment, a series of quakes began to get bigger until there was a deafening crack, and the earth began to fall away from beneath them.

A torrent of water swallowed them, and they began to sink. They tumbled for a few minutes until finally coming to a rest on the ocean floor.

"How deep are we?" Micheal asked.

"Approximately 3200 feet down. Look at this." She motioned for him to come and take a look.

"What am I looking at?"

"Atlantis is gone! Sunk below the sea. And look at that..." She pointed out a clear sign of movement from where Atlantis had been.

"It's a tsunami!"

"A mega-tsunami! The readings say the initial waves are over a mile high!" She was stunned.

-November 12, 1952 BC

"So Plato was right. Atlantis sank into the sea in a day. That day was September 24, 1952 BC. The islands of Atlantis had been the last vestige of the pre-flood super aquifer. The aquifer that had helped cause The Flood of Noah. Now the concussive force of two 10 Megaton nuclear detonations caused the last supports to fail."

When the 50-mile-wide islands collapsed into the sea it generated a mega tsunami that was initially over a mile high. A tsunami of at least several hundred feet washed up on every shoreline in the world. If the nuclear blasts didn't kill them, the tsunamis likely did. Most of the more than 3 billion people died in this double apocalypse. And now the nuclear winter is beginning to set in."

Our pod protected us from the initial apocalypse, but now we are stuck on the bottom of the ocean. Even if we weren't, we need to survive another five years until our time wave arrives. What are the odds of that in a world of chaos?"

Even if the Atlantean age was to end, I didn't want to be the reason. But here we are. We gave them the nuclear bomb. We failed to retrieve it. And I have come to believe that killing Katherine sent George over the edge. So while he was the one who technically pushed the button. I might as well have pushed it for him."

I feel like Sarah Connor from Terminator. Every night, I close my eyes and see the nuclear holocaust I created."

Julie stopped writing for a moment as the tears were falling on the paper. She took a deep breath and then continued.

"How much do we really know about our history? Especially ancient history. Rome? Greece? Egypt? Atlantis? To history, Atlantis is just a myth. But then, most myths have a basis in fact, as we know. People have long questioned if there was an advanced civilization in the past. One mostly forgotten by time. It is said, that history is written by the victor. But what if there is no victor?"

PS: Micheal has been my rock through the storm of 40 years of marriage in the timeline. I love him now more than ever.

PPS: I usually conclude a volume of The Book of Avalon when we leave a timestop. But we missed our original jump. So, I had to reopen this volume. But now I've decided to close it again. Because we've reached the end of an age... The Age of Atlantis...

-I'm Lady Avalon, Aphrodite, Julie Hall. And this is The Book of Avalon, Volume 6...

SESOSTRIS

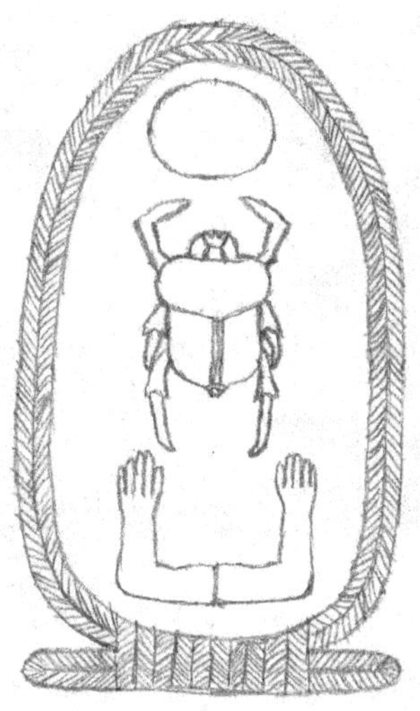

"**Y**OUR GOD ON EARTH..." Vizier Intefiqer announced him to the crowd of thousands bowing before him.

Pharaoh Sesostris stepped out as a living God to the people of Egypt. "People of Egypt, I come before you to present my son, your God, Amenemhat, who shall join me this day in ruling dominion over you..."

Amenemhat stepped forward. "With my father, your God on earth. We shall lead you to a bright future of prosperity and glory!"

Sesostris retired to his private chambers. Bringing his son into the reign guaranteed the perpetuation of his deity on earth dynasty. It made him contemplate his legacy. He had actually ruled Egypt in the long-forgotten advanced age, which was all destroyed in a terrible war. A holocaust that nearly ended humankind.

He barely survived the tsunami, the 10-year winter, and the decades-long temperature swings. He had also had to endure the mass starvation and violent chaos.

After nearly two generations, he finally restored order through force of will. And his Egypt had risen from the ashes of the apocalypse.

So, nearly 30 years after the double apocalypse, most of the memory of Atlantis had been lost. He pulled from his prewar experience to establish his divine right to rule. He had once known some actual gods. The Atlantean God of Wisdom and Knowledge, Koios. And the Atlantean Goddess of Love and Beauty, Aphrodite. So, he would become a God in the eyes of his people. And he would bring order to the chaos.

He raised his son in blessed ignorance of humanity's horrible history. He raised him to truly believe himself as divine.

Only a few people left in the world remembered their true history. And he thought it was better that way. He decided to let the old world die and fade to legend. He would rewrite their history. And the world would be born anew, a world in his image.

<<<<>>>>

ATLAS OF ATLANTIS

1ST AGE OF ATLANTIS

226 PF (3812 BC) – ATLANTIS FOUNDED
238-281 PF (3800-3757 BC) – WARS OF THE 12 MONARCHS
281 PF (3757 BC) – UNION OF THE 12 (ATLANTEAN EM-
PIRE)
328 PF (3710 BC) – FOUNDING OF BABYLONIAN EMPIRE
728-738 PF (3310-3300 BC) – GREAT ATLANTEAN-BABY-
LONIAN WAR OF EMPIRES
738 PF (3300 BC) – EXECUTION OF EMPRESS CYRA OF
ATLANTIS
740 PF (3298 BC) – PROPHECY OF THE GODS BY SETH THE
PROPHET
757 PF (3281 BC) – COMING OF THE GODS
757-762 PF (3281-3276 BC) – REIGN OF THE GODS
1233-1238 PF (2805-2800 BC) – DAON'S WAR
1400-1500 PF (2638-2538 BC) – ATLANTEAN INDUSTRIAL
REVOLUTION
1481 PF (2557 BC) – KHUFU'S PYRAMID COMPLETE
1569 PF (2469 BC) – START OF ATLANTEAN TECH AGE
1581 PF (2457 BC) – START OF ATLANTEAN SPACE AGE
1666-1669 PF (2372-2369 BC) – WAR OF APOCALYPSE
1669 PF (2369 BC) – THE FLOOD

2ND AGE OF ATLANTIS

1863 PF (2175 BC) – THE CONFUSION
1978 PF (2060 BC) – BRITISH EMPIRE FOUNDED
1985-2085 PF (2053-1953 BC) – EUROPEAN CONQUEST

2084-2086 PF (1954-1952 BC) – GLOBAL WAR
2086 PF (1952 BC) – DOUBLE APOCALYPSE(NUCLEAR EX-
CHANGE/MEGA-TSUNAMI)

ATLANTEAN MEASURES OF TIME

-12 MONTHS OF 30 DAYS, DIVIDED INTO 3 10-DAY WEEKS
-YEAR ENDS ON THE WINTER SOLSTICE
-YEAR RESETS AFTER 5 OR 6 DAY "DEATH FESTIVAL"
(THANASEL)
-YEAR PF(POST FALL OF THE ELDERS)

MONTHS	DAYS
1- KOIOSEL	1- HELIDAY
2- PHOESEL	2- SELEDAY
3- KRONOSEL	3- POLODAY
4- RHEASEL	4- EODAY
5- KRIOSEL	5-PROMEDAY
6- THEASEL	6- LETODAY
7- HYPERISEL	7- EPIMEDAY
8- TETHYSEL	8- ASTERDAY
9- OCEANSEL	9- ATLASDAY
10- THEMISEL	10- HECDAY
11- IAPESEL	
12- MNEMOSEL	

ATLANTEAN ALPHABET

VOWELS

- X - A/t
- X - E/d
- X - I/t
- X - ah
- X - Uh
- X - eE
- X - ooh
- X - U/t
- X - oo
- X - aw
- X - Ir
- X - Ar
- / - eA
- % - eye
- /. - ow
- /' - oi
- ./ - oh
- % - eer
- ./' - Air

CONSONANTS

- + - F
- + - S
- + - H
- + - V
- + - Z
- + - sh
- + - Th/i
- + - Th/o
- + - vi/S/ica
- + - P
- + - T
- + - C
- + - B
- + - D
- + - G
- | - Ch
- ¡ - J

- — - M
- · - N
- ·· - nG
- ⊥ - R
- ⊥ - W
- ⊥ - Y
- ⊥ - L
- ⊥ - pi/LL
- ⊥ - Q

PUNCTUATION

- o - PERIOD
- C - QUESTION
- Ɔ - COMMA
- ∧ - EXCLAMATION
- ◉ - COLON
- > - HYPHEN
- < - SLASH
- ( ) - QUOTATION

THE WORLD 757 PF(3281 BC)

WORLD POPULATION   5 BILLION

ATLANTEAN EMPIRE POP   1.2 BILLION

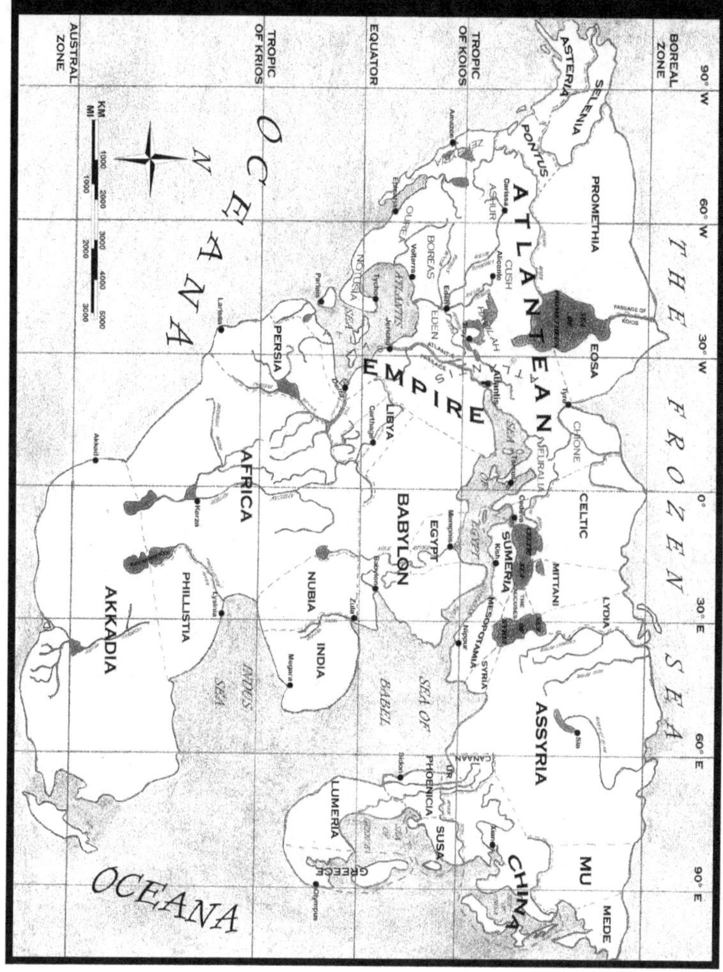

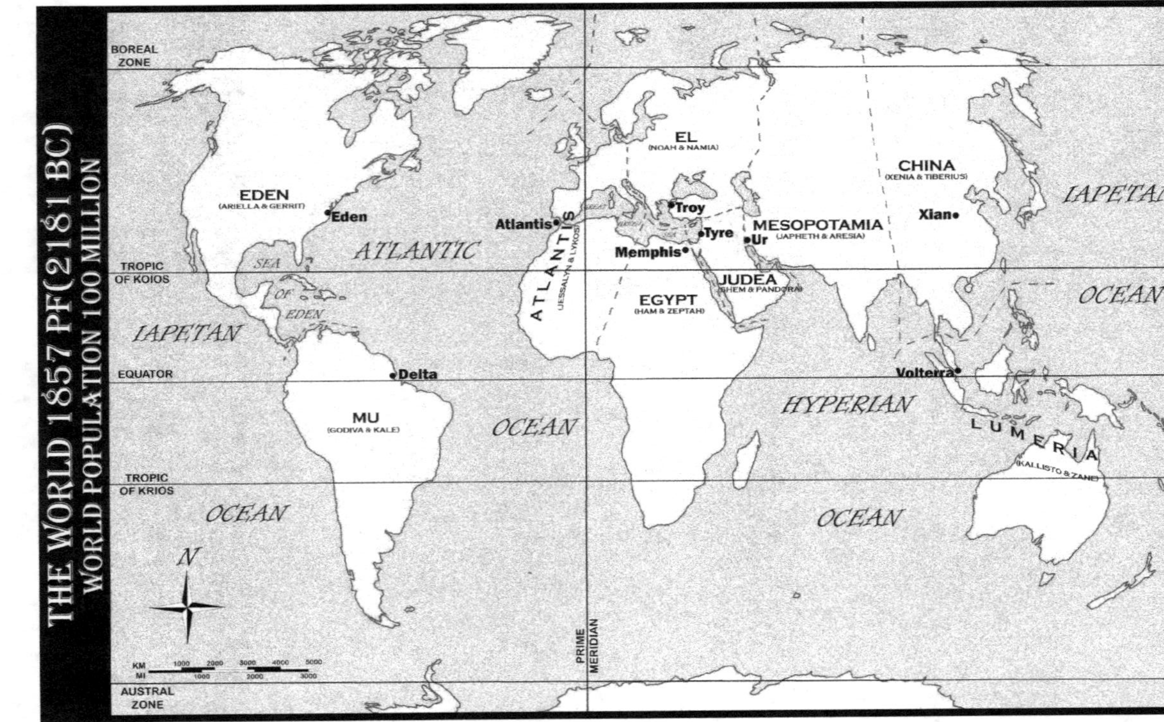

THE WORLD 1857 PF(2181 BC)
WORLD POPULATION 100 MILLION
BOREAL ZONE
TROPIC OF KOIOS
EQUATOR
TROPIC OF KRIOS
AUSTRAL ZONE
EDEN
(ARIELLA & GERRIT)
Eden
ATLANTIC
SEA OF EDEN
IAPETAN
MU
(GODIVA & KALE)
Delta
OCEAN
OCEAN
ATLANTIS
(JESSALYN & LYKOS)
Atlantis
Memphis
Troy
Tyre
Ur
EL
(NOAH & NAMIA)
MESOPOTAMIA
(JAPHETH & ARESIA)
CHINA
(XENIA & TIBERIUS)
Xian
EGYPT
(HAM & ZEPTAH)
JUDEA
(SHEM & PANDORA)
IAPETAN
OCEAN
HYPERIAN
Volterra
LUMERIA
(KALLISTO & ZANE)
OCEAN
N
KM
MI
1000
2000
3000
4000
5000
1000
2000
3000
PRIME MERIDIAN

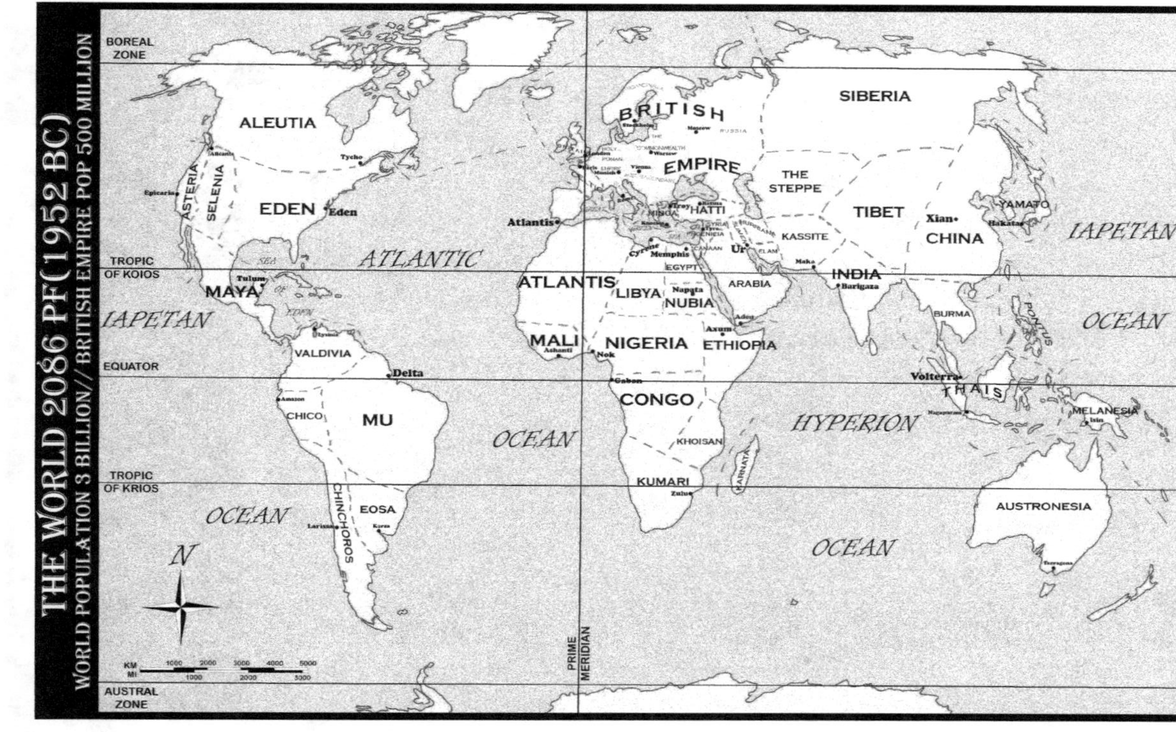

THE WORLD 2086 PF(1952 BC)
WORLD POPULATION 3 BILLION// BRITISH EMPIRE POP 500 MILLION
BOREAL ZONE
TROPIC OF KOIOS
EQUATOR
TROPIC OF KRIOS
AUSTRAL ZONE
PRIME MERIDIAN
IAPETAN
IAPETAN
ATLANTIC
OCEAN
OCEAN
OCEAN
HYPERION
KM
MI
1000
2000
3000
4000
5000
N
ALEUTIA
ASTERIA
SELENIA
EDEN
Eden
Tycho
Epicaria
MAYA
Tulum
VALDIVIA
Delta
Amazon
CHICO
MU
CHINCHOROS
EOSA
Larissa
Kora
BRITISH
EMPIRE
Stockholm
London
Warsaw
COMMONWEALTH
RUSSIA
THE STEPPE
SIBERIA
TIBET
Xian
CHINA
YAMATO
Hakata
KASSITE
INDIA
Barigaza
BURMA
Atlantis
HATTI
ATLANTIS
LIBYA
NUBIA
Napata
Memphis
Cyrene
EGYPT
Ur
ELAM
ARABIA
Axum
Adua
Moka
ETHIOPIA
MALI
Ashanti
Nok
NIGERIA
Gabon
CONGO
KHOISAN
KUMARI
Zulu
KARNATA
Volterra
THAIS
PONTUS
Nagapranii
MELANESIA
Isin
AUSTRONESIA
Tarragion

ATLANTIS 757 PF(3281 BC)

POPULATION 38.1 MILLION

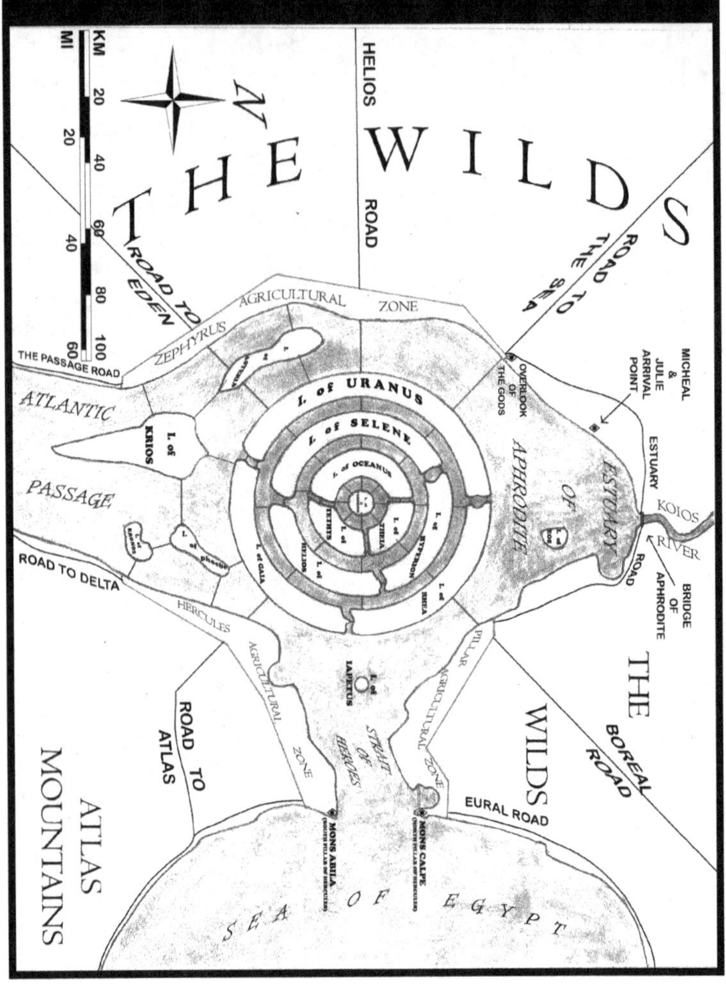

ATLANTIS
2086 PF(1952 BC)

CITY POPULATION 36 MILLION
COUNTRY POPULATION 320 MILLION

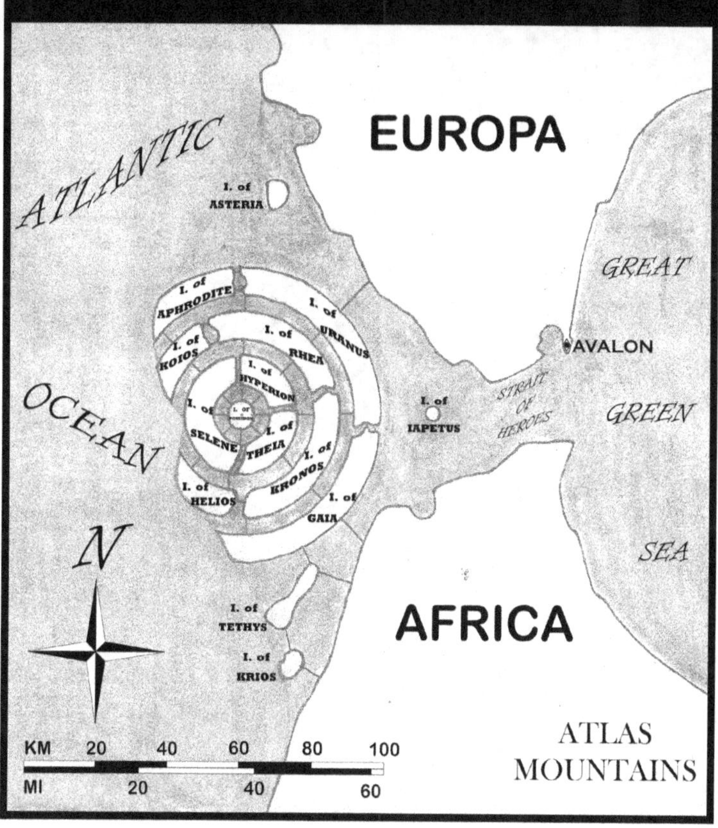

ISLAND OF POSEIDON

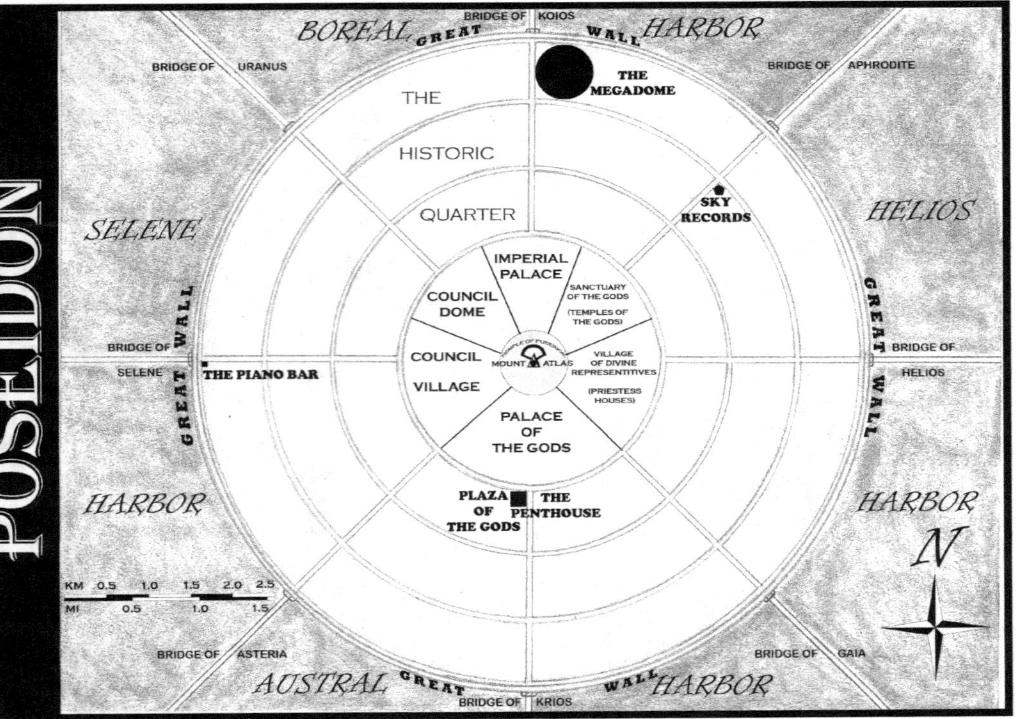

ACKNOWLEDGMENTS

MAREN JENSEN
APOLLO BLAKE – EDITOR
LINCOLN WRITES
KJYRSTEN ASHDOWN
DIANA TINGEY
RALPH and CHARLOTTE JENSEN

ABOUT THE AUTHOR

S TEPHEN JENSEN GREW UP fascinated by the world around him. He spent his childhood studying science and history. In his youth, he became interested in the stories and worlds of Sci-Fi and Fantasy. As an adult, he's spent the last couple of decades traveling the world to see the history and cultures firsthand.

All of this fostered his imagination to create his own fantasies and worlds in his head. The last few years he's put pen to page to bring some of these stories to life.

The AVALON SERIES is the culmination of this life journey. He lives in Salt Lake City, Utah.